The pilot's body was held in place by the safety harness

Bolan reached out to help, but stopped when the Black Hawk began to spin out of control. Turning toward the side hatch, he worked the lever. It moved smoothly, but the hatch refused to budge an inch, held in place by the pressure of centrifugal force.

Bracing a boot against the minigun, Bolan grabbed the lever with both hands and exerted all of his strength. It felt as though the universe was rapidly spinning around him. The Black Hawk was a sitting duck, and the next burst of shells would blow him out of the air.

"Come on, you stubborn son of a—" The lever bent slightly, then the hatch moved and he was thrown from the spinning helicopter....

Read by Dad
for
Patti Ann
1970 – 2013
Loved + missed
forever

Don Pendleton's Mack Bolan®

Shadow Strike

A GOLD EAGLE BOOK FROM
W♦RLDWIDE®

TORONTO • NEW YORK • LONDON
AMSTERDAM • PARIS • SYDNEY • HAMBURG
STOCKHOLM • ATHENS • TOKYO • MILAN
MADRID • WARSAW • BUDAPEST • AUCKLAND

Recycling programs
for this product may
not exist in your area.

First edition January 2012

ISBN-13: 978-0-373-61550-6

Special thanks and acknowledgment to
Nick Pollotta for his contribution to this work.

SHADOW STRIKE

Printed in U.S.A.

By taking revenge, a man is but even with his enemy; but in passing over it, he is superior.
> —Author Unknown

Heaping revenge on a wrongdoing solves nothing. Avenging an injustice is something else entirely.
> —Mack Bolan

PROLOGUE

Northwest Atlantic Ocean

"Remember what happened to the southern United States when that offshore oil rig ruptured?" a man asked, easing an ammunition clip into the receiver of an AK-47 assault rifle. "Now just imagine the same thing happening to every offshore oil ring on the whole planet. It would be..." He fumbled for the correct word.

"Catastrophic," a woman supplied, working the arming bolt on her own weapon. "But we're not going to do that to every oil rig in the world, just the ones around the British Isles. Maybe fifty or sixty million will die, not a couple of billion."

He grinned. "But still, something to think about, eh?"

"Oh, shut up and concentrate on your work," another man growled, removing the clip from his assault rifle to spray some military lubricant into the receiver.

Flying at maximum speed, three massive C-160 Hercules transport planes maintained a tight formation as they cruised dangerously low over the Atlantic, just below the American coastal radar net.

On the distant horizon a raging squall, a sudden summer storm, churned the ocean in unbridled fury, and choppy waves sprayed the bellies of the huge airplanes with layers of slick moisture that flowed smoothly away from the steady stream of air churned by the powerful Allison engines.

Inside the planes, the low hum of the turboprop engines was a palpable presence among the grim passengers, and conversation was difficult, but not impossible. They were all dressed in loose civilian clothing, totally inappropriate for long-distance air travel, and heavy fur parkas.

"So…was this the first time you ever…you know?" a bald man asked, his voice tight with emotion. There was a bloody bandage on the side of his head where an ear had been, and his fur collar was stained dark red.

"Killed anybody?" a woman replied, her hands busy reloading an AK-47 assault rifle. "Yes, of course." The curved magazine slid easily into the receiver, and with a jerk of the arming bolt, the deadly weapon was ready for business again.

"First time for me, too," another man added, disassembling his own weapon to clean the interior.

"Never saw so much blood in my life," an older man whispered.

"Shut up and concentrate on your work," the first man growled, irritably touching the bandage. Then he savagely jerked out the clip from his assault rifle and placed it aside.

The entire group had been practicing for the past hour, disassembling an old AK-47, only to put it back together and then take it apart once more in an endless learning ritual. Naturally, all of them were familiar with hunting rifles and such, but nobody had any military training. How could they? Iceland had no army or navy, only a national police force. This bizarre Russian weapon, a combination of a 7.62 mm machine gun and 30 mm grenade launcher, was as foreign to them as the dark side of the moon. As was murder.

Killing for food, they understood. That was part of life.

However, taking the life of another human was something horribly new, and most of them looked a little queasy from the recent slaughter. True, it had been necessary, but still extremely disagreeable.

Located at the extreme rear of the lead Hercules, the fifty men and women were jammed uncomfortably between the hydraulic exit ramp and a solid wall of wooden cubes that filled the rest of the huge cargo transport.

Each squat cube was roughly a yard square, and bore no manufacturer logo, designation or shipping label. Nor was there a manifest, customs sticker or duties seal. The identical wooden boxes were completely blank, aside from a few smears of drying blood, an occasional tuft of human hair and the all-pervasive smell of industrial lubricant.

At the front of the plane, only inches away from the colossal mound of crates, was a short flight of metal stairs that led to the flight deck. Underneath the deck was a utilitarian washroom and a small metal room that once had been an ammunition bunker for a twin set of 40 mm Bofors cannons. But for this trip it had been converted into a crude electronics workshop. The noise from the engines was noticeably less at this location, yet the three people clustered in the cramped room hadn't spoken for hours, ever since hastily leaving the burning warehouse.

"So, is it done yet?" a portly man finally demanded, grabbing the hexagonal barrel of an old-fashioned Webley .445 revolver and breaking open the cylinder to remove the spent shells. He dumped them into a metal waste receptacle, and the brass tinkled musically as it rolled about on the bottom. Though he was a large man, the three-piece silk suit he wore hung loosely from his wide shoulders, and a series of holes cut into his leather belt accommodated a recent dramatic weight loss. On his right wrist was a solid-platinum Rolex watch that shone mirror-bright, while a cheap gold-plated wedding ring gleamed dully on his left hand. Although only middle-aged, he seemed much older, with deep lines around his mouth and eyes, and his curly dark hair was highlighted with wings of gray at the temples.

"Only glaciers can move mountains, Thor," muttered the slim woman bent over the workbench clamped to the metal wall. Her pale hands moved among the complex circuitry of an electronic device, soldering loose wires into place and attaching computer chips with the innate skill and speed of a surgeon.

"What does that mean?" growled a skinny man attaching a large drum of 12-gauge cartridges to the bottom of a Vepr assault shotgun. The deadly weapon mirrored its new owner, bare-bones and deadly, possessing nothing that wasn't absolutely necessary to the single goal of eradicating life.

His hair was so pale that he almost appeared bald, and he was painfully clean-shaved, with a small bandage covering a recent nick on his shallow cheek. He was wearing a camouflage-colored military jumpsuit, and one of his boots bulged slightly from a folded straight-razor tucked in the top for dire emergencies.

"It means, Gunnar, that we shouldn't bother the professor when she's busy," Hrafen Thorodensen answered, thumbing a fifth round into the cylinder. With a snap of his wrist, he swung up the barrel and closed the British-made weapon.

Gunnar Eldjarm scowled, resting the Vepr on a shoulder. "You shouldn't snap a revolver shut like that, Thor. It damages the catch."

"Only if I do it a lot," Thorodensen replied. "But with any luck, two days from now I can throw it away and never touch another damn weapon."

"And if we fail?" Professor Lilja Vilhjalms asked, expertly inserting another circuit board into the rapidly growing maze of electronics.

Midnight-black hair trailed down her back in a thick ponytail that almost reached her trim waist. A pair of thick horn-rimmed glasses dominated her otherwise lovely face.

"If we fail, my dear Lily, then we'll all be dead, which will achieve the same result," Thorodensen said, pulling a folding jump seat from the curved wall. "Now, please finish up quickly. We will reach our next target soon."

"Target?" Vilhjalms asked in a whisper, her hands stopping cold. "But I thought—"

"Yes, yes, we will try to legally purchase the equipment, of course," Thorodensen interrupted with a curt gesture. "But if there are any complications, then we shall take what we need."

"At any cost?"

"Yes, at any cost."

Putting aside the soldering gun, the woman made one last plea for sanity. "Please, Thor, the Americas aren't our enemy."

"Wrong," Eldjarm stated coldly, brushing back his hair. "The friend of my enemy is my enemy."

Removing a cigar from inside his suit, Thorodensen grunted in somber agreement. He didn't really care for this new blood-thirsty aspect of his childhood friend, even if it did help in this dirty little war. However, as the old saying went, needs drive as the devil must. Which he always took to mean that, sometimes, in extreme cases, the end actually did justify the means.

Withholding a sigh, Lilja Vilhjalms tactfully said nothing and returned to the arduous task of assembling the sonar scrambler. She didn't care for the name of their little group, Penumbra, and had no idea if they were on the path of righteousness or damnation. Sadly, there was no other course available. Win or lose, right or wrong, this was their destiny, and revenge was as inevitable as death itself.

Outside the windows, the sky began to darken as the three Hercules raced away from the thunderous storm and slipped into twilight, heading directly into the coming night.

CHAPTER ONE

Brooklyn, New York

Lightning flashed and thunder rumbled in the stormy sky. A cold rain fell unrelenting on the dark city. Rivers of car headlights flowed in an endless stream along the regimented streets of south Brooklyn, while traffic lights blinked their silent multicolored commands.

The ragged shoreline of Sheepshead Bay was brightly illuminated by the bright neon lights of countless bars, restaurants and nightclubs skirting the choppy Atlantic, where oily waves broke hard against ancient rocks and modern concrete pylons. Tugboats churned across the bay, guiding huge cruise liners out to sea, and even more massive oil tankers to the industrial dockyard.

As silent as the grave, a black Hummer rolled to a stop near the mouth of an alley, and the driver turned off the headlights, but kept the engine running. For several minutes, Mack Bolan, aka the Executioner, did nothing, closely studying every detail of the area, from the flow of the dirty water in the gutters, to the shadows on the window curtains of nearby apartment houses.

The rain pelted hard across the neighborhood, visibly dancing on the sidewalks and hitting the patched pavement of the streets with a sound oddly similar to a steak sizzling on a griddle. There were few pedestrians about at this late hour, only a couple drunks staggering home, and a lone prostitute huddled under the tattered awning of a cheap hotel.

The rest of the wet street was lined with parked cars. Every store window was protected by a heavy steel gate, every wall adorned with garish graffiti, and the few bus kiosks were made of military-grade bulletproof plastic, the resilient material still scored deeply in spots by knives and car keys. No messages had been etched into the plastic, just random scars to signify that nothing was allowed into Sheepshead Bay without the permission of the locals.

There were no security cameras in evidence anywhere, but Bolan did a careful sweep of the vicinity with a hand-held EM scanner just to double-check. When the electro-magnetic device read clean, Bolan tucked it away under his waterproof poncho, turned off the engine and stepped from the vehicle.

Bolan was a big man, well over six feet tall, and while he carried 220 pounds, he moved with the grace of a jungle cat. For the mission this night, he was wearing black clothing and shoes, and a black leather duster that hung to his knees.

Walking to the next corner, Bolan glanced around the dead-end street, and almost smiled at the glowing oasis of light in the Stygian gloom, the Golden Grotto. Electric signs flashed digital photos of various dancers whose clothing melted away to reveal their many delights, but always stopped at the exact limit that the law allowed. Most of the dancers were blonde, even the Latinas and Asians.

Music thumped from inside the building, and the parking lot was filled with a wide assortment of cars. A uniformed doorman stood under a wide canvas awning, and kept close attention on the rows of vehicles. Even from this distance Bolan could tell the man was armed.

The rest of the street was deserted, which wasn't surprising, since Bolan knew Michael Tiffany owned all the buildings in the area, and deliberately kept them empty of tenants so that there would be no nobody to complain about the noise and blazing lights of the Golden Grotto Gentleman's Club. Even the warehouse situated on an old jetty was dark. The squat brick structure was shiny from the thundering downpour, and was Bolan's real goal for this night. Getting there would be far trickier than it appeared.

However, Bolan found it odd that the warehouse didn't look as if a dozen people had died the previous day. There was no sign of any gunfire or explosions. Interesting.

Heading for the club, he straightened his leather collar and used a thumb to break another ampoule of whiskey taped to the underside. The reek of potent liquor briefly flooded the air, then was washed away by the unrelenting rain.

Pretending to stagger along the sidewalk, Bolan got to the door just as the burly doorman opened it and waved him on inside.

"Good evening, sir," the man declared.

Mumbling something unintelligible, Bolan shuffled past, noticing that the fellow was wearing a bulletproof vest under his raincoat, along with an Uzi submachine gun.

As the glass doors closed, Bolan was hit by a tidal wave of noise, smoke, light and steaming hot air that reeked of hard liquor, stale sweat and cheap perfume. Every wall was covered with mirrors, and a disco ball hung from the ceiling, radiating a galaxy of moving star points.

The club was spacious, filling the entire ground floor of the converted warehouse, but it was still packed to the walls, with cheering customers at every table, waving and leering at the naked dancers gyrating on three different stages. The signs outside displayed only as much flesh as the law allowed. Inside was another matter entirely.

A completely nude woman was walking off the first stage, her hands stuffed with dollar bills, while two Asian women were just starting to remove their schoolgirl outfits on the middle stage, and a young black woman wearing tooled boots, chaps and a cowboy hat strode out onto the third, to be greeted by a crescendo of loud country music and wild hoots from the drunken crowd.

Smoothing back his soaked hair, Bolan grunted in wry amusement. Nonstop entertainment meant it was harder for a paying customer to realize it was time to leave and go home. There were no wall clocks in sight, and the front door was partially hidden behind a barricade of plastic plants. Las Vegas had been using these tricks for decades, and apparently Tiffany had decided to copy the big boys. Smart. But then, nobody had ever said that Mad Mike Tiffany was a fool, just ruthless.

The cushioned leather stools along the curved hardwood counter were mostly empty, as the management wanted the drunks sitting in chairs and not falling onto the floor. A dozen waitresses rushed back and forth from the bar to the patrons, steadily relaying overpriced drinks. They wore matching outfits of fishnet body stockings, leather boots and white satin bowies.

"Table, sir?" a pretty redhead asked, coming out of the smoky darkness. The name on her plastic ID badge read Shelly.

Her smile could have illuminated Broadway, but her eyes were dead, telling an age-old story that Bolan had encountered far too many times in his travels.

"No, thanks," he replied. "I'm here to see Tiffany."

Inhaling sharply, Shelly stiffened at the open use of the name, then forced a friendly smile back on her face.

"Part of the new security team?" she asked with a tilt of her head. Then, stabbing out a finger, she poked his duster and found the holstered Beretta underneath. "Yeah, I can see that you are."

Bolan was impressed, but said nothing. New security team? Maybe something had recently happened here that had scared Mad Mike. Had somebody tried to ice the man, or had it been something even worse?

Looking about, Shelly leaned in closer. "You know, we're all still kind of upset about that. So many of his people dead…" Suddenly, she looked frightened and took a step backward.

"Hmm, what did you say?" Bolan asked with a stone face. "I was looking at the dancers and didn't hear a word you said, darling."

Relaxing at the obvious lie, Shelly blessed him with a smile, a glimmer of the girl she had once been peeking out from the overlaying years of abuse. "Come on, the vault is this way," she said, turning to briskly walk away.

Checking for any oddly placed mirrors that might be hiding a surveillance camera, Bolan stayed close, watching the crowd as much as the waitress.

But nobody seemed to be paying him any undue attention. Every gaze was locked on the Asian women, who were naked by now and oiling each other in a pretend wrestling match.

When they reached a curtained alcove, Shelly parted the black drapes, and Bolan observed that they were very heavy and thickly coated with a tan foam on the inside to retard the ambient noises of the club. Beyond them was a short hallway and another set of soundproof curtains. Past that in a small room lined with metal lockers, two large men were sitting at a table, playing cards. One had a beard, the other a Mohawk, and they were both openly armed, automatic pistols tucked into shoulder holsters, their jackets draped over the back of their chairs.

Keeping his back to the wall, Bolan read both of them as low-level guards, just some muscle to keep out the drunks. Next to them was a second door, made of solid steel and equipped with an alphanumeric keypad.

"Hey, Chuck," Shelly said in greeting. "Meet the new guy."

"No names," Bolan said. "Not yet, anyway."

Both men kept playing cards, but shifted position in their chairs for faster access to their weapons. Okay, they were big, Bolan noted, but not completely stupid. Too bad for them.

"You the mechanic from Detroit?" asked the man with the Mohawk, shifting the cards in his hand.

"Don't ask stupid questions," the bearded man said with a sneer, sliding a hand inside his jacket to scratch his stomach. "Whatcha want, Blackie?"

Bolan grunted. That was a not-so-subtle reference to him being a Black Ace, a professional killer. "I'm here to see Mad Mike," he replied in a bored voice.

The two men broke into laughter, and Shelly went pale, as if just speaking the nickname could get you killed. Looking nervously at the three men, she abruptly turned and departed, closing the soundproof curtains in her wake. Soon the hard clicks of her high heels faded away.

"Okay, what's your business with the boss?" asked the bald man, rising from the table. Something under his shirt jacket hit the Formica table with a metallic thump.

Bolan showed no reaction but immediately changed his tactics for gaining entry. These men were wearing military body armor, not a cheap bulletproof vest like the doorman. These weren't guards, but street soldiers. Muscle for the boss.

"Don't worry about it." Bolan chuckled, drawing the Beretta and firing twice.

Each man jerked back as a 9 mm Parabellum slug slammed into his chest directly above the heart. As the slugs ricocheted away, the guards doubled over, gasping for breath and clawing for their own weapons. Stepping closer, Bolan swung the Beretta fast, clubbing them both across the back of the head, and they dropped to the floor like sacks of dirty laundry.

It would have been faster and safer to simply execute the guards. But since Bolan didn't know for sure that they deserved death, he would allow them to live for the time being.

Removing a pair of 10 mm Glock pistols from their shoulder holsters, he tossed them into a wastebasket.

Checking the guards, he found a transceiver on the bearded man, along with a throat mike and earplug. Plus an access card. Tucking in the earbud, he switched on the radio, hoping it was already on the correct channel. There was only silence. Damn.

Going to the wall, Bolan searched alongside the door until finding a disguised access slot in the woodwork. He slipped in the card, and a panel slid back, revealing a glowing sheet of plastic with the outline of a human hand. He grunted at that. A biometric refusal system. That was pretty high tech for a Brooklyn gun dealer. Suddenly, he had a very strong suspicion that his tip from Leo Turrin was right on the money, and that something big had happened here yesterday, something a lot more dangerous than selling cheap Taiwanese revolvers to gangbangers.

Looking over the unconscious men, Bolan chose the one with the better shoes. That meant he was probably getting paid more, which translated as holding a higher position in the criminal organization.

Pressing the hand of the man against the panel, Bolan heard a soft chime, and the armored door slid into the wall.

Directly ahead was a long hallway illuminated with bright halogen lights and lined with closed doors. The walls were brick, the floor terrazzo, and there were no security cameras.

Dropping the limp body in the path of the door to prevent it from closing, Bolan shrugged off his leather duster and drew both his weapons. The Beretta 93-R machine pistol rested comfortably in his left hand, while the right was filled with a .50-caliber Desert Eagle. Quantity and quality. A very deadly combination.

Easing along the hallway, he strained to hear any noises, but there was only the soft whir of the air-conditioning system blowing a warm breeze from hidden vents, then the radio earbud crackled.

"Chuck, we've got a reading that the damn door is wide open," a man growled in annoyance. "Check it, and see if that idiot Bobby dropped something in the jamb again, will ya."

Touching the throat mike, Bolan grunted in reply. Ahead of him a door opened and a man stepped into the corridor, a case of U.S. Army HEAT rounds cradled in his arms.

He gasped at the sight of Bolan and dropped the case to go for a mini-Uzi holstered on his hip. The Executioner stroked the trigger of the Beretta and the weapon fired, the sound suppressor reducing the report to a discreet cough. The man fell back into infinity, his brains splattered across the brick wall.

"The damn door is still open!" the voice said as the radio crackled. "What the fuck are you two morons doing up there?"

Up there, eh? Thanks for the directions, Bolan thought, stepping into the room. It was filled with wall shelves packed solid with cases of Glaser Sure-Kill, Navy SEAL Daisy Cutters, Black Talon cop killers and Army HEAT rounds, all strictly illegal for civilian use. Especially the high-explosive armor-piercing tracers. There was even an empty carrying case for an HK XM-25. Now, that was real trouble.

Pulling a cigarette pack from his jacket pocket, Bolan pulled off the arming strip, then slapped the disguised explosive charge against the middle case of HEAT rounds. Those would do the most damage when the plastic-wrapped wad of C-4 detonated.

Checking the next room, Bolan found it full of crates of U.S. Army M-16 assault rifles, M-79 grenade launchers, and several cases of mixed hand grenades. He primed a second pack of cigarettes.

Taking a couple of HE grenades, Bolan dropped them into a pocket. Turrin had been right, and wrong. This wasn't just a supply depot for the local Mob, but a major league black-market weapons dealer. Now, Bolan was eager to find Tiffany and discover exactly what had happened that made him increase security to this level.

"If you two assholes are fucking the new girl instead of standing your post, the boss is going to feed your balls into a fucking woodchipper!" the voice on the radio said furiously. "Now, answer me right fucking now, you losers!"

Too late for that, Bolan thought, removing the safety tape from around the handle of a flash-bang stun grenade. He yanked the pin free and tossed the sphere up the corridor toward the strip club. It landed directly on the back of the unconscious guard and rolled into the alcove.

Turning away, Bolan sprinted for distance. A few seconds later there was a thunderous explosion and a blinding flash. Instantly, every fire alarm started to howl, then white foam gushed from sprinklers in the ceiling.

"Red alert," a woman said calmly over a speaker inside the drop ceiling. "We have an explosion in section 12.

Repeat, explosion in 12. Everybody topside clear the club and seal the doors. Allow nobody access. Nobody!"

"Mr. Tiffany, I sent Harry to get a crate of grenades," a man said over the radio. "The blast might have been him, sir."

"That old drunk?" another man growled. "If the asshole is still alive, shoot him in the head! Now clear the club and seal the doors! The last thing I want is a bunch of firemen charging in here!"

The voice was low and throaty, almost garbled, and Bolan couldn't tell if it was from a man, a woman, or computer-generated. But that fit the description of Mike Tiffany.

"No problem, sir!" the man replied promptly.

Satisfied that all the civilians would soon be gone, Bolan sprinted for the end of the corridor. From this point onward, anybody else he encountered should be an employee of the arms dealer, and fair game.

Reaching the end of the corridor, Bolan paused before an elevator, frowned, then stepped through an open doorway that led to a stairwell. Even over the fire alarm, he could hear several people running up the steps. Pulling out another grenade, he left on the safety tape and simply dropped it over the railing. The sphere hit the metal steps below with a ringing crash, then started bouncing along, impelled by gravity and inertia. A few seconds later, the unseen men began shouting curses, then running away fast.

Pulling out a second grenade, Bolan started to remove the safety tape, then heard a sound from behind. Dropping the grenade, he drew the Beretta and pivoted at the hip.

A large man in a yellow raincoat was running down the corridor, working the pump action on a 12-gauge shotgun. Instantly, the Executioner fired twice, the double report lost in the clamor of the alarm.

The shotgun discharged harmlessly into the wall as the first round knocked it aside, then the man jerked backward as the second 9 mm bullet punched a neat black hole in his forehead. Slowly, he crumpled to the floor and lay down as if going to sleep.

Suddenly, the soldier heard the sound of people running up the stairs again. This time, Bolan pulled the pin on an HE grenade, counted to three, then dropped the bomb over the railing. The metallic sphere hit the stairs with a hard metallic ring, and somebody cursed.

"Grenade!" a man yelled.

"Ignore it!" another countered gruffly. "That last one wasn't even live!"

A split-second later, a violent explosion filled the stairwell, and fiery chunks of human remains vomited into view. A smoking hand still holding a gun smacked into the concrete wall, and a tattered shoe arched over the railing to land in the corridor.

Quickly starting down the stairs, Bolan hopped over the grisly remains of the guards and kept moving. Unfortunately, he could feel the stairs swaying, and cursed the fact that the builder had merely attached them to the wall with pinions and wires, instead of anchoring them properly to the masonry with thick steel bolts. Now there was a chance that the staircase would tumble to the bottom level with him on it. However, the elevator was a guaranteed death trap, so he had no choice.

Increasing his speed, Bolan holstered the Beretta, using both hands to steady his hasty progress down the shuddering stairs. Pinions were ripping free from the wall moorings, the support cables lashing about like insane snakes, hissing as they whipped through the air. He was hit twice in the back, his life saved by the Threat Level IV body armor under his jacket. Then he caught a cable across the face. The sharp pain blurred his vision for a moment, and he tasted blood, but kept moving. Speed was his only defense now.

As he neared bottom, the last flight of stairs gave a low groan and twisted sideways, closely followed by a horrible crashing sound that steadily built in volume and power.

Jumping the last eight feet, Bolan hit the floor in a crouch and dived at the exit. The fire door resisted for a second, and just for a moment the soldier thought this was the end. Then the portal crashed open and he half fell onto soft carpeting. A split second later, a deafening avalanche of stairs, cables, stays and corpses arrived, blocking the doorway completely as it formed a ghastly pile of debris.

As Bolan started to rise, a dozen armed men charged into view from around a corner. Drawing the Beretta 93-R, the soldier emptied the magazine into the group. Faces disappeared, and hot blood splashed the wall as the chests of the guards were torn open under the barrage.

Dropping the magazine, Bolan slammed a fresh one home as a second group of gunners appeared. But these men were carrying M-16 assault rifles and wearing body armor.

As the guards paused at the sight of the carnage, Bolan threw himself to the floor and quickly shifted targets. Firing 9 mm rounds across their exposed knees, he brought them down screaming and cursing, white bones and gore erupting from the hideous wounds.

Rolling to a new position, Bolan drew the Desert Eagle and stroked the trigger. The big bore handcannon boomed louder than doomsday in the enclosed confines of the hall, the muzzle-flame extending for almost a foot from the pitted maw of the oversize weapon.

The head of the first man simply broke apart, his life gone in a microsecond of high-powered annihilation. Then the nose of the second man vanished, just before the back of his head exploded, the men behind him caught in the spray of bones and brains.

Temporarily blinded by the gory material, the other guards rubbed at their faces and fired back randomly, mostly hitting the floors and ceiling, and occasionally one another.

Constantly moving and shooting, Bolan continued to ruthlessly exterminate each of them, one after another, until the corridor was again empty.

Swiftly reloading both his weapons, Bolan took this opportunity to press the button on the remote detonator clipped to his shoulder holster, then toss the device away.

Moving onward, the soldier stayed low and close to the walls, gunning down everybody he saw carrying a weapon, as well as every security camera that came into view.

Pausing at an intersection, he fired the Desert Eagle into the ceiling, dislodging several foam acoustical tiles to expose raw concrete and several thick power cables. He grunted at the sight. Those would lead either directly to the power room or to Tiffany. A fifty-fifty chance. He went to the right.

Sure enough, at the far end of the corridor, Bolan saw a group of men with military weapons clustered around an unmarked door. As they turned, Bolan shot the two men in front, then dived to the side. Caught by surprise, the guards took a moment to fire back, their assault rifles sending a fiery maelstrom of steel-jacketed lead along the corridor. But Bolan was already safely behind the corner, and unwrapping a grenade.

"Surrender or die!" he yelled, yanking out the arming pin and releasing the safety lever.

"Fuck you, cop!" somebody snarled in reply. "Come and get us!"

As the guards cut loose with another barrage, much longer this time, Bolan threw the military sphere as hard as he could at the opposite wall. It bounced off the bricks and went around the corner.

A man cursed, another screamed, then the antipersonnel grenade detonated in the air, sending out a hellish corona of stainless-steel fléchettes. Just for a second, Bolan heard the hiss of their trajectory, then there was only silence.

Pulling a mirrored dental probe from his inside pocket, he glanced around the corner to check the damage. There were tattered bodies in sight, but none remotely resembled human beings anymore, just piles of ground meat in cheap suits. Then he spotted a disembodied arm holding an XM-15. Bolan scooped it up and slung the deadly weapon across his back.

Stepping over the ragged corpses, the soldier heard one of the mutilated men give a low groan, and he quickly fired a mercy round from the Beretta to end the torment. Just then, the overhead lights went out, casting the corridor in near absolute blackness.

Cracking open a chemical glow stick, Bolan tossed it onto the bodies, then blew off the lock to the office door with a single booming round from the .50 Desert Eagle. The thundering rip of an auto-shotgun answered, a dozen cartridges discharged in a single, continuous volley.

Even before it stopped, Bolan tossed in an unprimed grenade. The bomb hit the carpet and rolled out of sight. He heard a man curse vehemently, and swung around the jamb.

Standing behind a huge wooden desk was a short bald man, a tailored silk shirt almost unable to contain his amazingly muscular frame. He appeared to be made out of nothing but bulging muscles and scar tissue. On the brick wall were several certificates from local charities, and a framed picture of the short man standing with his arm around the recently elected congressman who was rumored to be in the pockets of organized crime. Tiffany was clean-shaved, and had a puckered scar across his throat where a Jamaican drug lord had tried to behead him and failed. That was what gave the arms dealer his characteristic growl for a voice.

"What the fuck…a fake!" Tiffany snarled, dropping the spent drum of the Atchisson and reaching for another from a pile on the desk.

"Don't do it, Mike," Bolan said softly.

Tiffany froze with his hand less than an inch from the ammunition drum. Slowly, he looked up to squint into the darkness.

A long moment passed, then he curled his lips into a snarl and tossed away the Atchisson. It landed with a clatter on the carpeting, right next to the smoking ruin of a computer. The cover was off, and an electric stun gun was resting inside the complex wiring, molten plastic dribbling from the hard drive onto the floor.

"Okay, you got me, feeb," Tiffany growled, raising both hands. "But you took too long, and my computer has bizarrely crashed." He grinned as if he had just won the battle. "Now, read me my rights and call me a fucking lawyer."

"Okay, you're a fucking lawyer."

Tiffany scowled. "What was that?"

"I'm not with the FBI," Bolan stated, cracking alive another glow stick while advancing. "And I'm not here for your records, or to arrest anybody."

"That so?" Tiffany muttered. "Well, you sure aren't here to zap me, or else you would have tossed in a live grenade."

Biding his time, Bolan said nothing, letting the arms

dealer work out the details for himself. Interrogation was an art, not a science.

"You don't really think I'm going to rat out my contacts for a shorter jail sentence?" Tiffany barked in a cold laugh.

"Mad Mike, the Brooklyn Terror? That possibility never even entered my mind," Bolan stated honestly, pressing the hot barrel of the Colt against the man's cheek.

The skin sizzled at the contact, but aside from a slight furrowing of his brow, Tiffany gave no indication that he felt anything. Finally, Bolan removed the weapon.

"Okay, now that you've had fun, what the fuck do you want?" the dealer demanded, rubbing the spot with his fingertips. "Money? I can get you that. More than you can spend in a dozen lifetimes!"

"Wrong again, Michael," Bolan whispered, making the other man strain to hear the words. This was an old interrogation technique that almost always worked.

"Weapons?" Tiffany snorted in disdain. "You didn't have to ace half my staff to cut a deal for some guns! What do ya want? Stinger missiles, C-4 satchel charges? I can even get you a PEP laser, if you give me a week."

Bolan had started to speak when he saw Tiffany's eyes widen in delight. Instantly, the soldier's combat instincts flared and he spun out of the way with both guns blazing.

A big man stood in the doorway, aiming an M-16 assault rifle. He stumbled backward from the triphammer impact of the .50-caliber round from the Desert Eagle ricocheting off his chest, the shirt tearing to reveal body armor. Then the triburst of 9 mm rounds from the Beretta walked across the man, tearing away more cloth, then punching through flesh and bone.

As the riddled man fell, the M-16 cut loose a wild hellstorm of 5.56 mm cartridges, then the M-23 grenade launcher shoved beneath the barrel boomed, the 40 mm shell shooting harmlessly down the hallway.

Before the concussion stopped, Bolan spun and fired the Desert Eagle again.

Caught with his hand in a drawer, Tiffany shrieked in pain as the top of the desk exploded into splinters. He jerked back his arm, his wrist bristling with slivers. "Son of a bitch!" he snarled.

Kicking aside a chair, Bolan went around the desk and yanked open the drawer. Inside was a sleek, black Glock machine pistol and several ammunition clips.

"Now, I thought we had an understanding, Michael," Bolan said, dropping the magazine of the Desert Eagle to slam in a fresh one.

Watching the magazine fall to floor, Tiffany went pale. "Okay, okay! Sure, no problem, we got a deal!" he replied, backing away until he was flat against the wall. "Ask away. Whatever you want. I'll tell you everything!"

Bolan stood perfectly still and said nothing. Then he slowly raised the Desert Eagle and took aim.

"Sweet Jesus, what the fuck do you want to know?" Tiffany yelled, a touch of fear in his voice at last. "I'll talk already! Just tell me what you want to know!"

Unfortunately, Bolan had no idea exactly what he wanted to know. So there was only one way to play this, cold and hard. "Tell me about what happened a few days ago," he demanded, leveling the Beretta.

After inhaling deeply, Tiffany let his breath out slowly. "Oh…that. I should have known. Well, I'll be fucking delighted to roll over on those assholes. They paid half a mil in advance, but when I delivered the goods, they released mustard gas and took everything…and killed fifty of my best men. Fifty! Even the fucking rats in the rafters were dead before the air was clear enough for me to get back inside the warehouse!"

"The warehouse on the wharf outside?"

"Yeah, bunch of locals also bought the farm. Some bums, a few gangbangers and two of my cooks."

Civilians had died; that upped the ante. "Sorry for your loss," Bolan said in a graveyard voice. "Keep to the important details."

"Yeah, sure." Slowly reaching for a wall switch, Tiffany turned on the lights. He blinked as they came on. Bolan didn't.

"There were twenty or so of them, but one guy was in charge," Tiffany said, sitting down in a plush leather chair. Wisely, he kept his hands in plain sight. "A foreign guy, nice dresser, platinum Rolex and such."

"Name?"

"Mr. Loki."

Now, that was a new one. "More," Bolan said.

"Loki spoke really good English, but with a weird accent, like nothing I've ever heard before," Tiffany said with a shrug. "Know what I mean? Not Israeli, German, French or anything normal like that. Something else."

Which left most of the world's population. "What did he purchase?" the soldier demanded impatiently.

"Junk."

Bolan scowled. "Drugs?"

"No, I mean real junk," Tiffany repeated. "Tons and tons of it. The oldest, cheapest crap I had in storage. I was figuring on dumping it all on some third world warlord who didn't know napalm from orange juice, who didn't know a revolver from a cruise missile, but this guy had cash in hand, bags and bags of euros. He wanted all of it, but didn't have quite enough cash. So we cut a deal and—"

"And he used gas and took all of it."

"Every fucking thing in the warehouse! Let me tell you, there is no honor among thieves anymore."

"There never was. Define junk, Michael."

"Antiques, man. Cold War stuff. AK-47 assault rifles, and some World War II bazookas. Honest, freaking bazookas!" He paused, and a shadow briefly crossed his face.

"Don't lie to me now," Bolan warned, thumbing back the hammer on the Desert Eagle.

Tiffany shrugged in resignation. "Okay, they stole the guns. They had arranged to buy just a couple hundred land mines."

"What kind of land mines?"

Reaching down to the ruined desktop, Tiffany pushed away some papers to reveal a wooden box. He flipped the top and took out a slim cigar. "Not land mines, underwater mines," he stated, biting off the end and spitting it onto the floor. "You know, the sort of things Britain used to chain to concrete blocks and line the Channel with to stop Nazi U-boats. Mines, man."

Yes, Bolan knew all about underwater mines. North Korea used them by the thousands to blockade their own harbor to prevent NATO or South Korea from invading. Underwater mines were one of the deadliest defensive weapons in existence. But why did Loki want so many of them?

"I need more," Bolan prodded.

Lighting the cigar tip, Tiffany inhaled deeply, then exhaled dark smoke. "Sure, sure, no problem. They were Iranian mines, M-39s."

"Any idea what he wanted the mines for?"

"I don't stay in business by asking questions," Tiffany told him, touching his wounded arm.

Fair enough. "How many mines?"

"All of them, couple hundred."

"Exactly how many, Michael?"

"Okay, okay, six hundred and fifty."

Six hundred underwater mines...that was enough to blockade the entire city of New York. "What did they use to haul them away, trucks or a freighter?"

"A Hercules transport. Big-ass seaplane."

Interesting. "Describe the buyers."

"Two men and a woman. She was pretty, and had the biggest tits I've ever seen."

Considering that he ran the strip club overhead, that was quite a statement. "And the men?"

"Loki was tall, good-looking, like George Hamilton, the actor. Old, but classy."

"And the other?"

"Just a mook. Street muscle. Skinny, with cold eyes, like there was nothing inside but hate and hunger."

A trigger man. Possibly a bodyguard. "Anything else?"

Tiffany hesitated. "Not all of my guys were dead when I arrived. One of them managed to whisper that he heard the fuckers talk about bringing a squall to the world."

"Interesting. Did he say a storm or a squall?"

"Squall. Now, in my business, that is both a sudden summer storm and an incredibly expensive piece of Russian navy hardware. It's a kind of underwater missile, a rocket-powered torpedo."

Tiffany paused as if waiting for Bolan to deny that such a thing could possibly exist. When that didn't happen, he added, "I don't carry any of those. Don't know anybody who does! The damn things malfunction half the time. They've killed more Russians than anybody else. Still..." He shrugged.

Bolan felt as if an important piece of a puzzle had just clicked into place. North Korean mines and Russian torpedoes. Somehow those two were connected. Was Loki going to declare war on the rest of the world? That made no sense whatsoever. Something very odd was going on here, and Bolan had a bad feeling that a lot more innocent civilians were going to die if he didn't figure this out fast.

"Okay, we're done," he said, holstering the Beretta. "I leave, and you go out of business, because if we ever meet again…" He didn't finish the promise and saw in the other man's eyes that it was not necessary.

"Yeah, sure, no problem." Tiffany sighed, crushing out the cigar in a glass ashtray. "Always wanted to retire to… ah…Florida?"

"Mike, I don't care where, just leave tonight," Bolan stated, walking backward out of the room. "Leave tonight."

Staying in the chair for several minutes, Tiffany plucked splinters from his aching arm while debating his options. Standing, he started to reach for the Glock in the drawer, then abruptly changed his mind and turned to move the picture of the congressman and reveal a small wall safe. Twirling the dial, he opened the door and began stuffing packets of cash into his pockets.

"Smart move," Bolan whispered from the darkness outside.

Trying not to shiver, Tiffany emptied the safe, then headed directly for the nearest emergency exit. First a bunch of foreigners wipe out his dock crew, and then some hardcase blows open his Brooklyn operation like he was the wrath of God. It was obviously time for him to find a nice tropical island someplace where the rum flowed freely and the native girls wore only smiles and sunshine.

Keeping his expression neutral, Tiffany waited for the elevator doors to sigh shut before finally allowing himself a brief smile. At least he had been able to bluff that big son of a bitch about one thing. Loki hadn't stolen a couple hundred of the North Korean mines, but four thousand!

Enough to blow the city of New York out of the water, or sink a dozen battleships.

But that was his problem now, Tiffany smugly thought, rearranging the packets of cash stuffed into his clothing.

Suddenly, a figure in the darkness blocked his way. "Half a mil in advance would mean a cool million dollars for a couple hundred underwater mines that sell legally for a grand apiece," Bolan said from the shadows. "Not even you overcharge that much, Michael. What else did they get?"

His elation melting away, Tiffany felt a cold fury well within him, and he made a desperate grab for the Glock. There was a bright flash of light, a brief pain, and he fell forward into an inky blackness that seemed to extend forever.

Returning to his car, Bolan saw drunk men staggering away into the night, then heard police sirens and fire trucks wailing in the distance. The club parking lot was empty by now, and even the doorman was gone.

Stowing his weapons in the truck of the car, Bolan drove off into the hard rain. He had allowed Tiffany to lie about the amount of mines stolen only to salve the man's ego. Let subjects think they outwitted you on a small point, and they'd spill their guts about all the rest. That trick usually worked, just not this time. Bad luck, nothing more.

When he was several blocks away, Bolan turned onto Flatbush Avenue and headed toward Manhattan. Okay, Mr. Loki had obviously taken a lot more than a couple hundred underwater mines. Maybe it had been several thousand. The big question was, what did Loki plan to do with enough military ordnance to launch the Empire State Building into orbit? The possibilities were endless, and he didn't like any of them.

As the car rumbled across the Brooklyn Bridge, Bolan

flipped open a cell phone and tapped in a memorized number. It was answered immediately.

"Yeah?" a sleepy voice said with a yawn.

"Striker here," Bolan said brusquely. "We need to talk."

"Where?"

"Flintstone." Then the soldier closed the phone and tossed it out the window. It hit the steel lattice of the bridge and shattered, the pieces falling through the grating to sprinkle into the turgid waters of the Hudson River.

CHAPTER TWO

Azores Islands

The sea foamed white and clean before the cutting prow of the HMS *Reliant,* while behind the destroyer a school of bottlenose dolphins played in the churning wake.

Staying close to the *Reliant* were three heavily armed frigates. Their overlapping Doppler radar ceaselessly swept the sky above, and state-of-the-art sonar probed the murky depths below. The missile pods were primed, depth charges and torpedoes were ready for action, and sailors stood on the decks cradling L-85 assault rifles. But they lounged against the gunwales, kept their faces to the sun and mostly talked about women.

The entire crew of the convoy was fully prepared for battle, but expected nothing more serious than a mild case of sunburn to happen. Everybody knew the monthly trip to South Africa was about as dangerous an assignment as standing guard at Buckingham Palace when the royal family was away on vacation. Boring, but necessary for the general good of the United Kingdom.

It was early in the morning, with the sun still low on the horizon. But the sky was clear, the wind warm. And standing on the flying bridge of the *Reliant*, Captain Olivia Taylor, wearing a pair of nonregulation sunglasses, was watching the dolphins splash and play, and occasionally feed on the smaller fish that were attracted to the churning foam, incorrectly thinking it was food. Evolution in action.

Opening a bottle of suntan lotion, Taylor spread some on her exposed arms and neck, working up to her cheeks. This assignment was a cakewalk, as her American father had liked to say, a task so easy it would border on dull if it hadn't been for the vital nature of their cargo.

Roughly a hundred years ago, Great Britain had owned most of South Africa, and was making a serious attempt to get the rest of the continent, when the Boer War erupted, closely followed by Zulu uprisings. Then there was the Great War, World War II…and every conflict seemed to whittle down their African holdings a little bit more until they were reduced to being landowners in just a few locations.

Closing the cap on the bottle, Taylor had to smile. But those last few were choice locations, indeed. Snug in the bowels of her destroyer was the yearly run from the Imperial Gold Mines UK Limited—a hold full of gold bullion worth millions of pounds. Which was why the Royal Navy had been assigned to convey the gold from Johannesburg to London, the final destination being the main vault of the Bank of England, the most impregnable fortress this side of Fort Knox in the United States.

"Cup of tea, Skipper?" a young officer asked, stepping onto the flying bridge. He was carrying two large plastic mugs, the bottoms oddly curved.

"Lord, yes, James! My thanks," Taylor said with a smile. Taking the mug, she drained half of it in a single gulp. "Ah, like blood to a vampire!"

Chuckling, Lieutenant James Jones set his mug on the railing of the platform. Its curved bottom fit perfectly over the steel pipe and locked into place with a snap. "Now, that sounds like a line from a bloody Hammer film back in the seventies."

"Ah yes, Christopher Lee and Peter Cushing."

"To be honest, Skipper, I was thinking more along the lines of those curvy Hammer Girls, and their rather famous low-cut gowns."

She took another sip. "I'm sure you were, Lieutenant. To each his own. Peter Cushing is more to my liking. The nearer the bone, the sweeter the meat!"

The officer laughed. "As you say, Skipper, to each their own."

Just then, a wing of fully armed RAF striker fighters streaked by overhead.

"Cheeky bastards, rattling our chains like that," Jones muttered, squinting at the disappearing jets.

"Just doing their job, Lieutenant," Taylor replied, finishing off her tea. "Any sandwiches in the galley?"

"Yes, ma'am. What would you like?"

She laughed. "I'll get them myself, James. No sense—"

Unexpectedly, a loudspeaker bolted to the armored wall of the warship crackled to life. "Captain to the bridge, please! Captain to the bridge!"

With a sigh, Taylor hurried inside, passing off the empty mug to a waiting rating. The young sailor took it, saluted and scurried away.

"Trouble?" Taylor asked the room in general.

Control panels lined the room, a dozen computer screens showing the exact state of everything important on the navy ship, from the temperature of the main bearings in the Rolls-Royce engines, to the amount of 30 mm ammunition left in the bunkers for the forward Oerlikon miniguns. A dozen men and women were sitting at their posts, heads bent solemnly over the controls like priests in prayer.

"Unknown, ma'am," said an ensign, rubbing the back

of his neck. "But with this much glimmer in our belly, I thought it wise to be safe instead of sorry."

"Fair enough," Taylor said, pushing back her cap. "Status, please, chief."

"We're traveling the exact same route we took going down to South Africa," Chief Michelson replied crisply, his gaze locked on a glowing sonar screen. "We know every hill and rock under these waters, and there's something new below. Something big."

"A dead whale?" Jones asked curiously. He had followed the captain inside.

"No, much larger than that, sir. Sonar says irregular shapes, mounds of it. Could be a wrecked ship."

"Damn. Have there been any storms in the vicinity, or known pirate attacks?" Taylor asked. "If a commercial vessel sank in these shallow waters, there could be survivors about. What about it, Ears?"

"Possibly a civilian wreck, Captain," the sonar operator replied. Eyes tightly closed, he held the earphones in place with both hands. "But it would have to have been a small ship, maybe a fishing boat or pleasure craft. I'm not hearing any metal below, just lots of wood and plastic."

"Sounds like a speedboat to me," James stated, crossing his arms. No metal meant there was no threat to the convoy. "Ears, what's the depth?"

"Five hundred meters, and rising," the sonar operator called out briskly, hunched before the glowing computer screen.

"Lieutenant, send out a couple of hovercraft... No, belay that," Taylor said with a grimace. "Uncork a Lynx helicopter and do a sweep for any survivors. Hundred meters, three hundred and five. Move quick now."

"Debris spotted in the starboard water, sir!" an ensign

interrupted, touching his headphones. "Multiple lifejackets, broken wood and general flotsam!"

"Get that Lynx flying, Lieutenant," Taylor snapped, sitting in the command chair. All around her banks of video monitors strobed into life, showing every aspect of the colossal vessel. "Helm, increase speed to maximum. Chief, have one of the frigates stay behind and conduct a full S and R op."

"Search and rescue, aye, aye, ma'am," he said with a brisk salute. "But may I suggest—"

Just then, the entire destroyer rocked from the force of a powerful explosion.

"What the bleeding hell just happened to my ship?" the captain demanded, glancing at the overhead monitors. A forward compartment was taking on water—not much, but steadily. A port side depth charge launcher had gone offline, and two of the crew had vanished, last seen near the anchor chain winch.

"Unknown, ma'am!" the sonar operator reported crisply. "Sonar is clean. There is no hot noise in the water! Repeat, no hot noise!"

"Thank God for that. What about radar?" Taylor demanded, twisting her head.

"Clean and clear, Skip," the ensign replied. "Five by five. Whatever is happening is coming from below."

"The water is clear," Ears repeated sternly.

"Well, something just hammered us like a Christmas bell!" Jones snarled, just before a second explosion shook the vessel, closely followed by another, then six more in rapid succession.

Reaching up, the captain grabbed a hand mike from an overhead stanchion. "All hands hear this, all hands hear this, battle stations! I repeat, battle stations!" she snapped. "This is not a drill. We are under attack!"

Instantly, Klaxons and horns began to hoot all over the destroyer, and swarms of sailors poured out of hatchways to surge across the tilting deck and take their assigned positions at the weapons stations.

"How could you possibly know this is an attack, and not a catastrophic mechanical failure?" Jones demanded, grabbing on to a stanchion as the ship shook again, even harder this time.

"That wreckage on the ocean floor," Taylor growled in reply. "It had to be a trick to make us stop!"

The ship rocked again as a water plume rose off the starboard side.

"But we accelerated!"

"Then let's hope we escape!"

By now, the overhead monitors showed several breaks in the primary hull, with multiple compartments taking on water faster than the gauges could read. One engine was already dead, and screaming was coming from the galley.

"Helm, evasive tactics!" Taylor said calmly, her heart wildly pounding. "Sparks, call Gibraltar for rescue! Engine Room, all pumps to maximum!"

Just then, there came a deafening explosion, and one of the escort frigates rose from the ocean on a boiling column of steam and flame. As the stunned bridge crew of the *Reliant* watched, the frigate broke in two, spilling crew and machinery into the water.

"Are we being nuked?" Jones demanded, blood flowing from the palm of his clenched fist. "Did we hit a ruddy volcano?"

"I have no idea," Taylor said honestly, her hands pressed firmly to the cushioned arms of her chair.

Another powerful explosion shook their vessel, and a sailor yelled as he went over the side. Several water columns appeared alongside another frigate, and the armored hull ripped open wide to show the burning decks inside, broken human bodies flying away in chunks. Diesel fuel and oil spread across the choppy waves like thick blood. The second frigate was listing badly to the side, while the third was already nose deep in the water and quickly sinking.

"Ma'am, the *Cardiff* is gone," the radar operator said in an emotionless voice, his face deathly pale.

"What in the… Captain, sonar is dead!" Ears called out, staring in horror at the screen. It was glowing a solid, featureless green, every attempt by the onboard computers completely overwhelmed.

"Well, fix it!" Captain Taylor bellowed, as the destroyer rocked again and a water plume rose high on their port side. Honest to Jesus, if she didn't know any better she would have sworn that was an underwater mine!

Ears held out his hands, his fingers hovering inches away from the complex controls. "But I don't even know what's wrong, Skip! This…this is impossible!"

"Fix it anyway!" Jones demanded, as yet another explosion shook the warship.

"Forget target acquisitions! Every station fire blind into the water!" Taylor shouted into the hand mike. "Weapons Officer, set depth charges for—" That was when she saw a dozen metallic spheres rise to the surface of the ocean surrounding the convoy. They were covered with short, dull spikes and…

Mines! The convoy was being attacked by bleeding underwater mines! she realized in shock. But any British navy ship could withstand the concentrated attack of a dozen conventional mines, maybe twice that number!

Except that as she watched, more and more of the dark spheres appeared on the waves, dozens upon dozens of them, until they made the sea look like a cobblestone street.

Taylor could barely believe the sight. It was a nightmare come true. There had to be thousands of them! There wasn't a ship in the world that could withstand that sort of mass attack. But how had the things gotten so close? Had the sonar been sabotaged? That was the only logical answer, because otherwise it would mean that—

The entire ocean seemed to erupt into a solid sheet of flame as the jostling mines clanged into one another to start a hellish chain reaction, a nonstop series of bone-jarring blasts that filled the universe. Briefly, men and women screamed as there arose the terrible keening of tortured metal being twisted out of shape. But even as Captain Taylor dived for the self-destruct button that would de-stroy the communications code in the main computer, she felt the ship heave upward, and for an unknowable length of time there was only pain and chaos.

FIGHTING HER WAY back to consciousness, Captain Taylor found herself waist deep in water, with the strange sensa-tion of being in an elevator that was descending. Sinking, my ship is sinking! But that was difficult to confirm at the moment. Her left eye wasn't working, her chest ached and both legs felt oddly numb. The ceiling lights were gone, but a couple of the emergency wall lights had survived intact and were emitting an eerie green luminescence.

Glancing around, the captain discovered that she was trapped in an air pocket on the bridge—the inverted bridge. The deck was above her head, and she was awkwardly standing on the ceiling. Smashed electrical equipment crackled from the control boards, blood was everywhere, and pieces of her command crew bobbed about in the water like fishing chum. A jumbled array of tattered arms and legs swirled in the water, then the head of Lieutenant Jones floated by, his face contorted in a final scream. Her stomach lurched at the grisly sight, but she banished those thoughts, and concentrated solely on staying alive. Her job now was to destroy the main computer and then escape from the sinking wreck. Of course, the only two exits were blocked by folded layers of crushed steel, but that wasn't her main concern at the moment.

As Taylor feebly splashed her upside-down chair toward a sparking controls board, she noted that the only reason she was still alive was that the windows were all still intact, the bulletproof plastic merely scratched. She felt a sudden jarring from below, and loose sand swirled outside the windows. They were at the bottom already?

Creaking and groaning, the *Reliant* began to settle into place, the crippled vessel warping around the steel-reinforced shell of the bridge.

"God bless all navy engineers!" the captain panted, then gasped at the sight of moving lights outside the windows. In growing astonishment, she saw a dozen scuba divers swimming along the murky seabed, heading her way.

Wild hope of rescue flared just for a second, until she realized those were nonregulation diving suits, and the masked strangers were carrying acetylene torches and crowbars.

In a surge of cold adrenaline, Taylor fought her way through the morass of body parts to reach the glowing SD button, smash the glass covering and press hard. She felt it click, and there was an answering thump through the water from the pressure of the explosive charges cutting loose. Now the military codes of her nation were safe, the communication chips and data files utterly destroyed. Whoever these bastards were, they would learn nothing from those molten remains!

Just then, a scuba diver riding an underwater sled drove into view, and she bitterly cursed at the sight of a net being dragged behind the sled. The nylon threads bulged with gold bars…and corpses, the faces of the dead sailors familiar to her. These weren't enemy spies, but common, ordinary thieves—and for some unknown reason, body snatchers.

"Filthy bastards!" Taylor screamed in white-hot rage.

As if hearing the curse, the driver slowed and looked about for the source. He seemed quite startled to see the live naval officer on the other side of the cracked window. Then he smiled and waved hello.

Sputtering expletives, Taylor irrationally drew her sidearm and fired all fifteen rounds. However, the 9 mm slugs merely smacked into the heavy plastic and stayed there like flies in amber. The resilient material that kept in her precious air supply also prevented her from reaching out to the thief.

Grinning behind his face mask, the skinny driver waved again and continued on his way.

Raging impotently, the captain holstered the pistol, unable to think of anything else to try at the moment.

Forcing herself to remain calm, she tried to conserve oxygen, biding her time as the strangers looted the *Reliant* of its entire cargo of gold bullion, and then departed.

She waited a few extra minutes just to make sure, then surged into action. Rummaging among the dead crew, she found a pocketknife and started scratching details of the thieves into the tough plastic—their numbers, descriptions and type of weapons carried. But then the skinny driver unexpectedly returned.

Quickly, the captain moved away from the window, but it was already too late. Reaching into a canvas bag slung at his side, the skinny man pulled out a WWII limpet mine and clumsily attached it to the plastic. He set the timer, smiled, threw her a salute and swam away once more.

Trapped inside the wreckage, Captain Taylor could do nothing but curse until a bright flash of light filled her universe.

Flintstone, Maryland

TURNING OFF THE MAIN ROAD, Hal Brognola skirted the little town of Flintstone and drove the rented truck into the vast rolling countryside of Maryland. The old vehicle rattled and clanked at every pothole and gully, and the big Fed hoped he wasn't leaving a trail of broken parts all the way back to his office in the Justice Department.

Occasionally checking the GPS on his dashboard, he finally took an unmarked dirt road that snaked into the hillsides to finally end at a long-abandoned stone quarry. Windblown leaves covered the ground, ancient garbage was scattered everywhere, and the sagging remains of huge machines slowly rusted away into indecipherable mounds of debris.

Coming to an easy stop, Brognola set the parking brake, but left the engine running in case of trouble. A stocky man with graying hair, the big Fed could still bench-press his own weight at the gym. Although, to be honest, it did seem to take more of an effort these days to achieve those results.

As head of the Sensitive Operations Group for the Justice Department, he normally wore a two-piece suit, but this day Brognola was in less formal attire—a denim vest, red flannel shirt, worn pants and leather boots. Flintstone was a hardworking, blue-collar town, home to a cement factory. Nobody wore a suit around here, not even the mayor.

Easing a S&W snub-nosed revolver out of a shoulder holster under the vest, Brognola thumbed back the hammer, but stayed behind the wheel, listening to the soft clatter of the engine. Nothing was moving in the jagged expanse of the stone quarry. There wasn't a tree, a bush or even a stray dog, just rocky desolation. Even the construction shacks and mill had collapsed into jumbled piles unfit for anything but burning in a wood stove.

The sole exception was a colossal lifting crane, the long box girder neck extending over the main pit. For some reason it reminded Brognola of a gallows, and sent a shiver down his spine. The message he'd received from Mack Bolan had used all the correct code prefixes. But codes had been broken before, and the big Fed had more than his share of enemies. The list seemed to go on forever these days, and the only thing getting shorter was his tolerance for the bloodthirsty sons of bitches who broke the law, and then demanded its protection.

"Choose one or the other," he growled softly, involuntarily tightening his grip on the checkered handle of the .38 Police Special.

Just then, he heard the soft rattle of a rock tumbling down a mountain of broken slabs. Instantly, Brognola turned in the exact opposite direction, with the S&W level and two pounds of pressure on the six-pound trigger.

"I see sitting in an office hasn't slowed you down in the least." Bolan chuckled, stepping into view from behind a granite boulder.

"Not yet, anyway." Brognola grinned, lowering the barrel of his weapon. "Okay, what's with meeting out here in the middle of nowhere? I mean, for God's sake... Flintstone?" He snorted. "I had to check two maps before I even found the place!"

"Too many new faces in D.C.," Bolan said, pulling a small black box from his belt and moving it slowly about. "We need privacy."

"You checking for bugs?" Brognola asked incredulously, then clamped his mouth shut and looked around at his car. Slowly, he turned off the engine, and thick silence descended.

A minute passed, then another.

"Okay, we're clear," Bolan announced, tucking away the box. "This EM scanner was built for me by a friend at JPL Laboratories, and has twice the range of anything the Farm can come up with." The Farm was Stony Man Farm, home base for the Sensitive Operations Group. "It also jams cell phones and digital recorders, and sends out an ultrasonic pulse to check for any parabolic reflectors."

"What's the range?"

"Half a mile."

"That should do the trick," Brognola stated, tucking the revolver into its shoulder holster and climbing out of the car. "You don't trust anything, do you?"

"Just a few old friends," Bolan replied with a smile, extending a hand, and the men shook.

"It's been a while since we last met face-to-face, Striker," Brognola said. "I've had an awful lot on my plate."

"Yeah, so I've heard." Bolan released his grip. "Come on, I have a camp set up over here. Canvas chairs, sandwiches and beer."

"Now you're talking," Brognola said amiably.

Following a zigzagging path through the field of broken slabs and boulders, Bolan finally led Brognola into a small clearing. There were a couple of canvas chairs set up near a foam cooler. There was also a battered canvas backpack on the ground nearby, an M-16/M-203 assault rifle combo lying on top.

"Expecting company?" Brognola asked, scanning the nearby rocks for suspicious movements.

"Just prepared for it," Bolan said, sitting in a chair and

flipping back the lid of the cooler. Inside was a six-pack of beer, a couple deli-wrapped sandwiches, several grenades and a 9 mm Heckler & Koch MP-5 submachine gun with a sound suppressor attached.

Brognola tried not to chuckle. The man never missed a trick. "Okay, the last I heard you were in Brooklyn checking on a smuggling ring."

"It's out of business."

Yeah, Brognola knew what that meant. The smugglers were dead and buried.

"So what were they moving? Drugs, illegal aliens, slaves, DVRs, pornography...?"

"Weapons."

He frowned. "Saturday night specials or—"

"Damn near everything, including North Korean underwater mines."

"Damn! How many?"

"Couple of thousand."

"Who the hell would want those in Brooklyn?"

"You tell me," Bolan said, and gave the man the full details of the matter.

"Loki...nope, never heard of them," Brognola said, massaging his jaw. "That's the Norse god of mischief, right?"

"Pretty much. Not necessarily evil, just a pain in the ass. Which makes me wonder if the thieves were sending a message with the name."

"As if they want people to know who stole the mines?" Brognola said with a snort. "I don't like those implications. Sounds like a suicide message. Maybe it was a mistake."

"That's not how I read it, and Loki was good enough to take Mad Mike in his own backyard."

"Yeah, good point. Amateurs, but not fools."

Bolan then told him about the Squall.

"The combination of old weapons and advanced technology bothers me. Any idea what they're planning?"

"Wish I did," Bolan said. "Hal, are there any known terrorist groups that operate out of Iceland or Greenland?"

"Hell no. Those countries don't even have armies! They've got nothing worth stealing or blowing up. Nothing major, anyway."

"Then this might be a personal matter."

"Swell," Brognola said with a scowl.

"Did you bring the files?" Bolan asked.

"Of course." The Fed reached inside his flannel shirt to remove a plain white envelope. "A couple of these needed presidential clearance, but the White House owes you big time, so no problem there."

"Good to know." Bolan started riffling through the top secret documents. Where his fingers touched the paper, it turned brown. "Damn, all these are dated yesterday. Anything happen within the past couple of hours? Anything in water? Mysterious explosions, ships lost at sea, river tunnel collapse…anything odd like that?"

"Sorry, no," Brognola said, then frowned. "Wait a minute, yes, there was. Just a couple hours ago a British naval convoy went missing off the Azores, all hands lost."

"Any reason given?"

"An unexpected storm."

Finishing his sandwich, Bolan arched an eyebrow. "A summer storm…near the Azores Islands at this time of year?"

"Well, that's what the prime minister is saying," Brognola said with a shrug. "Anyway, the British navy went absolutely ape-shit over the sinking, and scrambled two wings of RAF jet fighters out of their base on Gibraltar to sweep the area."

"Not helicopters?"

"Nope."

"It's impossible to rescue drowning sailors in something flying at Mach 3," Bolan stated, crumpling the paper into a ball and depositing it back into the cooler. "The jets were doing a recon, not a search and rescue."

"Obviously. Think those stolen mines sank the convoy?"

"Could be."

A cold breeze blew over the mountains of boulders, carrying the smell of distant plant life mixed with the reek of diesel fumes.

Bolan leaned forward. "Okay, Hal, what was stolen? A member of the royal family, a new type of message decoder, nerve gas or nuclear warheads?"

"Give me a minute." Pulling out his smartphone, Brognola tapped in a number and held a terse conversation. Then he texted somebody else and made another call.

"They stole gold," he stated at last.

"Just gold?" Bolan asked.

"A lot of it. According to my contact in MI5, the convoy was carrying a full consignment of refined ore from the Imperial Gold Mines UK down in South Africa."

"How much gold are we talking about?"

"Hundreds of millions of dollars' worth, maybe more. The Brits aren't talking. The *Reliant* was a big ship, and those are very lucrative mines."

"Damn well guess so."

"Now, the U.S. Navy had an attack sub in the area patrolling the deep waters, and offered to help with the search and rescue," Brognola said slowly. "But the British government refused any assistance."

"On an S and R?" Bolan frowned. "Those jets were looking for the thieves."

"That would be the logical assumption."

"Any chance the RAF blew them out of the water?"

"No way. The Pentagon had a Keyhole spy satellite orbit over the area only minutes behind them. If the Brits blew up anything, even a submarine, we would have seen the oil slick and flotsam."

Furrowing his brow, Bolan said nothing for a few minutes. "Tiffany said that the people who stole his mines used a Hercules transport. A Herc could carry a hell of a lot of bullion. If the terrorists are hauling gold, they'd need more than one. Any reports of a couple of Hercules planes being stolen recently? That would give us someplace to start looking for the thieves."

"Not that I've heard. But if they rented the aircraft, then they wouldn't be considered missing for days, maybe weeks."

"That would be the smart move," Bolan said.

"Striker, this is starting to stink to high heaven of a French stepladder."

"That possibility occurred to me," Bolan growled, setting aside the remains of his sandwich.

"Swell." Brognola sighed, throwing the squashed beer can at the cooler. It hit the plastic rim and bounced inside.

A "stepladder" was an old French police term for a street mugger who used a rock to smash the window of a hardware store, to steal a stepladder to rob a house through a second-story window. He then sold the purloined jewelry to buy enough explosives to blow open a bank vault, and used that cash to bug a truckload of drugs that he then sold for millions to a dealer. Throw a rock and become a millionaire. All it took was guts, brains and a complete lack of morals.

"Did they take anything else from the sunken ships?" Bolan asked.

"If you're referring to the rods in the nuclear power

plant, no, nothing like that," Brognola said, shaking his head. "The destroyer and frigates were all diesel."

"Glad to hear it. Any of the crew missing before the convoy left port?"

"Unknown. Think it might be an inside job? You could be right. There have been traitors before, and for a slice of hundreds of millions of bucks…" Brognola's voice faded away.

"The big question has to be how did the thieves know where to ambush the convoy?" Bolan asked. "The route had to have been secret."

"Well, once, very long ago, I was assigned to help guard a delivery of gold from the United Kingdom to Fort Knox. Nothing big, about half a ton." He smiled. "They hid radio transmitters inside the wooden pallets so that the gold could be tracked every step of the way."

"Any chance the Brits have upgraded their system and now have GPS microdots on their gold?"

"Sure. Probably on the pallets, and hidden inside the gold itself. Try to melt down a bar, and the heat would trigger a micropulse signal. Five minutes later, you're surrounded by the British army, asking for their property back."

"Unless you melt it inside a Faraday cage to block the signal."

"Think Loki is that smart?"

"They have been so far," Bolan said. "Now, I'm willing to bet that the British MI5 are already checking on the company that manufactured the GPS dots, to see if anybody called in sick today, or recently died in a car crash."

"Nothing we can do to help them there," Brognola stated honestly. "And if Loki can safely remove the tracking dots, then they can sell the bars anywhere, on street corners if they like."

Bolan scowled. "Not without the British being informed. I'd be very surprised if they don't already have a huge reward posted across the internet for any information about the thieves, no questions asked."

"True. Which means Loki will have to sell it on the black market, and get a fraction of the real value."

"One or two hundred million is still a boatload of cash."

"Damn straight. Okay, where can they go? Switzerland?"

"No, the Swiss banks are riddled with spies working for Interpol these days," Bolan stated, leaning back in the chair. "And in spite of all the electronic banking done, the need for hard commodities like gold and silver is very much alive and well. The biggest underground banks are in Ecuador, Pakistan and China."

"Ecuador?"

"It's the Switzerland of South America."

Brognola almost smiled. The man knew the damnedest things. "Okay, but that's only for trading small amounts of gold, right? Where could Loki go to unload so much gold in one shot?"

"Without getting a half-ounce of hot British lead in the back of their heads?" Bolan said. He didn't speak for a moment, his mind filled with a swirling hurricane of half-truths, rumors and outright lies, about the hidden world of criminal finance. Stealing the gold was only half the job. Now Loki would have to convert it into something usable, and more importantly, untraceable.

Propping his fingertips together, Brognola patiently waited.

"Barcelona," Bolan said at last, rising from the chair and starting to pack away the campsite. "But I'm heading for Albania."

"Why?" Brognola demanded in confusion.

"To talk to the people who actually own the secret banks of Spain," he told his old friend.

CHAPTER THREE

Barcelona, Spain

The blazing sun shone mercilessly on the bustling metropolis of Barcelona. The streets and sidewalks seeming to reflect the waves of searing heat like parabolic mirrors until the entire city appeared to be shining.

Traffic had slowed to a crawl, and most of the pushcart venders had closed shop. There was no sign of tourists, and even the locals had abandoned the daylight to seek the cooler realms of basements and air-conditioned cafés.

At a small private airport located far outside the city limits, three Hercules seaplanes sat baking on an isolated strip of cracked asphalt. One of the big planes was closed, its ramps rigidly locked in position. The other two had their access ramps fully descended, the shadowy interior of the aircraft dimly visible through the wavering heat from the ground.

Dripping sweat, twenty men and women surrounded the hulking aircraft, AK-47 assault rifles carefully balanced in their gloved hands. The Icelanders had stripped down as far as decorum allowed. Everybody was wearing tinted sunglasses, their pale, exposed skin oily with suntan lotion.

The gold had been divided into three parcels, and now each plane contained roughly a hundred million dollars' worth. The sheer numbers made Hrafen Thorodensen feel slightly drunk. But it was nothing, a drop in the ocean, to what Britain would end up paying for their inhuman greed.

"Well, any sign of them yet?" Gunnar Eldjarm demanded, tying a handkerchief around his head to stop the sweat from pouring down his face and washing away the sunscreen.

"Speak of the devil," Thorodensen replied, lowering a pair of binoculars.

A small dust cloud was coming their way from the west, and as it drew closer, he could dimly see an armored truck accompanied by a dozen motorcycles. The riders were masked in combat gear, body armor and mirrored helmets, and Thorodensen tried not to imagine how hot it had to be for the guards, in that heavy equipment. Still, he did appreciate their professionalism.

The truck and escorts braked a hundred feet away from the idling planes, and a second later the wake of dust arrived, to flow over the area like desiccated fog. The Icelanders started coughing, but held their positions, alert for any treachery by the infamous Spanish bankers.

Before the armored vehicle had fully stopped moving, the rear doors burst open and out rushed a dozen men carrying an assortment of weaponry—American assault rifles, German autoshotguns and Russian grenade launchers.

Watching timidly from the shadows inside one of the big planes, Professor Lilja Vilhjalms marveled at the open display of ordnance, and double-checked the EM scanner in her hands for any sign of a tracer signal or microburst. She had personally neutralized the GPS dot from each bar of gold, and destroyed them inside a standard microwave oven. The clever British had thought of everything but that. As her old science teacher had liked to jokingly say, advanced technology was just so damn primitive.

Climbing out of the cab of the truck, a slim man stepped

onto the shimmering tarmac. Dressed in a three-piece business suit, he carried a small laptop slung at his side, and had a leather briefcase in one hand. If the heat had any effect on the dapper man, it wasn't noticeable.

"Good morning, Mr. Loki!" he called out, casually walking forward. "I am Hector Gonzales. Lovely day, is it not?"

"Yes, wonderful day. Spain must be the home of God," Thorodensen said diplomatically, trying not to breath too deeply. Then he added, "Gibraltar."

"Malta," Gonzales replied with a smile. "Well, now that's done, shall we proceed to business? How much of a deposit are you making this time, sir?"

"One hundred million dollars in gold," Thorodensen said, glancing at the closest Hercules. "And I need another hundred million converted into German bearer bonds."

"Please accept my hearty congratulations on your success in such a slow economy," Gonzales said, swinging up the laptop and typing away. This wasn't their largest account, but it was most definitely in the top ten. "Does the gold need to be, ah, washed?"

"Yes."

"Very well. Then after our usual fee for the service, your deposit will be…thirty-four million dollars. Correct?"

"Correct," Thorodensen growled, trying not to bridle at the open thievery. The money was flowing away like water running downhill, and they were still a long way from their final goal. But every journey started with a single step.

At a gesture from Gonzales, the bank guards swarmed forward, advancing upon the two open Hercules as if the airplanes were an enemy position, their weapons constantly sweeping for danger. Gonzales strolled up the ramp of one and patiently waited while a pair of guards broke out laboratory equipment and inspected every gold brick for purity.

When the amount was confirmed, the guards relayed the gold bars into the armored truck, and Gonzales ran off a receipt from a small printer attached to the laptop.

"Here you are, sir." He smiled as he passed over the slip. "And here are the bonds you requested. If there is anything else?"

"Yes, please transfer one million dollars to this numbered account," Thorodensen said, handing over a sealed envelope.

"With pleasure, sir," Gonzales replied with a toothy grin, tucking it away inside his jacket. "Hope to see you again soon. Have a pleasant flight!"

Forcing a smile to his face, Thorodensen nodded in return, and didn't allow himself to relax until the armored trucks and guards had disappeared once more into the distance.

"I have trouble believing that you just gave the Spaniards a million dollars as if it was pocket change," Gunnar Eldjarm muttered, resting the Vepr on a shoulder.

"Have no fear, old friend. That amount is all the bastards will ever get from us," Thorodensen stated, passing over the briefcase. "Now, take these bonds to France and purchase five more Hercules seaplanes. We will meet you at the established coordinates off the coast of Sardinia in sixteen hours. If we are not back from Greece on time, leave immediately for Peru. Wait there for two days, then leave. Spend the gold in good health."

"No, I'll come find you!"

Starting back into the airplane, Thorodensen smiled tolerantly. "Thank you, old friend. If we have not returned by then, it means we are dead." He stopped to place a hand on the shoulder of the bony man. "Don't take any chances, Gunnar. Trust nobody, and keep to the plan! Wait two days, then disappear. You know where to purchase false identity papers in New Zealand?"

Resting a foot on the access ramp, Eldjarm gave a curt nod. "Yes, the Two Billies Tavern, just outside of Christchurch. There are new names and passports waiting for all of us." He stressed the last words.

"And with luck we will retire to the Gold Coast of Australia, and live in luxury and peace for the rest of our lives. But that can only be accomplished by adhering to the plan!"

"Thor, when you were the Icelandic ambassador to the United nations, where you this much of a pain in the ass?" Eldjarm asked with a friendly scowl.

"Of course!" he said with a laugh. "How else could I have ever gotten anything done, representing a country without an army?"

Muttering under his breath, Eldjarm swung away from the plane and strode off. Half the armed Icelanders followed, and the rest strode into the open Hercules after their leader.

As Thorodensen started for the flight deck he was joined by Professor Lilja Vilhjalms. She didn't say anything, but from her tense expression, he could tell that she was deeply concerned about something important.

"What is wrong, Lily?" he asked, using his private name for her. The two of them had been very close once, sex partners, but not really lovers. These days they were much closer than that, partners in crime. The evaluation of their relationship amused him.

"Your plan is so complex," the woman stated, moving closer to the big man. "Selling your home to rent the planes, making the mustard gas to steal the mines, and now... Are you sure it is not going to unravel?"

"No, my dear, everything is under control." Thorodensen laughed, draping a friendly arm across her shoulders.

She thrilled at the contact and ached to touch him back, but restrained herself for the moment. They were in view of the others. Perhaps, once they were on White Sands... "So, we are not going to be caught?"

"By those fat fools in NATO? That would be impossible, Lily. Impossible!"

Vilhjalms frowned. "Yet you once told me that nothing is impossible to a strong will."

That caught Thorodensen by surprise. He started to speak, then merely grunted in reply as they started up the steel stairs to the flight deck of the massive aircraft.

Durrës, Albania

FLYING TO A PRIVATE airfield outside of Durrës, Mack Bolan bribed officials to get a locked trunk through airport security, then rented a Range Rover with four-wheel drive and drove toward the capital city, Tirana.

Albania was the heroin hub of the world, supplying the narcotics to most of Europe. The Fifteen Families even had a sweetheart deal arranged with the drug lords of Colombia. They exchanged heroin for cocaine, and each group expanded its sphere of influence. A win-win situation, unless you were one of their customers, forced into thievery, prostitution or worse, just to maintain your supply of the deadly substances. Bolan considered them all narcoterrorists, and removed them from this world as quickly possible. But at least for today, he needed the willing assistance of the murdering sociopaths.

The rolling countryside was beautiful, with rich fields of soybeans, cotton, wheat and endless herds of grazing cattle. However, the roads were much less noteworthy. They were mostly paved, but not always, and were often so steep that the sidewalks had been replaced with concrete stairs. The tough Range Rover took the steep inclines without noticeable effort, aside from a few assorted rattles and a lost hubcap.

Traffic was light, mostly pedestrians, and a few small trucks hauling produce. But Bolan carefully marked the location of every military vehicle.

Albania had once been a kingdom, then Communist, and now was supposedly a democracy, but that was a lie. The entire nation was owned, body and soul, by the Fifteen Families, the largest and most powerful crime family in existence. They made the old Mafia look like a sewing circle. Albania was ruled by a secret dictatorship that used the military to control the police. The reason Bolan rarely tangled with them was because their main concerns were inside Albania. He felt sorry for the enslaved Albanian people, but never fooled himself into thinking that he could save the entire world. That was madness.

Traffic become thicker near the capital city, but the roads didn't improve much. The majority were made with cobblestone, dating back to the Middle Ages. Very picturesque for the tourists, but not practical. Occasionally there was a smooth stretch of pavement, a remnant of the days when the Soviet Union ruled the tiny nation. But most of the streets were in very poor condition, dotted with deep potholes. More than one car was abandoned alongside the road, with a wheel bent sideways, the axle broken in an unexpected encounter with a particularly deep depression.

Standing on a small raised platform, a young policewoman in a crisp uniform and bright orange gloves was expertly directing vehicles around a traffic circle. She instantly noted that Bolan was a tourist and smiled as he passed. He grinned in return, but noticed that her smile quickly faded as she returned to work.

Just then, a limousine raced past the police officer, clearly going way over the posted speed limit, veering in and out of lanes without regard for the other cars, and generally ignoring every rule of safe driving. She bridled at the sight for a moment, then turned her back on the vehicle with a sigh.

Watching in his rearview mirror, Bolan guessed the limousine was owned by a member of the Fifteen Families, and noted that the vehicle rode low on military-grade, bulletproof tires. The limo was armored. He almost smiled at that. In the trunk of the Range Rover was something he had brought along from Brooklyn for just a target.

Hopefully, he wouldn't have to use it. On the plane ride from the States, Bolan had placed a few phone calls and managed to set up a meeting with Rezart Kastrioti, a high-level member of the Fifteen Families. Bolan was posing as a representative for a cartel of American manufacturers to negotiate safe passage for cargo ships carrying Detroit-made cars to Europe. As always, the Fifteen Families were happy to talk business with rich Americans—if the price was right. Bolan should get what he wanted in only a few hours, and then slip quietly away. However, he knew from experience that it was wise to plan for what the enemy could do, not just for what they might do. Hence the XM-25 in the trunk.

The city limits of Tirana were marked by a sharp improvement in the road surface. It was a beautiful municipality, with its tan brick buildings and red tile roofs, and carried a sense of age. Everything in the country felt old, even if it was brand-new. He had encountered such a feeling before many times, mostly in third world nations where poverty was rampart, but also in Detroit, the so-called Rust Belt of the Midwest.

Circling the crumbling remains of an old Roman fortress, Bolan easily spotted his destination in the distance, the glass-and-steel structure rising from the older stone buildings as if a starship had landed in a junkyard. The King Zog Hotel had been built into the side of a small mountain. The slanted glass facade sparkled brightly, and even from a distance he could see a heliport on the rooftop.

The hotel was named after a legendary president of Albania, a gentle and wise man so deeply beloved by the people that they had given him the nickname King Zog. He had tried to stop the invasion by the Soviets, and failed, but his heroic battle still gave heart to the people.

Parking a short distance from the hotel, Bolan walked around the block a few times, casually dropping small packages into trash bins and down storm gratings. After checking the signal on the remote control, he returned to the Range Rover and drove to the front of the futuristic hotel.

For the meeting he was wearing business chic: a Hugo Boss three-piece suit, with a raw silk tie and gold Citation wristwatch. He had a miniphone clipped to his ear, and a fake prison tattoo of a spiderweb stenciled on his neck to indicate a rough-and-tumble past. His shoes were Italian, his sunglasses French and his briefcase burnished steel. His usual weapons were riding their accustomed positions, but he also was carrying a brace of knives in case some silent kills were necessary.

Underneath everything else, Bolan was wearing a ballistic T-shirt. It would stop only small-caliber rounds from penetrating, and his bones would still break, but under the circumstances he couldn't wear any type of proper body armor. That would be an insult. And he needed to gain the trust of these killers.

Stepping out of the vehicle, he left the door open and flipped the keys over a shoulder. From a nearby kiosk, a teenage valet rushed forward to snag them in the air, muttering apologies for not being more prompt.

"Don't worry about it, kid." Bolan chuckled, pulling out a wad of cash. Peeling off a hundred euro note, he let it drop. "Just park it close."

"Absolutely, sir!" the valet gushed, beaming over the colossal tip. "I wash, too! Good job!" One hundred euros was a month's wages.

"Yeah, sure, whatever," he said, dismissing the matter with a wave. "Just don't scratch the paint or I'll break your legs."

"Yes, sir! No, sir! Thank you, sir!"

Heading for the front door, Bolan noticed the armored limousine from the traffic circle parked in a handicap zone. Standing around the vehicle were four large men openly carrying Uzi submachine guns, with spare clips jutting from their belts like samurai swords. One of them had a dead white eye, and a military-style hand mike dangled over the shoulder of his white linen suit. Bolan instantly marked him as the crew chief.

The men watched him closely, shifting to a more aggressive stance, but Bolan ignored the street soldiers as if such a sight was an everyday occurrence. He would wager five-to-ten that the limo belonged to Rezart Kastrioti, the man he was supposed to meet in a few minutes for lunch.

Stepping through a revolving door, Bolan felt as if he was entering another world. The structure was hollow and rose impossibly high, the rooms arranged along the outer rim. By craning his neck, the big American could see straight to the vaulted roof some fifty stories above.

The air was cool and clean, smelling faintly of jasmine. Lush plants grew in orderly abundance, and carpeted steps led to a spacious lobby that stretched nearly the length of a football field. Glass elevators rose and descended at several locations, liveried staff rushed about carrying trays, and soft instrumental music played from hidden speakers. Bolan identified it as something by Debussy. Signs pointed the way to the indoor golf course, water park, brothel, restaurant, casino and skeet shooting range.

A score of elegant people moved through the lobby, the men in tailored business suits, the women in skimpy dresses that showed a wealth of cleavage and displayed long legs. Everybody was deeply tanned, and accompanied by secretaries, assistants, armed bodyguards, aides, butlers and maids, while nannies herded small children or pushed babies in strollers.

Bolan pretended to check his watch, barely able to believe the ebb and flow of people. It was more like opening night at the Metropolitan Opera than a simple Tuesday morning. Was this some national holiday he didn't know about? That could be a major problem.

That was when he noticed the carefully disguised video cameras. They were everywhere, overlapping one another's ranges. There was absolutely no way anybody could go anywhere unnoticed. This was prison level security. Bolan realized that this wasn't merely some random hotel; it had to be owned and operated by the Fifteen Families. The King Zog was most likely the nerve center of Albania, a safe haven of luxury and comfort for the criminal elite, far from the misery and strife they caused.

Instantly, he changed his plans for an emergency escape. There were far too many innocent bystanders in the line of fire to do a blitz of any kind. Which left him only one option if things went wrong. But hopefully, he wouldn't have to do anything that extreme.

Radiating confidence, he coolly headed for the restaurant. Appearing as if from nowhere, smiling waiters bowed and removed a velvet rope to usher him through to a private section. A young waitress gave a curtsy in passing. Bolan stayed in character and merely grunted in return.

Just past an array of private booths, Bolan found another part of the restaurant had been sectioned off by a wooden trellis covered with a thick blanket of live roses, a secret world hidden within the mob terrarium. Inside the decorative arbor were a dozen tables, all empty except for the largest. That could accommodate twenty, but there were only two settings, on opposite sides. Sitting at the head of the table was a short fat man in a reclining office chair, his dirty shoes on the linen tablecloth. Rezart "The Hacksaw" Kastrioti was puffing on a black cigar, a SIG-Sauer pistol peeking out from a shoulder holster under his tailored suit. The man was clean-shaved, including his head. A diamond twinkled from his right earlobe, and his left shoe had a extra-thick bottom, indicating that that leg was slightly shorter than the other.

Possibly from having rickets as a child, Bolan guessed. Which meant he had been poor once, but wasn't anymore. He had to have worked his way up the organization, by being either smart or ruthless, probably both. That told Bolan a lot about the man.

"Get your damn feet off the table!" Bolan snapped.

With a start, Kastrioti instinctively obeyed, not used to being ordered about by anybody but his direct superiors in the organization. Then he scowled and started to go for the pistol under his jacket, until Bolan burst into laughter, sat down in a chair and put his own feet on the table.

"Stop hogging all the room." He chuckled. "Is that how you treat a guest?"

Breathing deeply, Kastrioti did nothing for a long moment, and Bolan started to think he had read the man wrong. Then Kastrioti snorted a nasal guffaw and slapped the tabletop with an open palm.

"I like your style, Yank!" He laughed, pointing a finger across the table. "You take no shit! Me, too! I am Rezart Kastrioti! Welcome to my country!"

Never had Bolan heard that phrase used so accurately. It *was* his country, every rock, tree and bush. "A pleasure." He smiled and gave a salute. "Now, do you want to talk business first or—"

"Business always first," Kastrioti stated, pushing aside a plate to fold his hands on the table. "Afterward we shall have wine, women and song, eh?"

"Sounds good to me."

"Agreed!" He smiled, then went darkly serious. "So… pirates have been bothering your ships. That is not good for profits. How can we help? Do you want armed guards on the ships, or military escorts, or—"

Bolan interrupted. "What I told my representative this meeting was about, and want I really want to talk to you about are two entirely different things." Swinging his feet to the floor, Bolan slid the briefcase across the table.

Scowling, Kastrioti looked at the case while thoughtfully rubbing a ring on his thumb. Then he reached out to turn the case around and flip up the lid.

"Nice," he whispered, fingering the stacks of cash before he closed the case again. "Very nice, indeed. Okay, Yank, what is it you really want? Slaves, drugs or guns?"

"Just some information."

"What kind of information?" Kastrioti asked in a calculated manner, pouring a crystal goblet of dark red wine. He took a sip and waited.

"Somebody stole my property," Bolan said, letting a hint of anger enter his voice. "I want it back."

Kastrioti gave a nod. "As is only proper."

"Unfortunately, I don't know who has it," Bolan said, observing a subtle movement on the other side of the rose trellis. His combat instincts flared, and he casually slipped a hand into his pocket to press the button on the remote control.

"That is a shame," Kastrioti said.

"But you do know how it is."

"Indeed," the man replied, twirling the glass to inspect the wine in the overhead lights. "And I have this information because…?"

"Because they just made a sizable deposit in a Spanish bank," Bolan said. "Your bank."

"Me? I do not own a bank." Kastrioti laughed, looking over the rim of the goblet. "But I may have a cousin who does. Several cousins, in fact." He took another sip. "What does this thief look like?"

"I have no idea."

"Then how—"

"He just deposited several million in gold bars," Bolan stated, resting his elbows on the table. "That can't happen every day, even to the Fifteen."

Sipping more wine, Kastrioti gave no reaction to the mention of the organization. "No, it does not," he said, setting the goblet aside. "Yes, I am aware of this person. The sum was truly impressive. But there is a small problem."

"Which is?"

"You have not paid me anywhere near as much as he has deposited. Thus, he is more valuable to me than you."

There was more movement on the other side of the roses,

and Bolan distinctly heard the telltale click-clack of an arming bolt being pulled into place. Once again he changed the escape plan. Yes, this was a private little world, perfect for some bloody business far from the view of everybody else.

"At the moment, you're correct," Bolan said smoothly, shifting his weight. "But you see, in regards to the billions involved—"

"Billions?" Kastrioti interrupted in surprise.

Bolan smiled. "Of course! Did you—" Instantly, he surged upward, heaving against the heavy table with all his strength.

The candles and silverware went flying, while the heavier plates and wine bottles slid toward Kastrioti to crash in a noisy pile. Snarling curses, the Albanian toppled backward in his chair, but came up in a roll with the SIG-Sauer drawn.

"Freeze," Bolan gritted, pressing his Beretta into the base of the fat man's neck.

Startled that the voice came from behind him, Kastrioti started to turn, then stopped, easing his finger off the trigger of the deadly pistol.

"Smart move," Bolan said. "Now drop it."

"This is not good business, Yank," Kastrioti muttered, letting go of his weapon. It hit the soft carpeting with a dull thud. "Simply tell us who you are working for, and you can leave alive."

"Do the other one, too," Bolan ordered, digging the barrel in deeper.

Kastrioti reached down to pull a small .32 Remington from an ankle holster.

"You really shouldn't have put your feet on the table," the soldier said, tapping the weapon out of the hands of the other man with the Beretta's barrel. "Now, kick it away."

Sullenly, Kastrioti complied.

"Okay, call off your boys," Bolan commanded, watching the shadows move on the other side of the trellis. "Or you're the first to die."

For a moment, Kastrioti did nothing, panting deeply from the exertion of controlling his anger. "Not a chance in hell," he growled, and dived to the floor.

A split second later, the entire trellis exploded as a dozen automatic weapons cut loose, spraying a hailstorm of high-velocity lead across the private alcove.

CHAPTER FOUR

Mazagón, Spain

"Bah, this smells like death," a man announced, sniffing the stiff collar of his British uniform. An L-85 assault rifle was slung from his shoulder as per regulations, and a canvas belt of spare 5.56 mm magazine clips was strapped tightly around his waist.

Placing both hands behind his back, Thorodensen stood rigidly at attention. "Nonsense! All these uniforms have been thoroughly washed several time. They are absolutely clean."

The man wearing the uniform of a CPO gave no reply, but his expression clearly stated that he completely disagreed with the former Icelandic ambassador, as did several other members of the group.

"I love this heat!" a large woman said, smiling into the warm sun.

"Dear God, I miss snow," a small man growled in reply, wiping a sheen of sweat off his brow.

The ancient ridge of cooled lava had been smoothed over time by the crash of the gentle waves, yet the landscape still held a certain aspect of raw power that reminded the people of their distant home.

The dozen armed members of Penumbra stood in an orderly row, NATO equipment bags stacked neatly off to the side. Behind them rose a hulking concrete building situated at the extreme end of a rocky peninsula. Every door to the NATO disposal facility was made of solid steel, with three different types of locks. There were no windows whatso-ever, and two massive chimneys rose from the middle of the structure like the horns of a demon. The entire grounds were enclosed with an electrified fence topped with razor wire, and a radar antenna spun nonstop on a nearby hill, where a SAM bunker was hidden.

The shore was lined with antipersonnel mines, a sunken WWI battleship blocked the narrow harbor, and a state-of-the-art NATO sonar sensor was hidden among the barna-cles, rust and colorful coral.

The best way to approach the place was along a narrow road, a twisting ribbon of asphalt studded with concrete tank traps, edged with more land mines, and lined with rows of steel spikes fully capable of rendering even bul-letproof tires into ragged shreds.

The exit ramp from the main highway was normally closed with a steel barrier designed to stop a modern-day tank, along with a secondary spread of steel spikes jutting from the pavement that would shred tires.

"I hope everything goes well this time," Professor Vil-hjalms said, hunching her shoulders. "Brooklyn was a di-saster."

"Yet we did get the mines, correct?"

"That is true," she hedged. "But still…"

"Everything will be fine, Lily. The staff of the facility accepted my credentials, did they not?" Thorodensen said, minutely adjusting his cap. The insignia of a commander was stitched on the bill. "And why should they not? The papers are real enough. They were just not assigned to me." He turned to smile at her tolerantly. "Everybody is gone, and we're here alone. What could possibly gone wrong?"

"The unknown is what frightens me," Vilhjalms said,

glancing out to sea. Their Hercules seaplane was moored just over the horizon, well past the reach of any ground-based radar. If all went well, they would be gone within the hour. If not, escape was only minutes away. That gave her some solace.

Nervously, she tugged on the heavily starched uniform again. This had been the largest shirt among the dead sailors. However, it had been designed for a man, and it simply didn't fit conformably across her more ample feminine contours. In an effort to flatten her breasts, she had removed her brassier. That helped, but not much, and now every step produced a very undignified jiggling effect. Everybody was trying not to notice, and she deeply appreciated the courtesy.

Trying not to be obvious, Vilhjalms glanced at Thorodensen, standing so close that she could almost feel the heat radiating from his body. The white uniform fitted him perfectly, of course. But then the man was built like a Norse god of war, and she wouldn't have minded at all if he had noticed her unbound freedom. Not even a little bit. On impulse, she bumped a soft breast into his bare forearm.

Curiously, Thorodensen glanced down. "Something wrong?"

Suddenly, they heard the low roar of truck engines in the distance.

"Here they come." She sighed, trying to cover the blunder. Science and math she understood, but clearly, seduction was not one of her many skills.

"And right on schedule," Thorodensen said with a smile. "Okay, people, stand at attention! Remember, from now on only speak English! Even among yourself. Understood?"

"Ja, samkomulag!" the men and woman answered in a ragged chorus.

"And what did I just tell you?" he bellowed.

"Yes, sir!"

"Better," Thorodensen growled, feeling a trickle of sweat going down his spine.

There was a loaded pistol at his hip, as well as an L-85 assault rifle across his back. More importantly, he had a remote control in his pocket. If necessary, he could destroy the entire facility, along with his own people and a huge section of the peninsula. But that would purely be a last resort, death instead of being captured. His fledgling organization, Penumbra, desperately needed this cargo. Without it, the plan fell apart completely, here and now.

As the convoy rumbled closer, Thorodensen noted in relief that it was a standard NATO formation, nothing special. There were three primary vehicles and a few escorts. The main three were massively armored NBC-class trucks, nuclear-biological-chemical proof, able to withstand any type of modern-day weapon, even a near hit from a tactical nuke. Of course, a direct hit would vaporize them, just like anything else. But where most armored vehicles would be torn to pieces and nearly vaporized, these resilient trucks could ride out the shock wave with the crew intact and alive.

"Trouble?" Vilhjalms whispered, licking her dry lips.

"Not in the least," Thorodensen said with a thin smile. Accompanying the four NBC trucks were two Hummers full of combat troops, and six motorcycle riders in full body armor. An Ashanti gunship hovered in the sky overhead.

Thorodensen grunted. That was normally more than enough protection for this type of cargo. Just not this day.

As the convoy got close to the exit ramp, Thorodensen waved a hand, and the Icelander in the guard kiosk operated the controls. Hydraulics thumped, and the flimsy-looking gate slowly moved out of the way.

The convoy braked to a halt at the kiosk, and the motorcycles spread out in a defense pattern. Saluting the guard, the driver of the lead Hummer offered a clipboard full of papers. Saluting back, the Icelander pretended to read them, gave a curt nod, then waved the convoy on.

"Pass," he said in a perfect Liverpool accent.

That caught the driver by surprise, and he beamed in delight. "Cor' blimey, you from the Puddle?" He laughed. "Me, too! Where were you stationed?"

Since he had already used the only English word he could say correctly, the guard merely scowled and jerked his head toward the facility. The driver glanced that way, and Thorodensen frowned darkly.

"Pass!" the guard repeated, stressing the word.

"Sorry, mate," the driver muttered, and shifted into gear once more.

"Wait a minute," a Turkish sergeant commanded, holding up a palm. "That's a British navy uniform. Why is the royal navy guarding a UN facility?"

Instantly, everybody in the convoy stiffened and stared intently at the lone guard.

With a sigh, Thorodensen reached into his pocket.

"Hey now, he's just some swabbie doing the task he was assigned," the driver said with a big grin. "Isn't that right, ya yellow-bellied whoremaster?"

Having no idea what else to do, the guard grinned back and winked.

"British my ass, it's a trap!" the sergeant yelled, working the arming bolt on a MP-5 as he swung the weapon around and fired.

The startled guard was blown off his feet as the hail of 9 mm rounds hammered across his chest.

Thorodensen pressed the first button on the remote control.

Instantly, the entire section of road lifted up on thundering columns of flame, twisted bodies and broken wreckage spraying outward for a hundred yards. The motorcycle riders were torn to bits, their flaming bikes tumbling into the electrified fence sending out torrents of sparks. Even the armored trucks flipped over, rising a dozen yards into the air before crashing back down sideways onto the ruined roadway. The NBC vehicles slammed into the pavement, but seemed completely unharmed; not even the windows were cracked.

Instantly, the Icelanders started to rush forward.

"Wait!" Thorodensen commanded, pressing the second button.

A split second later, a full salvo of surface-to-air missiles streaked out from the hidden bunker on the hill, and the Ashanti gunship erupted into a writhing fireball. As it fell, the props came loose and spun wildly away, while several rockets launched into the sea. They hit the water and violently detonated, sending out huge waves that crashed onto the rocky shoreline.

"Now, get those trucks open!" Thorodensen bellowed, striding down the road. "We have thirty minutes before reinforcements arrive!"

"Thirty?" Vilhjalms asked, already working the small EM scanner in her hands. "I thought our window was only fifteen minutes!"

"Before leaving the United Nations I managed a small reorganization of the tactical rescue forces in Spain," Thorodensen said grimly. "They're now less efficient than the French parliament on a Friday."

Grabbing their equipment bags, the Icelanders swarmed toward the burning vehicles, zigzagging through the smoldering maze of bodies and machines. Several of them were pulling on fireproof suits marked with the insignia of the British navy.

"Ah…which one of these was in the middle?" a man asked, glancing at the NBC trucks. "I've lost track."

"That one," Thorodensen said, pointing at the truck nearest the berm. "I memorized the serial number on the side."

"You think of everything," Vilhjalms said, minutely adjusting the EM scanner to jam every radio and cell phone transmission in the area.

"I try my best," he replied, almost too softly for her to hear.

Just then, one of the crackling bodies jerked about as a fast series of small explosions sounded, the spare ammunition clips of the dead guards igniting from the intense heat of a burning motorcycle.

Several of the Icelanders ducked for cover, one recoiling as blood erupted from his arm. Then another man dropped his assault rifle to grab his throat with both hands. Crimson fluid gushed from between his spasming fingers to spray the other cringing people.

"Lodiu!" a plump woman cried, pulling out a small medical kit.

But before she could reach him, the battered SAW machine gun inside a flaming Hummer rattled into action. Two more people fell with minor wounds, and the first man reeled as he was hit in the chest a dozen times, the big caliber rounds blowing out the back of his British uniform. He hit the churned ground hard and didn't move.

"Lodiu…" the medic whispered softly, reaching out as if to touch the fallen man. Then she inhaled deeply and turned away to assist those that could still be saved.

"My God, I knew his wife in school," Vilhjalms said, turning pale.

"Not now! Stay focused, woman!" Thorodensen commanded, stepping awkwardly over a smashed transmission. "Uther, Fallea, get those burning bars hot!"

"Yes, sir!" a woman growled, pulling down the hood of her flame-resistant suit.

Using an industrial scraper, she sparked the end of a short black bar held by a man in a similar outfit. The tip sputtered for a moment, then a white-hot flame gushed from the thermite lance.

Burning at nearly three thousand degrees, the thermite radiated an incandescent nimbus that was difficult to look at. Even the people in the fireproof suits cringed from the blazing dagger of fire.

Waddling forward, the man approached the first NBC truck and splayed the white flame from the lance across the seam of the back door. Then he did the same to the second truck.

Built to withstand even the staggering temperatures of thermite, the armored door resisted the assault, but the melting iron sheath of the thermite lance flowed red-hot along the edge, then darkened as the cool armor made it quickly harden.

Immediately, a series of hard thumps came from the people inside the truck, and the doors quivered slightly, but nothing more.

"Sealed!" the man announced, starting toward the last truck.

With a sharp crack, a small panel slammed open on the side of the truck, and the stubby barrel of a MP-5 submachine gun jutted into view.

With a curse, the man thrust the thermite lance forward. As the white flame washed over the MP-5, the steel barrel visibly dissolved. The ammunition exploded in a fast series of cracks and bangs, the man inside screamed and the partially melted weapon dropped from view.

Rushing forward, Thorodensen shoved the barrel of his L-85 assault rifle into the red-hot gunport, and cut loose with the entire clip of 5.56 mm rounds. More screams sounded briefly, then there was only silence.

"Damn! The crew is dead!" Vilhjalms stormed, lowering the EM scanner. "Now how do we get inside?"

"That's not a problem," he replied, pulling out the remote control and flipping it over to quickly type on a miniature keyboard.

At first nothing seemed to happen. Then there was a dull metallic clank, and the near door hissed as it opened slightly.

"But...if you could do that..." Vilhjalms turned on the leader with a furious expression. "You always planned on killing these men!"

"It was necessary," Thorodensen replied curtly, pulling on a pair of insulated gloves and grabbing the latch. The gloves flamed briefly at the contact, and he tugged with no result. Placing a shoe on the bumper, he tried again, the fireproof sole smoking as he hauled the stubborn door aside.

The interior of the NBC truck was brightly illuminated by the ceiling panels. Four soldiers in NATO uniforms were splayed on the walls, their lifeless eyes staring into infinity, their uniforms reduced to red rags. A lieutenant dangled from behind the steering wheel, a cracked hand mike still in her twitching fingers. Tightly strapped along a cushioned rack were a series of small canisters, each marked with the biohazard symbol.

Pulling off his gloves, Thorodensen drew his pistol and fired once into the face of the driver. The twitching stopped.

"Get these canisters free, and be careful!" he directed, holstering the smoking weapon. "No more mistakes!"

Unable to turn off the thermite lance, the man simply tossed the blazing rod into a nearby ditch and pulled out a small acetylene torch. Abandoned alongside the road, the thermite lance continued to burn, melting rocks, pavement and steel rebars, until it was lying in a pool of bubbling lava.

"Are you sure about this?" he asked, narrowing the roaring red flame down to a stiletto of intense blue-white.

"No, I am not," Thorodensen replied honestly, using a hand to shield his face. "But if there is a puncture, we will be dead instantly, so success is assured."

Puzzled by the convoluted logic, the man shrugged and bent to the task. With extreme care, he cut away the restraining bolts holding down the cushioned straps, the flame never even getting close to the small silver canisters. As the final bolt melted, the straps fell away and a canister rolled free.

Moving fast, Thorodensen grabbed it before it could hit the wall underfoot. He flinched from the temperature, but said nothing as he passed it to a waiting man wearing gloves. The canister was gently placed inside an equipment bag.

"Is that one enough?" Vilhjalms asked from outside the truck.

"Yes, but we'll take two more as insurance," Thorodensen stated, stepping back to let the man wearing gloves do the delicate work. His own palms were bright red and blisters were starting to form.

The canisters were extracted with the care usually given to nuclear material, then the Icelanders quickly left the area. Thorodensen was the last to depart, placing a small black box inside the NBC truck.

Retreating to the harbor, the Icelanders waited only a few moments before a hovercraft crested the horizon and raced closer. It skimmed past the underwater blockades and scraped onto the rocky shore.

"Damn, we lost so many people," a woman said, trundling onboard.

Nobody else spoke, but their faces were a strained mixture of grief and grim joy.

"Take heart, my friends. That is nothing compared to the staggering number the accursed English will lose before we are done," Thorodensen growled, changing the settings on the remote control.

As the hovercraft left the shore, he impatiently waited until they were a hundred yards away before pressing the last button. A small explosion erupted inside the NBC truck, and a golden cloud swirled into view.

Instantly, the tattered corpses on the ground began to froth and bubble, their bones turning an obscene black before crumbling into dust. The paint flowed off the trucks, and the ragged remains of the rubber tires started to dissolve. The pavement started to boil, dark fumes rising high.

When it reached the burning thermite lance, the expanding golden cloud visibly spread far and wide. Suddenly, the grass on the hill was bleached a deathly white, the leaves fell off a tree, then a branch cracked and fell away. Startled, a flock of small birds took wing, but none of them escaped, the limp bodies tumbling to the ground to smack into the bubbling soil.

"What is that?" Vilhjalms demanded, feeling sick to her stomach.

"Something new from a Muslim terrorist group whose name I cannot pronounce properly," Thorodensen replied, tossing the remote control into the choppy water. "A NATO special forces team killed the terrorists, and sent this batch of their hellish brew here to be destroyed."

As a wisp of the golden cloud reached the shoreline, a

fox darted from its burrow beneath a bush. Instantly, the animal went still, both eyes turning dead-white before it toppled over, blood gushing from every orifice.

"Why aren't we using this on England?" a man demanded, yanking off his gloves.

"It would not kill enough," Thorodensen replied, turning to face the waiting seaplane. "This is merely another key." He didn't have the heart to tell his friends that this had actually been the easy part of the plan. From here on, things were going to get very bloody indeed.

The King Zog Hotel, Albania

MOVING FAST, Mack Bolan hit the floor just as the entire world seemed to erupt into rose petals and wood splinters from the arsenal of assorted weapons. There were more assault rifles, shotguns and pistols then he could tabulate under the circumstances.

Closing his eyes tight, he rolled to a new position, firing both the Beretta and the Desert Eagle. Everything was thundering chaos, but he concentrated on listening to the voices of the men operating the machine guns, and not the chattering weapons. Switching the Beretta 93-R to 3-round-burst mode, he fired an entire clip into the lush greenery behind a marble statue, and was rewarded with a strangled cry of pain.

As the machine gun stopped churning out rounds, Bolan charged, running over a chair and launching himself at the battered trellis. In a crash of splintering wood, he smashed through and collided with a burly man trying to staunch a bleeding wound in his arm.

In a wild tangle of limbs, they tumbled to the floor, and Bolan bashed the gunner unconscious with the hot barrel of the Desert Eagle. The man went still with a soft sigh, and Bolan snatched up the assault rifle.

Darting forward, he yanked a reserve magazine from alongside the barrel and rammed it into the rear breech. It clicked into place as he shouldered a small man aside, his shotgun discharging into the ceiling. The lights died with a shatter of glass, and Bolan vaulted over a trimmed hedge to land on a polished mahogany floor full of dancing people.

Dropping her martini glass, a mature woman screamed, a fat man cursed and a bald bodyguard went for a weapon under his coat. Swinging the stock of the assault rifle, Bolan clipped him hard in the jaw just as the Glock came into view, and the men reeled backward into an ice sculpture of the winged horse Pegasus. They both went down, the Glock firing off its entire magazine.

Kicking the bodyguard in the side of the head, Bolan grabbed the Glock machine pistol and thrust it into his belt. Just a little extra something to help tilt the odds more in his favor.

By now, the thirty-piece band had wisely stopped playing, and everybody was rushing toward the nearest exit. Only the disco ball in the ceiling kept spinning, sending out a twirling array of sparkling starlight. With combat skills forged in a thousand firefights, Bolan wasn't disoriented by the display, but the civilians seemed to go insane, blindly beating at one another, colliding with furniture and generally running amok.

Grabbing a spare ammunition magazine from the fallen bodyguard, Bolan almost smiled. This couldn't have been more perfect. Time to move.

Charging forward, he sprinted back the exact way he had come. Easily taking the low hedge in a single bound, he landed in a combat crouch, the assault rifle held steady in both hands. There was movement in the darkness, but he withheld firing until he saw the glint of silver and heard the telltale rack of a slide. The Imbel whined out a burst of a dozen rounds, and a big man crumpled, his Uzi submachine gun hitting the floor and skittering away.

Skirting the wall, Bolan was trying not to step on any of the glass to reveal his position, when a group of men charged into the room. Flashlights swept the area, glistening off the broken shards. Nobody spoke. There was only deep breathing and the occasional grunt.

Ducking behind a portable bar, Bolan stayed low and from between two rows of expensive liquor bottles, watched the group of men walk past. As they moved onward, the flashlights revealed that they were wearing body armor and carrying automatic weapons, mostly AK-109 assault rifles. These were shock troops, the elite of the street soldiers for the Fifteen Families.

Slowly standing, Bolan took aim and sprayed the rest of the magazine in a single burst, the rounds stitching a path of destruction across their heads, sending hair, scalp, brains and eyes flying away in a horrid spray.

Even before the bodies fell, the Executioner was in motion again, moving low and fast around the trellis, this time using the silenced Beretta to gun down everybody he saw who was carrying a weapon of any kind.

Just then, a series of loud explosions went off outside the hotel, closely followed by an amplified voice announcing in Albanian that the hotel was surrounded by Interpol, everybody was under arrest, and that they should come out with their hands empty.

From the darkness to his left, Bolan heard a man mutter a question. The only word he recognized was *Interpol*. The question was curtly answered by Kastrioti in a furious snarl.

Easing that way, Bolan could figure out what the conversation was about. Interpol had no authority in Albania, which was exactly why he had planted the recorders around the hotel. Just a touch of confusion to keep everybody off balance.

Skirting a marble pillar, he almost took out a waiter carrying a champagne bottle, but stopped just in time. The man stared at him in horror, then slowly set the bottle aside and raised both hands in surrender.

"Run for your life," Bolan whispered tersely.

Breaking into a sweat, the waiter started to tremble, and looked as if he was about to burst into tears.

Clearly, the servant didn't speak English.

"Sorry about this," Bolan muttered, and clubbed the frightened man with a short, swift stroke from the butt of the Imbel.

As the waiter crumpled, unconscious, Bolan nudged him under a table covered with silverware to try and keep him out of harm's way.

Suddenly, machine-gun fire chattered from every direction, closely followed by howling sirens and the deep throb of military helicopters.

At the top of his lungs, Kastrioti shouted orders, and dozens of people scampered away from the private garden, many of them yelling additional commands.

"Sounds like a hell of a party," Bolan said, pressing the barrel of the Beretta hard into the throat of the crime lord.

Kastrioti went stiff and started to raise his gun, then dramatically released the weapon. "If you wanted me dead, I would be so already," he stated. "So what is this, a kidnapping?"

"Exactly what I told you before," Bolan said, pulling the fat man into a corner. "I just want information."

"That bullshit story about the thieves was real?" Kastrioti scoffed in disdain. "Do you think I am stupid?"

Swinging up the Beretta, Bolan fired twice, smashing the lights, and darkness enveloped them.

"What I think is that you don't know the entire story," Bolan replied, holstering the weapon.

Breathing deeply, Kastrioti did nothing for a few moments, then barked a short laugh. "Okay, Yankee, you win. I talk, and you kill these people. Yes?"

"That's the plan."

"And what happens to their gold in my bank?"

"What gold?"

Slowly, Kastrioti smiled and sat in a chair. "The group calls themselves Penumbra. The leader is a man called Hrafen Thorodensen."

"Never heard of either of them," Bolan said. "What did the gold buy, new identities?"

"Bah, I do not handle such small things," Kastrioti said with disdain. "I am Family! Not some distant cousin, or country bastard."

Outside the hotel, the battle between the bodyguards and the recordings continued at full force.

"Good for you. So what did Penumbra buy?" Bolan demanded. "Weapons?" Deliberately, he kept the question vague.

"Vehicles," Kastrioti said, rubbing his neck. "Experimental armored-personnel carriers, XTV-99 Uberpanzers, made exclusively by, and for, the Swiss military."

The Uberpanzer was a supertank. "Okay, what's new about them?"

"They are ultralight," Kastrioti said, raising a hand. "Don't ask me how. Some kind of ceramic material. Very light in weight, but incredibly strong. Twenty millimeters… roughly an inch, yes?"

"Close enough."

"An inch offers better protection than a...foot of conventional steel."

Now that was impressive. "Okay, what's wrong with the Uberpanzers?"

"They are much too expensive to manufacture in the numbers wanted for national defense." Kastrioti scowled. "What does Switzerland need with an army, anyway? They are protected by their banks."

That was certainly true enough. "When is Thorodensen scheduled to get the tanks?"

"Tomorrow noon."

"Where?"

"Pebble Beach, Sicily."

That caught Bolan by surprise. "Then they're not buying the vehicles from you?"

"From the Families? No, we merely brokered the deal between him and the Mafia."

In the distance, police sirens started to howl, along with the clang of bells from fire trucks and the strident wail of ambulances. It sounded as if everybody in the entire country was heading for the Zog.

"It's good to be the king," Bolan chuckled.

"Of course!" Kastrioti grinned. "So, you now have what you want?"

"Yes."

"Then leave...with my blessings."

Just then, a group of men raced past the darkened trellis, and Bolan swung up his assault rifle. Kastrioti did nothing, and when the group ran on, he gave a long exhalation.

"Just one more thing," Bolan said, lowering the assault rifle. "Do I really even have to say it?"

Slapping a knee, Kastrioti snorted his piggy laugh. "Am I a child? If I tell the Mafia, you come back. If the information is not true, you come back. I understand." He leaned forward and offered his hand. "We have a deal, Yankee. You kill Hrafen, and I keep his gold. The Fifteen Families have been in business a very long time, and we know when it is wise to deal honestly."

Knowing the truth when he heard it, Bolan holstered the Beretta, took the man's pudgy hand and shook it briefly.

"However, if we ever meet again…" Bolan added.

"Of course! While I will happily dance at your funeral," Kastrioti said, wiping his hand clean on a handkerchief. "But that is just business. Nothing personal."

"It is always personal," Bolan countered, slipping farther into the shadows.

When he was alone again, just for a moment, Kastrioti felt the urge to shout for his guards. Then he shrugged in resignation and walked to the liquor cabinet to pour himself a very long drink. This had been a most interesting lunch. In spite of everything, he just made several million euros in gold. For that alone, he wished the big Yankee good luck in handling the Sicilians. They were grim, humorless men without the slightest hint of dignity or honor…unlike the noble Fifteen Families.

"To Family!" Kastrioti toasted, draining the glass, then dashing it against the rear mirror.

Both shattered in a deafening crash, and for just a second Kastrioti thought he saw the reflection of the Yankee standing close behind him in the broken shards. But when he turned there was nobody in sight, and an icy shiver ran down his spine.

CHAPTER FIVE

Johannesburg, South Africa

"Blue Team, go, go, go," the SAS lieutenant whispered into his throat mike.

Instantly, the sewer grating across the street popped open, and out surged five British soldiers in full combat gear. They crossed the street in only a　　seconds and, without stopping, jumped directly into a huge glass window of the office building.

The SAS operatives crashed through to land among the desks and file cabinets, their L-85 assault rifles sweeping for targets. Live microphones weren't allowed on this mission, as the technologically advanced thieves might be listening for a carrier wave. Silence was their main protection today. Silence, speed and surprise.

In perfect timing, a pair of RAF Lynx gunships lifted into view from behind the downtown skyscrapers and began to circle the building, their rocket pods aimed downward.

Various British intelligence agencies had confirmed that this was the off-site computer dump for the firm that manufactured the GPS microdots for Imperial Gold Mines UK, and the most likely location of the secret headquarters for the gold thieves. They were hiding in plain sight.

"This is the police!" the lieutenant said again, this time his words booming from every PA speaker inside the five-story building. "We have the place surrounded! Surrender, and come out with your hands raised!"

Just then, a soldier appeared at the broken window and frantically slashed a thumb across his throat, to try to warn the others to retreat.

"It's a bleeding trap!" he yelled through cupped hands. "Leg it, mates!"

But the heroic attempt was too late. A microsecond later the fifty crates of TNT wired to the PA system simultaneously ignited.

The high explosives were designed to crack open mountains, so the old brick structure offered no more resistance than a child's sand castle. A deafening thunderclap blew the entire office building apart, obliterating it at ground level and sending out a monstrous corona of destruction.

Every window within ten blocks shattered, cars flipped over and pedestrians went flying away like screaming autumn leaves. Unstoppable, the roiling concussion crushed the British gunships into gory wads of metal and flesh, and sent them tumbling into the nearby bay.

In dark majesty, a black mushroom cloud began to rise above the smoky field of fiery devastation as a maelstrom of assorted debris, smashed bricks, twisted bits of plumbing, and very small pieces of humans, rained down across the city for a hundred blocks.

Belice, Sicily

"WHAT THE… Flight 412, where are you going?" an angry voice demanded from the dashboard radio. "Stop! Come back, you fool!"

Ignoring the air traffic controller, Mack Bolan continued to guide the Cessna off the landing field, and finally parked it in the middle of a weedy field.

As sirens started to wail in the distance, he simply left the aircraft and sprinted into the nearby pine forest. The kind of weapons he would need to tackle the Mafia couldn't be bribed past the customs inspectors in Sicily. Or most anywhere else, for that matter. So he simply made the trade of abandoning the Cessna to get a backpack of heavy ordnance onto the island.

It was early in the morning, and the ground was firm, so Bolan made excellent time putting as much distance between himself and the tiny airport as possible. Slowly, the sun climbed above the treetops to warm the world, and the soldier let himself enjoy the run. The awakening forest was becoming infused with the tangy smells of wild oregano, pine and laurel. A heady combination.

For this mission, Bolan was armed for war, wearing a full set of Threat Level IV body armor, and covered with weapons, an ammo belt and assorted small equipment. His war bag included camping gear, with waterproof flares for starting a fire in the rain. A friend had once marveled how any soldier could carry an eighty-pound backpack and be able to run for an entire day. But that was just a typical day in the life of a foot soldier.

After a four-hour hike, Bolan paused on the crest of a grassy hillock to catch his breath and take a fast gulp of a sports drink. How anybody ever made it through basic without the stuff he had no idea.

Just then, the cell phone in his equipment vest gave a hard vibration, and he extracted it from behind his back.

"Cooper," Bolan said, flipping it open. There was no return number on the screen. But then his phone was also blocked.

"Hal here, Striker. Just heard from my British contact," Hal Brognola said in a grim voice. "SAS acted on intel and raided the suspected headquarters of the gold thieves."

"Johannesburg was an ambush," Bolan stated.

"Yeah, it was."

"But the SAS went in, anyway."

"Do or die, old buddy. Sometimes walking into a trap is the only way to get the bastards."

"Did the team learn anything useful?"

"Only how much damage three tons of TNT can do to a medium-size office building."

Scowling, Bolan wanted to ask if they were any survivors, but he could tell the answer from Brognola's tone. However, it seemed odd that Thorodensen would use that much TNT. It was massive overkill.

"Hal, check into any possible connection between Iceland and England," Bolan said. "I'm starting to get a bad feeling that this whole thing is a personal matter."

"Terrorism as revenge?" Brognola asked. "That sounds unlikely, but I'll look into it. Maybe Parliament has been stepping on somebody's toes."

"It has been known to happen."

"Got that right."

As an eagle flew by overhead, Bolan dimly remembered hearing a story about the London banks doing something in Iceland that really upset the locals, but he couldn't dredge up the details.

"Be sure to check the financial angle," Bolan suggested.

"Right," Brognola said. "How are you doing? Need anything?"

"Yes, any and all information on a Hrafen Thorodensen," Bolan said, and briefly explained what had transpired in Albania.

"Hrafen Thorodensen. Are you sure about that name? And he's fronting a terrorist organization called Penumbra?"

"Bet my life on it," Bolan replied. "Kastrioti was telling the truth. Or at least, what he thought was true."

"No, they can't be the same person," Brognola muttered, over the sound of shuffling papers. "But there was a… Yes, there was a Hrafen Thorodensen at the United Nations. He was Iceland's ambassador."

"What do you mean, *was* the ambassador? What happened?"

"He retired after his wife committed suicide. Something about the bank she worked at."

Suddenly, Bolan felt a tingle along his spine. "How do you know?" he asked. "That's hardly front page news."

"True, but Thorodensen… Oh hell, the guy was the UN liaison between NATO and Interpol."

"Good thing you keep track of all major law-enforcement personnel." Bolan sighed. "Damn, he was a cop."

"One of the biggest in the world. If he's crossed over, well, that would explain how he knows about the gold shipments, the black market…. Christ, what doesn't he know?"

"Concentrate on the wife," Bolan said. "Her death might tell us about his ultimate goal."

"I'll do my best. Stay loose, old buddy."

"Will do," Bolan replied, snapping the phone shut and tucking it away again.

Constantly checking a GPS and compass, Bolan made his way through the rolling hills, eating and drinking as he walked to save time. Even after three thousand years of cultivation, Sicily was a wild land, and he spotted the remains of several old Roman forts while crossing streams and skirting small farms. Time was tight, but he was on schedule, and he kept an even pace. The numbers were falling, and soon enough the blood would hit the fan.

It was almost noon by the time Bolan finally reached the sea. The sun was bright, but the air was cool, and he could taste the salt on his lips. Wonderful. According to scientists, humanity came from the sea, and just breathing the tangy air was like recharging his internal batteries.

Just off the coast, small rounded islands dotted the azure waters, rising like the shells of giant turtles from the shallows. The domed hills were green with vegetation and scattered with small white rental cottages. There was no sand on the shoreline; the beach was just a smooth bed of dark rocks, with blue waves gently splashing the polished stones. Schools of fish could be seen moving just below the surface—bluegills, anchovies and sardines, the last after the nearby island of Sardinia. Seagulls sat on the sagging remains of old wooden pylons from the time when Pebble Beach had once been a vibrant port. Now it was a deserted stretch of shore, haunted by memories of its past.

Staying low in the grass covering the top of a rolling dune, Bolan surveyed the area with his U.S. Army monocular. Just past a wooden bridge, a paved road led directly to a large flat field. The ground was smooth, bare of any tree stumps, rocks or vegetation—highly unusual on Sicily, where wild oregano grew in amazing abundance.

Ten BMW flatbed trucks sat idling along the side of the field, puffs of blue smoke coming out of the tall exhaust pipes to show that the diesel engines were running. The cargo was covered with heavy tarpaulins, lashed firmly into place. But the sea breeze pushed back a loose flap to briefly reveal the angled prow of an armored vehicle, before dropping back into place.

Bolan allowed himself a small grin. *Bingo.* On the flight over from Albania, he had read what information had been available on the Swiss XTV-APC 99, nicknamed the Uberpanzer. It was an ugly machine, designed strictly for utility. Little more than a squat box with angular sides and prow, it had a double row of huge tires making it able to ford any of the innumerable rivers that crisscrossed Switzerland like hatchwork. There were smoke generators along the sides, along with the stubby barrels of grenade launchers capable of sending smoke canisters for hundreds of feet in any direction. The gray-and-tan camouflage pattern would make the vehicles disappear in the swirling clouds, then the crew could retaliate with the deadly 12.7 mm coaxial Gatling machine gun mounted on top.

However, to climb the steep hills, the brutish vehicle had to be very lightweight, but also capable of withstanding the direct impact of contemporary antitank weapons, everything from the American LAW to a Carl Gustav. That had been accomplished by making ceramic armor.

The Uberpanzer was fast, light and extremely deadly, the perfect fighting machine. A hundred of them had been fully assembled before the unbelievable cost of the ceramic armor had finally forced the wealthy Swiss government to abandon the project, and instead go with more conventional reactive-armor plating and a standard aluminum frame.

However, what North Korean underwater mines, Russian rocket torpedoes and Swiss armored personnel carriers had to do with each other was a complete mystery. Was this Thorodensen trying to equip a private army? Nothing made sense yet, which meant there were still pieces missing from the puzzle.

Sweeping the area with the monocular, Bolan noted sentries blocking the access road, and parked a safe distance from the row of BMW trucks was a VW fuel tanker. On the opposite side of the crude landing field was a cobalt-blue Bentley limousine. The windows were down, and Bolan could just hear soft music playing. The driver was intently smoking a cigar as if it were a prescription from a doctor, while the smiling passenger in the rear was snapping his fingers in time to the beat and bobbing his head. He was clean-shaved, and gold flashed from both hands.

Focusing on the face, Bolan easily recognized Nunzio "The Sledgehammer" Degerrio. More heavily muscled than a stonemason, Degerrio always had a happy smile on his face, and didn't appear anymore dangerous than Santa Claus. It was a look that the brutal mafioso tried very hard to cultivate, as it was always a total surprise to his enemies when he cut their throats while still benignly smiling.

The last thing Bolan had heard about Degerrio was that he was in charge of counterfeiting credit cards in Palermo. But here he was handling a major deal with the Fifteen Families.

"This was a bad day to get a promotion, Nunzio," Bolan whispered, calculating the range and wind sheer.

Surrounding the sedan was a large group of men in heavy work clothes, many with patches on their pants, but every one of them cradling an M-16 assault rifle. Bolan counted fifty. That was quite a sizable group for a simple transfer of goods.

The Executioner wasn't overly concerned with the street soldiers. They were just warm bodies hired by Degerrio for this particular job and dismissed afterward. If there was any more muscle around the gunners, they would be out of sight under the tarpaulins with the Uberpanzers. Those would be the experienced men, professional killers held in reserve in case of trouble. Degerrio was ruthless, not a fool.

Basing a guess on the average size of an APC, Bolan guessed that each truck held two armored personnel carriers, making a total of twenty. That was enough rolling thunder to take over most small countries, which raised some interesting questions. Was Thorodensen planning a military junta back home? The possibility wasn't without some merit. Iceland didn't have a military, only a national police force, and the Uberpanzers would go through them like a reaper cutting down new wheat. Okay, Thorodensen used the mines to steal the gold to buy the Uberpanzers. That was logical enough, but where did the torpedoes come into play?

Checking the other dunes, Bolan wasn't surprised to find two men hidden among the trees and bushes. However, they were in sand-colored ghillie suits, and each was carrying a .50-caliber Barrett rifle. Now that was unexpected.

Bolan frowned. The Barrett wasn't a typical rifle for the Mafia. It was too powerful and required a lot of hard training to learn how to operate properly. Plus, those titanic 700-grain rounds would punch straight through his Threat Level IV body armor as if it were tissue paper. He had never heard of anybody who survived being shot by a Barrett, no matter what they were wearing. The cigar-size bullets could penetrate a brick wall a half mile away. Was the local capo expecting trouble, or was there some sort of a double cross in the works? Either way, a little hard intel would tell him a lot. Time for a recon. Stashing the Imbel G-12 on top of the sand dune as a fallback position, Bolan slid down the rear slope.

Crawling through a shallow gully, he circled the dune until reaching a gravel road closed with a chain. The rusty sign swinging from the chain claimed in Italian that the access bridge was closed for repairs. Except that the wooden bridge around the curve was in excellent condition. Sidling closer, Bolan rubbed a thumb along the edge of the sign, and a rust spot came off on his finger, showing clean metal underneath. A fake? Curious.

Retreating to a copse, Bolan dug out the EM scanner and did a quick sweep of the area. Almost instantly, he got a strong reading of radio chatter, and then of a sweeping radar beacon.

Then everything winked out and the screen went blank.

Instantly, he shoved the scanner into a belt pouch and drew both his handguns. Nothing seemed to be moving, aside from a few bushes swaying in the breeze. He concentrated on the thick green grass, which was where he would have gone to ground. The dry weeds would rustle and give away your movement, but the living grass would be silent.

The cresting waves could be heard in the distance, along with the low purr of the truck engines. Then a frog croaked from the weeds and hopped into view.

Everything seemed innocent enough. Bolan had a definite feeling of being watched, a sort of sixth sense that every combat soldier eventually develops. The snipers on top of the dunes couldn't see down there, which meant Bolan wasn't alone. But where were the others hidden, and why were they here? Could Thorodensen and his people have arrived early?

Suddenly, Bolan had a flashback to the Brooklyn slaughter, and wondered if the Icelandic ambassador was planning on doing the same thing here—arrange for a meeting, then kill everybody and simply steal the goods. It had worked once before. Why not again?

The soldier heard a slight sound behind him, and he faked to the left, then jerked hard to the right. Out of the corner of his eye he saw a stun gun wire fly past his face, the crackling prongs just missing his cheek.

Pivoting into a martial arts crouch, Bolan swept out a leg and tripped the camouflaged hardman. The stun gun went flying, but the female attacker hit the ground in a shoulder roll, and came up with a Beretta drawn. But Bolan already had both his guns up and ready. The two warriors paused, targets acquired.

Braced for an attack from behind, Bolan took a moment to study the woman. She was pretty, even with black-and-gray slashes of camouflage paint on her face. Her long black hair had been tied in a ponytail and tucked into her shirt, and she had a throat mike around her neck. She stood lightly, balanced on the toes of her combat boots, ready to move in any direction.

Aside from the Beretta, an MP-5 submachine gun was slung across her back, the barrel equipped with a sound suppressor. She also had a Gerber combat knife hanging upside down at her left shoulder in the quick-kill style of a commando. Several stun grenades were attached to her chest harness, and a triangular pouch hung alongside her belt buckle, exactly the kind that police officers use to hold handcuffs.

"Surrender your weapon!" she demanded in Italian, the words barely above a whisper.

"Sorry, don't speak a word of the language," Bolan lied. "Try again."

"Bullshit," she said in flawless English. "I saw you read the sign. Only a fool would learn to read a language but not speak it."

"Maybe I'm a fool."

"More likely you wish to learn if I am," she replied softly, shifting her stance. "Now surrender your weapon or die!"

Bolan gave no reply. Since there had already been plenty of time for her to use the Beretta, that meant either she could tell he was wearing body armor, or else she wanted things kept quiet.

Keeping the Beretta pointed at her chest, Bolan aimed the Desert Eagle straight up at the open sky and thumbed back the hammer.

"No! Please, don't!" she begged, raising a palm. "You

are interfering in a police matter. I am a special field agent for Interpol!"

"No, you're not," Bolan replied, easing down the hammer and holstering the weapon. "And neither am I."

Scowling, she looked him over. "The accent sounds American," she said suspiciously.

"Matt Cooper, Central Intelligence Agency," Bolan said, reaching into a pocket of his equipment vest to produce a leather booklet. He briefly flipped it open to show the photo ID and badge inside.

Holstering her weapon, she intently studied the booklet, but since it was legitimate, she could find no flaw.

"So…you're with the Orchestra," she said.

"The Company," he corrected. "The KGB is the agency that used to call itself the Orchestra."

She smiled. "My mistake."

Bolan said nothing. Mistake his ass; it had been a test, and a rather clumsy one. "Not a problem."

"I am Major Antonia Salvatore, NATO special operations," she said, unbuttoning a pocket on her shirt to pull out an identification card.

"And what is your team called?" Bolan asked, tucking his booklet away once more. "Or are you going to arrest Nunzio and his fifty goons over the hills all by yourself?"

Bridling at that remark, Salvatore started to marshal a lie. But she saw it was pointless and pursed her lips to give a low whistle.

Moving like ghosts from a grave, a dozen camouflaged soldiers rose from the tall grass, their ghillie suits and MP-5 submachine guns festooned with twigs and tufts of greenery. Every one of them had a finger on the trigger of their silenced weapon, but the muzzles were aimed at the ground.

"This is Recovery Unit Alpha, codenamed Black Thunder," she said with a touch of pride in her voice. "We specialize in recovering stolen military equipment."

"Such as experimental Swiss armor." Bolan didn't poise it as a question.

She crossed her arms. "Now how do you know about those?"

Bolan pointedly ignored that. "Perhaps we can help each other," he said, holstering the Beretta. "You primarily want the machines, while I want the people who stole them."

"What do you know about them?" she asked, squatting on her heels.

"They're called Penumbra, from Iceland."

"Iceland has terrorists?"

Bolan started to answer, but something caught his attention. The noise was just a vague buzz, like an annoying insect, but soon became a whine that steadily grew in volume into the low rumble of powerful engines.

"Ask them yourself," he stated, stepping into the shadows under a spreading olive tree. "Because here they come."

Quickly copying the move, Major Salvatore touched her throat mike and whispered something too low for him to hear. As if they were made of vapor, Black Thunder melted back into the waving grass and disappeared.

"What can we expect?" she asked, breaking out a pair of Zeiss binoculars. "How high-tech are they?" The sky was full of puffy white clouds and a blazing sun, so it wasn't surprising she could hear the plane but not see the terrorists. Then again, maybe they were coming in from the other side of the sand dunes, skimming low over the ocean waves to avoid any possible radar.

"They're armed with some vintage Kalashnikovs, and homemade mustard gas," Bolan said, unlimbering the angular XM-25 grenade launcher.

"Good to know," she replied, still surveying the sky, even while swinging around the MP-5 submachine gun. "So, does the CIA want us to catch this Penumbra in the act of dealing with Degerrio, or can we just kill everybody?"

Going by the numbers, Bolan activated the autolaser range finder. "I have no problem with dead."

"Excellent," she said, working the arming bolt. Then she touched her throat mike. "Lightning to Thunder, we have red on zero. Repeat, red on zero. No survivors."

Just then the sun dimmed, and everybody looked up in surprise.

Even wearing sunglasses, it took Bolan a moment to blink his sight into focus. Then he spit a curse and started running.

"Take cover!" he yelled, sprinting for the bridge.

A moment later, a formation of Hercules transport aircraft appeared out of the blinding sunlight, a strange golden mist spreading out in their wake to fill the entire sky.

CHAPTER SIX

As the rumbling Hercules circled the stretch of beach looking for a place to land, the Mafia street soldiers tried to not
appear impressed, even though for several of them from
the hill country it was their first close view of an airplane.

"Hey, look there!" a tall guard said, pointing at the sky.
"One of them is leaking fuel."

"No, all of them are," a husky guard growled, tightening his grip on the M-16 assault rifle.

"Strange thing to do just before landing," a stocky man
named Berto muttered, working the bolt of his weapon to
chamber a round.

"Bah, the pilots are probably just emptying the toilets,"
another guard said with a shrug, his own weapon cradled
in both arms. "The same way a train does just before pulling into a station."

Raising a hand, the first man squinted into the bright
sunlight. "That does look like piss," he agreed hesitantly.

Scowling, Berto said nothing, keeping his own counsel.
But he maintained a solid grip on the assault rifle. "Still
doesn't seem right," he said. "It is like they are pissing on
us, eh?"

The rest of the men muttered crude agreements, mostly
peppered with vulgar comments about all foreigners and
their general lack of hygiene.

Carefully making sure the boss wasn't looking in their
direction, one of the Mafia guards pulled out a crumpled

paper bag from inside his jacket and took a fast swig of the contents.

"Ah, better." He sighed, passing the bottle on to the next guard. "It's such a hot day."

"That better be vodka," another man muttered, throwing a nervous glance at the limousine parked on the other side of the sandy field. "If Degerrio smells alcohol on your breath…"

"Of course it is vodka!" The first guard smirked. "Am I a fool?"

"No comment," Berto whispered, passing along the bottle without taking a drink.

The first man snorted at that, then patiently waited for the bag to make the line and return. One little drink wasn't enough these days. It was a good thing he had stopped at a bar and had a few shots before coming to the beach. Standing still and doing nothing was such thirsty work.

"A Swiss APC." He chuckled. "Do you think aside from a cannon that it also has a folding blade to make a little hole in your belt?"

"Try making a hole in your head," a bony man corrected, stuffing a wad of tobacco into his cheek. He chewed it into place. "From what I hear these men of the north are stone killers, and not to be trifled with."

"Of course they are cold killers! They come from Iceland, no?"

"Actually, Iceland is very green, while Greenland is very icy."

"Is it? Well then…please go shit in your hat and punch it."

"Now, I find it curious," Berto said, "that they do not have enough planes. There is no way they have enough to carry twenty of the Swiss tanks."

"Armored personnel carriers."

"Whatever…oh, pass the bottle."

INSIDE THE COMFORT of the limousine, Nunzio Degerrio sighed and made a vague gesture to the driver.

"Enough, Emilio, please close the window." He sat back in the soft leather seat. "And turn the music on again."

"Yes, boss," Emilio replied, lowering a parabolic microphone and pressing a button on the dashboard.

As music began to play once more, Degerrio pulled out a slim gold case and lit an Australian cigarette. Armed men bickering among themselves like old woman in the market and drinking on the job. While he felt a strong obligation to offer these people work, which was only right and proper for their parents' years of service, he didn't ever have to offer them a second job. That was only common sense.

This was a savage business, and only the strong survived. Degerrio had been thirteen years old when he'd made his first kill. A stranger tried to sneak into his home to steal food. He'd hacked off the arm of the would-be thief with an old meat cleaver, then pried open the hand, and shot the man in the face with his own gun. His whole family had helped bury the corpse in the root cellar. His mother kept the cash in the wallet, his grandfather got the shoes and young Nunzio kept the gun.

A few years later, his sponsor had taught Degerrio the trick of using a long-range microphone to listen to men grumble. Most of the time it was just lies about women, but once it had revealed an ambush by Mossad agents who were very angry about a recent business transaction in their homeland between the Mafia and the Palestinians. The sponsor and his soldiers had shot their way to freedom using only handguns.

Blowing a smoke ring, Degerrio almost smiled. In those days, the Mafia was made of real men, proud and strong, whose revolvers seemed to be a part of their hands, removable only by surgery. They were crack shots, deadly and remorseless.

Nowadays, everybody carried assault rifles. Not because they were excellent weapons, but because nobody seemed able to shoot straight these days. Spray-n-pray was what it was called. Just keep throwing lead at the other guy until he fell down. It was pitiful. To call such men street soldiers was an insult to the others who had lived before them. Gone were the glory days, destroyed by attrition and Interpol.

"Sir, we have a message from Lucia," Emilio reported, touching an earbud. "She says…the missiles are set to fire at your command."

"Tell her to stay ready," Degerrio growled, puffing away steadily. "But not to move before I say to. Understand?"

"Yes, sir."

Women in the Mafia, portable radar, flying drones, minicomputers, cell phones, lasers, spy satellites… Degerrio checked the machine pistol holstered under his coat. There was a new type of Mafia struggling to claim its birthright among the foreigners flooding the crime world. The Jamaican drug lords were little better than wild dogs, using machetes to hack apart anybody who stood in their way. The Russians operated exactly like their Cossack ancestors, and he was often surprised that they didn't arrive charging over a hill, riding horses and waving spears.

Only the Fifteen Families understood honor and respect. Degerrio enjoyed working with the dignified Albanians. They were decent men, although he still looked forward to when the Mafia would slaughter all of them and seize control of their vast trade in heroin and weapons smuggling. But that was merely business. Nothing personal. The Mafia had started smuggling weapons to freedom fighters centuries ago. It was in their blood.

Swooping low over the grassy hill, the Hercules aircraft started to angle west toward the landing strip. But then abruptly changed course and started directly for the trucks and guards.

"At last, they are landing," Emilio said, both hands on the steering wheel. "They make us wait to score points, eh? To show they are strong?"

"Perhaps," Degerrio said, crushing out the cigarette. "Anything on the radio yet?"

"No, sir."

"Strange. Tell Lucia to stay alert. We may need those rockets.... Jesus!"

The fine golden mist jettisoned from the airplanes had finally arrived, sweeping across the sand dunes and the rocky beach.

Hidden among the tall weeds, the snipers were the first to die. Caught totally by surprise, they tried to run, but got only a few yards before they fell back into the weeds, and went forever still.

Expecting the smell of urine on the wind, the frowning guards stationed along the crude landing field were startled when the needles on the pine trees quickly turned a ghastly pale yellow and fell in droves. Busy at a salt lick, a lone sheep looked up at the rain of needles, shuddered and began vomiting blood, even as its hair started to fall off.

Shouting and cursing, the guards opened fire on the roaring planes, their assault rifles spitting out torrents of hot lead. Then the cloud reached them, and the screaming began as their skin burst open and their blood started to bubble. Their eyes went solid white, tongues turned black, and they fell in agonizing convulsions, thrashing and trying desperately to scream.

"Sweet Jesus, nerve gas!" Emilio gasped, quickly closing every window.

"Tell Lucia to fire!" Degerrio shouted, slapping a handkerchief over his face. "Shoot down those planes!"

The ordered was relayed; the driver's door of the VW cab slammed open and a pretty young woman carrying a Stinger missile launcher jumped to the ground. Stepping away from the tanker, she raised the missile to a shoulder and swept the weapon back and forth across the sky. Nothing happened.

"Boss, she cannot get a lock!" Emilio said in a rush. "Either the Stinger is malfunctioning or these Icelanders are jamming the radar. Is that even possible?"

"Tell Lucia to fire anyway!" Degerrio shouted through the embroidered cloth. "Then get me out of here before that gas arrives!"

"Yes, sir!" Emilio replied, doing both at the same time.

Even as the tires of the Bentley spun in the loose gravel, the woman knelt, aimed and fired.

In a rush of fiery smoke, the guided missile leaped away, to streak directly between two of the oncoming Hercules, missing them both by a wide margin.

"The idiot missed!" Degerrio fumed, looking backward.

"She said there was no lock…." Emilio started when an unexpected gust of wind blew some of the golden cloud across the limousine.

Instantly, the engine died in a sputter.

Muttering curses, Emilio tried to start the engine again, with no success, then threw the transmission into Neutral. For a long moment, nothing seemed to happen, then the limousine slowly started to roll along the sloping ground—moving backward.

"Idiot! We're heading for the cloud!" Degerrio yelled, trying to look out every window.

There came a dull thump as the limousine went over a moaning corpse that grew blissfully silent.

"Yes! Then we hit the ocean! The water should protect us, boss."

"So we drown rather than dissolve?"

"It buys us time to, ah…"

"Yes? To do what?"

"How the fuck should I know, you fat asshole?"

The heated conversation stopped as the rear of the limousine splashed into the salt water. Still moving, the limousine started to rock from side to side, even as waves crested over the trunk.

Trying the door, Emilio found that he couldn't swing it wide against the push of the waves. Then there came a horrible stink of chemicals as the cloud flowed in through the partially open door.

Grabbing his face, Emilio shrieked as watery blood and other vicious fluids dribbled between his dissolving fingers.

Quickly closing the bulletproof partition that separated the front compartment from the rest of the limousine, Degerrio saw a tendril of pale gold fumes snake out of the air vent, and knew that he was already dead. With forced calm, he drew the Glock, shoved the barrel into his mouth and squeezed the trigger. The back of his head vanished in an explosion of bones, brains and blood, the rear window splattering with his final thoughts.

Seconds later, the nerve gas flowed over the beheaded corpse, dissolving everything organic, and even changing the hue of the mobster's gold jewelry. Then the gas came in contact with the smoldering cigarette. Just for a moment, a searing fireball filled the interior of the limousine. Then it was gone, leaving behind only the steaming residue of charred bodies.

Undamaged, the stereo in the dashboard continued to warble classical music.

CROUCHING IN THE MUDDY water under the old bridge, Mack Bolan, Major Salvatore and the rest of Black Thunder studied the airplanes carefully as they made another pass over the beach. The wash of the planes spread the golden cloud farther across the landing field.

"That's not mustard gas," Salvatore stated, easing the biofilter mask across her face.

Covering her mouth and nose, the porous cone was generally used for fighting in a burning house, to give soldiers protection from the deadly fumes that came off burning wall-to-wall carpeting.

"Looks more like nerve gas," Bolan said with a frown. "But I don't recognize the color, or that weird melting aspect."

"Something new then," a sergeant stated, shifting his grip on the MP-5 machine gun.

Salvatore grunted. "Or more homemade crap from some half-ass chemist who doesn't know a ketone from a polymer."

From their position, Bolan couldn't see the trucks or limousine anymore. But he could clearly hear the wailing death cries of the guards. It sounded like something from the pit of hell.

Just then a woman ran into view from around a bend in the road, gurgling horribly. Her clawed fingers were tearing away the blistering flesh of what had once been her face. The skin came off in ragged strips, and red blood was gushing everywhere, but the woman didn't seem to notice or care. White foam was sizzling from her mouth, and her eyes were gone, the sockets full of a bubbling jelly.

As she ran across the bridge above them, Bolan tracked her passage with the Beretta. But the moment she came into sight again, the private next to him triggered a short burst from the MP-5, the hail of 9 mm Parabellum rounds stitching up her spine and ending her torment forever.

Unexpectedly, they heard a dull explosion, the sound oddly muffled, then warbling rock music rose above the low noise of the circling planes.

"What the fuck was that?" Salvatore demanded with a puzzled expression.

"Tell you in a moment," Bolan said, wading out of the water and up the sloping bank.

Crawling through the bushes, he stopped when the vegetation started to lose its green color, and broke out the monocular. The golden haze made it difficult to see many details, but there didn't appear to be anything alive on the makeshift landing field.

Even the truck engines had stalled, with spreading puddles on the ground telling the story of dissolved hoses, belts and vital gaskets. Then Bolan spotted the limousine with the skeletons inside. The bodies were smoking slightly, but not melting anymore. That told him everything he needed to know.

A movement from behind almost made him turn. Then Salvatore appeared, flanked by two of her soldiers.

"What's the situation?" she asked, breaking out a bulky pair of binoculars.

"Any thermite, or willy peter?" Bolan asked, ignoring the question.

"Willy who?" The private arched an eyebrow.

"That is American slang for white phosphorus," the sergeant explained. "No, sir, that was outlawed by the UN many years ago."

"Never hurts to ask," Bolan said, unlimbering the XM-25. Taking careful aim, he tapped the button for autorange and stroked the trigger.

The grenade launcher gave a hard thump, something

darted past the limousine, and then the fuel tanker violently exploded, sending shrapnel and flames far and wide. The concussion threw bodies high into the sky, then the explosion bizarrely redoubled in strength, becoming brighter and hotter. Now a sizzling corona pulsed across the landscape, reaching into the distant hills, out across the ocean waves, and rapidly extending along the curved roadway.

With a cry, Salvatore threw herself back down into the muddy gully, followed by the soldiers. Only Bolan didn't move, but studied the fiery destruction of the death cloud as the flames flew straight for him...only to see it die away before reaching the edge of the yellowing grass.

He tightly closed both eyes as the heat flash arrived, his skin prickling from the searing temperature. But a moment later it was gone, and a cool breeze blew in from the ocean, banishing any lingering traces of the volcanic maelstrom.

"Are you insane?" Salvatore growled, crawling back out of the gully. Her previously damp uniform was now coated with sticky mud, along with all her weapons.

"Some people think so," Bolan replied, watching the planes circle overhead.

"So, the nerve gas was flammable." The sergeant snorted. "Good call, Agent Cooper. It must be homemade. This would be useless in a war zone."

"Damn straight."

As the last traces of the firestorm faded away, one of the Hercules broke formation, banking around to start landing.

"Good God, they must think the gas ignited accidentally," the private said, already using a packaged moist towelette to clean his machine gun.

"There were several people smoking cigarettes," Bolan said. "It would probably take only one live ember to set off the whole cloud."

"When do we move, Major?" the sergeant asked, easing

back the arming bolt on his machine gun. It clicked into place with cold metallic certainty.

"When I say so, Liberman, and not a second earlier," Salvatore stated, slinging the MP-5 behind her back, and unholstering the Beretta at her hip. The gun was only wet, and fully operational.

"Why the delay?" the private asked eagerly. "We wait until they land, blow off the tires so that they can't escape, and then—"

"These are seaplanes," Bolan stated, "and this model can land on the beach or water." He gestured at the wide Mediterranean Sea washing onto the pebble beach.

"Besides, if those 40 mm Bofors cannons on the Hercs are operational, they can wipe us out in seconds," Salvatore added grimly. "I've seen a single Hercules armed with Bofors level an entire forest. Even NATO body armor doesn't mean much against that kind of firepower."

"It can't happen. Those are stolen civilian planes," Bolan said. "Useless they have a master gunsmith, there are no cannon onboard." Then he relented. "On the other hand, they did rob a warehouse full of military weapons. But even if they had Bofors, they'd require a master gunsmith to install them."

"They have a chemist," Salvatore retorted. "Why not a smith?"

Unfortunately, Bolan could find no reasonable argument against the possibility.

Bypassing the steaming ground littered with corpses and debris, the Hercules dropped low until it was skimming the ocean waves, then landed hard. Taxiing to the beach, it swung around and reversed engines until the tail was scraping on the pebbles. With a whine of hydraulics, the rear ramp cycled down, revealing people carrying AK-47 assault rifles, and wearing Royal Navy NBC environmental suits.

"Damn! That's what I was really concerned about," Salvatore said, hunkering lower. "If we charge, they can release more gas. Their people will be safe inside those damn suits, and we'll be coughing out chunks of our lungs."

Even as the figures in the Hercules walked along the ramp onto the beach, another Hercules landed on the sea, closely followed by two more.

"We can ignite the gas and fry ourselves," Sergeant Liberman said, shifting gears in midspeech. "Damn it, those NBC suits will even protect them from the heat flash!"

"Nuclear, bacteriological, chemical," the private muttered.

More people in NBC suits moved of a Hercules, their gloved hands full of fuel canisters. But others stood off to the sides, holding old-fashioned WWII bazooka or brand-new Atchisson autoshotguns.

"Clever. The bastards brought along their own fuel supply," Salvatore said dourly. "There's probably just enough in the Uberpanzers to show that the engines work, but not much more."

"Cheap, and stupid."

"Agreed."

Starting at the closest truck, a team pulled aside the canvas sheets covering the pair of Uberpanzers on the flatbed, and two other terrorists got busy putting a few gallons of diesel into the fuel tank.

Even before they were done, somebody inside the APC had the engine running, and they barely got out of the way before the Swiss juggernaut rolled off the back of the flatbed. It fell the three feet to the ground, sinking a foot into the hard soil, but kept on going as if the drop was no more than a speed bump, and of no concern whatsoever.

Driving over the bodies, the Uberpanzer rolled straight up the ramp and into the waiting Hercules, where more figures in NBC suits promptly started chaining it securely in place.

"Okay, what can we do, Major?" Liberman demanded, his body tense.

"Not a damn thing," Salvatore said in a hard voice. "We stand down and simply observe. Once they leave, we'll contact Interpol and…hey!"

Dropping his heavy backpack, Bolan was already on the move, running low and fast around the outside of the sand dunes. He had far to go and damn little time to get there.

Pushing himself for the maximum speed, the big American was breathing hard by the time he got to the far side of the landing field. Running carefully through the gooey puddles of dissolved animals, he reached the crest of a dune. Peering over the top, he easily found the remains of the NATO sniper, and just as quickly departed. The soldier had to have had the Barrett tucked under his arm when the nerve gas hit, and the rifle was coated with sticky fluids. Absolutely useless. It would take hours of detailed cleaning to make the weapon serviceable again. Bolan only hoped the other Barrett was in better condition, or he would have to scrub this mission. The XM-25 was good, but not against an APC, much less these expensive Swiss models.

Down on the beach, the first Hercules was taxiing away from the shore, and heading for the open Atlantic.

Reaching the second sand dune, Bolan was relieved to find the Barrett free of any residue from the dissolved NATO sniper. Unfortunately, the ammunition pouch was slick, the brass almost swimming in thick bodily fluids. All Bolan had were the ten rounds in the magazine.

Quickly checking it over, he worked the arming bolt to cycle through a round, and caught the cigar-size bullet before it dropped. The brass was spotlessly clean. Then he took a look through the Zeiss telescopic sights and saw only a blurred smear. Without a word, he got busy with spit and a handkerchief to clean the fouled lens.

In a roar, the first Hercules lifted off, and only seconds later another started moving away from the beach.

There was no more plant life in the area to use as protective cover, so Bolan went flat on his stomach and crawled to the crest of the dune. Looking like alien astronauts, the members of Penumbra were busy handling the Uberpanzers, along with stealing the occasional M-16 assault rifle from a dead Mafia guard.

It was impossible to see the faces of the people inside the NBC suits, so Bolan randomly choose the person waving his or her arms around the most. That would be Thorodensen or his second in command. Either was a good target.

Levering in a fresh round, Bolan listened to the wind, calculated the range and density of sea air, then aimed just to the left of the gesturing person and stroked the trigger. The Barrett rifle boomed louder than unchained thunder.

Down on the rocky beach, one of the people wearing an NBC suit flipped over backward and landed in a sprawl, internal organs exposed to the heavens.

At once, all the other members of Penumbra wildly cut loose with their weapons, randomly hammering the sand dunes, the dead forest, the few patches of inland vegetation that were still thick and green.

There was an answering cry of pain from the bushes near the wooden bridge, and then a dozen MP-5 submachine guns began a controlled barrage. Several of the Penumbra people fell under the assault, but then struggled to their feet again and clumsily fired back with their stolen weapons.

They had to wear body armor under the suits, Bolan realized, squeezing the trigger once more. Another figure leaped off the ground from the hell-hammer arrival of the 700-grain slug, life exploding outward in a horrid spray of blood and organs.

Every member of Penumbra on the beach swept their weapons along the top of the dune in retaliation. But Bolan had already dropped down the far side and was sprinting for his next position.

Now one of the people carrying an Atchisson ripped a swath through the greenery, the fléchettes shaking every leaf, petal and needle. But the distance was too great, and there was no sound of a hit this time.

Never once exposing themselves, Black Thunder responded with a flurry of grenades, the canisters landing among the corpses and spewing thick clouds of green and blue smoke.

Contemptuously, the terrorists waddled into the billowing fumes just as the round AP grenades detonated. Vivisected by the shrapnel, four of the terrorists fell in crimson finality, and the rest hastily retreated to the beach, endlessly firing their weapons at anything and everything. A person operating a bazooka launched another round, and a sand dune erupted skyward, the NATO soldiers hidden behind it briefly crying out in surprise, then going silent.

After circling a low dune, Bolan dropped on top, aimed and fired. Caught in the act of reloading the bazooka, the person in the NBC suit shrieked as he…no, as she spun, her left arm terminated at the elbow. Blood spurted from the ripped arteries, and she tried to staunch the flow with her cumbersome gloves. The effort was useless, and she crumpled, her moans becoming softer and weaker until stopping completely.

Screaming curses in an unknown language, another person grabbed the fallen bazooka and swung the weapon toward Bolan, then abruptly shifted targets and fired. The fat rocket streaked across the beach and field to slam into the wooden bridge. The explosion lifted the structure from the ground, spreading burning chunks of it far and wide.

The members of Penumbra cheered, and Bolan coolly put a round into the bazooka itself. The antitank weapon was torn from the grip of its operator, a glove and several fingers going with it, judging from the shrieks that followed. Nearly bent in two, the bazooka hit the ground and clattered along, small pieces breaking off until it came to rest alongside the depression made by the exploded fuel truck.

Just then another Hercules climbed into the sky, and two others started to swing around and come back, their engines building power as they swooped steadily lower.

Pausing to brace himself, Bolan fired the Barrett sniper rifle at the oncoming aircraft, and one of the engines burst into flame. Out of control, the huge airplane veered away, but leveled out again when the automatic systems cut the flow of fuel to the burning engine, and the flames died.

Working the arming bolt once more, Bolan put two more titanic bone-shredders into the nose of the Hercules, trying for the pilots. The prow was reinforced, but it wasn't a hardpoint like the doors and aft ramp. Since the nose was an impossible target, only the floor was armored against shrapnel. But if he had any success it wasn't evident.

Then the Hercules began to release a wide golden spray.

Dropping the Barrett, Bolan ran for his life across the beach. The noise of the plane got louder, and he was still too far away, so he also ditched the XM-25, then sprinted forward, to dive into the cresting waves. He cut deep into the shallow water and collided with a sharp rock, the blow almost forcing the air from his lungs. He was also sinking with alarming speed.

Fighting not to exhale, Bolan quickly got rid of the heavy body armor, then dug his hands into the grainy muck of the sea floor, trying to follow it deeper.

Swirling sand blocked his sight, and a darting school of sardines came out of nowhere, but Bolan stayed on course. He finally located the ancient Roman pylons looming from the murky darkness and eased himself around the far side of one, where he would be out of sight. The water's surface shimmered brightly less than a foot above his head, but if the gas was there even a quick peek could mean instant death.

Trying to ignore the burning in his lungs and the pounding of his heart, he retrieved a camping flare from his web belt and scraped it alive. The bright chemical flame illuminated the ocean for several yards. He knew that would make him a perfect target, but hoped the pylon offered cover. At least for a few precious seconds.

Keeping his hand safely underwater, Bolan inched the flare upward until it broke the surface. When nothing happened, he started to relax. Then there was a flash, and the atmosphere burned with blinding intensity, the radiating heat making his skin prickle even through the cool seawater.

When the flames eventually stopped, Bolan waited a few more seconds for any lingering traces of the nerve gas to dissipate, then surged to the surface and greedily pulled in a lungful of air. It smelled of the ocean, clean and fresh.

Glancing about, he didn't see anybody nearby, then instinctively ducked as a Hercules roared past overhead. Impatiently, he waited until it was gone, then used the flare again. But this time there was no reaction.

Swimming to the beach, Bolan staggered from the shallows and started running, thankful that he didn't have to deal with loose sand.

Checking over his remaining weapons, he heard the raging battle on the other side of the dunes long before it came into view. Black Thunder was using short, controlled bursts from its MP-5s.

Meanwhile, Penumbra was firing AK-47 assault rifles nonstop, the overlapping chattering steadily punctuated by the dull thud of 30 mm grenade launchers. Men and women were screaming and cursing, grenades boomed, a plume of sand blew high, and a Hercules flew by so close that Bolan almost ducked out of the way.

Rounding the dune, he saw that two of the flatbed trucks were on fire, the Uberpanzers draped in burning canvas. The rocky beach was strewn with fresh corpses, most of them wearing NATO ghillie suits. How was that possible?

Then an Uberpanzer rolled off the back of a flatbed, and a 7.62 mm machine gun mounted on top lurched into action. A withering hail of steel-jacketed lead swept across the landscape, chewing a path of destruction among the partially dissolved corpses.

Moving fast as the deadly weapon came their way, Major Salvatore and Black Thunder scattered, taking cover behind the other flatbeds and their own dead.

The machine gun never stopped shooting as the Uberpanzer rolled backward toward a waiting Hercules, golden arches of spent shells flying away to land with a musical tinkle on the smooth pebbles.

Although many of them were clearly wounded, the last members of Penumbra stayed close behind the APC, shooting around it, then ducking back again.

They might be amateurs, but they learned fast, Bolan noted, swinging up both of his handguns. That was bad news.

He cut down two of the terrorists with head shots before a second Uberpanzer joined the first, its machine gun driving the Executioner behind a burning flatbed truck. As he reloaded, Bolan saw the nearby corpse of a terrorist. The hood of the NBC suit was thrown back, revealing the face of an old man. Not just mature, or middle-aged, but genuinely old, maybe in his seventies. Just who were these people?

Ignoring that thought for the moment, Bolan crouched to shoot between the tires, both the Beretta and the Desert Eagle blazing away. Another terrorist fell, but the rest staggered away wounded, saved once more by whatever they were wearing under the bulky NBC suits.

A third Uberpanzer had joined the other two, and using a triangular formation they flanked the terrorists, working as rolling cover to escort them safely to the remaining Hercules. The rest of the big planes were already airborne, and spreading out in different directions to confuse any possible pursuers.

The soldiers of Black Thunder maintained steady fire, the ricochets bouncing off the armored side of the Uberpanzers, doing as much damage as snowballs. Switching the Beretta to full-auto, Bolan drilled an entire magazine at the people behind the APC, and scored only a few more flesh wounds. Between the Uberpanzers, and their body armor, the terrorists were hard to stop, and once they got off the ground and into the air…

But then Bolan smiled and holstered both weapons to break into a sprint. Once in the air, they would be sitting ducks. That was, if Degerrio was actually as much of a hardcase as Mafia legend claimed.

Skirting from wreckage to corpses, Bolan zigzagged across the battlefield as another Hercules took off in a roar. That meant there was only one plane left. Time to move fast. Upon reaching the partly submerged Bentley, Bolan saw that the vehicle was in poor condition, battered, busted and broken, the windows shattered and the tires gone, leaving only the shiny steel rims. But he was just interested in the trunk.

Wading to the rear of the limousine, he pressed a small wad of C-4 onto the lock, snapped off the timing pencil and stepped back. There was a loud bang and the hood flipped open, revealing several large trunks.

After briefly checking for traps, Bolan threw back the lid of the largest one. Inside, nestled in a thick cushion of gray foam, was a pristine Carl Gustav multipurpose launcher and four rockets.

Unfortunately, Bolan didn't find any AA projectiles, only antitank rounds. Probably so that Degerrio could stop Penumbra from using an Uberpanzer against his guards. Smart move, just not smart enough for Bolan's liking.

Loading in an armor-piercing projectile, the soldier rested the all-purpose weapon on top of the Bentley. The beach was clear.

Skimming along the waves, the last Hercules was just taking off, the pontoons dripping with sheets of water, and it banked hard to join the other escaping planes.

"Bring it down!" Major Salvatore snarled, walking out of the billowing smoke from a burning truck.

Taking a deep breath, Bolan waited what felt like a very long time, until the wind was blowing in just the right direction, before he released the safety and squeezed the trigger.

A huge blast of smoke came from the aft of the long tube, then a lance of fire extended from the front, the rocket slamming directly into the Hercules's vulnerable hull alongside the armored door. The antitank rocket was traveling so fast it actually came out the other side of the plane before exploding, the blast sheering off a wing and igniting the thousands of gallons of aviation fuel.

Engulfed in a writhing fireball of gargantuan proportions, the Hercules briefly disappeared, then the engines reappeared, tumbling free as the rest of the huge plane thunderously exploded. Chunks of machinery soared away, and two angular boxes shot out of the flames, tumbling and turning as they fell. One of the Uberpanzers hit the ocean like a meteor, a white plume rising high as it punched deep into the salty water.

Tumbling end over end, the next supertank slammed into the beach, with much more disastrous results. The armored prow dug halfway into the smooth pebbles before the chassis folded like an accordion. The tires exploded, the hatches burst open and a red goo sprayed out, lumpy with heads, boots and small pieces of equipment.

"Think any of them survived?" Salvatore asked.

"Not a chance in hell," Bolan growled, hefting the heavy Carl Gustav onto a shoulder as he squinted into the sun. "But it looks like the rest of the bastards got away clean."

"Not yet they haven't," Salvatore growled, lowering the machine gun and touching her throat mike. "Big Dog to Jaws. Scramble! Repeat, scramble!"

CHAPTER SEVEN

As the rest of Black Thunder began to gather around them, Bolan started to ask a question, but then he heard a familiar noise. Turning, he saw a Black Hawk helicopter streaking their way out of the distant hills.

Lowering the rocket launcher, Bolan smiled. Correction. This was a different model helicopter than what he normally used as transportation. There was no mistaking the side-mounted weapons pods, or the outlandishly long sensor probe on the right side, extended like the lance of a medieval knight riding into battle. This was a UH-60 Black Hawk Penetrator, something new from the Department of Defense. Unlike the regular model, which could carry ten people and equipment, the Penetrator had a crew of three, two pilots and a gunner. The rest of the helicopter was filled with ammunition hoppers for the M-134 7.62 mm miniguns, GAU-19 12.7 mm Gatling guns, and 70 mm Hydra rocket pods.

As it rapidly grew in size, Bolan checked to see if it was carrying any AGM-114 Hellfire laser-guided missiles, but those had been wisely replaced with extra fuel tanks.

Putting the Carl Gustav aside, Bolan swung up the monocular and easily found the escaping Hercules. The aircraft were flying due west toward the open sea. In only a few minutes they would be gone from visual range.

"I'm coming along," Bolan stated, tucking away the monocular.

"You've earned it," Salvatore declared. "But can you fire an M-134?"

"Yes, as well as a GAU-19…even with the new modifications."

Briefly, she smiled. The man knew guns, that was for sure. "Okay, you're in."

"Radar still dead?"

"Yeah, it is. The radio, too," the major replied, checking an EM scanner. "Caval! The bastards must have left the jammer behind to keep us quiet. Find that fucking thing, and turn it off!"

"Yes, Major," the private replied with a salute, then dashed away on the hunt.

"Davis, give me your grenades!" Salvatore ordered, tucking away the useless scanner. "Caramico, all of your ammunition, please!"

Dutifully, the men passed over the requested items, and the major refilled her belt pouches.

With his own belt feeling uncomfortably light, Bolan wished he could do the same. Unfortunately, nobody in Black Thunder was carrying a Desert Eagle, and he could see the XM-25 lying in a puddle of congealing human remains. With a snort, he shrugged off the bandolier holding spare 25 mm rounds.

"Here you go, sir," Liberman said, proffering a fistful of spare 9 mm magazine clips for his NATO-issue Beretta.

"Much appreciated," Bolan said. "How many of your people died?"

"Too goddamn many," Liberman replied with a grimace. "Those assholes are lousy shots, but they must be wearing Threat Level V body armor. We kept hitting them, and they kept not dying."

"Can the chatter, ladies," Salvatore snapped. "Smith, Gutman and Lilkilolani! Run back to our Hummer, drive out of this goddamn jamming field and radio in a full report to Brussels."

"Yes, Major!" a corporal replied with a crisp salute. Then the three men turned to sprint inland toward the tall green mountains.

"Peterson and Dobrinski! Search for any wounded and gather dog tags."

Nodding, the grim man and woman took off at a run across the battlefield.

"Sergeant, you stay here with everybody else to sweep the area for the dead," Salvatore continued, removing her cap. "Take everything they're carrying, and I do mean everything!"

"Wallets, watches, wedding rings, nipple rings, fingerprints and tattoos." Liberman rattled off the litany as if he had done so a thousands times before. "Cell phones, too, if they were stupid enough to carry a live one into battle."

"They probably were!" Salvatore snorted. She brushed back her hair, then rammed the cap back into place. "Don't bother with the Mob goons. They're just local muscle. But I want to know who these new arrivals are, and where they come from!"

"Yes, Major!" Liberman replied. "If I can't get a print from their fingers, I'll pull the teeth from their mouths."

She gave a hard smile. "Good man."

"What if any of them are still alive?" a private asked, scratching at his neck. There was a shallow furrow there from a near miss, and his shirt was dark with blood.

"None survived," Salvatore stated, pulling out a pair of sunglasses and setting them into place. "Understand?"

"Yes, Major," the private replied.

Just then, the Black Hawk arrived, hovering overhead for a few moments to allow the people on the beach to clear a landing area. As they got out of the way, it gracefully descended.

"You and you, get out!" Salvatore commanded with a jerk of her hand. "I'm taking your place!"

With a nod, the copilot and gunner clambered out of the helicopter and held the door as she climbed inside.

Going around the chopper, Bolan pulled open the hatch and got in back.

"And who the fuck are you?" the pilot growled, resting a gloved hand on the Beretta holstered alongside the seat's ejector lever.

From the voice and figure, Bolan could tell she was female, and remembered that NATO had a lot of women, most pilots with sterling combat records.

"Lieutenant, say hello to Matt Cooper from the CIA!" Major Salvatore announced, buckling on a safety harness. "He's a friendly, Goldman!"

Removing her helmet, a very pretty Asian woman scowled at Bolan, then nodded. "If you say so, Major," she replied, sliding the helmet back into place.

"Goldman?" Bolan asked in surprise, taking the gunner position.

"Lieutenant Yuki Goldman!" she answered in a mocking tone, flipping switches on the overhead controls.

As the Black Hawk lifted, she turned. Her features were partially hidden behind the mirrored face shield, giving her an oddly inhuman appearance. Then she grinned. "What, don't I look Jewish?"

"As kosher sushi," Bolan replied with a chuckle, checking the feed on the enclosed ammunition belts.

Aside from the Hydra rocket pods, the Black Hawk was equipped with a pair of 12.7 mm Gatling guns that were operated by either the pilot or copilot. But there were also two 7.62 mm electric miniguns controlled by a rear gunner.

"Damn it, radar is still jammed," Salvatore growled, pushing buttons and twirling dials. "Have to do this the hard way. Head due west, and get hot!"

"I was born hot," Goldman replied, one hand on the yoke while the other changed settings on the control board. Meter needles jumped and lights flashed.

"Okay, now we're also sending out a jamming field," she announced. "If they try to drop their field to get a lock on us, it won't work."

"Good to know," Salvatore said, as the helicopter banked sharply. A few loose items on the floor rolled to the side. "How's our ammo?"

"Enough to bring down King Kong! What are we hunting, Major?"

"Seven Hercs!"

As the big GE engines continued to build in power, the Black Hawk steadily accelerated. There was only sparkling blue sea below them now, the coast of Sicily dwindling quickly into the distance.

"Nice big targets," Goldman said casually, running a test on the primary weapons systems. Whole sections of the control boards came alive, glowing indicators showing the status of the Gatlings, miniguns and rockets. "Are the Bofors cannon live?"

Salvatore shrugged. "Unknown, but most likely not."

"However, they do have some form of nerve gas," Bolan added. "So under no circumstances fly directly behind them."

"This bird is NBC rated," Goldman answered, glancing at the open hatch. "But not now, eh? Okay, we play it safe, Cooper."

"Much appreciated," Bolan replied, sliding on a headset and throat mike.

For several long minutes there was no further conversation inside the helicopter, everybody concentrating on getting ready for battle. On the main control board, the radar screen remained clear, the luminescent arm sweeping around and around, showing no blips or bogeys.

"If you don't mind my asking," Bolan said, "Why don't you have any missiles?"

With the hatches closed, normal conversation was possible inside the helicopter. But he needed the hatch open to fire the minigun, and the rushing wind was deafening. At its top speed of roughly 200 mph, the Black Hawk was literally sealed inside a personal hurricane.

"Say again?" Salvatore demanded, glancing into a small mirror mounted on the overhead control board.

"Why are there no missiles on board?" Bolan repeated.

"The supreme commander of NATO didn't want the Swiss Uberpanzers damaged!" Goldman said, her lip curling in disgust.

"Why not?" Bolan demanded curiously.

"Politics," Salvatore replied, as if expelling a rotten piece of fruit from her mouth.

"Smart move, eh?" Goldman added mockingly.

"A soldier should always plan for combat!" Bolan countered, snapping a safety rig onto a wall stanchion.

"Thank you, Sun Tzu!"

The wind was buffeting him hard, his wet clothing whipping about with stinging force. Bolan was chilled to the bone, but there was nothing he could do about that. Taking advantage of the lull in combat, the Executioner slipped on a parachute and dug out a high-calorie energy bar. He washed it down with a few sips of water from his canteen.

There should have been a helmet for the door gunner, but it was nowhere in sight. Then Bolan spotted a pair of sunglasses and grabbed them. They were mirrored, which helped cut the glare of the sun off the water, but the blue coloring made the distant sky murky, and that was a liability.

"By the way," Bolan added, "the Hercs are also carrying two Uberpanzers each."

"Good, that will seriously slow them down," Goldman replied. "Anything else I should know?"

"Yes, there they are," Salvatore said, gazing through binoculars. "West by southwest. Altitude, fifteen thousand feet."

Using the monocular, Bolan looked, but all he saw were scattered clouds. Then he found a brief break in the cover and there they were, seven Hercules still flying in formation.

"Range is five miles, and closing," Goldman stated, swiveling her head to stare at the distant planes.

"Not close enough for the mini," Bolan said, switching on the primary circuits for the electric weapon. Instantly, it came alive under his hands, the metal seeming to pulse with dangerous intentions.

"Not a problem," she replied, pulling back on the yoke.

Throwing out an arm, Bolan barely had time to brace himself between the door frame and an ammunition hopper before the Black Hawk banked hard and fast in a dangerously tight curve. The twirling blades overhead abruptly changed pitch as the twin GE power plants surged in volume. The throb of the mighty engines was a palpable presence inside the chopper.

Raising the prow, Goldman pushed the helicopter to the limit and then beyond, while a dozen gauges hit the redline and started blinking a warning. The aircraft punched through the cloud layers and emerged into brilliant sunshine. The Hercules were only a short distance away, slightly ahead and off to the side.

"Which one should we go after?" Goldman asked.

"There's no way of telling the command ship," Bolan declared. "It's a crap shoot which has Thorodensen on board."

Twisting in the chair, Salvatore looked hard at Bolan. "Thorodensen...the ambassador?"

"Former ambassador," he corrected.

"Damn diplomats always did make my ass itch," she announced, studying the planes. "Okay, they're now in range."

"From NATO with love," Goldman announced, thumbing a red button on the yoke. Both Hydra rocket pods unleashed a stuttering barrage of 70 mm rockets.

The sizzling cluster streaked away, most of them completely missing the rear two Hercules. Then the last couple rockets slammed into the tail section of the third, blowing a ragged hole on the aft stabilizers.

Instantly, the huge aircraft lost control and started to angle away from the others. Aiming for the pilots in the cockpit, Bolan added a long burst from the minigun as the wind sheer visibly enlarged the breach until the rear fuselage started to warp and then tear, strips of material breaking away.

Immediately, all the Hercules started wildly launching countermeasures, flares and chaff filling the sky to confuse any incoming missiles.

With a snarl, Salvatore thumbed the firing controls on her yoke, and the 12.7-mm Gatling guns hammered out a concentrated spray of high-velocity death. A hundred holes appeared along the weakening body of the Hercules, then it burst into flames and violently exploded.

Chunks of burning debris tumbled into the clouds below as the Black Hawk swung around to dodge any possible shrapnel, then moved right back on a new attack vector.

Unexpectedly, three other Hercules slowed, and their rear ramps began to cycle down.

"Are they going to dump their cargo to try and escape?" Goldman demanded skeptically.

"I'd say the exact opposite is going to happen!" Bolan growled, the M-134 in his hands vomiting a steady stream of rounds.

Every tenth round was a tracer, and he moved the dotted line across another Hercules, stitching a line of holes in the nose. The control room windows exploded and the pilots inside threw up their arms against the storm of flying glass. Blood splattered the windshield, and the airplane angled sharply to the left before turning over in a barrel roll.

With cool deliberation, Goldman, Salvatore and Bolan raked the belly of the craft with their weapons, and the plane started nosing downward, spinning ever faster in a tight spiral until it fell behind and out of view.

"Fish in a barrel," Goldman said with a sneer, both shoulders hunched as if she had plunged a sword into the guts of an enemy.

Swaying from side to side, the two rear Hercules finally got their ramps fully lowered, and inside each plane an Uberpanzer could be seen, strapped tightly into place.

"Careful, these fish shoot back," Bolan said, releasing the trigger on the minigun to let the barrel cool. If he maintained a barrage for too long, it would start to melt, and then the back blast would blow the Black Hawk out of the sky.

"Shoot back with what?" Salvatore snorted. "Handguns and assault rifles?"

"Bushmasters," Bolan said.

Just then, a series of bright flashes erupted from the top of the chained APC, and a dark flurry of objects streaked by the Black Hawk.

"Clever! They're using the APC chain guns," Major Salvatore snarled, even as another cloud of 25 mm shells moved past the helicopter.

"I don't know that weapon," Goldman said honestly, maneuvering the helicopter to swing like a pendulum. "But this bird is proof against anything up to a 40 mm shell."

"Not fifty of them at once," Bolan told her, sending out another long burst from the M-134.

The Black Hawk dropped low and banked hard, just as the other Hercules sent off a swarm of shells that missed them by only a few yards.

"Maybe we should retreat," Salvatore suggested in grudging hesitation, the Gatling gun firing in short bursts.

"Jump if you want to, ma'am," Goldman snarled, releasing more rockets. "But I'm in for the count!"

The two Uberpanzers returned fire, the streams of shells crisscrossing in front of the Black Hawk as it briefly slowed, then surged forward once more.

"Cooper?" Salvatore asked, glancing into the mirror.

"I say that we take them here and now," Bolan growled, aiming above the other five Hercules.

The rain of falling bullets peppered the enemy planes, and an engine burst into flame. But then the automatic systems engaged, and the fire died as the fuel lines stopped pumping. The Hercules slowed, but then so did the others, maintaining formation to protect the wounded member, and now more access ramps were starting to lower.

"Okay, then!" Salvatore declared, alternately triggering the two Gatling guns. "Hell favors the brave!"

Just then, something hard rattled along the armored hull of the Black Hawk, and a hatch dented, but there was no penetration.

"That was close," Goldman muttered, raising and lowering the helicopter randomly.

"Close isn't a kill!" Bolan countered, starting to trigger a long burst, until the weapon abruptly stopped.

Doing a fast check, he found a live round jammed in the ejector port. He struggled to get it clear, but the bent casing was so hot that the brass had welded to the steel framework. Muttering a curse, he snapped free the safety harness and crossed the helicopter to the second minigun.

By now, land was starting to appear through the clouds under them. A coastline, cities, factories and fishing boats.

"Is that Sardinia?" Salvatore asked, switching ammunition hoppers for the Gatlings.

"Tunisia," Goldman replied, dropping the empty fuel pods to add some speed.

Unexpectedly, a bright flash of light appeared inside one of the Hercules, and seconds later something large streaked by the Black Hawk.

"That was a LAW rocket," Bolan said, as it went past the window.

"They launched an antitank rocket at a helicopter?" Goldman said with forced calm, releasing more of their own rockets. "Wonder where they got that half-ass idea?"

"From him," Salvatore said, the Gatling guns yammering again in mechanized fury. Streams of spent brass arched away into the wind, gold rain from the gods tumbling down into the cool blue sea.

"True, but I didn't miss!" Bolan stated, both hands shaking as he rode the bucking 7.62 mm minigun in a tight circle.

Holes appeared along a pontoon, and then a window cracked on a Hercules, but didn't shatter. In reply, two more of the airplanes began firing back with the Bushmasters on the Uberpanzers.

More slow rockets shot out from the interior of different planes, and Goldman easily swung out of their way.

Then one of them circled and started to come straight back toward the helicopter.

"Stinger!" she snarled, releasing chaff and flares.

There was a tense moment when it didn't appear that the heat-seeker was going after the decoys. But then it changed course and zoomed away, to vanish in the fleecy clouds.

"The bastards tried to fake us out with a couple of LAW rockets, then used a Stinger missile," Goldman snarled. "Damn near worked, too."

"They're amateurs, not stupid," Salvatore said, cutting loose the Gatlings for a prolonged barrage.

"I'm betting it won't happen again," Bolan said. "If they had a lot of missiles, they would have used them back in Sicily!"

"Here's hoping that you're right."

Suddenly, every Hercules started gushing pinkish fluids.

"Now, why are they dropping fuel?" Goldman said slowly. Then she sat up straight. "It's another trap!"

Sending the Black Hawk soaring away sideways, she barely got out of the way of the onrushing cloud. As it passed, the biohazard warning sounded loud and clear.

"Nerve gas again," Bolan said, spotting a blinking light on the dashboard. "They hid the gold-colored gas inside a cloud of fuel."

"Would it have killed us?" Salvatore asked with a frown.

"Probably just stall our engines," Goldman replied, briefly glancing down. "But over these mountains that would be pretty much the same thing."

Casting a fast look, Bolan saw a seemingly endless array of jagged mountain peaks, bare rocks, snow, ice for as far as the eye could see. "Tunisia?"

"Apollo Mountains," Salvatore answered. "Personally, I'd rather crash in Beirut."

"Okay, Jaws, charge straight at them," Bolan commanded, flexing his hands. "Just give me ten seconds of smooth flying."

Goldman smiled at the use of her military call sign. "I'll get you twenty, Mr. Cooper!" she declared, shoving the yoke to the last stop. "And my friends call me Goldie!"

"Then call me Matt!"

In a roar on controlled power, the Black Hawk shot forward with renewed speed. Rockets and lead poured from the racing helicopter, and the airplanes answered back with crisscrossing streams of 12.7 mm rounds and bursts of 25 mm shells.

Concentrating on the targets, Bolan couldn't see what was happening below, but to anything on the ground, the rain of high explosives had to have seemed like the end of the world.

Squinting in the rushing wind, Bolan fought a shiver, the cold seeping through every opening in his clothing.

"Almost in range again," Salvatore reported, shooting above the Hercules.

Just then, an object collided with the side of the helicopter in a hard bang. A few seconds later, a powerful explosion rocked the Black Hawk.

Craning her neck, Lt. Goldman tried to see what had hit them. "Holy shit," she whispered. "That was a limpet mine!"

"Good thing the magnets couldn't stick to our composite armor," Salvatore said, a scowl forming on her face. "That's not a distance weapon, so how the hell—"

She was interrupted by another hard clang, closely followed by an even louder explosion. The lights briefly dimmed this time, and one of the engines slowed, the speed of the helicopter drastically reducing. Then it came back as strong as ever, and they accelerated once more.

"They're overhead!" Bolan snarled, bending out of the hatchway to look straight up.

The spinning blades blurred his vision, but sure enough, there was another Hercules high above them, a thousand or more feet away. Even as he watched, something large rolled out of the open rear ramp to come hurtling downward. It was one of the North Korean mines!

Gambling everything on the military expertise of the Black Hawk designers, Bolan jerked the M-134 around and fired up through the rotating blades. He recalled how back in WWI, the Army Air Corps had linked the timing of their engines to the weapons, so that pilots could shoot straight ahead at the enemy in a dogfight. Hopefully, NATO had done the same thing for just this sort of an emergency, because if they hadn't...

Even though Bolan had the firing mechanism depressed hard, the normally superfast machine gun only chugged out extreme short bursts. But the combat rounds passed effortlessly through the blades, and the underwater mine thunderously exploded into a raging fireball.

Quickly, Bolan ducked back inside as a hail of shrapnel hammered the Black Hawk, sounding like a hail storm pounding on the roof of a civilian car.

"That got us!" Goldman snarled, dropping low, then banking high, to try to avoid the incoming ordnance. "The blades are fine, but we're leaking fuel like crazy."

"How bad?" Salvatore demanded.

"I'm already using the emergency reserve!"

"Damn!"

As another underwater mine fell past their windows, the other Hercules aircraft began moving back and forth, going around one another in a wild jumble. Now all of them started using the Bushmaster cannon atop their Uberpanzers to shoot back at the NATO gunship, filling the sky with 25 mm shells. Then more pink fuel was dropped, along with additional streams of golden nerve gas.

With no other choice, Bolan slammed both hatches closed. Half a heartbeat later, something slammed into one hatch and promptly exploded.

"Christ, we can't take much more of this!" Goldman growled, as several of the 25 mm shells detonated on the Black Hawk. They didn't breach the hull, but each blast rocked the damaged helicopter worse than before. "And if one of those big-ass mines gets hit by our blades, we're shit in a blender!"

"Land this thing before we fucking come apart!" Salvatore ordered in a whip-crack tone. "That is a direct order!"

A long moment passed in thick silence.

"Yes, ma'am," Goldman said bitterly. She'd started to turn away from the escaping planes when a cluster of 25 mm rounds peppered the windshield, the explosions resembling fireworks. The tough plastic held, but the flexible seams burst, and the windshield broke off, intact, to sail away.

Instantly, a monstrous wind buffeted the three warriors inside, and alarms sounded as the helicopter spun crazily, all aerodynamic stability gone. Gauges flashed into the red, oxygen masks dropped from the ceiling, and Salvatore tumbled sideways out the open cockpit door.

"Matt, jump while you can!" Goldman yelled, wrapping both arms around the yoke to try to regain control.

"Maybe if we work together..." Bolan countered, starting forward.

But before he could reach the copilot seat, more shells arrived to hammer the crippled aircraft across the prow. Several came in through the missing window, and Goldman didn't even have a chance to scream as the 25 mm shells tore her apart in bloody explosions. A loose shell went between the two front seats and impacted on the aft machinery, the blast catching Bolan in the back and shoving him against an ammunition hopper.

Forcing himself erect, he saw that the pilot was gone, only tattered pieces of her body still held in the seat by her safety harness.

He reached out to help, then stopped as the Black Hawk began to spin out of control.

Quickly turning toward the side hatch, the Executioner worked the lever. It moved smoothly, but the hatch refused to budge an inch, held in place by the ever-mounting pressure of centrifugal force.

Bracing a boot against the minigun, Bolan grabbed the lever with both hands and exerted all his strength. It felt as if the entire universe were rapidly spinning around him, but he concentrated on the task at hand. He had to get the hatch open fast. The Black Hawk was a sitting duck at the moment, and the next burst of shells would blow him out of the air.

"Come on, you stubborn son of a bitch...." Bolan growled. The lever bent slightly, then the hatch moved, and he was thrown out of the spinning helicopter.

CHAPTER EIGHT

Apollo Mountains, Tunisia

The cold air hit Bolan hard, and he immediately curled into a ball to reduce the wind resistance and increase his velocity. The next few seconds would make all the difference between the turboblades slicing him apart or escape.

The burning helicopter loomed large at his side, then was gone, and the soldier was alone, plummeting through the clouds.

A crumpling blast sounded high above him, and an instant later he was slammed by the concussion wave. It sent him hurtling out of the clouds with renewed speed, and abruptly, he was in the clear. Below him spread northern Tunisia, the jagged mountaintops reaching up like the clawed hands of a thousand stone demons.

Extending his arms, Bolan tried to catch the buffeting wind, and angle away from the ragged tors. For a moment he thought it was futile, then he was savagely jerked to the side by an arctic gust, and sent into a wild barrel roll, tumbling over and over.

Closing his eyes to prevent disorientation, he slowly counted to five, then locked his legs together and spread his arms. Almost instantly, his descent leveled, and he quickly looked about.

Burning wreckage from the destroyed Black Hawk was falling to the west, and a small parachute floating

downward to the east, not far from him. He started to call
Major Salvatore, then remembered the throat mike had
been ripped away. He could find her on the ground easily
enough.

A low roar could be heard over the whistling wind, and
Bolan frowned at the sight of the Hercules aircraft starting to curve around as if planning on coming back. Not
satisfied with blowing them out of the sky, Thorodensen
and Penumbra must want the NATO pilots dead, unable to
report anything to Brussels.

No time for finesse then, Bolan decided.

Curling into a ball once more, the soldier built more ac-
celeration, shooting toward the mountaintops like a cannonball. Spreading his arms again, he managed to angle
away from the snowy peaks toward a small lake nestled in
a lush green river valley. The shore was lined with deadly
pine trees, the archenemy of all paratroopers, and he could
see boulders in the river, and floating chunks of ice in the
lake.

Playing with the wind, Bolan aimed himself toward the
lake, then grabbed the rip cord of his parachute and yanked
hard.

Nothing happened for long moments, then the chute appeared, fluttering above him in ragged strips, torn to pieces
by the exploding 25 mm shells back in the helicopter.

With his heart wildly pounding, Bolan calmly reached
for the emergency chute on his chest and gently pulled the
ring. Instantly, the canvas pack parted, silk billowed and a
small parachute blossomed overhead. It was the most beautiful thing Bolan had seen in many long years.

As the harness jerked under his arms and crotch, Bolan
immediately slowed. He was still traveling much faster than
desirable, or even sensible. But with Penumbra on his tail,
the numbers were falling.

His monocular was blocked by the straps of the emergency chute, so Bolan craned his neck to look over the rapidly approaching land below, memorizing any important features for later. Unfortunately, there was far too much open country, which offered little or no cover from the approaching airplanes. The forest would be his best bet. Now all he had to do was get there alive and in one piece.

Breathing deeply for several moments, Bolan supercharged his lungs with oxygen, then crossed his arms over his chest to form a barrier and keep water from shooting up his nose and drowning him in the first few seconds of immersion. Locking his legs together, he angled his boots toe-first to minimize impact trauma.

The lake swelled before Bolan, and he hit the water hard, the impact rattling his teeth. The water was unbelievably cold, and had to be runoff from melting snow on the mountains. That was sheer bad luck. But then again, he might have been forced to try to land in the river among the boulders.

As he sank fast, the bitter cold hit Bolan like tiny daggers, stabbing every inch of exposed skin. He ignored the pain and concentrated on avoiding any sunken tree branches.

When he began to slow, Bolan slapped the release of the parachute and started to swim away from the silk at full speed. The gleaming white material was designed to float and thus serve as a marker to help a search and rescue team find the downed pilot. But now it would only serve as an excellent target for the Penumbra gunners.

Something came at Bolan from the darkness. He started reaching for the knife on his hip when the colossal salmon turned, startled, and swam away at great speed.

Bolan kept going, using only small kicks of his boots, to prevent the generation of waves on the surface, which would reveal his position. Nobody in a jet fighter would ever be able to see small disturbances, but at minimum ground speeds, a Hercules would offer far too good a view of the lake. Just one of those North Korean mines could stun everything in the water, including him, and two would crush him like an empty beer can.

With his lungs already starting to strain, Bolan forced himself to think about less stressful times in an effort to reduce his heartbeat and conserve oxygen.

Suddenly feeling mud beneath his fingers, the soldier grabbed handfuls of muck and started crawling along the lakebed, following the natural incline upward until he broke the surface. Greedily, he drew in deep lungfuls of cold air as he crawled onto dry ground, past small mounds of pristine snow.

Looking around for cover, he found only a mossy log nearby. Crawling past it, he saw a wide-open field of tall grass, studded with clumps of spiky teasel.

"Matt?" a voice whispered.

That was the major. Bolan started to respond when a shadow crossed the field, followed by the low rumble of airplane engines from above. Moving fast, he rolled away just in time to feel the ground jump from the arrival of high-velocity rounds, then hear the distant chatter of a machine gun.

Coming to rest alongside a tree stump, Bolan drew the Desert Eagle as the field suddenly sprouted fiery explosions from a barrage of 25 mm shells raining from above. In the forest, branches snapped off trees and leafy tops fell away. Startled birds took flight, only to be obliterated.

Patches of the ground danced from the savage arrival of the 7.62 mm rounds, then more 25 mm shells. Rocks shattered, logs exploded and then the sky cleared and the three Hercules were gone, climbing high once more.

Dashing into the river, Bolan took refuge under the cover of a large boulder. He was already partially numb, so the rushing water really didn't worsen his condition. However, he wisely kept flexing his fingers and toes to maintain circulation.

Mentally, Bolan did a fast inventory of his available weapons. He still had the Desert Eagle and Beretta, along with a bandolier of spare shells for the XM-25. A fat lot of good those would do him at the moment. He also had a few flares, a knife, several garrotes, and a couple small, shaped charges of C-4 designed for blowing open locks. All of which were absolutely useless for fighting an airplane traveling at more than 300 mph.

Bolan froze as he heard the steadily increasing whine of a large plane in a power dive. As expected, a Hercules appeared above the lake, swooping low, then climbing once more. It was a rattling pass to scare him and Major Salvatore out of hiding. Bolan knew that would never work on veteran soldiers. But maybe he could use Penumbra's lack of combat experience against them somehow. There was an old adage that a professional soldier armed with a wooden stick could always kill the civilian playing with a sword.

Shivering in the cold spray, Bolan inspected the Desert Eagle for any damage or blockage. It was dripping wet, but otherwise fine.

After wading across the river, Bolan darted across a grassy field and into the dark woods. Taking a position between two thick trunks, he braced his hands against the rough bark and settled in to wait.

Soon enough, another Hercules came into view, only higher this time, and two of the North Korean underwater mines rolled off the rear access ramp to fall toward the lake. The boxy Uberpanzer inside came briefly into view, along with some armed people still wearing their stolen NBC suits.

Expertly tracking the moving airplane, Bolan emptied the Desert Eagle. The distance was too great for sound, but he saw one of the terrorists jerk backward, blood gushing from a shoulder, while two others dropped flat, one rolling down the ramp to tumble away into the lake below.

Moments later, the North Korean mines cut loose below the icy surface of the water, sending up huge plumes of churning steam and smoke. Ducking behind the largest tree for cover against shrapnel, Bolan cursed when he saw the tattered remains of the corpse hurtle away in numerous directions. There was no way he could extract any data from those tiny pieces. He'd be lucky to find an intact finger to get a usable print. Unfortunately, a good effort meant nothing in this deadly contest, where the winner got to live and the loser went into the ground. Which gave him an idea.

Darting from the safety of the forest, Bolan made it back to the river and waded across the foaming stream once more. If anything, it felt even colder this time, but he kept moving until reaching the grassy field. Mobility was his greatest asset. The airplanes were fast, but they couldn't turn on a dime, while he could.

Lying among the prickly weeds, Bolan reloaded his weapon while listening for the sounds of a Hercules. When he heard the muted rumble, the soldier charged across the field, jumping over patches of snow, icy puddles and fallen branches. He'd made it only halfway when a shadow crossed the field. Instantly, he dodged to the left, a split second before the arrival of a burst of 25 mm shells from a deadly Bushmaster. As the aircraft were armed at the rear, the shadow of each Hercules gave him a full second to move before coming into view of the terrorists inside the plane.

The Bushmaster spoke again, and he raced to the right, then back to the left, putting all his strength into an irregular zigzag pattern to throw off the gunners. The ground churned from the arrival of bullets and explosive shells, but none got close to Bolan. The soldier made it back under the protective branches of the big oak trees before the Hercules banked away. He emptied the Desert Eagle again, but this time scored only a couple of flesh wounds. None of the terrorists fell down, much less tumbled out of the plane.

As the aircraft moved off into the distance, a bush stirred near a small creek and Major Salvatore peeked out from the foliage, twigs and leaves stuffed into her hair and clothing as camouflage.

"Still alive, I see," she said, watching the sky. "What about Goldman?"

"Dead," Bolan said bluntly, reloading again. "Are you armed?"

She blinked several times. "Not really, just a pistol and knife. How about you?"

"The same."

"Damn." She sighed.

Bolan scowled at that, but then they both ducked as a Hercules came out of the sky to swoop dangerously low across the trees. As it passed, both Bolan and Salvatore raised their guns, but the rear ramp had been cycled shut.

"Another damn rattling pass," Salvatore said, blinking yet again. "I saw some caves to the right… No, I mean the west…." She pointed to the north with a wobbling hand.

"Toward the lake?" Bolan asked suspiciously.

"Yeah, that way." She made a vague gesture.

"Major Salvatore," he snapped, in his best top-sergeant voice, "cadence count!"

"Do what?" As she asked, a trickle of blood came out

of the flowers in her mussed hair, to flow across her dirty face. "Sure…six…ah…four…"

"Stay where you are," Bolan commanded. "I'll be right there!"

"No…" she said, blinking. "I'll come to you."

"Stay right where you are, Major! That's a direct order!"

"Yes, sir," she muttered with a scowl.

Extracting himself from the trees, Bolan didn't waste any time trying to answer. Her disorientation had obviously come from a strike to the head. Probably from a tree branch, since she'd landed in the forest. He had been grazed several times while underwater, and only narrowly escaped being knocked unconscious himself.

Unfortunately, head wounds were tricky. There could be huge amounts of blood and the soldier would be otherwise fine. Or there could be only a little trickle, and a few minutes later the person might drop dead. If Salvatore had a concussion, Bolan needed to get her someplace warm very fast, and keep her awake at all cost, or else she might fall asleep and never wake up again.

High overhead, the Hercules aircraft disappeared into a cloud bank and circled the jagged mountain peaks. Explosions followed in their wake, creating a small avalanche of rocks, snow and earth.

Moving low and fast, Bolan ran in a zigzag pattern along the edge of the trees, where he could move faster. Birds took flight, revealing his passage, so he quickly returned to the same location and took off in a new direction to scramble the trail. The terrorists in the Hercules would see the birds, and try to track him through their flight patterns. He could use that, but not twice. Whatever else could be said about Thorodensen, the man was smart. At the moment, Penumbra had everything going in its favor. The only real hope Bolan had was to outthink them on the ground.

Suddenly, the huge airplanes reappeared from the clouds, quickly descending and spreading out in a classic attack formation. There was no doubt that this time they were coming in for the kill.

Weakly standing, Major Salvatore raised her Beretta and started shooting at them.

Instantly abandoning his battle plan, Bolan turned on a heel and sprinted back across the open field. Jumping over a log, he dived across a muddy depression, only to land on his feet and keep running. The planes were almost within range when he finally reached Salvatore and tackled her to the ground. She cried out and they rolled away from the bushes and across an icy creek. Her Beretta went flying as Bolan kept the wounded women in motion, until reaching a small boulder alongside the foaming river.

"My gun…!" she cried, trying to stand upright.

With no other choice, Bolan swung an arm across the back of her knees to bring her down hard. Then he stood, slung the woman across his shoulders and erupted into action, sprinting across the snowy ground toward the woods once more. Weakly, she struggled to get free, and he tightened his grip.

Almost instantly, distant chain guns began singing their deadly song, and trees shuddered from a hail of 25 mm shells, green needles and brown bark exploding from the splintering trunks.

Putting everything he had into the desperate sprint, Bolan maintained the course, and made it back into the dark shadows only a heartbeat before another Hercules started chewing up the field they had just crossed. As the big American kept going, the entire forest seemed to be filled with thunder and explosions, whole trees toppling over from the relentless pounding.

More than once, Bolan felt something hot smack into his

back or legs, and he could only hope that Salvatore hadn't taken any shrapnel for him, and was still alive.

Pausing to catch his breath near a small clearing, Bolan saw a second Hercules come down from the sky, but this time it was crossing the path of the first. He grunted at that. Bracket fire! They were learning from their mistakes.

Moving to a copse of old oak trees, Bolan eased the woman onto a bed of leaves and started shoveling handfuls of them over her as covering. It wasn't much, but the best he could do under the circumstances.

"Cold…" Salvatore whispered, shivering as she closed her eyes.

"Stay awake!" Bolan demanded, slapping her across the face.

Just for a moment, her eyes cleared in furious rage, then she seemed to comprehend what was happening, and looked frightened. "L-leave me…." she croaked, then sagged once more, her eyelids fluttering.

Drawing the Desert Eagle, Bolan fired twice into the air, then place the hot barrel against her cheek.

She gasped at the stinging touch and jerked away. "You son of a bitch!" she snarled in a remarkably normal voice, fiercely rubbing the spot. Then she weakly smiled. "Thanks."

"Anytime."

The shadow of a Hercules raced by overhead, the wash shaking the treetops.

"Use these…." she said, fumbling for a pair of grenades on her military harness.

Accepting the canisters, Bolan sprinted away, pulling the pin on one of the thermite grenades, but keeping a firm grip on the arming lever. Approaching the edge of the forest, he whipped the canister forward as hard as possible, and watched it sail away high over the river, to land amid some waving teasel. Booming flames erupted, throwing out a corona of scorched earth and numerous dead frogs. Then Bolan paused. Hadn't he asked about thermite back on the beach, and nobody had any? Curious.

Moments later, the Hercules returned, their weapons mercilessly hammering the field and river. The barrage continued for an inordinate length of time before the planes moved onward. Less than a minute later, two more Hercules arrived to do the exact same thing to the same area, then moved on to blast random patches of grass and the lake.

Ramming the last grenade into the crook of a tree, Bolan took off, circling a clearing until he was at the far side. Kneeling in the snow, the soldier squeezed off a single round from the silenced Beretta. The tree branch cracked, the grenade fell and rolled down the sloping ground toward the lake. A few seconds later, it exploded on the shoreline, sending wild flame and chemical thunder echoing along the river valley.

Within moments, the Hercules converged on the area, dropping several mines and releasing a large greenish cloud.

Mustard gas, Bolan realized, just like they'd used back in Brooklyn.

Which meant that they were out of the deadly nerve gas, because this would have been the perfect opportunity to use it. One less danger to deal with. Now all he and the major had to do was hide until the terrorists departed.

Luckily, there was no place those big planes could land. The lake was too small and the river had way too many boulders. The rest of the hilly landscape was covered with trees and small cliffs. And bold as they were, if the terrorists tried to parachute into the valley, Bolan would take them out before they ever reached the ground.

Taking advantage of the brief lull in the aerial attacks,

he dug out the monocular and did a fast sweep of the terrain. If there were any caves nearby, they should be in the cliffs.

Surprisingly, he spotted a dozen caves—most of them inaccessible, located hundreds of feet off the ground. Those would be impossible to reach without rappelling equipment. Bolan guessed they'd been made by underground rivers, probably from snow melting in spring. He had seen something similar in Finland and Siberia. Ice caves.

However, there were a few small openings near ground level, and one was positioned directly under a jutting cliff. Perfect cover from an aerial strike.

Watching the crisscrossing planes overhead, Bolan chose his window, then raced into the woods. Major Salvatore was exactly where he had left her, and she was sound asleep, softly snoring. Damn!

Slinging her roughly over his shoulders again, Bolan gathered the last of his fading strength and took off once more. As he left the shadows, the soldier heard the Hercules get noticeably louder. But he ignored that and put everything he had into a full sprint, running headlong for the cave.

The distant wasn't great, certainly no more than a thousand feet, but it felt like miles to Bolan as he charged across the field. His progress slowed slightly as the ground sloped, the slight incline feeling impossibly steep, and Bolan realized he was about to collapse from exhaustion. Just a few more yards, soldier, he thought grimly.

As he neared the mouth of the cave, the Hercules let loose its arsenal, the barrage hammering rock chips off the protective ledge overhead. Diving forward, Bolan yelled as if in mortal pain, then broke off abruptly as he and Salvatore rolled into the darkness.

Remaining motionless on the hard rocks, Bolan watched

the slice of sky outside. A Hercules swooped low past the cave, the gunner trying to get an angle inside. But the cliff was too deep.

Long minutes passed, but Bolan kept perfectly still, despite the cold from the ground digging into his back. The sound of the airplanes retreated into the distance, and still he played dead.

"I—I…th-think they b-bought it," Major Salvatore whispered, her teeth chattering.

"No reason why they shouldn't," Bolan replied, prying himself off the ground. "How long have you been awake?"

"S-since w-we l-l-landed in h-here," she replied. She was shaking all over.

"At least you're awake again," Bolan said, reaching out to touch her bloody forehead. The skin was hot and sweaty. That was a bad combination in these low temperatures.

Breaking out his last flare, he got it working and placed it near the shivering woman. Reaching out to cup her hands around the sizzling flame, she gave a heartfelt sigh as the frozen cut on her head started to bleed again.

"Be right back," Bolan said, stiffly rising to stagger back into the bright sunlight.

There was no reply.

When he returned in a few minutes with an armload of firewood, the major was gone. A smeared trail of fresh blood led deeper into the cave, and as Bolan dropped the tree branches he distinctly heard a low animal growl, followed by the crunching of bones.

CHAPTER NINE

On the flight deck of the Hercules, nobody spoke for a few minutes. There was only the sound of the powerful engines and the dull throb of the radar jammer.

"Do you think they're dead?" Lilja Vilhjalms asked, looking down at the river valley receding into the distance.

"You heard the scream," Hrafen Thorodensen replied confidently, thinning the fuel mixture to the engines. "We have all been hunting enough to recognize a death cry when we hear it."

"I don't know," Gunnar Eldjarm muttered, standing in the hatchway to the flight deck. "These people are tricky. I don't trust them." He was still wearing the NBC suit, the hood pushed back to reveal his face.

"Do you want to make another pass?" Vilhjalms asked in concern. Her own suit was folded on the floor, open and ready, just in case it was needed again.

"No, we have to keep going," Thorodensen stated, keeping both hands on the steering yoke, while checking their location on a GPS graph. "We're already too far behind schedule. Damn those Mafia fools! I should have expected betrayal on their part."

"We were also going to betray them," the woman said hesitantly, removing the pencil from her hair to make a note on a clipboard about fuel consumption.

Taking a compass bearing, Thorodensen snorted. "That is beside the point. We have a mission to accomplish! They were only common thieves, and thus of no matter whatsoever."

That statement startled her, and she said nothing for a long time. "Gunnar, how many people do you think we..." Vilhjalms stopped, unable to finish the query. "I mean, how many did they—"

"Fourteen are dead," Eldjarm replied gruffly, pulling off his NBC suit and kicking it into a corner. His bulletproof vest was dotted with shiny gray blobs. "The Mafia bastards got three of us. Those soldiers shot six more, and the rest were taken out by that big fellow with the black hair." He gave a low grunt. "He was a hell of a marksman."

"He murdered our friends!" Vilhjalms cried out, returning the pencil to its accustomed place.

"Death is part of life," Eldjarm said, taking the Vepr from a wall peg and slinging it across his back. "I can still admire his expertise, even though I would not care to face him again."

"Then it is a good thing he is dead," Thorodensen muttered. "Lily, can you still manufacture the new armor with our loss of personnel?"

Personnel. She tried not to scowl at the impersonal word for their friends and colleagues. "I can't say for certain," she hedged, tucking a loose strand of hair behind her ear. "It all depends upon the condition of the laboratory."

"We could use more nerve gas," Eldjarm interjected, a touch eagerly. "Perhaps a short trip to Greece..."

"Sorry, old friend. There is no time to steal fresh supplies," Thorodensen said, tapping a flickering fuel gauge with a finger. "We will simply have to make do with what little mustard gas we have for the next part."

Eldjarm shrugged. "It'll get bloody."

"When does it not?" Thorodensen said, changing their

course, until the Hercules was flying exactly along the equator.

Deep in thought, Vilhjalms sat quietly for a long time. Watching her two colleagues check over the details on the next part of their mission, she began to wonder what had happened to the men she used to know, and how their noble goal had become so scrambled. Were they still on the side of justice? Or had Penumbra crossed the line, and become the terrorists that the media was starting to call them.

Gazing out the window, she admitted that she didn't know the answers to those important questions, and she suddenly felt very alone in the world.

DROPPING THE BRANCHES, Bolan grabbed the dying flare and drew the Beretta. Thumbing off the safety, he quickly started forward. His boots echoed on the stones, and the crunching noise abruptly stopped.

The cave continued back for several yards, then abruptly bent to the left. The passage opened into a much larger cave, its roof covered with glistening stalactites. The air smelled musty, like wet leather, and there was a steady drip of water somewhere in the distance.

Bolan sniffed hard, but there was no telltale reek of blood. But that was no comfort; he knew some wild animals preferred carrion to fresh meat. The major could already be dead and stuffed into a crevice to rot for a few days before the animal feasted.

"Major Salvatore!" Bolan shouted, but there was no reply.

Just for a moment, he did nothing, unsure of his next move. He was exhausted, and could feel sleep tugging at his eyes.

"Major!" he called, and something large growled in reply.

Squinting in the gloom, Bolan braced himself for the charge. Seconds later, a huge brown bear lumbered out of the darkness and into the sizzling light of the flare.

Snarling in rage, the bear swiped its claws toward Bolan, who barely managed to leap out of the way and avoid having his head smashed open.

"Major!" he shouted again, unwilling to fire a shot in the murky gloom and risk hitting the woman.

"Matt…" a voice croaked from off to the side.

Now that he knew her approximate location, Bolan triggered the Beretta, the report of the silenced weapon no louder than a hard cough. The bear grunted at the arrival of the 9 mm round, and retreated slightly. Then it rose on its hind legs, bellowed even louder than before and charged.

Pivoting out of the way, Bolan put two rounds into the bear's head and four more into its huge shaggy body. Nimbly turning, the snarling animal snapped its jaws, grabbing for the gun, then swiped at the soldier's legs with a paw the size of a catcher's mitt. Constantly in motion, Bolan avoided the crippling blow and switched the Beretta to 3-round-burst mode.

As the animal tried again to bite him, Bolan emptied the magazine into the belly of the beast. The 9 mm hollowpoint rounds ripped off chunks of hide, exposing the thick layers of hard muscle underneath, but didn't achieve penetration to the vital organs.

Screaming in pain, the enraged bear jumped for Bolan. Once more he stepped aside, but one of the creature's legs slammed into him, and he went down, the flare he held skittering away into the blackness. It stopped alongside the rough wall of the cave, highlighting a large collection of cracked bones, and a bloody Major Salvatore trying to crawl out of the kill zone.

As the bear rushed forward, Bolan drew the Desert

Eagle. Waiting until the last possible moment, he put a single .50-caliber round directly into the animal's left eye. The booming report echoed wildly inside the confines of the cavern.

Jerking backward, the bear growled as it pawed curiously at the missing orb, sticky fluids tricking down its face.

Bolan cursed the poor light in the cave. The bullet hadn't penetrated the dense skull of the animal, only ricocheted off. The bear lurched forward once more, snarling insanely.

Walking backward, Bolan hammered the face of the beast, triggering single rounds again and again into the missing eye. Suddenly, the bear stopped, as if reaching the end of a steel chain. Swaying slightly, it exhaled deeply, then lay down and went still.

Retrieving the nearly dead flare, Bolan checked for signs of any other bears, then went to the major. She had collapsed again, a hand at the empty holster on her hip. Checking her for any new injuries, Bolan was thankful to see that she had only been clawed on the shoulder, most of the damage absorbed by the body armor under her camouflage-colored ghillie suit.

Dragging her to the front of the cave, he used the last sparks from the flare to start a small campfire. After consuming another energy bar, he limped outside for more wood, constantly adding fuel until the flames were a crackling bonfire, the heat of which soon removed the chill from the cave's stone floor and walls.

As he slumped against the rough rock, Bolan could see the dense smoke snake along the ceiling and pour outside. If the airplanes returned, their pilots would know there were survivors, but he was too tired to do anything about that at the moment. Just needed to grab a short nap, and then...

At the sound of a gunshot, Bolan came awake with the Beretta in his hand. The campfire had dwindled down to a glowing pile of ash and charcoal, the reddish light making the cave seem to be painted in blood.

Standing at the mouth of the cave, Major Salvatore was slowly shooting into the darkness outside. Every round invoked a yelp of pain and assorted angry growls.

Joining her at the opening, Bolan looked into the night. There were several animals moving about, and a few still shapes on the sloping ground.

"Wolves," Salvatore said unnecessarily, as one of them let loose a long, drawn-out howl. "They must have been attracted by all the noise from the fight."

"Plus the dead bodies," Bolan added grimly, stroking the Beretta's trigger. A wolf flipped over backward and tumbled down the slope, to disappear into the night.

Unfortunately, the rest of the wolves didn't go after the corpse. They continued to patrol back and forth before the cave, occasionally making a brief charge forward, only to abruptly change course and move off again.

"Pack hunters," Salvatore said, firing twice. In the brief muzzle-flash, the family of wolves were clearly visible. Then darkness returned, and there was only the reflection of the moon in their eyes and on the shimmering lake. The sky overhead was full of twinkling stars, a blanket of heaven's glory.

"The fire is almost dead," Bolan said, risking a short burst from the Beretta. A wolf yipped in pain and scampered away, wounded, but not dead. "Got a lighter, flare, matches—anything like that?"

"Nothing," she replied. "Which means we need to keep this one going, or freeze to death."

"Okay, cover me," Bolan said, calmly walking out of

the cave. Caught by surprise, the wolves retreated a little, constantly snarling.

Unleathering the Desert Eagle, Bolan shot to the left and the right, herding the wolves into a tighter group. Then he cut loose with the Beretta 93-R, the bursts of rounds from the machine pistol tearing into the animals. A few wolves escaped into the night.

"I got your six," Salvatore said, standing at the mouth of the cave. "Get the wood!"

Holstering his weapons, Bolan started for the forest, until a wolf unexpectedly jumped out of a bush, jaws wide. Dropping low, the soldier rammed a fist into the throat of the beast, and it hit the ground hard, gurgling horribly.

Red light flared from inside the cave, and Salvatore appeared, wearing only her body armor and a T-shirt. Her burning shirt hung from a long stick and cast a wide nimbus of illumination across the cold landscape.

Snarling, the wolves backed away. Then one launched itself forward, going straight for the major. She grunted as the animal grabbed her forearm, and she dropped the makeshift torch. In spite of the poor visibility, Bolan decided to risk a shot, but then she dived forward in a shoulder roll.

The major landed on her feet just as the wolf twisted free and landed upside down in a patch of snow. While the animal struggled to get back on its feet, Bolan fired from the hip, and the wolf's head exploded.

Yipping in terror, the other wolves bolted away into the night. Recovering the torch, Bolan and Salvatore checked over their weapons as they listened carefully for any further tricks from the pack. But their howls faded into the distance, then grew silent.

"That's the last we should see of them," Bolan muttered, trying to stop his teeth from chattering.

"I just hope we don't attract the attention of another bear," Salvatore said, rubbing her arm. Thankfully, the bite she'd sustained was minor.

Bolan snorted a laugh.

"What's so damn funny?" she asked, breaking out a small medical kit from her belt.

"Tell you later," he said, holstering both guns.

Bolan helped Salvatore to clean and bandage her wounds, then helped with his, and together they shuffled off to scavenge every dead tree branch and chunk of wood in the vicinity. After rebuilding the dying campfire, they made a stack of spare branches to dry near the blaze. Then the major went outside again, heading for the lake.

"Found these," Salvatore announced when she returned, dropping her rumpled parachute on the floor. "Not much of a blanket, but better than nothing."

"Any survival gear?"

"Most of it was lost in the lake," she said, biting her lip. "But we still have a couple MRE packs, water, a flare gun, desalition straw for drinking seawater and an inflatable raft."

"Excellent." Bolan smiled. "I thought dinner was going to be grilled bear in wolf sauce."

"Might prefer that. You haven't tried spaghetti à la NATO yet," she retorted, pulling the rip cord on the raft.

With a low hiss, the device quickly inflated, and she shoved it into the mouth of the cave. It wedged in tight, and the evening breeze eased noticeably. However, the smoke from the fire immediately began to gather at the top of the cave.

"Not much of a door," Bolan said, removing the lace from a boot. "But it should keep out most of the chill." Using the lace, he lashed down the top of the raft, so the smoke trickled out once more.

"Sadly, there was no sign of your chute," she said, spreading out the silk of her parachute near the fire to dry. "That would have come in handy."

"We'll be fine in the morning," Bolan said, tossing another branch onto the fire. "We have plenty of wood, but tonight is going to be rough. The temperatures here drop below zero, especially this high in the mountains."

"It is a little chilly," Salvatore said, fighting a shiver.

Reaching out with both hands, Bolan vigorously rubbed her bare arms to try to restore some circulation. The major felt cold to the touch, but soon grew a little warmer.

Nodding her thanks, she smiled. "Beef stew or spaghetti?" she asked, fanning out the shiny food packs. The waterproof Mylar envelopes were covered with cooking instructions in English, Spanish and French, the official languages of NATO.

"Either is fine," Bolan said, hunkering down near the crackling flames.

Adding a few drops of water from their canteens to the crystal heaters inside the Meals Ready to Eat packs, Bolan and Salvatore waited until the envelopes began emitting wisps of steam, then broke out the plastic "sporks" and dug in with gusto. While they ate the hot meal, their clothing dried out, but the stink of animal blood canceled out what small comfort that brought. There was a lake nearby, but the howling wind outside precluded any notion of washing their filthy clothing, dressed in only their shorts.

When the meal was over, they each savored a precious cup of hot coffee, then went outside to use the bushes. Preparing for the night, they once more sealed the cave as tightly as possible, then carefully cut the parachute in two. Each of them took a piece, and got as comfortable as possible on the cool rock floor, removing their boots and gun belts, but keeping their weapons close at hand.

Sleep came quickly.

CHAPTER TEN

Butterfly Island, French Territory

As a rosy dawn arrived, the blue ocean moved below the wing of rumbling Hercules like a conveyor belt, endless and unchanging. There were no ships in sight, much less any islands. There was only open water for hundreds of miles, a salty wasteland void of any details except the transitory waves and ethereal winds.

"At last, there it is!" Gunnar Eldjarm cried out, pointing a bony finger.

"Precisely on schedule," Hrafen Thorodensen said, judiciously reducing their speed and starting to cycle down the landing gear.

Straight ahead was a small green island of swaying palm trees and white sand beaches. Small hills of cooled lava rose off to one side, and a large lagoon spread out invitingly on the other. There were a few concrete runways, and a couple brick buildings dotted with bird nests. But everything else had been reclaimed by the jungle, engulfed by flowering vines and blankets of thick green moss.

"Butterfly Island," Lilja Vilhjalms said, checking the folded map on her clipboard. "It is hard to imagine that France once spent billions here, and then abandoned it completely."

"And who knows better than us about financial downturns?" Thorodensen said curtly, taking a hand mike and thumbing it alive. "Attention, all pilots and crews! Our target is due west, and approaching fast. Maintain formation! This needs to be short and sweet. They're better trained than us, so our only advantage is surprise. Don't waste it being squeamish!"

"Kill or be killed," Eldjarm muttered, working the arming bolt on the Vepr autoshotgun.

"Exactly!" Thorodensen declared, then repeated the line. "Be ruthless or die. We commence in one minute. Get ready."

"Here we go," Gunner said, leaning forward, his face bright with excitement.

Scowling, Vilhjalms looked away in revulsion. She had no idea who this new person was, but her childhood friend was clearly gone, replaced with this bloodthirsty maniac. When the great plan was finished, and everything returned to normal, Vilhjalms grimly decided that she would have to kill Gunnar. She would do it as painlessly as possible, of course, but she couldn't allow this…thing…to wander the world, a threat to innocent people.

As the Hercules circled around the island, Vilhjalms could see people on the beaches, driving Jeeps and walking along the jungle trails. There were some boats docked in the lagoon, and even a couple small planes parked in the grass alongside a short runaway of cracked pavement.

"Get ready…and…release the mines," Thorodensen said into the hand mike.

Laughing softly, Eldjarm pressed a button on the console. They heard a low rumble from the rear of the huge airplane, followed by a high-pitched whistling that quickly faded away.

There was no indication of what was happening behind the Hercules, but Vilhjalms heard the explosions, and as the aircraft banked for another pass, she could see spherical mines falling from the other planes. Designed to sink armored battleships, the North Korean weapons obliterated anything they hit, throwing out huge gouts of fiery debris, flipping over cars and uprooting trees. However, none of the brick structures had been hit by any of the mines, only open ground, the streets and lagoon. Every ship at the dockyard was on fire and rapidly sinking, black plumes of smoke rising high to mark each kill.

Down on the ground, screaming people were rushing about, heading for cover. Only a few began firing upward with handguns. But even if the bullets could reach the Hercules, the small-caliber rounds would do no damage.

"All right, that's enough!" Thorodensen yelled into his hand mike, throttling back the engines. "Now, get ready, people! We want as little damage to those buildings as possible!"

Buildings, not people. Wisely, Vilhjalms said nothing.

"See you later." Eldjarm chuckled, releasing the safety harness.

"Good luck, old friend," Thorodensen said, hanging up the mike.

"Bah, who needs luck?" the younger man replied with a smirk. Slamming open the door, he left the flight deck and began whistling as he scrambled down the metal stairs to the main deck.

"He's gone insane, you know," Vilhjalms said softly, hugging the clipboard as if drawing strength from the documents.

"Good, we can use a madman," Thorodensen growled, dropping the flaps and feathering the props. "Brace yourself, my dear, this is it!" Streaking low and fast, the Hercules flashed over the waving palm trees, then the lagoon, and quickly descended toward the old runway.

As the cracked pavement swelled in the windows, Vilhjalms realized that they were coming in much too fast, and braced herself for a fiery crash. But just as a scream boiled up into her throat, Thorodensen pulled back on the yoke with both hands, the tendons in his forearms visibly swelling. Ever so slightly, the nose of the aircraft lifted, and there was a hard jerk as the tires touched down on the runway and bounced off. Then Thorodensen did it again, and this time the aircraft stayed down, the brakes squealing in protest as it angled off the strip and onto the grass.

Almost immediately, another Hercules landed and moved off to the side, to allow room for the next. The last aircraft was skipping along the runway when the aft ramp of the first finished cycling down, and an Uberpanzer rolled into view and onto the grass.

A heavy machine gun fired from the jungle, and a line of bullets bounced off the armored sides of the APC, leaving behind gray streaks. Steadily accelerating, the Uberpanzer changed direction and charged toward the hidden defenders. The machine gun kept firing, and seconds later the APC rolled over the lush bushes to crash through the sand bag walls. Instantly, the machine gun stopped firing, and men briefly screamed. The Uberpanzer burst out of the jungle, the military tires leaving crimson tracks in its wake.

Charging out of the planes, other Uberpanzers spread across the landscape, crashing through sand bag barriers, crushing Jeeps and brutally running over people even when they threw aside their weapons and surrendered.

Inside the Hercules, Vilhjalms covered her ears to muffle the sounds of gunfire and screaming. Then she slowly turned as Thorodensen laughed.

"Look at them run!" He chuckled, checking the load in his Webley revolver. "Justice is sweet, is it not?"

"Justice," Vilhjalms repeated, as if never hearing the word before today.

Rising from the chair, Thorodensen looked down at her. "What else would you call this?" he asked, gesturing out the window with the weapon.

Unable to think of a reply, she merely shrugged and started turning off all the electrical systems on the plane to conserve battery power. Soon enough Penumbra would enter the final phase of the plan, and then she would have to decide if she would actually help Hrafen to finish this madness, or try to escape.

Which, she realized suddenly, would probably mean her death.

Apollo Mountains, Tunisia

WAKING SOME TIME after dawn, Bolan and Salvatore had MREs for breakfast, then made their way carefully down the treacherous side of the mountain to the icy lake.

No matter where they looked there were no remains of any downed terrorists, only a few ragged pieces of cloth, along with the occasional watch or tattered shoe.

"Our wolf friends consumed everything but their guns." Salvatore sighed in disappointment.

"None of which are of any use to us," Bolan added, casting aside an AK-47 with a clearly bent barrel.

"So much for getting their fingerprints." Salvatore buttoned the collar of her ghillie suit. The camouflaged material was dry from the campfire, but still streaked with assorted filth from the firefight yesterday.

"Then we need to get back to Sicily."

"Agreed."

"I'll call us a cab," Bolan said, rummaging about for his

cell phone. He frowned at the feel of loose parts and pulled out a handful of wreckage.

"Mine caught a round," he said, dropping the material on the ground. "Better check your own."

Reaching into a pocket, Salvatore flipped open her device and pressed a few buttons. "Completely dead." She tossed it into the lake.

"Okay then, we walk. The shore should be the closet place to find a radio."

"Or steal a boat," Salvatore said, glancing at the towering mountains to the southwest. "I was thinking that maybe we should continue to play dead. Without an encoded military radio, any broadcast we send for assistance would be heard by everybody in the region."

"Smart move. Nobody will come hunting for the dead," Bolan said, "and we'll find no help in these mountains."

She hurried along in his wake.

As THEY LEFT the mountains, the climate got noticeably warmer, and Bolan and Salvatore shucked off their heavier garments.

The going was easy, but it still took them until noon to reach the shore. After that it was relatively easy to steal some clean clothing, then find a bar. The nameless town was small, scarcely more than a dozen buildings, the two largest being a tavern and a machine shop of some kind.

Hiding their weapons, Bolan and Salvatore strolled into the tavern, bought a few drinks and easily made contact with the local smugglers to obtain passage on a westbound fishing vessel that for the right price was heading due east toward Sicily. Bolan made the payment with a black Amex card tucked into the sole of his boot.

The bartender who took the payment raised an eyebrow at the sight of the elite card, but made no comment as she ran the charge through a very old style scanner attached to a telephone landline. The hums and clicks of the ancient modem fumbling to make a connection were almost nostalgic to Bolan.

"Receipt," the bartender said, handing over a dirty slip of paper.

Nodding his thanks, Bolan tucked the card and receipt into a pocket.

"A black Amex card has no limit," Salvatore said, as they walked from the ramshackle tavern. "And I thought your country was critically short on funds."

"Maybe it's a personal card."

"Does that mean Matt Cooper is your real name?" she asked out of the corner of her mouth.

Crossing the muddy street, Bolan only shrugged in reply.

At the far end of a concrete dock, past a fishing shack that reeked of hardwood smoke, they found the *Sweet Dreams,* a weather-beaten trawler full of splinters, its hull in desperate need of refinishing. The battered vessel looked as if it might fall apart and sink at any moment.

"Is this camouflage for the harbor patrol?" Salvatore guessed, tromping along a wooden plank that extended from the dock to the deck.

"No, for the pirates in the area," Bolan corrected. "They attack anything that might have any value."

"Even this piece of shit?"

"Absolutely."

"They can't be very smart then."

"Already said they were pirates," he stated, sitting down on a wooden crate near the gunwale. "That's about as low as you can go before scrapping the bottom of the criminal barrel."

"Guess so," Salvatore said, looking over the crew. There were twice as many people on the deck as a vessel that size needed, and she eased a hand inside her stolen coat to slide off the safety of her Beretta. Only ten rounds remained, so if trouble came, she would have to make every shot count.

In perfect harmony with the vessel, the crew were burly, unwashed, bearded men in heavy nylon parkas and roll-top boots with small patches of fur adhering to the cracked leather. All of them carried a long knife tucked bare into a belt outside their jackets. The bald captain, looking down from the wheelhouse, wore a thick turtleneck sweater, and sported a sleek, nylon shoulder holster carrying a shiny, nickel-plated, .357 Magnum Colt Python.

At a shouted command from him, the crew cast off the mooring lines. A small gasoline engine sputtered to life, and the trawler sluggishly moved away from the dock. Once they were a good distance from shore, the little engine stopped, replaced by the muted rumble of diesel engines from belowdecks, and the *Sweet Dreams* proceeded at a greatly increased clip.

"Now we at sea, perhaps search woman for contraband." A bearded sailor laughed, his English barely recognizable through the thick accent.

Without a comment, Salvatore turned from the gunwale and stepped in close to grab the much larger man by the belt and wrist. Bending at the waist, she then flipped him over a shoulder in a judo move. The sailor hit the deck hard, the air exploding out of his lungs, his fishing knife sliding across the deck to splash into the water.

With a snarl, he started to rise, and the major landed on his chest with both knees, the point of a shining Gerber combat knife pressed against the throbbing jugular vein in his throat.

"Go ahead and try," she growled in his ear.

Some of the crewmen hunched their shoulders as if preparing for a fight, and Bolan switched the Beretta from single-shot to burst mode.

"Ha! Good woman!" The fallen sailor grinned widely. "Take me easy. Real lady. I like!"

"Thanks, but I don't date sailors," Salvatore said, sheathing the blade and climbing off his huge body.

As the others roared with laughter, the sailor stiffly rose, rubbing a sore arm. Then playfully punched the major in the biceps. "Good woman!" he repeated, before rejoining his comrades.

Watching from a window in the wheelhouse, the captain tucked away the Colt Python and started to light a corncob pipe.

"It seems that you're a hit," Bolan said with a chuckle, removing his hand from the grip of the deadly 9 mm machine pistol.

"All men are like mules. First you hit them, then you kiss them." Salvatore exhaled in disgust. "You're included in that, you know."

"Sure as hell hope so."

The rest of the journey across the Strait of Sicily was uneventful, and both Bolan and the major got some rest, taking turns grabbing a catnap under a tarpaulin to keep off the spray from the bow while the other stood guard.

The Mediterranean was clear of traffic all the way to the horizon, aside from the occasional Swedish cruise liner, or lumbering Egyptian oil tanker. Halfway there, the captain offered them overpriced mutton sandwiches sealed inside plastic containers. Politely turning down the questionable repast, Bolan and Salvatore consumed candy bars they'd purchased at the oceanfront tavern.

Several hours later, the *Sweet Dreams* approached the southern coast of Sicily, far from the scene of the earlier battle between Black Thunder and Penumbra. Roughly a mile offshore, the trawler was stopped by the Italian coast guard in sleek fiberglass speedboats, the neatly uniformed sailors each carrying a Beretta ARX-160 assault rifle. However, the dapper captain never even stepped onto the Tunisian vessel.

Staying behind a crowd of the crew, Bolan and Salvatore watched as a large net bag of what appeared to be greasy sausage was exchanged between the ships using a bosun chair, and the smiling captain waved the smugglers onward.

"Sausages?" Salvatore asked, easing her stance.

"The toll used to be cigarettes," Bolan commented with a shrug. "Times change."

As the coast guard tactfully disappeared over the horizon, the *Sweet Dreams* pulled in close to shore. Climbing down a rope ladder, Bolan and Salvatore splashed into knee-deep waves and waded onto the rocky shoreline.

"It's a long walk to Pebble Beach." Salvatore sighed, watching the Tunisian trawler rumble quickly away.

"Which was why I asked to be dropped off here," Bolan said, starting forward.

"Local friends?" she asked curiously, keeping abreast.

"Not quite, no."

Cresting a low dune, Salvatore snorted at the sight of a sprawling resort town full of busy cafés, taverns, a noisy brothel, and even a small disco, closed for renovations.

Putting two fingers in his mouth, Bolan let loose a shrill whistle. "Taxi!" he yelled with a wave.

CHAPTER ELEVEN

Butterfly Island

Smoke from a dozen small fires drifted across the landscape, partially hiding the score of crushed bodies strewed about on the ground.

Standing in the commander's hatch of an APC, a member of Penumbra steadily fired the coaxial chain gun in short bursts, ruthlessly cutting down anybody who tried to run away from the Icelanders.

Walking along behind the Uberpanzer, Thorodensen checked under parked Jeeps and inside toolsheds for anyone hiding.

Staying close to the former ambassador, Lilja Vilhjalms held a handkerchief to her face and tried to breathe through her mouth. The air reeked of death, the horrible coppery tang of freshly spilled blood mixing with the wretched aftereffects of slaughter. Feces, blood, gunpowder and diesel fumes—the combination of smells was making her dizzy and nauseous. And when her stomach clenched hard, she dashed into a stand of flowering bushes surrounding a tall palm tree.

"Lily, are you wounded?" Thorodensen asked, striding toward her when she stumbled back into view.

"F-fine! I'm…I'm fine," she replied, wiping her mouth clean on the cloth, then tossing it away.

Just then, another APC rumbled by, its armored chassis

splattered with fresh gore, and tufts of human hair sticking to the forward prow.

"My God, how can we do this to people?" she yelled, almost bursting into tears. "It's inhuman! Monstrous!"

"We aren't doing anything to people," Thorodensen snapped, firing his AK-47 into a dark alley. "These are pirates! The worst type of murdering scum on the planet!"

There came an answering cry of pain from the passage, and a young man stumbled into view with most of his throat gone, blood spurting everywhere. There was an AK-105 assault rifle slung across his back, and a canvas bag at his side.

"Pirates are also people!" she stormed furiously.

"No, they are just mad dogs, and will be treated as such!" Thorodensen growled, firing again, a much longer burst this time. "Death is all they deserve!"

As the riddled corpse fell, Thorodensen turned to walk away, rummaging in his pockets for another magazine. When he didn't find any, he went back to recover the AK-105. It was much lighter than an AK-47, and then he saw that it fired 5.56 mm NATO rounds, and not the old-style 7.62 mm Russian ammunition. Thorodensen frowned. He much preferred a large caliber weapon with decent stopping power than this wimpy toy.

Checking inside the man's canvas bag, Thorodensen was delighted to find a dozen fully loaded clips, as well as a single 40 mm round for a grenade launcher, which wasn't attached to the assault rifle.

Just then, an APC rumbled to a halt nearby, and the rear doors slammed open. Wearing sunglasses, Gunnar Eldjarm stepped into the sunlight.

"Is the base clear?" Thorodensen demanded, slamming a fresh clip into the AK-105. The newly acquired weapon felt strange to him, off balance, and there were still smears of blood and brains from the original owner on the wooden stock.

"Not yet," Eldjarm muttered, sending a long burst from the Vepr into a smoke-filled doorway.

A pirate stumbled into the sunlight. His left arm was gone at the shoulder, spurts of bright red blood arching high and away from the severed arteries.

Falling to his knees, the man overcame the horrible shock and started screaming in high-pitched wails of agony, his right hand clutching the strings of flesh at his shoulder in a futile effort to staunch the torrent of life.

Turning away, Eldjarm strolled off to look for any more survivors, as Vilhjalms started forward to help the dying man.

Scowling in disapproval, Thorodensen raised the AK-105 and fired a single round into the pirate's face.

Startled, the woman stopped short as the pirate threw back his head, pink brains splashing across the cinder-block wall. Still mouthing words, the twitching corpse fell flat and went still.

"I remember when we were children, and you two boys refused to remove the hook from the mouth of a fish," Vilhjalms stated, opening and closing her empty hands.

Firing another 12-gauge cartridge through a glass window, Eldjarm turned his head and scowled. "What does that mean?" he demanded curiously.

From inside the building, a pirate stumbled out the broken window, his body slashed from the shards of flying glass. Weakly gesturing, he croaked something about gold, then crumpled into a twitching heap.

"Nothing. Forget I ever mentioned it." Professor Vilhjalms sighed, gazing on the stranger who had the face of his friend.

Shrugging in response, Gunner triggered two more

blasts from the Vepr across the sandy street. A garbage can exploded and a wounded pirate rose into view with both hands held high.

"Surrender, I surrender!" he yelled in English, tossing away his assault rifle. "You speak English, right? Mercy, please! I beg surrender!"

Laughing cruelly, Eldjarm fired the Vepr into the man's belly, then walked away whistling through his teeth.

Shaking her head, Vilhjalms said goodbye to her childhood friend and continued walking behind Thorodensen, not because she wanted to, but because she didn't know what else to do. Their lofty plan for revenge on England seemed like a pipe dream now, withered and dead, melted away like winter snow in the spring.

It took the members of Penumbra several hours to clear the assorted buildings of the pirate base, including the secret dockyard at the lagoon, and the Quonset hut in the jungle, where they had an old Bell & Howell helicopter parked.

"According to the work sheet, there are eighty men on this island," Thorodensen said, thumbing through a list. "How many bodies do you have?"

"Sixty-three," Vilhjalms replied, pulling a notepad from a pocket and checking the tally. "No, sixty-four."

Just then, somebody screamed in the distance, the sound stopping abruptly.

"Make that sixty-five." Eldjarm laughed, adjusting his new sunglasses before strolling away with the Vepr resting on a shoulder.

"Hrafen, honestly, I'm starting to think that Gunnar is losing his mind," Vilhjalms muttered, tucking the notepad away once more. "He actually seems to like all this bloodshed. I've heard of people, soldiers, policemen, going crazy after a battle, but I never thought it was real!"

"That is irrelevant," Thorodensen snapped, tucking the clipboard under his arm. "The important matter is that we are going to be behind schedule, because now we must assign guards to watch for the return of any of the fifteen remaining pirates, who'll be seeking revenge."

"You think they might come back after all this?" Vilhjalms asked. "Are you serious? I would start swimming for Argentina and never look back!"

"But then, you are intelligent," Thorodensen stated bluntly. "Which cannot also be said about any pirate."

Just then a Jeep pulled around a whitewashed building, the rear stacked with corpses like firewood. When the driver stopped, a woman got and rushed over, while the vehicle pulled away again.

"Anything wrong, Hoxha?" asked Thorodensen.

"Sir, we found something," she said, licking dry lips. Her platinum hair was pulled into a tight bun on top of her head, and her clothing was speckled with blood.

"More pirates?" Vilhjalms asked with a sigh.

"Absolutely not pirates," Hoxha replied cryptically. "They're… I mean…" She looked at both of them. "Perhaps you had better come see for yourself."

"Of course," Thorodensen said, gesturing for her to lead the way.

Following the woman into a concrete blockhouse set off by itself, Vilhjalms realized that it was the pirate's fuel dump. The building was filled with hundreds of bright yellow five-gallon canisters marked with the international symbol for flammable material.

"I'm pleased that none of the pirates was smart enough to consider bolting himself inside here with a box of matches," Thorodensen commented in passing. "We would have been forced to cut a deal with the criminal. If this depot ignited, half the island would be awash in flames!"

"Perhaps we should consider such a plan," Vilhjalms said hesitantly. "Just in case of trouble."

Dismissing that possibility with a snort, Hoxha led them through a rusty steel door and down a brick-lined corridor. The tunnel seemed to go on forever. The brickwork was deeply scored in several locations, penetrating all the way through five courses of masonry to reach a smooth stone liner underneath.

"This is a blast tunnel," Vilhjalms stated, reaching out to brush her fingertips along the round walls. "It channeled the exhaust of the launching French rockets away from the control rooms and safely out to sea."

"They made a blast tunnel into a fuel dump," Thorodensen said gruffly. "I told you pirates were stupid."

"Really? How could bricks and concrete withstand those kinds of pressures?" Hoxha asked.

"They could not for very long," Professor Lilja replied. "But the liner is ferroconcrete, sometimes called gunnite, an expensive mixture of cement, epoxy glue and powered steel."

"You're making that up," Hoxha said accusingly.

Vilhjalms shrugged in reply, not overly concerned with changing the opinion of the woman.

Side vents were set into the tunnel every hundred feet, most of them merely blackened holes filled with glassy carbon deposits. But ahead was a light, and voices could be heard. Just then, a foul smell reached them, and everybody made a face.

"Did the pirates also use this place as their lavatory?" Thorodensen asked, coughing into a fist.

"In a manner of speaking," Hoxha replied, pushing open another steel door.

The next room was large and circular, the walls made of a smooth ceramic brick. Though its original function was unknown, the pirates had used scrap iron to section it into small, padlocked cells. Each contained a bare wooden cot, a waste bucket and a prisoner.

Each prisoner was dressed in different attire—ballgown, tuxedo, bikini, business suit, hiking shorts. Obviously, the pirates had captured them from a variety of locations, and never considered giving them clean clothing to wear.

"This is deplorable," Vilhjalms muttered.

A dozen cells, and ten with prisoners, Thorodensen noted. This was most definitely not good news.

"Thank God you're here!" a tall woman cried, stretching an arm through the bars. "Get us out of here before those lunatics come back!"

Thorodensen took a step backward. "It is not as easy as that," he said, a hand worrying the checkered grip of his Webley revolver.

"Not easy? What are you talking about?" an elderly man demanded, hobbling forward. "These pirates attacked our yacht weeks ago! Surely, you must have been sent by my corporation to rescue us?"

"Sorry, I have no idea who you are," Thorodensen said, releasing his grip on the weapon.

Immediately, all the prisoners started shouting and waving their arms.

"Be quiet!" Thorodensen bellowed over the din. "One at a time, please!"

In ragged stages, the clamor eased away, and the prisoners meekly looked at one another, waiting for somebody else to start.

They'd been broken like animals, Vilhjalms realized. Beaten and starved into submission.

"You first," Thorodensen said, pointing at a plump, matronly woman.

"My name is Dame Elizabeth Scott!" she said proudly. "Now please release us at once!"

That made all the Icelanders scowl. Her name sounded British, and so did her accent and complete lack of manners.

"I don't think they're going to do that, my dear," an elderly man stated, stroking a greasy mustache. He was wearing the remains of a tuxedo,

"You are correct," Thorodensen said, displeased. Mostly at himself. He should have assumed that the pirates would have prisoners, hostages for ransom, or even slaves, for sexual release, and for doing the dirty jobs around the island—mucking out sewage pipes and scraping barnacles off the boats. The necessary things nobody would do without being coerced.

"What do you mean?" The woman seemed genuinely confused. "They aren't here to rescue us?"

Inside another cell, a pretty young woman sharply whistled. "Ignore those old fools," she said tersely. "Set me loose! I'm nobody, but I'm rich and can pay you a fortune!" She was wearing a ball gown of some kind, but was dirty and unkempt, with dark roots showing in her blond hair.

"How long have you been down here?" Vilhjalms asked, crossing her arms.

"Two months, four days."

"I don't think so," the professor countered bluntly. The ballgown didn't fit the young woman, and not simply because she had lost a lot of weight. It had never been fitted to her figure.

"It's true!"

"Okay then, what was the Tokyo market at when you were captured by the pirates?" Vilhjalms asked, sliding both hands into the pockets of her jumpsuit.

Surprised at the bizarre question, Thorodensen looked at the professor, then slowly smiled. Very clever.

The young woman paused. "It's been so long," she muttered, biting a thumbnail. "I really don't remember anymore."

"She's a liar," Thorodensen said, dismissing her with a wave. "Probably put in here by the pirates to watch over the other prisoners."

Anybody worth millions would know the fluctuations of the international stock market as well as a normal person would his or her own telephone number. Thorodensen and his wife had just become millionaires when the prime minister of England made the Icelandic bank crash, and they had watched the daily stock market reports like a farmer did the weather reports. It was a vital part of their life. Ipso facto, this woman wasn't rich.

With a snarl, she drew a small pistol and kicked open the unlocked cell door. "Okay, you fat fool! Everybody up against the wall, or else—"

There was a sharp retort of smoke and flame, and the side pocket of Professor Vilhjalms's jumpsuit exploded. Gushing blood, the young woman fell back with a hole in her cheek. Gurgling horribly, she returned fire, but missed the professor, the 9 mm round hitting the brick wall, to ricochet harmlessly.

Feeling something snap inside her mind, Vilhjalms pulled out a Remington .22 pistol and emptied it into the spy until she sprawled lifeless on the dirty floor. "Lying bitch!" she screamed, then broke into tears.

"Shoot her again!" a man growled hatefully, his knuckles white as he clutched the iron bars.

"Enough!" Thorodensen command. "Lily, we will discuss this later."

Still holding the gun, she nodded.

"Hoxha, please get that out of here!" he continued. "Throw it away with the other pirates."

"Yes, sir!" she said, giving a salute and dragging the corpse away.

"As for the rest of you…" Thorodensen paused, buying time to gather his thoughts, a trick that had served him well for many decades of service at the UN.

"Hey," a small man said. "Hey, I know you."

That stopped Thorodensen cold, and he turned to stare sideways over a shoulder. "Do you?" he whispered.

Under the hard gaze, the man went pale and backed into the shadows. "No, no, sorry, my mistake," he said hastily. "Thought you were… My mistake!"

"Then be quiet," Thorodensen snapped, turning to leave. "I will consider what to do with the rest of you later."

As they closed the door, Hoxha returned, carrying a mop and a bucket.

"Hoxha, your new task is to guard these prisoners," Thorodensen directed sternly, closing the steel door to cut off the cries for clemency.

"Not a problem, sir," she said. "Should I sleep out here on a cot or…"

"You can have three of our people to help, once we get the main arc furnace up and running," Vilhjalms said, taking out a handkerchief to wipe her hands, as if they were covered with filth. "But until then, for God's sake be careful!"

"Careful…of those scarecrows?"

"They are desperate and will offer money, sex, anything to get free," Thorodensen said. "They will also kill without pause or mercy, so be alert!"

"Yes, sir!"

"On the other hand, they can have all the food they want, extra blankets, clean water and soap, books, anything they wish," Vilhjalms interjected. "Anything within reason, that is. But no visitors! I will hold you personally responsible."

"Nobody will rape the fools," Hoxha replied, setting down the mop and bucket. "My sister was sexually attacked on vacation in Mexico, and…" Her expression turned dark. "Nobody will harm the prisoners."

"Good." Thorodensen knew about the woman's personal tragedy, and nobody was a better guard for a thief than a man who had been robbed. It became a personal matter, not merely an assignment. His training as an ambassador was serving him well as a criminal, and the irony wasn't lost on the man.

"And get some ventilation in there," Vilhjalms added, fanning a hand before her face to try to dispel the pungent reek coming under the door. "If necessary, break a few holes in the walls, but nothing larger than a fist! Understand?"

"Yes."

Turning on a heel, Thorodensen walked back up the reeking corridor. The combined smells of human waste and gasoline were now explained. The fuel was actually a buffer to hold back the terrible stench of those poor imprisoned souls.

Reaching the courtyard, he stood still for a few minutes, letting the clean, salty air from the sea wash away the aftereffects of the makeshift prison.

"Lord, I could use a beer," Vilhjalms said out of the blue.

"This is not the time for drinking," he said sternly. "Although, considering what you did in there—"

"It's to clear our throats," she interrupted harshly.

"Really?"

"My brother works in construction and always has a beer when he comes home, to clear the taste of cement dust from his mouth. It seems only logical that it would also work with human waste."

"The things you know."

Suddenly, a screaming man holding a machete dashed into sight with a speeding APC hot on his tail. Standing in the cupola of the armored vehicle, Eldjarm was firing short bursts from the 7.62 mm machine gun just behind the pirate, to urge him on to greater speed.

"Stop wasting ammunition!" Thorodensen shouted through cupped hands.

Scowling, Eldjarm fired once more, ending the chase abruptly, and the APC rolled over the body just to make sure.

"Any idea what are we going to do about the prisoners?" Vilhjalms asked, fingering the empty weapon in her pocket.

"For the moment, we need to keep them incarcerated," Thorodensen said, starting across the sandy street. Some of his people were already at work clearing away the corpses, and making piles of weapons. "But once this is all over, we'll send them home in one of the launches used by the pirates."

He paused with a frown. "Pirates. In this day and age. Simply incredible."

"Hrafen, aren't we pirates, too?" she asked softly.

He shot her a stern look of disapproval. "Get your lab ready," he snapped. "After I tally how much the pirates have in their vault, I'll call the Russians and arrange to pick up the merchandise."

"Why not have them make a delivery?" Vilhjalms asked. "If they sell such things, it is only logical that they have a means to transport them."

"True. But the fewer people who know where we are located, the better."

"I suppose. How do you know such criminals, anyway?"

Heading for the airfield, Thorodensen laughed. "My dear professor, I worked with the United Nations for over thirty-five years!" he exclaimed. "The only people I ever met were criminals!"

Starting along the street, Vilhjalms drew the Remington and started to clumsily reload the little automatic pistol. Something strange had overwhelmed her back there in the roundhouse, and she wondered if she was starting to descend into the same pit of madness as Gunnar. Or if there was still a chance for her to find some way back to the light, and escape from the terrible trap of seeking justice through the bloody venue of revenge. Only time would tell.

Pebble Beach, Sicily

ONLY MINUTES LATER, the cabdriver dropped them at the closed road leading to the private beach. As it drove away, both Bolan and Salvatore drew weapons.

"Something is very wrong here," he said, walking toward the access road. The chain was down and partially buried in the sandy soil.

"No, everything is wrong," the major replied, leveling the Beretta.

On the other side of the gully, the wooden bridge was completely gone, blown to pieces and burned into ash. Yet brass shell casings sparkled from the dark residue. The shells were of different sizes, clearly stating that there had been a firefight here after the terrorists had flown away.

Quickly separating, the two swept around the big sand dune and come out on opposite sides. This area seemed untouched, exactly as they remembered it. Which was completely wrong.

"Why didn't my people clean up the bodies?" Salvatore

muttered, proceeding carefully among the melted corpses and smashed equipment. Then she stopped and cursed.

Bolan darkly scowled. A dozen NATO soldiers were spread out on the ground in a row, in spite of the industrious activities of the local sand crabs, lizards and black crows. Nature was a self-cleaning machine, even more ruthless and efficient than the humans who claimed mastery of the world. The soldiers' weapons were gone, knives and sidearms, too. Each of them had been cut numerous times across the arms and face, then shot in the back of the head, execution-style.

"Those dirty sons of bitches," Salvatore said, brandishing a fist toward the west. "Those filthy bastards came back to torture my people, then shot them down like dogs!"

"No, I don't think so," Bolan said, studying the ground. "These holes were made by a small bullet, a .22, or maybe a .25 caliber."

"Professional hit men use that caliber," she replied, her expression undergoing a fast series of changes.

"Is everybody present?" Bolan asked, feeling the mounting pressure of time. "Anybody missing?"

Walking slowly among the dead, Salvatore made a count. "Sergeant Liberman is gone," she said. "Maybe he got away and is hiding in the hills?" The words were positive, but her tone didn't carry any hint of conviction.

"Maybe," Bolan said, bending down to lift a small bag into view. "Toni, were any of your people carrying 12-gauge stun bags?"

"No, we had some rubber bullets," she replied, tilting her head. "But never got a chance to use them."

Squinting against the bright sunlight, Bolan looked across the landing field and beach. "Which means that whoever did this was here very recently," he said, tossing her the object.

Salvatore made the catch and blinked. The stun bag was still warm from being discharged from a shotgun. "This was fired no more than ten or fifteen minutes ago," she said in amazement.

"They must have waited until noon for us to come back," Bolan noted. "Then gave up, shot everybody and left with a prisoner to question later."

"You mean, torture in a basement somewhere."

"Yes."

"Think Nunzio had a backup team?" she asked, crushing the bag in a clenched fist.

"Only one way to find out."

"How?"

"We go look for him," Bolan stated, starting toward one of the burned trucks.

Still sitting on the back of the flatbeds were several of the Uberpanzers, covered with black ash from the burned canvas sheeting.

"You have got to be kidding," she muttered.

"Never more serious," Bolan replied, using a knife to slash away the last threads of the restraining rope.

"But we can't use those," Salvatore said, holstering the weapon. "Even if we knew where the Mafia took Liberman, there's no fuel!"

"There has to be enough to start the engines and show the buyer that they work, as well as drive them off the flatbed," Bolan said, rolling up his sleeves. "Not much more than that, of course, but if we empty all the fuel tanks we should get a couple gallons."

Frowning, Salvatore started to speak, then looked at the stun bag in her palm. Casting it away, she brushed back her hair. "We'll use this one," she said, going to the cleanest APC. "It has the least amount of fire damage."

Only a few minutes later, the Uberpanzer stuttered to life and rolled off the flatbed with a hard jounce.

"Where to now?" Salvatore asked, clinging to a ceiling strap. The dashboard gauge barely registered the small amount of fuel they had gathered, but at least it wasn't precisely on zero.

She found it surprisingly roomy inside the armored vehicle, but then it was designed to carry an armed platoon with full backpacks and ski equipment.

"Nunzio comes from Palermo, so that was our best bet," Bolan said from the driver's seat, flipping a series of switches. With a muffled roar, the engines accelerated, the entire APC vibrating softly.

"Then his people will be using the southern highway," she said hesitantly.

"Which is why we're going due east," Bolan countered, throwing the APC into gear.

With a lurch, it started forward, running over the corpses and assorted wreckage. There was no time for any niceties if they were going to save the sergeant's life. Every second wasted meant less fuel. Time was now their enemy.

"East?" Salvatore asked. "Across open country?"

"What's going to stop us?" Bolan asked, as the APC bounced down into the gully and up the other side.

"Pity we don't have any ammunition for the coaxial gun," the major said, rapping a knuckle against the ammunition bin. The metal gave a hollow boom.

"Don't need any," Bolan retorted, banking sharply. The APC curved around in a tight arc, smashing aside a small tree and plowing through the crumpled debris of a crashed Hercules.

"What, are we going to ram the Mafia?"

"At least we'll have the element of surprise on our side," Bolan said grimly, shifting gear.

"That's for damn sure. What's our speed?"

"Don't ask!" Bolan drove across the paved road. A second later, the tank crashed through a guardrail to the sound of splintering wood.

There was a slow-moving river on the other side, and he plunged straight into the water. Just for a moment, Salvatore thought they were sinking, then the Uberpanzer hit the riverbed and surged forward once more.

They rolled up the opposite bank, crushing a stand of trees under the armored prow. Then the APC churned across a wide field of lilies, the military tires chewing up the ground, and spewing out flowers in a high spray.

"Okay, let's head 'em off at the pass!" Salvatore shouted, then added a war whoop.

Struggling to control the powerful machine, Bolan could only grunt at the reference to the old cliché from bad Westerns. However, in this case it was true. If luck was on their side, this might just work. Probably not, he admitted privately. But there was no other choice but to try.

Beyond the field of flowers, a wide stretch of golden wheat gently waved in the breeze. The tank's destruction of the fence between couldn't be heard over the rumble of its diesel engines.

Checking the compass, Bolan plowed onward, until the major cried out, "Two o'clock!"

Looking up, he grunted at the sight of a huge American-made harvester trundling across the field, the front blades spinning as they cut a wide swath through the crop. Swerving fast, Bolan skirted the farm machine, as the driver inside the glass cab on top screamed curses in gutter Italian. The Uberpanzer rolled on across a dirt road, then careened off a tall woodpile, sending logs flying far and wide. Bolan swerved the vehicle around a stone cistern, and crashed through a wooden gate.

Beyond the gate, the APC traveled for a short while on a paved road, but when it curved away, Bolan kept going straight. Next came flat, open countryside. Perfect! Then he spotted neat rows of headstones and realized it was actually a graveyard. He hesitated for a moment, reluctant to desecrate the place, then decided that saving the life of a man was worth it.

Slamming the pedal to the floor, Bolan shifted into high gear. The big Detroit engines roared in response, and the Uberpanzer accelerated. Ancient limestone gravestones exploded into dust before the ramming prow, and the granite statue of a winged angel actually took flight for a moment, before crashing to earth and shattering into a million pieces.

Looking up in surprise, a large group of people wearing black gasped at the sight of the APC. Several drew pistols from inside their clothing and started shooting.

Dodging around the mourners, Bolan was impressed at the number of times they hit the APC, but the small caliber bullets merely ricocheted off the ceramic armor, without the usual musical twang.

"Now we've pissed off half of Sicily," Salvatore said, buckling on a safety harness.

Crashing through an iron fence, Bolan saw more smooth roadway ahead, seamless concrete that stretched straight for what looked to be miles. Rush-hour traffic filled four wide lanes.

Immediately, he steered right and started barreling down the middle of the highway, keeping the double yellow lines centered under the APC.

"What in hell are you doing?" Salvatore demanded, aghast. Then she nodded. "Right, we're ahead of them."

At the sudden appearance of the Uberpanzer, most of the oncoming drivers swerved sharply away, giving the military juggernaut a wide berth. But the majority of the southbound traffic didn't move, and Bolan was forced to slow.

"Christ, we don't even know which car has Liberman," Salvatore stated, trying to look into the backseat of a passing sedan. She saw young children playing video games.

"The tracks that went over the chain were from new tires, set well apart," Bolan answered curtly, swinging around a VW minibus full of terrified nuns. "So we're looking for something bigger than a limousine."

Bigger? Frowning in consternation, the major reached out to hit the red horn button on the dashboard. Not a single southbound car moved aside, while several of the drivers laughed and made rude gestures.

"Shoot your gun," Bolan directed sagely.

Shoving the Beretta out the gunport, Salvatore fired several rounds into the sky.

As if by magic, the lines of traffic parted, bitter experience having trained the drivers to disappear fast when guns were drawn. In a matter of seconds there were no other vehicles on their side of the highway.

"I see a limo!" she cried, pointing at the oncoming traffic.

"Tires are too worn," Bolan growled, just as a police car appeared from the bushes, lights flashing.

Drawing the Desert Eagle, he fired twice out a gunport, and the front tire on the squad car blew. Braking hard, the cop fishtailed to a fast stop, blocking both southern lanes.

"You're good," Salvatore commented drily, tucking away her useless pistol.

"Been chased before," Bolan stated. "Just never in an APC on a highway."

"First time for everything... How long do you think before the police call for backup?"

"Minutes, maybe less."

"Wonderful," Salvatore said with a sigh, squinting into the distance. "Hey, what about them?"

Topping a rise in the highway ahead of them was an enormous stretch Hummer escorted by four sleek motorcycles.

"Looks about right," Bolan said, when the cavalcade abruptly angled off the road and crashed through some bushes, to start racing across a stony field. "I'd say that we have target acquisition." He flashed the headlights before cutting sideways through the oncoming traffic.

Already wary of the huge APC on the roadway, the northbound cars and trucks instantly swerved out of the way, horns blaring, drivers and passengers screaming and cursing. As the Uberpanzer crossed the berm, Bolan was glad not to hear any fenders crunch or glass shatter.

"Okay, now what?" the major Salvatore asked, reaching over to pull the Beretta from Bolan's belt holster and rack the slide.

"Hold on," he growled, shifting into high gear and pushing the accelerator all the way to the floor yet again.

CHAPTER TWELVE

Slowly, the afternoon sun began to set behind the rumbling Hercules as it streaked along the equator.

Sipping coffee, Hrafen Thorodensen was sitting at the controls of the big transport plane, while in the copilot seat a lovely young Icelandic woman with the unlikely name of Slvanna Svanna labored to confirm their exact heading, using a pad and pencil.

"Ground speed and air speed, combined with magnetic heading of… Why do I need to know this?" she bitterly complained for the hundredth time. Her long platinum hair was tied in two pigtails knotted together behind her head.

"Because sometimes technology fails," Thorodensen replied patiently. "If the GPS stops working, then how will you know where to fly?"

"By using a compass and sextant?"

"Is that your answer, or another question?"

"Ah…both?"

"Get back to work," he ordered. Someone knocked on the door to the flight deck. "Come in!"

The door opened, and a man held out a slip of paper. "Sir, we received a coded message from Cobra Fourteen."

"Our spy in NATO?" Svanna asked, looking up in surprise.

"I'm busy, please read it," Thorodensen said, thinning the fuel mixture to the port side engine, and switching from an exhausted tank to a full one to carefully maintain the balance of the huge airplane. Flying a Hercules was rather like trying to drive a cement mixer around a parked car.

"'The CIA agent is alive and still coming after us,'" the man read.

"Are you serious?" Svanna asked with a scowl.

"That's what the message says." He paused, uncertain. "Should we call back Gunnar to handle the matter personally?"

"There is no need," Thorodensen said, checking the GPS. "Gunnar is of more use in Brazil. Besides, I already have the CIA situation under control."

Palermo, Sicily

MOVING AT BREAKNECK SPEED, the oversize Hummer banged and jerked across the uneven ground of the abandon farmland. A headlight shattered and a hubcap came free to roll away ahead of them.

The drivers of the four Ducati motorcycles tried to stay abreast of the luxury vehicle, but the sleek two-wheelers, designed for street racing, were unable to traverse the wild landscape. Hitting a large rock hidden in the weeds, one driver went flying over the handlebars to crash into a second one. The men went down, tangled with the motorcycles in crimson ruination.

The Uberpanzer zoomed in fast, its eight wheels churning up the earth and spraying it backward like brown exhaust fumes.

Braking to a stop, the remaining two motorcycle drivers turned to start shooting at the APC with chattering machine pistols, arcs of spent brass flying high. The hail of bullets harmlessly peppered the Swiss tank, which plowed on between them, sending men and machines tumbling away.

Inside the Hummer, everybody muttered curses and got their weapons ready.

"I suppose we shouldn't have left the highway!" snarled a man in the passenger seat. An underboss for Degerrio, the capo was dressed in a black business suit, and had both hands wrapped around the gold head of an ebony walking stick. Diamonds twinkled from every finger and an earlobe.

"Your plan sounded good at the time, boss!" the driver replied through clenched teeth, frantically dodging watery potholes and derelict pieces of farm equipment. "What should I try now?"

"Drive faster!" the capo snarled, tightening his hands on the walking stick. In the distance was an old farmhouse, but he quickly dismissed that as useless. If they tried to make a stand there, the APC would simply crash through the plaster walls and crush them like a spider under a boot.

Lowering the side windows, four of the street soldiers in the rear started firing Uzi machine pistols at the APC, but the streams of 9 mm rounds ricocheted harmlessly off the angular prow.

The fifth man was struggling to load a rocket launcher, but his lack of familiarity with the weapon, combined with his inability to read the attached instruction booklet, written in German, were seriously hampering his efforts.

"Why are they not shooting back?" one soldier growled, trying to ride his bucking Uzi into a tighter grouping. "They have cannons, yes?"

"Because they do not wish the harm our prisoner!" the driver retorted, twisting the wheel to avoid colliding with an ancient tree stump.

A fender scraped the bark off the stump in passing, and a dark swarm of bees poured out to rally against the supposed invader.

"Then we have an ace in our hand," the capo said, lowering the stick and pulling out a Heckler & Koch .357 Magnum pistol. "David, haul up the prisoner and let them see! Joseph, when they slow down, immediately circle around! We can lose them on the highway!"

"Yes, sir!" the driver growled, twisting and jerking the steering wheel as if in a wrestling contest.

Moving straight as a laser beam, the APC rolled through the bees, slamming aside the rotten stump.

"Come here, soldier boy," David snarled, grabbing the unconscious man by the collar.

But as he tried to pull the sergeant up from the floor, Liberman suddenly stood and rammed his forehead into the man's face. There was an audible crunch of bone, and David recoiled, with blood gushing from a badly broken nose.

"You prick!" he snarled, whipped the sergeant across the side of the head with a pistol.

Moving fast, Liberman almost got out of the way, but the weapon still landed a glancing blow that made his vision blur. In spite of the handcuffs on his wrists, the sergeant reached out with both hands to grab the mobster's throat and bury his thumbs into the soft flesh on either side of the trachea, alongside the Adam's apple.

Unable to draw a breathe, David fired the gun, blowing out the back window, then shooting the sergeant in the leg. Grunting in pain, Liberman tried to hold on, but his fingers slipped and he fell back onto the bucking floor.

"Don't kill him, you idiot!" the capo bellowed from the front. "We need him alive!"

"I know! I know!" David angrily replied, smacking the NATO soldier again and again with the pistol until he stopped moving, bleeding profusely from the mouth and nose.

Laughing in triumph at finally loading the rocket launcher, the fifth mobster swung the weapon out a side window, aimed and fired. Smoke and flame blasted from both ends of the squat tube, and the antitank rocket streaked away to crash directly on the prow of the oncoming APC. The rocket burst into a million pieces, but there was no explosion.

"What the fuck happened?" he demanded, looking at the tube.

"We're too close!" the capo snarled, working the slide on his own weapon. "The warhead of the rocket does not arm until after a hundred feet!"

"Bah, it is useless!" another mobster snarled, firing the Uzi at the tires of the APC. He kept hitting them, but the bullets merely disappeared into the material.

"I'm not sure even a standard rocket could penetrate that weird ceramic armor," another mobster added, slamming a fresh clip into his Uzi.

"Shut the fuck up!"

"Yes, boss!"

"Fire another rocket!" the driver shouted. "But this time, turn the launcher around! Shoot the rocket toward the sky, but try and put the backwash into the view slots. It'll fry the people inside alive!"

Savagely grinning in understanding, the fifth man quickly reloaded the rocket launcher and leaned out the window, just as the APC rammed into the side of the Hummer. The mobster screamed as the armored steel prow sheered off his arm, and the rocket launcher went flying harmlessly away.

Gushing a torrent of blood, the mortally wounded man began pawing at the ruin of his shoulder, shrieking insanely.

In cold deliberation, the capo turned and shot him in the heart. He fell back with a gasp and went still.

A moment later, the APC hit the Hummer again, ripping off a bumper, removing a sideview mirror and shattering several windows.

Desperately trying to get back to the highway, the Mafia driver attempted to dodge the next strike by fishtailing the massive vehicle. He almost succeeded. The APC only smacked them a glancing blow, ripping off a door.

Still firing his Uzi, one of the street soldiers fell out of the vehicle and under the spinning wheels of the Uberpanzer. His scream was mercifully short as the APC rammed them again, buckling in a passenger door.

The tires on the Hummer exploded off the rims as the vehicle was shoved sideways across the ground. The mobsters inside rattled about like dice, and the air bags exploded into action even as the engine sputtered and died.

Muttering curses, the capo and the driver shot their handguns into the restraining bags, then tried not to breathe the hot gases that belched out from the ruptured balloons. But they still caught a whiff. Oddly, it smelled exactly like burned firecrackers.

Stumbling out of the smashed Hummer, they tripped on the uneven ground, but staggered erect again with their weapons drawn. The APC was parked only a few yards away.

As the remaining street soldiers clambered out of the crashed Hummer, the capo heard the purring engine of the APC loudly sputter, then stop. He blinked at that. It had almost sounded as if the damn thing had run out of gas.

"Let's see who's inside," the Mafia driver snarled. But he took only a single step before a knife was suddenly jutting from his throat. Gurgling horribly, the man dropped his Glock and tried to remove the blade.

"No, leave it!" another mobster yelled.

The driver either didn't hear the warning or was simply too far gone to care. As the knife came free, red blood spurted out with every beat of his heart. Grabbing his throat, the driver tried to staunch the flow, and failed. Weakly, he stumbled away, moving slower with every passing second until falling into the weeds.

Another knife took a man in the stomach, and he doubled over, groaning into death. Then a gun fired, and a third man's head fell back, most of his face soaring away.

"Cover me!" the capo yelled, scrambling back into the Hummer. A moment later, he reappeared, pushing the unconscious body of Sergeant Liberman ahead of him as a shield.

"Okay, whoever you are!" he shouted. "I've got a gun to the head of your man!" He waited, but there was no response. "Let's cut a deal!"

"No deals," Bolan said, stepping around the APC and firing both weapons. The other two men died on the spot, their guns unfired.

At the sight, the capo put the barrel of his H&K pistol under the chin of the limp NATO soldier. "Stop right there, or this man dies!"

With both weapons at the ready, Bolan stayed perfectly still, but said nothing, waiting to see how the situation would unfold. A warm breeze blew across the field, carrying the smells of wildflowers and car exhaust.

"You got two guns," the capo snarled. "Can't throw a knife with your feet, right? I wanna see the other man now!"

"Right here," Salvatore said from the other side of the Hummer.

Startled, the capo started to turn, then quickly swung back. Already Bolan was yards closer, and a cold panic hit the underboss. God almighty, the big man moved like a panther!

"Over here, bitch!" the capo shouted, his eyes darting about. "I want to see both of you!"

A long minute passed, then the major appeared from behind the APC, her ghillie suit streaked with fresh mud.

"Look, I killed your men, you killed mine, that squares our account," the capo said, sweat forming on his brow. "So, you leave, I'll set him loose and we go our separate ways. Fair enough?"

"Now," Bolan said softly, the word almost lost in the breeze.

"Now what?" the capo demanded, just as Sergeant Liberman rammed his elbow backward, then dropped to the dirt.

Gasping for breath, the capo got off only a single round before Bolan triggered the Desert Eagle, the .50 Magnum hollowpoint round damn near removing his entire head.

As the capo's corpse slid down the battered chassis of the Hummer, Liberman rolled over, his chest splashed with fresh blood.

"Son of a bitch got me," he groaned, pressing both hands tight to his stomach. "Oh God, it feels like my guts are on fire...."

Rushing forward, Salvatore briefly inspected the wound, then started to open her ghillie suit, only to stop. The shirt underneath was just as dirty as the suit, and she had used everything in her small medical kit back in the Apollo Mountains.

"Quick, find me something to use as bandages," she commanded, pressing her hands tight against the bleeding wound. Blood seeped between her pale fingers, and Liberman groaned.

Briefly, Bolan looked over the dead mobsters, then dismissed their ragged clothing as unusable. He did, however, grab a cell phone. Knowing there was nothing in the APC, he went to the Hummer and forced open the rear hatch. Inside he found spare ammunition, more weapons, some assorted tools, bottled water and two spare tires.

"These are still sealed. The water should be sterile," Bolan said, tossing over a bottle. "Clean the wound, and I'll check the farmhouse."

She made the catch and removed the cap with her teeth. "This is going to hurt," she whispered, pouring the contents over the wound.

From previous experience in-country, Bolan knew various emergency numbers. Checking the phone's GPS application, he called for an ambulance and gave their location.

Then he sprinted across the field, his long legs eating up the distance. But even before he reached the low stone wall marking the farmyard, he knew the house would be useless. The windows were dirty, the plants in the flowerpots withered and dead.

But since there was nowhere else to look, he kicked open the front door and ran inside. The living room was bare, stripped to the walls, without even a rug on the floor. The kitchen was the same, but there were dirty towels in the bathroom, probably left behind by the owners.

That gave him an idea, and he checked the hallway closet. Inside was a roll of toilet tissue, a used bar of soap, some spare lightbulbs and a stack of hand towels. Exactly what was needed!

Taking a towel from the middle, he cut it into strips, then sprinted back to the Hummer and thrust them at Major Salvatore. She took them and expertly bandaged the stomach wound.

"It won't help much," she said, securing the loose ends.

"I can't make a tourniquet without killing him in the process."

"I'm fine...never better...." Liberman whispered, his skin deathly pale. "Could I have some of that water?'

"With a stomach wound?" Bolan asked. "Not a chance, brother."

"Was I shot in the stomach...?" he whispered, looking down. "Funny, I don't feel a thing...."

"He needs a hospital fast," Salvatore said, cradling his head.

"I already called it in. The medics'll be here in a few minutes," Bolan told her.

"Excellent!" Salvatore declared with a grateful smile, just as she heard the distant howl of a siren. "Damnation, they'll save the sergeant, but hold us for days, maybe weeks! If we're going to stop Penumbra, you have got to leave."

"Why would they put us in jail?" Bolan demanded curiously, then he frowned. "This mission wasn't authorized by NATO, was it?"

"Not officially, no. The locals like to handle the Mafia by themselves. No outsiders allowed."

A pissing contest. Great! All this trouble over the Sicilian police trying not to look foolish to the rest of the world. Bolan appreciated the effort, but not the results.

"B-before you go..." Liberman said, holding out a trembling hand. "Found this in ...the wreckage...plane...."

Gently, Bolan took the object and saw that it was a memory chip from a cell phone.

"Didn't the Mafia search you?" Salvatore asked in surprise

"Not carefully," he whispered. "Just looked for weapons."

Bolan tucked the chip into a pocket.

"Don't go naked," Salvatore stated, jerking her head toward the bodies near the crashed Hummer.

Nodding, Bolan checked them over and recovered several magazines for the Uzi machine guns. Thumbing out the 9 mm rounds, he reloaded the magazines for his own Beretta. Then he checked the capo and removed a suit of expensive body armor.

After pulling it on and adjusting it to his size, he hauled out the monocular to check the new arrivals.

Coming fast along the highway was a conga line of blue-and-gold cars with flashing light bars on their roofs.

"It's the Guardia di Finanza," he muttered, lowering the device.

The Guard was responsible for dealing with crimes of a financial nature, including drugs and smuggling.

"The Guard?" Brushing back a loose lock of her hair, Salvatore scowled. "How many?"

"I'd say all of them," Bolan replied without any trace of humor. Unconsciously, he rested a hand on the Desert Eagle, then released the weapon. He wouldn't fire on them. "Time for me to go."

"Before you do," Major Salvatore said, stepping close. She reached behind her neck and slid something over her head.

"For luck," she said, pressing it into his palm.

Looking down, Bolan saw that it was a Saint Christopher medal, and started to object. Then he saw the honest concern in her face and decided otherwise. Every soldier would like a little help from a higher power.

Tucking the religious icon into a pocket, Bolan climbed onto one of the undamaged Ducati motorcycles. "Live large," he said, kicking the engine alive.

The major seemed taken aback by that goodbye, as if only now understanding that they would probably never meet again. She opened her mouth to speak, then clamped it shut and just gave a curt salute.

A dozen blue-and-gold vehicles screamed off the highway, sirens wailing and lights flashing.

"Stop! Police!" a woman shouted in Italian over a megaphone, her voice echoing across the open field. "Stop!"

"Arrivederci," Bolan muttered, twisting the handlebar controls. The L-Twin engine roared with power. Popping the clutch, the soldier made the Ducati jerk upward in a wheelie to distract their aim, then surged forward, leaving behind a wake of dark exhaust.

CHAPTER THIRTEEN

Butterfly Island

After the pirate base had been secured and patrols arranged, Professor Lilja Vilhjalms gathered her people and proceeded directly to the hidden dockyard at the lagoon.

As expected, the boat repair shop was in excellent condition, and equipped with everything from an anvil to microcalipers. For obvious reasons, the pirates couldn't have their vessels repaired at a regular shipyard, so would have gathered everything necessary for any contingency. All of which Penumbra could now use for its own purposes.

First checking for booby traps, and thankfully finding none, Vilhjalms and her team then scrubbed and cleaned the equipment, then recalibrated everything. Nobody was surprised when most of the lathes, planes and even the drills were slightly off center.

"How did these idiots ever manage to repair anything?" a man asked, wiping a sleeve across his greasy face. The cloth left behind an even wider smear of industrial lubricant.

"Fucking pirates," a woman drawled, putting a wealth of information into the two words. Pulling her arm out of a hydraulic press, she cast away a bent screwdriver.

Raising his head from within a grease pit, a man looked around. "Where the hell is that lazy bastard Bardh?"

"Dead," another woman replied without emotion, testing the connections on a pressure hose. "A pirate stabbed him in the back."

"Oh. Damn."

"Fucking pirates," the first woman repeated with a snarl.

"Less talk, more work," Vilhjalms chided, busy replacing the breakers on an electrical dynamo. The carbon scoring was almost deep enough to function as an insulator, and she was amazed that the machine hadn't simply arced into a short circuit that killed everybody in the shop.

"Need a hand with that?"

"Yes, please!"

In a relatively short time, the shop was in order, and the Icelanders ran a final check over the electrical wiring, heat shields and mechanical controls of a small arc furnace. This one piece of equipment was absolutely crucial. If the furnace malfunctioned, or couldn't get hot enough, then all their plans ended here and now in failure.

"Okay, turn it on!" Vilhjalms shouted, using asbestos gloves to pull down the visor on her helmet.

"Cutting in primary circuits now," a man announced, throwing a series of switches.

Across the shop, the hulking furnace slowly began to register internal heat, then radiating waves of warmth, and soon the indicators were registering in the thousands of degrees.

"This works fine!" the professor said in relief. "Okay, shut it down and let's get the first test sample ready."

"Lily, how do we know what temperature the armor will melt at?" a short man asked. There was a bandage on his arm and fresh stitches on his cheek.

"We don't know," she replied, pushing up the shield and removing the gloves. "This is going to be trial and error.

That's why we needed so much of the Swiss armor. I estimate we'll lose about half the ceramics before we get the melting process perfected."

"Fair enough."

"Arian, start banking the forge. We'll need to run an outgas sequence to check the purity," Vilhjalms ordered, feeling a rush of elation at the project finally beginning. "Xhevat, begin to disassemble the tanks—"

"Armored personnel carriers," the woman corrected.

Impatiently, the professor dismissed that with a wave. "Whatever they're called! Just bring me the armor in as many small pieces as possible. Make a pile over by the lathe."

"Should we tell the ambassador about our progress so far?" Xhevat asked, hitching up her jingling tool belt. A 9 mm Glock pistol was tucked in among the wrenches and calipers.

"No, he's gone to deal with the Russians," Vilhjalms replied, going to a huge whiteboard set between the lavatory and a grinding wheel.

"What about Gunnar?"

"He's gone to Brazil to…well, you know."

Using double-sided tape, the professor attached a sheaf of papers to the whiteboard, spreading them out flat. First, she put up a detailed set of engineering blueprints, then a set of electrical schematics, and then mechanical overlays.

"The Loki," she whispered, smoothing the sheets with her hands as if caressing a lover. "The ultimate weapon!"

"If it doesn't explode and kill us," Arian commented drily, pushing a cart filled with oxyacetylene tanks.

"We will find a way to make it work," Vilhjalms said confidently, using a pencil to mark a small correction in the complex equations. She had no real training in steam-powered machines, but felt sure she could work out the details in time. That was all she needed, just a little time....

Palermo, Sicily

BOLAN ACCELERATED across the bumpy field in a roar of controlled power, the 160 horsepower engine of the Italian motorcycle purring softly even as it sent the sleek Ducati 1098 speedster hurtling forward at maximum velocity.

The jerks and bounces threatened to throw him off the motorcycle, but Bolan clung on to the handlebars and tightened the grip of his thighs. Considered the fastest production motorcycle in the world, the Ducati was too powerful for cross-country riding.

Just then, the supercharged bike slammed into an unseen gully, and Bolan thought he was going to launch into space. But the Ducati came crashing back down, and he wobbled onto the highway. With smooth pavement under the tires, Bolan felt the automatic high-speed transmission kick in, and now he really took off, the speedster reaching 60 mph in three seconds flat. Then it cut loose.

In only a few moments, Bolan left the Guard pursuers. But the four police sedans suddenly surged forward, zooming in and out of traffic while maintaining a standard chase formation.

Steadily accelerating, Bolan outpaced the much larger police cars, lowering his speed only on the curves, when it was absolutely necessary. The smooth, molded body channeled the flow of air comfortably around his legs, and the curved console communicated every aspect of the humming power plant this road rocket deemed to call an engine.

However, as he took a sweeping curve, Bolan noted that the fuel gauge was registering half-full, but was also visibly dropping as he accelerated. There was no smell of gasoline, nor a noticeable leak, so he could only assume the Ducati traded speed for mileage. He would have to outmaneuver the police quickly, or they would capture him when the engine ran dry.

Bolan heard a machine gun, and he felt a bullet flash past his face. Clearly, they wanted him dead, not alive. That changed matters entirely.

Zooming across a bridge, he saw a country road below instead of the expected river. Braking hard, he threw out a leg and tilted into a sharp turn. Leaving the highway, he curved through a field dotted with construction markers, then slowed even more as he sent the Ducati down the steep embankment and onto the smaller road.

In a few minutes, he saw a small town on the horizon and braced himself. Sure enough, as he entered the city limits the pavement stopped, to be replaced with granite cobblestones. Charging along the bumpy street, Bolan sounded the horn and flashed the headlight as a warning. But the people on the sidewalks and sitting at the cafés only glanced up, mildly curious.

Drawing the Beretta 93-R, he triggered a burst into the sky. The same as before, everybody ran for cover.

Darting through the center of town, Bolan began to hear police sirens again, and looked about for a likely escape venue. Choosing a corner store closed for the holidays. Wondering exactly what holiday they were celebrating, Bolan put a burst from the Beretta into the window. As the glass shattered, the 9 mm rounds continued on, to take out the other window and send a shower of twinkling shards blowing across the street.

Swerving dangerously close to a splashing fountain, Bolan slowed even more as he drove directly across the broken glass, zigzagging to avoid a punctured tire.

Moments later, police cars came screaming around the

corner and across the field of glass. Almost instantly, one began veering wildly, then crashed into a stone wall. The next went straight over glistening shards and promptly blew a tire. In the rearview mirror, Bolan saw the patrol car start to slide along the street.

However, the two cars following braked hard and shot off into alleyways, soon reemerging from different directions, sirens howling.

Bending low, Bolan tried to gain some speed. Two down, two to go.

Rifle fire ricocheted off the cobblestones alongside the motorcycle. The soldier quickly swept to the left, and then immediately back to the right. As he repeated the maneuver, another burst hammered the exact location he had just vacated.

Swinging low around a corner, Bolan careened off the granite cornerstone of a bank, the fiberglass shield over his legs cracking from the impact. But as he shot down the side street he was out of the line of fire. The police started yelling over a PA system once more, calling for him to surrender.

Okay, that had bought him a few seconds, but not much more. Bolan had to get out of range double quick. A brief glance in the rearview mirror identified their weapon—a compact Beretta ARX-160. Brand-new and state-of-the-art, the rifle was chambered for a regulation 5.56 mm NATO round, but it also carried a 40 mm grenade launcher, and if they decide to unleash those his ride would be drastically cut short. Bolan consoled himself that it was highly unlikely the police would use high explosives in this densely populated area.

A low stone wall alongside the road violently exploded, and a cloud of debris peppered Bolan and the Ducati. The windshield scored a crack, the headlight shattered, and he felt something very hard smack his shoulder. However, there was no accompanying spread of warmth, which meant there had been no significant penetration. He was just bruised from the flying stone fragments. Good enough.

Turning another corner, Bola frantically ducked as a street cop swung a blackwood baton at his head. He missed, but the soldier streaked away with a newfound respect for the Italian police. If nothing else, they were determined.

Sounding the horn, and firing the Beretta to clear the way, Bolan cut through a market and emerged in a small courtyard fronting an old church. It was flanked by two other buildings of similar height, the front doors of which were wide open, as were those of the church. That gave him an idea.

Twisting the accelerator on the handlebars, Bolan rattled up the marble stairs, pleased to not see anybody inside the church. But shooting through the doorway, he accidentally rammed the poor box. It burst apart, spewing coins everywhere, and the motorcycle's cracked windshield shattered from the barrage.

Losing control for a moment, Bolan careened off a wooden pew, the front fender breaking into pieces and flying away. Struggling to control the Ducati, he ended up in the middle of the church, streaking between rows of pews.

The police cars couldn't follow him inside, but the officers would be on foot, and in this confined area, those ARX rifles would give them a lethal superiority in firepower.

Sitting in an office, at a desk stacked with books, a young priest gasped as Bolan streaked by, then popped another wheelie to start climbing a curving bank of ancient stone stairs. The jarring impacts were brutal, but nothing compared to his earlier journey across the farmland, and Bolan managed to stay on the speeding bike. He was forced to slow when the handlebars scraped a wall, but he reached the second story still moving.

At the opposite end of a long hallway was a beautiful stained-glass window of Saint Francis feeding the birds. Throwing the Ducati forward at full speed, Bolan ducked to protect his face as the motorcycle crashed through the window in a deafening rainbow explosion.

Then he was airborne and dropping fast.

Lifting himself off the molded seat to protect his groin, Bolan crashed onto the roof of the next building, the impact rattling his bones. Skittering out of control, he braked hard and threw out a leg to avoid hitting a huge air conditioner, then banked around a glass skylight, startling a flock of sleeping pigeons.

Coming to a brief halt, Bolan checked himself for any broken bones, then reloaded the Beretta and blew off the lock on the roof access door.

The trip down these stairs was much easier and faster than his previous climb, after which he rolled slowly across a lobby full of screaming people, and out the front door.

Reaching the street, Bolan headed for the highway once more, the sirens of the police cars in pursuit soon falling away into the distance. However, as he rolled along the access ramp, he heard an entirely new siren, a hooting blare. In the remaining pieces of his sideview mirror, Bolan saw a pair of Ferrari motorcycles charge out from behind a billboard advertising the premiere of a local TV show.

The headlights of their bikes flashing, the two motorcycle cops cut loose with standard-issue Beretta pistols, one of the 9 mm rounds zinging off the handlebars less than an inch away from the Executioner's wrist.

Charging off the next bridge, Bolan cut the engine and

coasted into some bushes. Lying down, he waited for the sound of the motorcycle cops to fade into the distance, then straightened the Ducati and rode off once more. But moments later he heard the Ferraris return.

Ignoring the low level of fuel in the tank, Bolan put the pedal to the metal and unleashed the unbelievable speed of the Ducati on the smooth road to gain a few precious minutes. Of course, the police had broadcast his position over their radios, but there was nothing he could do about that. He had to handle one disaster at a time.

Hastily cutting across a used-car lot, the soldier then zigzagged through a maze of alleys and side streets until coming to the top of a sweeping hill. Turning off his engine, Bolan coasted down the back street, applying the brakes only when necessary. His speed became quite considerable, and he startled a sweaty cook hauling out some trash, along with numerous street cats, before reaching an enclosed backyard. There was laundry drying on the lines, and he appropriated serviceable clothes. That looked to be in his size. Then he grabbed a black wool blanket.

Using his belt knife to slit a hole in the worn fabric, Bolan donned it as a makeshift poncho and rode away again, feeling somewhat obvious. However, nobody he passed on the streets or sidewalks seemed to pay any attention to the big man in the strange cape riding the battered Ducati.

At the end of the street, Bolan discovered a large shopping mall overlooking the beach. A real beach this time, with white sand that had obviously been imported from somewhere else. There were numerous people playing in the surf or tanning on blankets. Many comely Italian girls weren't wearing tops to their swimsuits, in the fashion of most Europeans. At the jiggling display of healthy youth, Bolan allowed himself to be distracted for a moment, then jerked back to reality at the approaching murmur of the Ferraris.

Even if he could traverse the soft sand, a seawall cut off his access to the beach, and the police were coming down the only road. Left with a single other route, Bolan kicked the Ducati alive once more to ride slowly through the café, trying to avoid hitting the customers, while making as big a mess in his wake as possible, knocking over umbrellas and empty chairs.

Numerous people screamed at him in numerous languages, and one large man threateningly brandished a wine bottle. Bolan flashed the Beretta, and the man dropped the bottle and ran. Wise move.

It took the soldier precious seconds to blaze a safe trail through the morass of tables and reach open space once more. Meanwhile, the police sirens got steadily louder.

Trying not to draw any more attention, Bolan started driving leisurely along a shady street lined with little shops, until he heard the distant bark of a Beretta and felt the impact of the bullet on his back. Instantly, he surged forward, trying to build speed even while swerving in a random pattern. Damn, these Italian cops were good! It was no wonder the modern-day Mafia feared them so much.

Talking on a cell phone, a beautiful woman strolled out of a candle shop. She was carrying a wicker basket of fresh bread on her arm, and pushing a baby carriage.

Veering, Bolan struck a telephone pole, the impact making him temporarily lose control of the speeding bike, while his knee went numb.

Fighting to regain control, he realized this time it was hopeless, and he dived from the vehicle. Toppling over, the Ducati skidded along until it crashed into a fountain. The limestone basin shattered as if it were glass, and the water gushed out across the brick-lined street. On top of the fountain, a bronze statue of a man brandishing a sword started to wobble, then came straight down on the Ducati, flattening it. The fuel tank burst and the gasoline ignited from the sparking engine, but the fire was almost immediately extinguished by the flood of water.

By now, everybody in the piazza was screaming and running away, except for a couple heavily muscled stevedores, who calmly rose from a tiny table outside a tavern and started walking toward Bolan, cracking their massive knuckles.

Getting to his feet, the soldier took refuge behind a vehicle illegally parked in a handicap zone, and put a burst from the Beretta in front of the two men. The silenced pistol coughed gently, the 9 mm rounds ricocheted noisily off the cobblestones, but that only made the pair approach faster.

Just for a moment, Bolan considered putting a round into their legs, then decided the risk of accidentally killing them was too great, and instead decided to unleash the Desert Eagle.

Turning to look up the street, Bolan squeezed off a shot, and the wooden block under the wheel of a small fruit cart exploded into splinters. Even as the owner made a desperate grab for the handle, the cart lurched and started forward, shaking and clattering on the uneven bricks. Apples and bananas went flying, along with bottles of spring water and an astounding amount of loose change.

At its rapidly approach, the burly stevedores paused, then started to turn away. The fruit cart hit a depression and flipped over, sending a wild corona of colorful shrapnel pelting across the piazza.

Taking advantage of the distraction, Bolan was already inside the Bugatti, trying to hot-wire the ignition. Incredibly, the determined stevedores were on the move again, this time armed with wooden table legs, and scowling as if they fully intended to murder him right there in the street. Which they probably did, Bolan realized in cold certainty. In a town this small, they might very well be relatives of the fruit dealer, who was screaming for the police at the top of his lungs.

Just then, the motorcycle police arrived. Seeing the squashed fruit, they immediately braked, trying to avoid the splattered mess. But their tires slipped on the juicy pulp, and the bikes toppled over. Expertly, the drivers dived off and rolled away as both machines slid out of control.

With the engine still running, one motorcycle smashed into a bookstore, cracking the window, and the other went directly into a fuel pump of a corner gas station. In a strident crunch of metal, the pump was ripped from the island—but nothing gushed from the broken fuel lines. Inside the station the fat man behind the counter sighed in relief and released his hand from the bright red emergency cut-off button.

Revving the Bugatti, Bolan hit the gas pedal and raced away from the piazza, just as the police officers pulled out their sidearms and began banging out a steady barrage of copper-jacketed lead. The 9 mm rounds pounded the old Bugatti, removing the sideview mirror and knocking loose two hubcaps.

Ducking low in the seat, Bolan fishtailed the vehicle to try to throw off their aim. But the cops hit it twice in the trunk and then took out the rear window before he was able to swing around a stone wall for protection.

Circling the shopping mall, Bolan skirted the beach, then took a fork in the road back to the highway. But this time he headed north, hoping to avoid any roadblocks the police may have set up earlier. Unfortunately, the battered

Bugatti stood out from the rest of the traffic. He needed another vehicle immediately.

A dozen plans flickered through his mind, and Bolan chose one involving the least possibility of harming innocent civilians. Taking the next exit, he headed directly for downtown Palermo, and the main headquarters of the Guardia di Finanza.

CHAPTER FOURTEEN

Dakar, Senegal

Maintaining formation, the three Hercules transports flew at top speed over the Atlantic Ocean. Below the aircraft, the shiny waves were quickly becoming darker, and choppy, sure signs that land was near.

"And there it is." Slvanna Svanna exhaled in relief, both hands tight on the wheel. Her silvery-white hair had become loose during the long flight, and now hung freely down her back, the ends swaying with her every motion.

"Exactly on course, and on schedule," Thorodensen said, checking their flight path. "Well done, indeed."

"More luck than skill," Svanna replied with unaccustomed honesty.

Located on the extreme western edge of the African continent, Senegal was a well-known hotbed of criminal activity. Nothing conducted locally, of course, but with the right connections, anything could be purchased along the dockyards of Dakar, from advanced weaponry to slaves. Those were mostly white females these days, many of them teenagers from Western countries.

"You choose our base of operations very well, sir," Svanna said. "Fuel cells to the west, weapons to the right… everything we need is on the equator, close at hand and ripe for the taking!"

"Readiness is everything," Thorodensen said. He went

back to checking their position on the charts. There were radar beacons for the big commercial flights coming and going from Dakar International, but this was a more covert assignation, and he was forced to use dead reckoning. "Let's see, there's a buoy near a rocky island.... Check. And two tall smoke stacks from a meat processing plant to the northeast...again check..."

Folding away the chart, Thorodensen said, "Head for that river. Stop at the first dockyard."

"Aye, aye, skipper."

"That's navy talk. We're in a plane."

"But it's a seaplane, right?"

"I should have brought along Hoxha," he muttered, picking up the hand mike. "Beta and Gamma, this is Alpha. I'll arrange for the delivery, you keep distant and prepared for trouble. Over."

"Gamma to Alpha. Sir, what if something does go wrong, over."

"Then release the mustard gas, steal the torpedoes and give us a burial at sea," Thorodensen directed bluntly. "This mission is more important than any one of us. Understood?"

There was a short crackle of static.

"Gamma to Alpha, understood, sir. Wilco, over."

Her face half masked by hair, Svanna glanced sideways. "'Wilco'? I do not know that word."

"It is an affirmative. Short for 'we will comply.'"

"Ah. Very strange is English," Svanna said with a frown. "Complex, and many weird spellings. I much prefer Icelandic."

"As do I, my friend," Thorodensen replied, taking control·of the plane for their final approach.

Setting down in the murky harbor, the three Hercules coasted along together for a while, then separated, Beta and Gamma staying in the deep water, ready to leave at a moment's notice, or to attack.

Taking his time, Thorodensen parked the airplane at an old wooden dock. Even from this location, he could see that the wharf was covered with packing crates of assorted sizes, and he could even begin to guess which of them were for Penumbra.

Meanwhile, Svanna tried not to compare this African location with Sheepshead Bay in Brooklyn, and failed. It was a dump, plain and simple.

"Company, two o'clock," Thorodensen said, turning off the engines and locking the propellers.

Trying not to be obvious, Svanna glanced sideways out the copilot window. There was nobody on the wharf, or dock, but on the roof of the closest warehouse there had to be an easy dozen men, a few black, but most white, and all of them heavily armed with assault rifles, pistols and machetes.

"We should have brought along Gunnar," she muttered, checking the draw of the Glock tucked into her belt. The 9 mm machine pistol had been appropriated from the pirate arsenal, and her jacket pockets bulged with spare magazines.

Turning on the running lights, Thorodensen almost smiled. "Those were just to scare away the locals. The black market thrives on repeat customers, just like any other business. We're quite safe…as along as the Russian thinks this is merely the start of a long and highly profitable arrangement."

Removing the safety harness, he stood and stretched. "As an ambassador, I have done something similar many times before, over hotly contested treaties."

That seemed to somewhat reassure the woman, and she followed him down to the main deck. Six of the largest members of Penumbra were gathered there, armed similarly to the guards on the warehouse roof—with rifles and pistols, knives and grenades, along with full body armor. Two stood beside a motorized cart of the kind used to transport diesel engines or generators. However, this day it was heavily loaded with a dozen large steel trunks, each bound with thick chains.

Leaving one man onboard as a guard, Thorodensen led the others down a bouncing plank to the dock, and on to the warehouse. The motorized cart nearly veered into the water at one point, but the man driving it swerved in time, and there was no damage done.

As Thorodensen and his entourage approached, the entire front of the warehouse slid aside to reveal a door. Standing inside the building were five people, four men and a woman.

The man in front of the others was dressed in a white linen suit, with a matching Panama hat. His face was badly scarred, a streak of white cutting across a full mustache. A huge revolver of unknown design was tucked into a leather holster at his hip, the grip facing outward for a reverse draw.

Then Thorodensen recognized the weapon from a forbidden list issued by Interpol. It was a Russian-made Pfeifer Zeliska .600 revolver, the most powerful handgun in the world, and impossible for most people to use without blowing off their own face. He smiled. The gun alone identified this as the man in charge, Colonel Pyotr Belgurovski, formerly of the Spetsnaz, the elite special forces for the defunct Soviet Union.

The other men were obviously workers, their clothing rough and worn. But their weapons gleamed with fresh oil, and each had a certain aura that Thorodensen recognized as the confident air of a seasoned killer. These weren't novices in the art of dealing wholesale death.

For just a flickering moment, Thorodensen wished that Gunnar had indeed come along. There were few people in the world who could match his growing insanity, and any trained professional would fear that. Fear was always a good card to have on the table for any negotiation.

On the other hand, the woman with them was…unique. Even as a trained diplomat, Thorodensen was hard-pressed to find any phrase to describe her that didn't involve the word *ugly*.

She wore no makeup of any kind and was very bony, with ropy muscles that bulged from too much exercise, the mark of an endorphin junkie. She wore loose combat trousers and a skintight T-shirt that showed off her nearly complete lack of breasts. Her pale brown hair was cropped in a military buzz cut, a gold tooth gleamed in her mouth and a scarf tied around her throat almost hid a puckered scar that went all the way around. Her hands were empty, but two Heckler & Koch pistols were tucked into her belt, along with a sheathed knife. A second knife jutted from her left boot.

Privately, Thorodensen recognized the scar on her neck as the mark of a noose. She had been hanged, but survived. Intimidating.

"King Agamemnon," Colonel Belgurovski said loudly.

"Argos," Thorodensen replied.

"Welcome to Dakar!" Colonel Belgurovski said with a wide grin, spreading his arms. "Ident codes are such a bore, but a necessary prerequisite for new business, eh?"

"As you say, a bore," Thorodensen replied politely.

"Please allow me to introduce my head of security, Ludmilla Moscow."

The woman gave an incoherent grunt.

"A Russian with the last name of Moscow?" Svanna asked curiously.

Moscow fixed the Icelander with a stare that sent a chill down her spine. "Nickname," she growled.

"But come along, sir! Come along!" Belgurovski said, turning with a wave. "You must be eager to see the merchandise."

"Yes, I am, Colonel."

"No titles, please! Just call me Pyotr."

"Thorod…Thor. Just Thor."

"Like the god of war, eh?"

He chuckled. "The ancient Norse god of thunder, but close enough."

There were numerous stacks of crates on the wharf, but the colonel went directly to a pile alongside the warehouse wall. A guard pulled off the tarpaulin to reveal a stack of long wooden cases, eerily resembling coffins.

Thorodensen blinked. No, those actually were coffins.

"Coffins?" Svanna asked incredulously.

"An excellent way to move material past border guards," Belgurovski said with a grin.

"Nobody bothers the dead, even in Africa," Moscow added. She had a surpassingly sweet voice, almost musical.

Thorodensen gave no reaction to that, and Svanna coughed to hide a laugh. It was no wonder Moscow didn't like to talk. A voice like that, coming out of her skeletal face, was comical, and seriously reduced her menacing air of reproach.

Taking a pry bar from a shelf, one of the guards opened a coffin. Inside was a torpedo with a blunt end, the crown of the prow rising and falling in an irregular pattern. Thorodensen knew it was this strange shape that caused a cavitation effect underwater that formed a vacuum. Propelled by a rocket engine, the Russian Squall torpedo was fully capable of reaching the staggering speed of 300 mph.

The mathematics and science were far beyond his understanding, but Thorodensen had seen the weapon work, and read stolen reports from both the United States Navy, and the Russian special forces. The Squall was very much real, and feared around the world.

Of course, such radical technology had many limitations. The Squall had to be hard-fired into the water, already moving at 100 mph. Too slow and it sank, then exploded. Too fast and it burst apart, then exploded. But under the right conditions, the torpedo was nearly unstoppable.

Sheathed in Swiss APC armor, hidden by a NATO sonar scrambler, and powered by NASA fuel cells, it will be unstoppable, Thorodensen mentally added, running a hand over the satiny smooth hull of the deadly weapon. Invisible, and invincible! The perfect weapon for smashing England forever!

"May I take it that you approve?" the colonel asked.

"Yes, I do," Thorodensen said with a smile, then snapped his fingers. Two of his people drove the cart closer, turned off the electric motor and removed the chains.

Belgurovski nodded, and two of his guards walked over to open a trunk. Inside were rows of gold bullion stacked to the lid. The next seven held the same, but the last two contained other material: trays of jewelry, and stacks of cash from a dozen different nations.

"Now that's a lovely sight," the colonel said, as a guard handed him a gold bar. He hefted it in his hand. As always, the precious metal sent a tingle through his body, even more pleasant than the weight of a woman's breast.

"If these are good, then we have a deal," he said.

Taking the gold, Moscow knelt to pull out a small kit

from a pocket and start to run a few basic tests. A man began riffling through the cash, while another went directly to the jewelry and began studying the assorted items with a magnifying glass.

"They're good," Thorodensen stated, as a seagull flew by overhead. Everybody glanced up for a brief second, then back at one another, hands on weapons.

"Birds," the colonel said apologetically, releasing his grip on the Pfeifer Zeliska.

"The cash and jewels are real," his man announced.

"As is the gold," Moscow said in an oddly strained voice, acid fumes rising from where she had just tested the purity of the bullion.

"Excellent!" Petrov said with a broad smile. "Pierre, load the merchandise onto the plane, please!"

The man touched two fingers to his forehead and strode away.

"Thor, it was a pleasure meeting you," Belgurovski said. "I hope we can do more business soon."

"As soon as possible," Thorodensen lied, shaking his proffered hand.

The transfer of goods took only a few minutes. Unwilling to test the limits of his good fortune, Thorodensen departed immediately. His plane was still skimming the waves when it was joined by the two other Hercules, and they disappeared together into the night.

"ALL RIGHT, what was wrong with the gold?" Belgurovski asked, turning away from the ocean.

"Some of this gold already belongs to us," Moscow said, handing him a bar. "I recognize the marks."

"Do you?" he said, rubbing a thumb over a small depression in the lower corner. His people used the same molds for melting stolen gold into new bars, as his father had fifty years ago. With his love of the metal, the colonel knew every tiny imperfection in the mold better than his own face.

"We have not made any bars in several months," he said thoughtfully, hefting the gold. "Could this be from that batch we sent to your cousin Fernando for that last delivery of slave girls?"

"Yes, it could."

"Is it on every bar?"

"No, about half. The rest bear the royal crest of the United Kingdom."

That caught his attention. "The British shipment that sank?" Belgurovski said, his smile turning into a frown. "Then it would appear that Thor and his people sank a convoy of British warships to hijack a huge shipment of bullion, then somehow managed to involve Fernando in their scheme. I assume they killed him if they have his gold."

Looking back out to sea, the colonel scowled. "So the question is, what happened to the rest of the British gold? Did they lose it or purchase something else first? Something even more valuable than the torpedoes…" His voice trailed away in thought.

"I don't know and I don't care," Moscow growled, reaching for the knife on her belt. "They killed my cousin!"

"Most likely, yes."

"Then I want blood!" she yelled, losing control for a moment.

"Which is only right and proper," the colonel said soothingly. "But first we must know what happened to Fernando, as well as all that lovely British gold. Agreed?"

"Agreed," she muttered, releasing the knife.

"Good." Pulling out a small box from his pocket, Belgurovski checked the signal it was receiving. The device was a remote control detonator, his own invention. If buyers should decide to attack to try to get back their funds, he simply pressed a button and the C-4 high explosives hidden inside the coffins containing their goods would promptly detonate. It was a fail-safe against thieves. However, it also worked as a tracking module.

"They're flying due west," the colonel said, minutely adjusting the controls.

"Straight for Fernando's island," Moscow growled.

"Which will make it easy to find them." He tucked away the box. "Now, if they merely stole the gold from Fernando, then we do nothing. It is not our concern if he cannot protect his own property."

"Of course," she said. "But what if they killed him first?"

"Then we cut out their hearts as revenge, and take back our merchandise," Belgurovski replied. "But only after we find out what happened to all that British gold."

"That blonde woman is mine to question," Moscow said a little too quickly, too eagerly.

"As you wish." Turning, he strode for the warehouse. "Pierre, break out the hovercraft! I want fifty men fully armed and ready to leave in five minutes!"

Palermo, Sicily

NEARING THE CITY, Bolan wasn't overly surprised to pass a strip mall with a supermarket, tanning salon, liquor store and all the usual niceties. The locals didn't want the ancient purity of their beloved island sullied by the modern world, yet they still wanted every convenience possible. But that seemed to be the eternal dichotomy of Italy—they wanted nothing to change, but everything to be brand-new.

Heading downtown, Bolan passed the headquarters of

the Guardia di Finanza and continued on to city hall. Driving around the block, he soon found the expected parking garage located nearby for the use of politicians. Going to the middle level, he parked the bedraggled Bugatti near the stairwell, and left the engine running for the ease of any would-be thieves.

Heading to the next level, he removed the security camera with a single round from the silenced Beretta, used his EM scanner to disable the alarm on a Lamborghini, and climbed inside. Unlike the old Bugatti, the ignition lock of the Lamborghini was very sophisticated, so he simply smashed it open with the butt of the Desert Eagle, hot-wired the circuits, then used the EM scanner to make the sensor believe that the chipped key had been inserted.

The massive 12-cylinder engine started with a gentle purr, and Bolan eased out of the garage, paying the guard at the booth a hefty fine for losing his admission ticket.

Easing onto the main thoroughfare, Bolan did the same as everybody else and completely ignored the traffic laws. Every driver seemed to be trying to ram the next vehicle, and things got rather exciting before Bolan managed to leave downtown and return to the strip mall.

At the supermarket, he purchased a double espresso, a meatball sandwich and a prepaid cell phone. Then he went to a gas station and filled the tank. Just in case.

Eating and drinking while he drove, Bolan headed far outside of the city, away from any possible electronic sensors, before parking at a rest stop. Getting out of the car, he used the public restroom, then sat beneath a spreading olive tree and placed an international call.

The rest area was perched on a cliff overlooking a rocky beach, a true postcard view. A gentle sea breeze ruffled the leaves, and ripe olives fell to the ground with a thump. Picking one up, Bolan inspected the hard fruit, then tossed it away. Olives had be treated in several different ways before they were anything close to being edible. A fresh olive had the consistency of a coconut, and was about as tasty as a nine-volt battery.

As the expensive minutes ticked away, Bolan watched the bar on the cell phone rapidly descend toward zero. But just before he was about to be disconnected, he heard a series of hard clicks, and the phone suddenly registered unlimited time.

"Yeah," Hal Brognola demanded gruffly.

"It's me," Bolan replied, resting his back against the smooth bark of the tree.

"Damn glad to hear that you're still alive," Brognola said. "I heard some wild stories about NATO shooting you down in Tunisia!"

"Close. It was the other people, Penumbra. Except that we lived."

"We?"

"A friend came along. She's caring for a sick brother," Bolan said succinctly.

"Understood," Brognola replied.

"At the moment I need a Bear," Bolan told his old friend. Aaron "the Bear" Kurtzman was the chief computer wizard at Stony Man, a master hacker. There were few computer experts his equal anywhere.

"Not many friendlies in that part of the world," Brognola said slowly. "Or at least not many who aren't nestled in a well-cushioned pocket of a dark hand."

Bolan grunted at that. The Black Hand was a very old term for the Mafia. Brognola was showing his age and his intelligence at the same time.

"But I do know a woman, a dog lover," he continued. "A mirror expert, to your west. Skinny little lady, no glasses."

A mirror expert meant Bolan should reverse everything

Brognola said. Okay, there was a computer hacker to the east, fat, tall, a man who wore glasses. Bolan wasn't sure what the dog lover comment meant. The hacker liked cats? Maybe his name was Katz, or something similar.

"Is there a call sign?" Bolan asked.

Brognola gave him a phrase to memorize. "Anything else?"

"Not at the moment," he said, terminating the call. Then he tapped in the number for information, asked in Italian the show times for a local movie theater, then closed the cell phone and tossed it off the cliff. It dropped for a long time, then hit the rocks below and disintegrated into its component pieces. Nobody could ever trace the call now.

Returning to the Lamborghini, Bolan checked the glove box for a map, and spread it out to look for what Brognola had been talking about. Something about computers to the east. He was already on the east coast, so east would actually mean northeast, or southeast....

Spotting a name, Bolan smiled. There it was, the little town of Catania, the home of Catania University, the oldest and most respected college in Italy. How Brognola had that information at his fingertips, Bolan had no idea, but his friend had never let him down before. There was a very simple reason why Hal was one of the top cops in America. He was the best.

The drive to Catania was short and rather enjoyable. The stolen Lamborghini hummed along the coast road, and Bolan finished his meal while enjoying the fresh salty air. The wide Ionian Sea stretched to the horizon like a blue carpet, with small sailing ships and colossal freighters moving in stately grace across the azure waves.

Reaching the outskirts of the college town, he swung past the busy dockyard, to circle around a centuries-old Roman fort that had visiting hours posted, and a fast food restaurant specializing in genuine American home cooking.

Mount Etna, a live volcano, dominated the horizon, fleecy white clouds hovering around the icy cap on top. It was very beautiful, and boasted some of the best skiing in the world. However, every now and then Etna erupted in molten geysers of red-hot lava that poured down the sloping sides and rushed headlong into the sea, destroying everything in their way. But a few months later, everything was picturesque and lovely again.

Parking the car in a lot, Bolan watched as a laughing group of German tourists ambled by, their arms draped with heavy fur parkas, skis, boots and poles.

Shaking his head, Bolan turned away in wry amusement. To each his or her own.

Purchasing a camera and a city map, he trod the streets of the city, trying to blend in with the milling crowds. The camera around his neck helped the disguise, since it was the international sign for tourist.

Curiously, there were a lot of Americans wandering along the winding streets, but an equal amount of French and Japanese, plus a dozen other assorted nationalities. Which was not too surprising. Catania was a historic city. A couple centuries earlier, it had been flattened by an earthquake when Mount Etna erupted. However, the incredibly stubborn citizens had used the broken rubble of the town to completely rebuild their beloved city exactly has it had been before the quake, which explained the millions of tiny cracks in walls that seemed strong enough to resist cannonballs. That alone was enough to make it a tourist destination, the indestructible city of Catania.

Whistling through gold-capped teeth, a police officer strolled by, swinging a blackwood baton from the end of a worn leather strap. He stopped to give Bolan a hard stare.

Smiling widely, the soldier lifted his camera to ask a silent question. The police officer did nothing for a moment, then tolerantly struck a pose and waited for him to take his picture. Touching the baton to his cap, the cop strolled away, stopping briefly to ticket a car parked in a fire zone.

Taking his time going around the corner, Bolan waited a full minute before continuing onward. The local cops were either fully in the employ of the Mafia, or fanatical hardliners sworn to crush their ancient enemy. At the moment, he wanted nothing to do with either.

A thousand-year-old obelisk in a small piazza directed him to the Latin Quarter, and soon he saw the old stone edifice of Catania University. Located just off a public square, the university was a bustling place with students from every walk of life, young and old, rich and poor. Some were dressed in the very latest fashions, while others were wearing rebel chic, blue jeans, T-shirts and bikers boots. The only unifying aspect was that everybody had a cell phone.

There were no police in sight here, only some campus security who seemed more interested in talking about sports than watching for potential troublemakers, which was fine with Bolan.

The marble entrance hall to the university was cool and well-illuminated, the light coming from electric fixtures and huge bay windows. The floor was a mosaic of wild shapes and it took him a few moments to recognize the spirals as the ancient elements of matter—earth, water, fire and wind. He was walking over the past to reach the future. Bolan wasn't much for symbolism, but appreciated the effort.

Checking a wall directory in the lobby, he found the location of the main computer lab, and started for bank of elevators. On the way, a group of young women walked by in designer skirts so short they were almost belts. Along with most of the males in the hallway, Bolan politely paused to admire the view.

Surprisingly, a dusky beauty with ebony hair smiled back at him and winked. With a pretend sigh, Bolan touched the third finger of his left hand, where a married man would wear a wedding ring. She shrugged in return and blew a kiss, then hurried off to rejoin her friends. They all started giggling, and glanced backward as Bolan headed for the elevator.

"If you change your mind…" the young woman called out in heavily accented English.

Stepping into the elevator, Bolan scowled in disapproval at the pretty student and sternly wagged a finger. All of them laughed while they walked away. Bolan grinned as the doors closed.

On the bottom floor, he walked into a cold, sterile hall, but then cold was the best friend of a computer. It helped the primary circuits work faster.

Another directory lead him to a small office at the end of the wide stone corridor. To the left were a dozen cubicles filled with people hunched over computer monitors and industrially typing away, or talking on telephones. To the right was a clear Plexiglas door, where a shiny brass plate bore the name Dr. Philip Geraldo, along with a long string of alphabet clusters to show his numerous degrees.

Pushing open the office door, Bolan wasn't surprised to find the air inside even colder, so much so that his breath was visible. Beyond a second Plexiglas wall was a tall plump man sitting at a complex console of monitors, switches, dials and an oddly curved keyboard.

Softly, almost imperceptibly, Bolan could feel a faint vibration in the floor from a working supercomputer. It was probably buried deep underground, safe from any possible thermal pollution. The Plexiglas barriers were unusual, but he assumed they had something to do with keeping in the cold without disturbing the beauty of the century-old building.

Knocking on the inner door, Bola entered without waiting for a response. "Excuse me, Dr. Geraldo?" he asked, closing the door.

"Get out, I'm busy," the man replied, his hands never ceasing their typing on the keyboard.

"I'm a friend of Hal Brognola," Bolan said.

The typing ceased instantly, and Dr. Geraldo spun in the chair, stopping himself by planting both feet on the floor. He was wearing a heavy denim shirt, old-fashioned overalls and oversize sneakers. A pair of wireless glasses perched on his head, and a silver wedding band gleamed from his left hand. Whether it was platinum, silver or simple hematite, Bolan had no idea.

"What an interesting thing to say as an introduction," Dr. Geraldo commented, his hand resting on the mouse near the keyboard. A finger lay on the right-side button. "And how is my old friend?"

"Hal says that you still owe him nine hundred million lira for that round of beer, ya cheap Neapolitan bastard."

Bursting into laughter, Dr. Geraldo took his finger off the mouse and rose to offer his hand. They shook, and Bolan was surprised by the remarkable strength of the computer scientist.

"It has been a long time since Harold Brognola sent anybody to seek my help," Dr. Geraldo said with a laugh, his big belly shaking. "And the last was a tall black fellow who chewed a pipe and challenged everything I said!"

Yes, Bolan knew that man well. "That would have been Professor Huntington Wethers, another mutual friend. Tops in his field."

"So I assumed!" Geraldo chuckled. "And hunt me the professor did! I was wounded like a deer, through the heart, with his cold logic." He reclaimed the chair, and it squeaked under his weight. "After so many years of students kissing my ass, it was a breath of fresh air to be told that I wrong about anything!"

Then he frowned. "Even though I totally disagreed with the Yankee!"

In spite of the pressure of time, Bolan felt himself warming to the genuinely friendly scientist.

"So, what is it Harold said I can for you, Mr...." He paused to gesture in the air. "Smith... Jones..."

"Cooper, Matt Cooper."

He smiled. "Pleased to meet you."

Reaching into the his pocket, Bolan carefully extracted the damp handkerchief and took out the memory chip.

Scowling deeply, Geraldo accepted it like a ticking bomb. "Where has this been?" he muttered. "Down the sewers of Rome?"

"Swallowed by a NATO soldier."

"To keep it safe from the rightful owners, I would assume," Geraldo said slowly.

"No, they were anybody but the rightful owner."

"I see." He frowned again. "Stomach acid is very corrosive. There has been significant damage...." Lifting the lid of a small machine, he placed the tiny chip on a glowing gridwork and lowered the lid once more. On the console, one of the monitors flashed to life, now displaying the chip as it came apart to reveal the inner network of microcircuits.

"Cheap design," Geraldo muttered. "Japanese? No, South Korean. Mass produced... This is from a cell phone...."

"Can you recover any data?" Bolan asked, pulling a chair closer.

"That I cannot say yet," Geraldo replied, sliding his glasses down and moving closer to the monitor. Taking a light pen, he started drawing on the glass, creating new connections inside the virtual display.

"What kind of a supercomputer is this? I've seen a Cray and a Dell Thunderbird…."

"This is an IBM Blue Gene, the most powerful computer in the world."

"The Dell is faster."

"Faster does not mean more accurate!"

Diplomatically, Bolan conceded the point, even though he knew of several hackers in Virginia who would most strenuously disagree. "Can you help me?"

"Already working on it," Geraldo said, minutely adjusting the complex controls.

"Doctor, lives are in the balance," Bolan urged gently.

"Hunger does not make pasta cook faster," Geraldo stated.

Which Bolan translated as "go away, I'm busy." There was a knock on the outer wall, and the soldier turned to see a pretty woman wearing thick horn-rimmed glasses sliding some envelopes through a slot in the Plexiglas. Easing his stance, Bolan smiled, and she smiled in return, showing unsuspected dimples. Then she blushed and hurried away, clutching the rest of the mail tightly to her chest.

"You seem to have made a conquest there." Geraldo chuckled, typing silently on the keyboard. "Quilla does not take to most people. She is what you call an acquired taste."

"Quilla?"

"A common name here."

"Great legs."

"Absolutely! Not to mention her magnificent breasts. But then—"

"All breasts are magnificent?" Bolan hazarded.

"Certainly! How could the good Lord have made them otherwise?" Geraldo said, drawing new lines on the monitor. A section of the broken chip pulsed to life, and numbers began to rapidly scroll along the bottom of the screen. He stopped typing as a flashing red icon appeared on the monitor.

"What is this?" he hissed suspiciously. "Is this chip live? No, of course not." He looked over his shoulder. "Are you making a call on a cell phone?"

"I don't have one," Bolan replied. "Why? What's going on?"

"Something is trying to send a signal to the outside world," Geraldo said, glancing around. "It is blocked, of course. These are not just thermal walls, they are also a Faraday cage, protection from students trying to use wireless technology to steal tests answers or change their grades." He seemed embarrassed. "Such things happen."

"In America, too."

"No EM signal can enter or leave my little world here. But something is certainly trying."

In a cold rush, Bolan slowly reached into his shirt and extracted the Saint Christopher medal. Hoping he was wrong, he dropped it to the floor and crushed it under his heel. There was a crunch of hard plastic.

Lifting his shoe, Bolan cursed at the sight of smashed electronics that he recognized as a standard tracer circuit.

"Get everybody out of the building," he commanded, going to the wall and slapping the fire alarm.

Instantly, lights began to flash and a siren started to howl. Down the hallway, people leaped from their desks and hurried to the closest exit.

"What are you doing?" Geraldo demanded, removing his glasses.

"Keep working," Bolan growled, pulling the Beretta.

Just then, the air vents slowed and went still, then the ceiling lights winked out. Flashing yellow lights lurched into operation, showing the way to the exit doors.

"This is impossible! The college has a power source independent of the city," Geraldo said, slamming both hands on the dead keyboard.

"I've been followed," Bolan told him, clicking off the safety and working the slide to chamber a round.

There was only one possible explanation for the tracer in the medallion: Salvatore was a traitor and working for Penumbra. That explained a lot of odd things that had kept happening during their running battles with the Icelanders—missed shots, the thermite and such. Then Bolan cursed himself for a fool. He had left the wounded sergeant in her care! That meant Liberman was dead.

There was a muted ding and Bolan heard the elevator doors open. Around the corner came Major Salvatore, closely followed by four large men dressed in black suits, their hands holding automatic Heckler & Koch G-11 caseless assault rifles. She was in civilian clothing now, and her new companions weren't cheap street soldiers this time. Bolan knew the type at sight. Cold merciless eyes and a cool demeanor—they were professional hit men for the Mob.

"Kill them both," Salvatore said, working the arming bolt on an MP-5 machine gun, the barrel tipped with an acoustical silencer.

Grabbing Geraldo by the collar, Bolan dragged him to the floor just as the hit men swung up their Heckler & Koch assault rifles and unleashed a hammering barrage of mm steel-jacketed lead.

CHAPTER FIFTEEN

Compose Island, Brazil

A prolonged rumble of stentorian proportions shook the entire tropical island. Monkeys screamed in terror from the trees, and a thousand parrots took flight, looking like a living rainbow trying to return to the blue sky.

At the extreme end of the island, the umbilical cables disconnected from the Russian rocket, and it slowly rose from the launch pad to climb ever faster into the clear sky. A huge fan of fire washed across the launching area, directed out to sea by resilient tunnels of ceramic brick and ferroconcrete.

Situated off the northern coast of Brazil, the little known Compose Island sat like a green jewel in a shimmering blue sea. Most of it was wild jungle full of little monkeys, flowering vines, spiders the size of dinner plates and more snakes than could be counted in a lifetime. But past a low series of hillocks left by an ancient volcano was a smooth expanse of hard ground that extended all the way to the eastern shore and its white sand beaches.

A long time ago, the tropical island had been a secret paradise for the rich and elite from Rio. But then the government took over and converted it into the primary launch facility for Brazilian Space Agency. Exploration and scientific research weren't their primary concern, making a profit was, and most of the rockets they launched carried telecommunication satellites for cable networks, or spy satellites for the smaller members of the international community.

However, after the 9/11 attacks in America, members of the agency decided to build a more public launch facility on the extreme southern coast of Brazil, and simply remove this one from the maps. The project took millions of dollars and several years to complete. But eventually information about the island was erased from the internet, with every mention on every web page completely eradicated.

Gantries rose taller than the palm trees, and swarms of personnel in NBC suits trundled about relaying delicate electronic components and dragging along insulated fuel lines. Radar dishes along the hillside steadily tracked the climbing rocket, and the ground crew briefly cheered, then went back to their assorted jobs.

These days space travel was merely a business, with corporations paying enormous funds to have new, better, faster communication satellites put into orbit to replace the older models.

"What's next?" a technician asked, sliding off her fire resistant helmet. A wild explosion of ebony curls bounced free and cascaded down her back.

"How about a little private time in the fuel shed?" the man asked hopefully.

She scowled.

"Or we could have lunch," He quickly backpedaled with a grin. "After that we prep that Hungarian…ahem… weather satellite for launch this evening."

Fluffing out her hair with splayed fingers, the woman snorted. "Weather satellite, my ass," she stated. "Any idea what it really is?"

"No idea whatsoever," he said with a shrug. "And that

isn't our concern. The Hungarians pay on time and in cash, so we launch whatever they send us."

"Pay us enough and we'll put a dead whale into orbit," she said with a sigh, then stopped and tilted her head. "Do we have a shipment coming in today?"

"No, why?"

"I hear planes," she stated, cupping a hand to shield her eyes from the blazing sun. "A lot of them. Big planes…"

Coming in low and fast, barely skimming the waves, three Hercules transports appeared over the horizon, heading straight for the secret launch facility.

"Those are very big planes," the man agreed, taking advantage of the moment to step closer to the beautiful technician.

"Too damn big," she muttered, whipping out a cell phone and punching in the number for their main office in Brasília. She scowled when the screen remained blank. There weren't any bars at all, almost as if the call was being blocked somehow. But that wasn't possible…was it?

"Sound the spill alarm," she said quickly, a terrible sense of dread tingling down her spine.

"Do what?" he asked, puzzled.

She showed him the dead phone. "Sound the alarm for spilled fuel! Alert the base!"

"But they're just some cargo planes," he stated, then abruptly stopped.

The Hercules began dropping large round objects that thunderously exploded upon contact with the ground. Men and machines were sent flying with each fiery detonation, then a partially fueled Indonesian rocket broke free from its gantry to fall over. It hit the concrete apron and exploded into a fireball of gargantuan proportions, the flames licking out to reach the supposedly safe construction shack and communications building. A hundred windows shattered at the arrival of the shock wave, the pitiful screams of the people inside the buildings mercifully cut short.

Clawing for the radio on his belt, the man thumbed the transmit button, and a piercing howl came from the speakers.

"Jammed," he whispered. "They're jamming both radio and cell phones."

"We're a fucking launch facility, goddamn it!" she screamed, tightening both hands into fists. "What do they want here? We don't have anything of value!" Then she turned on him. "Do we?"

"No, nothing!" he stated, ducking as the airplanes zoomed overhead.

However, no bombs, or whatever the things were, dropped on the hillside, or in the jungle. Only the coastal facility was being hammered. Already a dozen small buildings were on fire, and the main field scattered with smoking bodies, smashed equipment and chunks of broken concrete.

Tears welled in the technician's eyes at the terrible sight of death and destruction. "What do you assholes want?" she screamed impotently at the planes began another bombing run. "Why are you here?"

LANDING AT THE AIRFIELD in a squeal of tires, the C-130 Hercules transport came to an easy stop, and the rear ramp cycled down. An Uberpanzer rolled onto the tarmac, Gunnar Eldjarm standing in the commander cupola with both hands on the grip of the 25 mm Bushmaster cannon.

"Head due south!" he said into a throat mike, then fired a brief burst of shells at a group of people running toward an idling Cessna plane. The high explosive shells tore the aircraft into fiery trash, along with the terrified scientists.

Rolling along an access road, the Uberpanzer slammed

open the locked gates and deliberately crushed the guard inside a small wooden kiosk as he took a picture of the APC with his cell phone.

"Fool," Eldjarm said in passing. "You should have run away!"

As the two Hercules continued the aerial bombardment, Eldjarm and his team rolled over the flaming debris and assorted destruction to reach a concrete blockhouse.

A single shell from the Bushmaster blew open the locked door, and Eldjarm stood guard in the cupola as a team of people swarmed inside. They soon returned with pushcarts loaded with sealed plastic boxes.

"Got them?" Eldjarm asked, studying the containers.

"Yes sir!" A man said with a grin, then fell back with blood on his shirt.

A dozen Brazilian security guards charged up from the beach came brandishing 4.5 mm Imbel caseless rifles. Taking aim as if on a target range, they knelt and fired, the angular rifles spitting flame.

As the hail of rounds peppered the Uberpanzer, Eldjarm swung the Bushmaster around and unleashed a long barrage of 25 mm shells.

The first dozen missed the cluster of security guards and only chewed up the sand in front of them. As they returned fire, more shells arrived dead on target, and they were annihilated in microseconds.

"Strip Dolf of anything incriminating, and load the damn fuel cell," Eldjarm commanded in a husky whisper.

His fingers tingled, his heart was racing and he physically ached to kill somebody again, anybody at all. He had never known this secret passion before, but now it had seized control of his life, and it was all that he wanted to do. Kill, and kill again.

Moving fast, the members of Penumbra packed the APC

with the plastic boxes bearing the famous logo of NASA from the United States of America.

Many years ago, NASA had created hydrogen fuel cells to supply clean electricity to space capsules, and then to the shuttles, and finally the International Space Station. Vilhjalms had tried to explain to Eldjarm how they worked, but all he could understand was that they had no moving parts, were absolutely silent and generated electrical power for months, with the only byproduct being clean, drinkable water. Absolutely amazing.

However, what worked in outer space would also work underwater.

Heading back to the airstrip, Eldjarm cursed as a bulky Huey helicopter lifted from the jungle and raced out to sea.

Probably trying to get beyond the radio jamming to call for help, he assumed. The markings on the hull were those of the Brazilian air force, not their space agency. Which meant Thorodensen had been wrong about the launch facility being protected only by the Brazilian AMX fighter-bombers they had destroyed in the first bombing run. A brief flicker of fear touch him, then Eldjarm dismissed the escaping helicopter. Even the crew were stupid enough to attack, how much of a real threat could one helicopter be?

Suddenly spinning, the Huey charged a Hercules and cut loose with a pair of M-60 machine guns, the tracer rounds visibly stitching across the blue sky. Immediately, the Hercules turned away, and the people inside responded with small arms, submachine guns and then a LAW rocket that missed the helicopter by only a couple yards.

Snarling in rage, Eldjarm swung up the Bushmaster and triggered a prolonged burst, even though he knew the helicopter was far outside the range of the 25 mm cannon.

With its M-60 machine guns still firing, the Huey launched a rocket from a pod attached to a landing rail. Banking hard, the Hercules tried to get out of the way, but was blown apart, burning wreckage tumbling into the beautiful sea.

"You dirty bastards," a member of Penumbra snarled, staring at the scene with open hatred.

"Come on, guys, get off the pot...." another muttered, a crate of NASA fuel cells still cradled in his hands. "Come on...."

As if in reply, three different types of SAM missiles spiraled up from the direction of the landing field and converged on the helicopter. Instantly, it began launching countermeasures, flares and chaff going everywhere. A radar-guided missile veered away, then so did a heat-seeker, but the other stayed on target, getting ever closer.

Eldjarm chuckled at the sight. The pirate arsenal had been well stocked with weaponry from a dozen nations. The pirates had been saving them to sell, but Eldjarm had wisely hauled along as much antiaircraft ordnance as possible on this mission just in case of trouble.

Dropping more flares and metallic chaff, the Brazilian helicopter attacked with both machine guns and rockets, swinging about wildly in an effort to escape when two more missiles rose to join the deadly aerial hunt. One of them was small and fast, the other large and slow.

With all the different exhaust trails mixing and converging, Eldjarm couldn't follow the details of the battle. But suddenly there was a huge explosion in the sky, and the fiery wreckage of the destroyed Huey plummeted back into sight. Tumbling and turning, it crashed on the white sand beach and exploded again.

"Okay, break time is over," Eldjarm commanded, releasing his grip on the Bushmaster. "Back to work! We've still got places to go, and millions to kill...."

Catania University, Sicily

THE FIRE ALARM WAS still honking as the hail of hot lead from the Black Aces slapped into the Plexiglas wall. But the 4.7 mm caseless rounds drilled into the soft plastic and stayed there.

Snarling in annoyance, Salvatore drew her MP-5 submachine gun and rattled off a long burst. The 9 mm steel-jacketed rounds punching through the outer wall, only to be caught by the second Plexiglas divider.

"Get out of my lab!" Dr. Geraldo bellowed from the floor, brandishing a stapler.

Rushing past the scientist, Bolan shoved the steel barrel of the Desert Eagle through the door handle, blocking it from opening. Then he rammed the muzzle of the Beretta 93-R out the mail slot and squeezed the trigger.

Caught in the act of reloading their weapons, the Mafia hit men dropped their rifles and jerked backward from the flurry of 9 mm Parabellum rounds, their expensive clothing ripping away to reveal the molded body armor underneath.

As they clawed for handguns inside their coats, Bolan switched weapons and coldly blew off their knees with .50 bone shredders from the thundering Desert Eagle. Cursing wildly, they fell, and Bolan stopped their cries with a single booming round to the face.

"There's more of them on the way, Matt!" Major Salvatore shouted, her back pressed tight against the transparent wall. She held a Glock 18 in both hands, palm on wrist in the style of a professional marksman.

"Hope they're better shots," Bolan replied, quickly reloading. She was using an odd grip for a 9 mm weapon.

Triggering short bursts from the Beretta, he was unable to train his weapons on her from this angle. The Desert Eagle could punch through the Plexiglas wall, but he knew in advance that she would also be wearing NATO body armor, and it would of much better quality than that worn by the hit men. Then again…

Firing twice, Bolan saw the slugs puncture the outer wall, and the major jerked at the arrival of the big bore rounds. But she didn't fall, nor was there any blood.

"Yes, it's Dragon Skin!" she shouted, with a little laugh. "Remember, I've seen you shoot!"

Bolan could see that she was starting to breathe heavily and flex her shoulders in pain. Even with a military-grade trauma pad underneath, not even Dragon Skin could prevent her from taking some damage, and he had deliberately shot the woman exactly where she had been wounded back in Tunisia.

Angrily firing the Glock at the ceiling, Salvatore tore loose a dozen acoustic tiles, only to reveal the solid granite ceiling. The soft lead rounds flattened against the ancient stone and ricocheted into the computer lab, doing scant damage.

"Try again, Toni! This particular building was built a hundred years ago to withstand earthquakes!" Bolan said to annoy her, then fired twice more through the wall. The first round hit her in the back, but she managed to spin out of the way of the second.

"I'm worse than any earthquake!" Taking refuge around the corner, Salvatore grabbed a fallen G-11 assault rifle, reloaded and raked the rows of desks in the main office with several bursts. The hail of 4.7 mm rounds destroyed laptops, spun away chairs and sent a blizzard of papers flying.

Then a man cursed and fell into view from behind a copy machine.

"Please..." he begged, displaying the bloody ruin of his hand. Several fingers were missing.

Without hesitation, she shot him in the face.

Jerking open the Plexiglas door, Bolan fired twice at the corner wall, but even the .50 rounds failed to achieve penetration.

Just then, a desk moved all by itself, the legs squeaking on the linoleum floor.

Firing in controlled bursts, Salvatore hammered it with 9 mm rounds, driving it backward along the floor. When the desk crashed into a huge decollator, there was a painful squawk, and Quilla stood with her arms raised.

"Please, I surrender!" she cried, tears on both cheeks. Then she flashed a hand forward, and something metallic spun across the room.

Bolan couldn't see around the corner, but he heard Salvatore cry out in pain. The Glock ripped into action, and she emptied the entire clip into the woman. Literally torn to pieces, Quilla collapsed behind the desk, leaving a wide crimson smear on the cracked wall.

Unexpectedly, the fire door slammed open and a police officer stepped into view, a flashlight in one hand and a drawn Beretta in the other.

"Run!" Bolan warned in Italian, but it was already too late.

As the beam came her way, Salvatore riddled the cop with 4.7 mm rounds and red geysers erupted over his body. The force of the caseless bullets pushed him back against the door, and he fell, sprawling halfway in the stairwell.

"There could be more fools on the way, or hiding under their desks," Salvatore growled, shoving a fresh clip into the G-11 rifle. "Just give me the chip, and nobody else has to die!"

"Is that why she's here?" Geraldo snarled, rising to grab a metal filing cabinet and awkwardly duck-walk it across the room to his console. Now protected by the cabinet, he sat down and started madly typing again.

As much as Bolan appreciated the efforts of the man, he could see the digital thermometer on the wall that registered the core temperature of the IBM supercomputer. With the power off, there was no more liquid nitrogen flowing. The machine was warming fast, and already dangerously close to crashing.

"Not going to happen, Penumbra!" Bolan shouted, shooting at a bubbling coffeemaker sitting on a side table covered with mugs and assorted snacks.

The glass pot exploded, spraying out hot coffee, and Salvatore cursed as she was splashed with the scalding contents. "So, I'm just a terrorist now, eh?" she muttered through clenched teeth.

"Surrender, and I give you my word you'll live to stand trial!"

"Not a chance in hell!" she snarled, triggering a long burst into the water cooler. The plastic jug didn't break, but the clear mountain spring water gushed out of the bullet holes. Flowing past the assorted corpses, the water took on a distinct reddish tint as it spread across the smooth linoleum.

Knowing his shoes would slip on the wet floor if he tried to rush around the corner to get the woman, Bolan had to quickly changed tactics and try something else. She was getting ready to leave, and unless he read Salvatore wrong, her departing act would be to toss in a grenade. That would kill everybody here, including him, but also remove any chance of her recovering the memory chip. Maybe it would be destroyed, maybe not. When she was ready to pay that price, all hell would break loose. Time to move.

Triggering single rounds from the Desert Eagle, Bolan smashed the hinges of the Plexiglas door. As it began to come loose, he grabbed the handle and started toward the ever-expanding puddle of pink water.

Turning the corner, Bolan saw Salvatore look up in surprise as she pulled the pin on a grenade. Her blouse was covered with blood, and a common letter opener protruded from her shoulder, just above the bulletproof body armor.

Firing around the door, Bolan got her twice in the chest with the Beretta. Driven backward, the major dropped the grenade as she clawed for the Glock. Shoving the door forward to fall on top of the woman, Bolan then stepped back around the corner, opened his mouth and covered his ears.

Less than a second later, a powerful explosion filled the office. Desks were flipped over, equipment erupted into pieces and ragged chunks of human flesh smacked into the wall.

Holding his breath against the billowing cloud of acrid smoke, Bolan proceeded back around the corner. Most of Major Salvatore was still intact under the Plexiglas door. However, her arms and legs were gone, ragged bits of the limbs strewed across the dirty floor.

"…Can't stop us…." Salvatore muttered through torn and bloody lips. "Still g-gonnna w-win…."

"We've already won," Bolan whispered soothingly. "Everything, all of it!"

Dreamily, Major Salvatore smiled. "Knew it'd w-work… j-just like…Norleans." With a shudder, she stopped trembling and went still forever.

"'Just like Norleans,'" Bolan repeated slowly, then comprehension flared. She had to have meant just like New Orleans, where an offshore oil rig had cracked a pipe and the spill polluted half the Gulf of Mexico, killing untold millions of fish and bankrupting hundreds of companies. It would take decades for the Gulf to recover.

Bolan suddenly knew this was what the Squall torpedoes were for…and the Uberpanzers. Replace the Russian armor with the lightweight Swiss ceramic, and the Squalls would be unstoppable, and even faster than ever, if that was possible. Send off a dozen of them into oil rigs around England, and the resulting spills would destroy the island nation. There was no way to estimate how many millions of people would eventually die in the resulting famine and riots. Afterward, what was there to stop Penumbra from doing it again to another nation? Or for that matter, attacking the offshore rigs of every nation, creating a worldwide famine, and soon afterward, full nuclear war?

Holstering his weapons, Bolan hurried back to the office and stopped just outside the Plexiglas wall. Through the empty doorway, he could see that the digital thermometer was registering in the danger zone, the metal file cabinet had been knocked over, and an eerily still Dr. Geraldo was sprawled across the console. A jagged piece of metallic shrapnel was sticking out of his neck, with red blood dribbling onto the keyboard.

Reaching for a wall phone to call for an ambulance, Bolan heard a musical ding, and a wireless printer on a shelf extruded a single sheet of paper covered with a long sequence of numbers, most of them zeros.

As he dialed an emergency responder, a single glance showed him that Dr. Geraldo had been successful. Those were directional coordinates, the latitude and longitude of every call made over the last month. Oddly, most of the recent calls seemed to have originated along the Earth's equator.

CHAPTER SIXTEEN

Butterfly Island

Sputtering and gasping, Hrafen Thorodensen awoke spitting salt water from his mouth.

Rudely shocked to full awareness, he found himself drenched in the stuff, and it burned in his eyes like acid. Desperately, he tried to wipe the fluid off his face, only to find that his hands refused to move, and all he could do was violently shake his head, like a dog coming out of the rain.

"Ah, awake at last, I see!" Pyotr Belgurovski said with a chuckle, stepping closer with the Pfeifer Zeliska gun in hand.

Ludmilla Moscow stood in the shadows, Thorodensen noted as he looked about in confusion. Standing nearby was Belgurovski, and a large number of people from the warehouse. Each was even more heavily armed than before, and now they were wearing body armor. That brought a moment of panic. What were the Russians doing here? And what was wrong with his hands? Rope… He was tied to a chair?

The room was dark, but as the fog of sleep left his mind, Thorodensen recognized he was in the basement of his cabin on Butterfly Island.

Upon originally discovering the place, he had naturally assumed it was the home of the chief pirate, as it was located away from the other cabins and barracks, was heavily fortified and had a secret tunnel in the basement that led to the lagoon. He had promptly claimed the place as his own, purely because it possessed a working air conditioner, and offered some small ease from the oppressive tropical heat.

"Why are you here?" Thorodensen asked, struggling against the ropes. But they seemed to have been tied by an expert, each leg and arm done separately.

"First things first," the Russian colonel said, holstering the monstrous handgun to light a cigarette. "I'm glad that you're smart enough not to yell for help. We brought along more people than you have, and all of mine are seasoned veterans, not academics, bookworms and scientists."

"They're patriots!" Thorodensen snarled, trying to rock the chair. But it had been securely bolted to the wooden floor, and proved immobile.

"Patriots? Please, they are fools." Belgurovski chuckled. "And you're the biggest one of them all."

Furiously, Thorodensen started to reply, then noticed Svanna was also tied to a chair only a few yards away, near the stairs leading to the upper level. He knew she had been on guard duty outside his home, protection from any returning pirates. Now the woman was also a prisoner, except that while he was wearing pajamas, she was stark naked, the ropes tied under her breasts forcing them upward as if on display.

Chuckling lustily, Moscow ran a finger along the bare breasts of the unconscious woman. The men present laughed and made lewd suggestions. Thorodensen fought back a wave of revulsion at the fondling, but took some small comfort that at least she hadn't been harmed.

"Very nice," Ludmilla whispered, pinching a nipple.

With a gasp of pain, Svanna awakened and wildly tried

to get loose. But her efforts proved as fruitless as his own had been.

"What the fuck do you want?" she snarled in Icelandic, then switched to English.

"Be quiet, bitch," Moscow said, grabbing her neck and squeezing.

Unable to draw breath, Svanna started to turn a dark red, her fingers and toes flexing helplessly.

"Let her live for now," the colonel said, not even looking in their direction.

"As you wish." Moscow removed her hands.

Gasping for air, Svanna glared hatefully at the other woman, then seemed to realize her condition and furiously blushed all over.

"Ambassador Thorodensen, I've been reading some of your paperwork upstairs, and it is fascinating. Absolutely fascinating," Belgurovski said, pulling a chair closer.

Turning it around, he sat and rested his arms on the back. "Do you really think that you can make a stealth torpedo capable of destroying offshore oil rigs in England from halfway around the world?"

"I have no idea what you're talking about," Thorodensen said, the lie coming naturally. "We were sent here merely to ascertain the whereabouts of a missing Icelandic diplomat. If you can assist us, there is a substantial reward and—"

Exhaling smoke through his nose, the colonel violently backhanded the man. "Never lie to me again," he said calmly, slapping him twice more.

Feeling his lip split open, Thorodensen said nothing as blood trickled down his chin. Back at the United Nations he had watched an instructional video on what to do if kidnapped. Primarily, it had said to stay calm and stay alive. Help was on the way. NATO would find him. However, that was no longer the case, and Thorodensen knew that his people were completely on their own.

"Look, clearly there has been a mistake," he mumbled, trying not to move his mouth.

"True, but the mistake was made by you," the colonel said, smoke trickling out of his nose as he pulled on a pair of leather driving gloves. "Fernando was my partner in crime, as they say."

"And my cousin!" Moscow snarled. "He was blood kin!"

"Just so," Belgurovski said, then punched the bound man across the face.

There was an explosion of pain, and Thorodensen felt his nose break, then streams of blood flow down his face and into his mouth, making it difficult to breath, much less speak.

Somehow the Russians had followed the Hercules back to the island, then slipped past the sentries by using the secret tunnel. The first thing I should have done was brick that tunnel shut, Thorodensen mentally chastised himself.

Sweat started dripping off him as he struggled to get a handle on the situation. He was used to dirty, hard-driven negotiations, and had thought that he could handle any situation. But no matter how bad things got, they were still conducted by men of honor, diplomats and ambassadors, presidents and kings. This criminal was insane!

More importantly, how had Belgurovski known about the tunnel in the first place? It wasn't as if… Of course! Slaves! The pirates took hostages for ransom, and if that wasn't paid, they didn't kill the people. That would be a waste of resources. Instead, they had to have sold the prisoners as sex slaves…to Colonel Pyotr Belgurovski, the biggest dealer of stolen goods in all of West Africa. Good Lord, Thorodensen was an idiot not to have considered that two major criminal operations this close together wouldn't have some kind of a working relationship.

"This is not good business," Thorodensen muttered, trying to radiated confidence, even though he was absolutely terrified.

"On the contrary, this is very good business," Belgurovski countered drily, lashing out with a closed fist again, punching him painfully on each ear.

"There's more gold!" Svanna blurted. "I know where it is hidden!"

"So do we," Moscow said, pulling the knife from her boot. The slim blade shone like polished sin in the reflected light of the overhead fluorescent tubes. "Which makes you useless."

"No, wait!" Thorodensen shouted, heaving against the rough coils.

"Such a pity." Ludmilla slashed the throat of the naked woman.

Gushing torrents of red blood, Svanna gurgled, struggling to breathe. As the blood formed a pool around her bare feet, she soon stopped fighting, and finally went limp, her head lolling to the side.

Thorodensen heard a noise escape his mouth, but didn't recognize it as anything human.

"Now, as for you, Ambassador," Belgurovski said, puffing on the cigarette. "Who is in charge of building this so-called supertorpedo, and where is the man in charge of what we will jokingly call your defenses?"

"Look, maybe we can cut a deal…." Thorodensen panted, trying to figure a way out of this dire predicament.

"He's stalling," Moscow said, cleaning the knife on the dead woman's platinum hair.

"But of course he is," the colonel said, touching the lit end of the cigarette to the Icelander's chest.

As the burning tobacco met his bare flesh, Thorodensen went stiff from the stab of pain that pierced his body. He was unable to speak for a moment, every thought driven out of his mind by the realization of the torture that was to come.

Puffing away, the colonel withdrew a cigarette lighter from his pocket, and a small case. Moscow snickered.

"Please …" Thorodensen whispered hoarsely. "D-don't torture me."

"Then answer my questions," Belgurovski said, flicking the wheel of the lighter.

At the sight, Thorodensen felt something snap inside his mind. "Lily!" he screamed. "Professor Lilja Vilhjalms designed the Loki, and Gunnar Eldjarm is in charge of security!"

"That wasn't so difficult, was it?" the colonel asked, blowing a smoke ring at the ceiling. "Now tell me about this sonar jammer."

"S-scrambler," Thorodensen corrected in a strained wheeze. "I stole it from NATO. It makes the torpedo sound like a school of fish."

"Hmm, clever. Very clever, indeed. Now tell me…why are you attacking England?"

Unable to stop himself, Thorodensen spilled the entire sordid story of how the prime minister of England had seized funds from Icelandic banks in the United Kingdom, claiming they were laundering money for criminal and terrorist organizations. That made the bank in Iceland collapse, and forced his wife to commit suicide rather than go to jail.

"Interesting. So, were your banks laundering money for terrorist groups?" Belgurovski asked, each word a puff of smoke.

"I don't know…maybe…" Thorodensen groaned, looking at the floor. "Who really knows such things?"

"Fool." Moscow snorted, sheathing the blade. "Half a fool, anyway."

"Agreed," the colonel said. "Thor, we shall help you build this Loki, and to strike at England."

"Why would you help me?" Thorodensen asked suspiciously.

"Because we're smart, and you are not." He chuckled. "Destroying the ecology for England is fine revenge, but nothing more."

He took a long drag, then tossed the cigarette butt away. It handed with a hiss in the pool of blood. "We will attack oil rigs across the globe, creating a worldwide ecological disaster that will destroy fishing for most of the planet. In turn, that will cause international famine, shortly followed by small local wars, and then global nuclear war as everybody tries to steal what little food there is remaining."

"But that's… Why would you do such a thing?" Thorodensen asked, barely able to believe the words. Unfortunately, he knew from bitter experience in global politics that the insane plan might just work. But where was the profit in creating global starvation?

"Why? Because afterward, I will be able to carve out my own private kingdom in South America, based right here on Butterfly Island." The colonel smirked, making a ritual of getting a fresh cigarette from the pack and lighting it. "Anything I want—foods, drugs, guns, slaves— my people can simply take by using a Loki." He grinned. "Good name, by the way. The god of mischief, correct?"

"You're mad," Thorodensen whispered in growing horror.

"Be that as it may, I still want your assistance in taking over the island from your people," Belgurovski said, gesturing with the cigarette. "This professor must be captured alive, along with her technicians."

"But everybody else goes," Moscow stated, crossing her arms. "Except for the ones that help us."

"Please, let them live!"

"Squeamish? Come now, you're already a mass murderer. What's a few more deaths, eh?" the colonel asked with a grin.

Making a fast decision, Thorodensen pulled in a lungful of air to scream for help. But before he could, strong arms locked his jaw shut in a viselike grip.

"I wasn't asking for your assistance, I was telling you what is going to happen," Belgurovski said, blowing on the end of the cigarette. "Now you must pay the price for disobedience."

The glowing tip come toward Thorodensen like the headlight on an express train, until it filled the vision of his left eye. Tears ran down his cheek as he felt the heat, and smelled the eyelashes burning—then the cigarette was removed.

"No, perhaps later." The colonel relented, returning the cigarette to his lips and puffing away. "For the moment, continue telling me about your people. Professor Vilhjalms—"

"Lily! I call her Lily!" Thorodensen muttered. "And Lily thinks Gunnar's gone mad. Lily calls it bloodsimple, but I don't know anything about that."

Glancing at each other, his tormentors shared a smile.

"Tell us more," Moscow whispered sweetly, draping a friendly arm across the man's shoulders, her knife resting on his bare skin. "Tell us everything…."

"Remember, nothing that shows!" Belgurovski warned sternly.

"Of course," she purred, sliding the knife down into his shirt and starting to cut.

The Equator

KEEPING ONE HAND on the vibrating yoke of the big seaplane, Mack Bolan used military binoculars to look out the window and scan the wide blue ocean below. Flat open water stretched in every direction, reaching all the way to the horizon, and there were no large ships of any kind in sight, nor any islands.

Even the sky was crystal clear, visibility unlimited, but aside from a flock of seagulls to the far south, he was alone in the wild blue yonder. Bolan would have preferred some cloud cover to hide his approach from the terrorists, but at least he could see them coming this time.

Prepared for full combat, Bolan was wearing a commando blacksuit, lightweight body armor and a weapons harness festooned with assorted death dealers—knives, garrotes and grenades, along with the Beretta and Desert Eagle. Lying on the deck was his big-punch weapon, a replacement XM-25 assault rifle, and the MP-5 submachine gun recovered from Salvatore. In the copilot seat was a parachute, a backpack and an inflatable raft, all set to go in case he was shot down again.

There had been scant time to grab supplies, but Bolan had been able to acquire some clean clothing, a thermos of hot coffee and enough dried sausage, hard rolls and Parmesan cheese to last him a month. The buxom young woman who ran the grocery store had been outraged that anybody would buy so much food without any wine, so Bolan had also purchased a bottle of Chianti, then given it away to a couple old men playing checkers on a street corner. They were delighted at the gift, and wished him the best of luck.

Scanning the sea, Bolan was starting to wonder if Thorodensen and Penumbra were operating out of a submarine. That would explain why they used a Hercules seaplane as transportation. It would also make his job of finding them virtually impossible. So he ignored that thought, and concentrated on finding some small atoll not shown on a standard map.

Hanging the Zeiss binoculars from a ceiling hook designed for just that purpose, Bolan looked over the digital gauges in the complex dashboard to check the fuel level, oil pressure and engine temperatures. But everything was fine. The twin Cyclone engines of the Grumman HU-16 Albatross were operating perfectly, the spacious interior of the seaplane filled with their low purr of controlled power.

The coordinates in the memory chip of the cell phone showed the owner had been at the last couple of known locations of terrorist attacks. He had also made several calls along the equator. Bolan was fully aware that the man might have been in transit at the time. But if not, then one of them might be the location of the terrorist base.

Unfortunately, there had been no seaplanes available for rent in Sicily. Even Brognola had been unable to pull a rabbit out of his hat this time.

With no other choice, Bolan had to waste precious time traveling to the mainland on a ferry filled with tourists, day workers, and Italians on vacation. The sound of children playing had been a reminder to Bolan why he continued his War Everlasting. He'd even managed to grab a short catnap on a deck chair, the Beretta hidden under a garish blanket decorated with Roman centurions.

The price negotiated for the aircraft was exorbitant, but Bolan had no room to haggle—no other seaplanes were available. He was grateful that he had used downtime during the past few years to learn how to fly. He couldn't handle a jet, but he was capable with two-engined planes.

The Grumman Albatross was a true amphibian plane, built to land anywhere. With a range of over three thousand miles, and a cruising speed of 150 mph, the aircraft was a favorite of bush pilots, insurgents, warlords and smugglers. Bolan had to agree. Although capable of carrying thirty passengers, the Albatross handled like a dream. It was also a civilian plane, which gave Bolan some protective cover. The Albatross shouldn't be seen by Penumbra as an immediate threat. Bolan only hoped that it wouldn't be necessary to test its dogfighting capabilities against the massively larger Hercules.

Slowly, the long hours passed, and each location he checked proved to be only empty water, the cell phone calls obviously made while in transit.

Off to the south, Bolan finally spotted an island, and to the north a cluster of atolls. His map listed the big landmass as Butterfly Island, formerly a launch facility for the French Aerospace industry, now long abandoned. There was no mention of the atolls.

Heading north-by-northwest, he circled the cluster from a distance, but couldn't detect any sign of habitation. There was no smoke, no visible roads, houses or docks. The beaches were smooth and undisturbed, and his EM scanner was detecting no large amounts of metal, and no radio or cell phone transmissions, much less any active radar. Oddly, the more the atolls seemed deserted, the more likely they would be as a terrorist base.

Bolan counted six atolls, two scarcely above sea level, the soggy land more swamp than anything, and one with a small but active volcano bubbling in the lagoon. Of the remaining three, he chose the largest and swooped in low over the waves to ease down in a gentle landing.

After motoring along the beach a ways, Bolan angled up a scummy green river, watching carefully for any rocks, tree trunks, or worse—underwater North Korean mines. The river soon snaked inland toward a small knoll. From there he would be able to see the entire atoll, and the next one over.

Pulling onto the shore, Bolan heard sand crunching under the pontoons. Once securely on dry land, he turned off the engine and waited to see if there was any reaction to his presence. The Albatross was anything but a stealth jet. Its 9-cylinder, 1,500 horsepower Cyclone engines made a lot of noise.

After slinging the XM-25 across his back, he hung the MP-5 at his side. Unlocking the door, he eased it aside and walked down the short flight of stairs. Keeping a careful watch, Bolan lashed the seaplane to a tangle of exposed roots. Obviously, the island was hit by some major storms for this sort of erosion to occur. He had better be long gone before another storm hit.

A gentle breeze carried a faint stink of sulfur from the underwater volcano, but it mixed rather pleasantly with the smell of green plants and the tangy sea spray. There were no sounds of life, not even of birds. The atoll seemed as lifeless as the dark side of the moon. Yet Bolan had the feeling of being watched. On a hunch, he cried out and fell to the ground, rubbing his ankle.

Instantly, a group of men charged from the bushes, waving machetes and crude clubs. Leaves and vines had been added to their tattered clothing as camouflage, and all of them were sporting several days' worth of beard. Several had automatic pistols holstered on their belts, but none of the weapons were drawn. Which meant they either wanted

Bolan alive or were simply out of ammunition. His guess was the latter.

Scanning the trees for snipers, Bolan made sure they were coming his way, and not running away from something else, then sent off a brief burst from the MP-5. The stream of copper-jacketed 9 mm rounds chewed up the ground directly in front of the men, and they instantly scattered, racing madly back into the thick foliage.

Going inside the plane for a minute, Bolan returned with the thermos and sat on the steps to have a cup of coffee. Whoever these poor devils were, they most definitely were not members of Penumbra. They were in rags and didn't look as if they had eaten for several days.

Placing the MP-5 within easy reach, Bolan sipped the cup of coffee he'd poured from the thermos, and waited. It wasn't long before a man shuffled from the bushes waving a red flag tied to a stick.

"If this is a parley, that's supposed to be white," Bolan shouted, still holding the warm plastic cup.

"It's all we had," the man answered back. He had a pronounced Spanish accent. "But yes, a parley!" He stopped just past the churned patch of bullet-riddled ground. "Are you a man of honor?"

"Is anybody?" Bolan replied, setting aside the cup. Then he picked up the MP-5 and released the arming bolt with a hard snap. "Feel safer?"

"You still have many guns," the man said with a gesture.

"And you have many friends," Bolan answered. "By the way, if I hear anything behind me, you're the first to die."

With that the man grinned, displaying amazingly white teeth. "Deal!" He laughed, planting the stick in the dirt. "I am Fernando Mescal, the leader of these men."

"Matt Cooper," Bolan replied.

"And you are?"

"The owner of this plane."

"And what a beautiful plane it is, *señor.*" Fernando brushed back his hair. "Is…is that coffee I smell?" There was no disguising the raw hunger in his voice.

Rising off the step, Bolan set the thermos halfway between them, then walked back to the plane. "Help yourself," he said.

Eagerly, Mescal opened the thermos and drank from it in a series of fast gulps. "*Gracias,* my friend." He sighed, then loudly burped. "Excuse me, we have not eaten for two days, and so much coffee on an empty stomach…" He shrugged in apology.

Going back to the plane, Bolan used a blanket to collect a small package of food from his supplies, and carried it outside. Mescal hadn't moved from his spot, and stared at the bundle with open greed.

"Eat slowly or it'll just come back up," Bolan advised, tossing over the blanket. As it landed, the knot came undone, and out rolled the bread, cheese and sausage.

With a cry, Mescal dived on the food, and a moment later, a crowd of men boiled out of the bushes to join the feast.

"You have saved our lives," one said, his mouth full of bread. "Whatever you want, ask, and it is yours!"

"I'd like some information," Bolan said, tossing over a canteen of water.

"About the big island?" Mescal asked, nodding in that direction. "*Sí, sí,* that was where we used to live, on Butterfly. We were pirates, robbing ships at sea and selling slaves."

Bolan arched an eyebrow at the frank confession.

"I make no lies," Mescal added, ripping off a handful of cheese. "We are criminals, yes, thieves and murderers!

But we robbed the foolish rich on their fat yachts, and only killed when necessary."

"But these pale blond people with their tanks and guns…" A short man made a dismissive gesture with a sausage, then bit off a large chunk. "Is good!"

"Only the best," Bolan said, resting his elbows on his knees. "Now, about those tanks. Can you describe them?"

"They were not tank, but armored personnel carriers," a black man said in a gruff voice, wiping a forearm across his mouth. "Eight wheels, 25 mm cannon, and squad support machine guns. Very similar to a LAV-25, but the armor looked odd, off-color, and I did not recognize this model."

"It's Swiss," Bolan said.

"Like the cheese?"

An Asian man looked up from nibbling. "This is Parmesan, you idiot."

"Not that cheese, the other cheese."

"Why would the Swiss attack us?" Mescal asked, sitting cross-legged on the ground. In his hand was a crude sandwich. He took a bite, chewed slowly and swallowed as if it was the most delicious food in existence. "As far as I know we have never robbed a Swiss ship."

"They aren't Swiss," Bolan said. "They're from Iceland, and only wanted your island to use as a base."

Astonished, Mescal lowered his sandwich. "They…they did not know we were there?"

"They didn't care. Just wanted the island."

"What for, eh?" Mescal demanded furiously. He sounded genuinely offended.

"I plan on asking them about that very soon," Bolan replied honestly. "Any chance you know a good way to sneak in close without being seen?"

In ragged stages, everybody stopped eating and looked

at one another. First, one man gave a nod, then another shrugged, and soon they all were nodding.

"You cannot get close in a plane," Mescal said, wiping his mouth. "The radar would see you a mile away."

"I have an inflatable raft."

"That will serve nicely."

"Any real defenses?"

"Yes. There are .50-caliber machine gun nests at the airfield and along the lagoon. Plus, a lot of MANPAD. Those are—"

"Man-portable defensives. What did you have, LAW rocket launchers?"

"Along with Redeye, Stinger, and a host of others," Mescal said quietly. "Once you are on Butterfly, what will you do next?"

"Kill the people that took it away from you."

The pirates murmured their approval of the idea.

"There are a lot of defenses, land mines, barbed wire, sensors. Very hard to get inside safely," Mescal said, rubbing his unshaved chin. "You'll need a guide."

"Actually, you'll need fifteen guides," the Asian man said, not posing it as a question.

Everybody had to go or nobody did, eh? Bolan had expected something like that, which was actually fine by him. The pirates would want revenge on Penumbra, and that would make a good diversion. Besides, Bolan didn't like relish the idea of leaving any of them alone on the atoll with the Albatross.

"Okay, we have a deal," he said, sliding the MP-5 off his shoulder. After dropping the magazine, he tossed them both to Mescal.

As they landed in front of the astonished man, everybody else stopped eating.

"However, I'm in charge. You follow my commands,"

Bolan continued, swinging around the XM-25 grenade launcher and giving the group a good look. "Anybody who lags behind, or fakes a wound, gets his head removed. No questions asked, no second chances."

"Agreed," Mescal said, retrieving the weapon and inserting the magazine. Working the arming bolt, he test fired a single round into the air. The report echoed across the lagoon.

"We'll need guns, too," a skinny man said, his face bright with eagerness.

"Those machetes will do for now," Mescal stated, cradling the weapon in both hands. "Okay, Cooper, when do we leave?"

"As soon as it gets dark," Bolan said, looking up at the sun. It was almost directly overhead. "Until then, better get some sleep. It's going to be a long night."

"Longer for some than others," Mescal said with a sneer, running a hand along the smooth barrel of the machine gun as if it were an old and dear friend.

CHAPTER SEVENTEEN

Butterfly Island

It was noon before Professor Lilja Vilhjalms finally roused herself from bed. She didn't find that surprising, as she had worked through the night until dawn.

The ceramic armor was proving much more difficult to control than previously expected. It was easy enough to melt; that wasn't a problem. But if cooled too quickly, it broke into a million pieces, useless to anybody but a manufacturer of grinding wheels. The trick had been not to quench the material, as you would steel, but to let it cool naturally. The process allowed the woman and her team to grab some much needed sleep, and even a meal. During the night, she had briefly awoken at the sound of the planes returning, and had wondered if it was Hrafen, or that lunatic Gunnar?

Strolling down the sandy street, Vilhjalms fought back a yawn even as she noticed that everybody in sight seemed tense and apprehensive. Had something happened to Hrafen? If those Russian criminals had harmed the man, she would make them pay dearly. It would be a simple enough matter to reset the coordinates on a Loki and blow their stinking warehouse into orbit.

Then reason prevailed, and she dismissed the matter entirely. If either of the men had been caught, or killed, somebody would have woken her immediately, as soon as the news arrived.

Entering the repair shop, she found Bordh making fresh coffee, and blessed the man with all her heart.

"Any word on what happened last night?" she asked, getting a sealed stack of styrofoam cups from a cabinet. Taking the pencil from her hair, she popped the plastic, and placed the freed stack near a plate of sliced nut cake.

"Good news. The torpedoes arrived," Bordh said, adding a clean filter and pouring in the grinds. "About five times as many as we expected, almost a hundred of them."

"That many? Hrafen must have cut an exceptional deal," Vilhjalms said, feeling a swell of pride. But tucking the pencil away once more, she frowned. "Or did he use the last of the mustard gas and steal them?"

"The gas was not used," Bordh replied as the hot water started to filter through.

"Excellent," she said, sniffing eagerly. "Have you had a chance to check on the new armor yet?"

"That was the first thing I did," he replied gruffly, filling a cup and drinking some immediately. "It fits perfectly. No further modifications will be needed."

"Wonderful news!"

"We have the first Loki already done," Bordh continued, adding powdered milk and sugar. "Some of the team has already started on the second."

"Even better!" Vilhjalms sipped her own coffee, feeling its wonderful warmth spread through her body.

"Now, tell me why you have such a long face," she said, looking over the rim of the steaming cup. "What has gone wrong?"

"Last night, Hrafen came back with some additional personnel," Bordh said hesitantly.

"Personnel from Iceland?"

"I would say no."

Just then, the door slammed open and four large men walked through the break room to grab coffee. Vilhjalms stared in surprise. They were completely unfamiliar to her, and carrying unknown weaponry.

"Hello," she said in Icelandic.

One of the men looked at her sideways and muttered something in a foreign language.

Was that Russian? she wondered.

"Sorry, I do not speak that language," she said, trying English.

"Good morning," he replied, grabbing some nut cake and leaving again.

The professor set down her coffee and rushed into the repair shop. It was a hive of activity, full of noise, heat and shouted conversations in several languages.

A long row of Squall torpedoes were arranged along one wall, dozens of them, the massive weapons resting in wooden cradles. A score of men, none of them known to her, were quickly removing the armored hull from the machines.

In a far corner, the arc furnace was blazing away, the workers tending them faceless in heat-resistant suits. Other men were preparing a mold for the molten ceramic, while still others were busy attaching finished sections to the skeletal framework of a naked torpedo. After that, a series of overhead chains hauled away the heavy explosive into another room, for final preparations and programming.

Catching the attention of somebody she did know, Vilhjalms spread her hands wide in a silent question. The man replied by jerking his head toward the little office. She rushed there immediately and yanked open the door.

Clustered around her desk were two more newcomers, and Hrafen. Vilhjalms felt a stab of concern at how pale he looked. Then she noticed how he was awkwardly standing. Her father and brothers had been big fans of boxing, and she recognized the stance as that of somebody who had been brutally beaten and was trying to hide the fact from others.

The others were a man and woman. He was darkly handsome in a white linen suit and matching Panama hat, although his mustache needed trimming. In contrast, the woman almost seemed deformed. She was dressed in the combat fatigues of a soldier, including boots and dog tags, and appeared to be skin and bones. In all honesty, Vilhjalms couldn't tell if she was male, female or something in between. A transgender? These days, it was more than possible.

"Hello," the woman said in an amazingly sweet voice. Then her gaze shifted downward, and she openly leered.

"Hello," the professor replied, primly closing the front of her lab coat and feeling very uncomfortable. With her exceptionally large breasts, Vilhjalms had been ogled by lesbians as often as by men. But this time her instincts warned that this bony little woman was something different, something twisted and evil, and not to be trusted.

"Ah, you awake at last!" The man smiled, looking up from a map of the world spread across the desk. "Good afternoon, Professor! I am Pyotr Belgurovski, and this is my assistant, Ludmilla Moscow. We have our own private reasons from wishing to see England destroyed, and have joined your crusade!"

"Isn't that right, Hrafen?" Moscow whispered.

"Yes, they are our comrades in arms," Thorodensen said, trying not move and rip open any of the stitches hidden under his clothing. Then he forced a weak smile.

Vilhjalms felt stunned that the former United Nations ambassador was behaving like a whipped dog. My God, what had they done to him? Then she went cold at the sight of the empty holster on his belt.

Glancing quickly around the office, she saw that every Icelander was unarmed, and all the new people were carrying multiple weapons. The tiny Remington .22 automatic pistol hidden under her jacket suddenly seemed the size of a mountain, but until somebody asked, she was determined to say nothing. It was obvious that the Russians had taken over the island and the project. She had no idea what that meant, and fear gripped her.

Pulling out a pack of cigarettes, Belgurovski made a little ritual of lighting one and blowing a smoke ring.

"So tell me, Professor," he said, sitting on a corner of the desk. "Does the weight reduction from the ceramic armor increase the speed of the torpedo?"

She was amazed at how well informed he was, but tried not to let it show. "We cannot know for sure until we do a field test," she replied, focusing her attention on the task at hand. "But my estimation is that it will double the velocity."

"Double?" the colonel repeated, tapping the grip on the Pfeifer Zeliska revolver he wore. "So they'll travel at six hundred miles per hour...even while underwater?"

"Roughly, yes. But converting them from a chemical jet to an electric turbine will lower their speed back to normal."

"But extend the range?"

"Enormously."

"How long with the chemical jets burn?"

"One hundred and twenty-seven minutes."

"Two hours? Fantastic," Belgurovski said, staring into the distance.

"Impossible," Moscow snorted.

"No, my friend. Russians invented the Squall, and

broke the underwater speed barrier," he gently reminded her. "These clever Icelanders have simply pushed it further than anybody believed possible. The lovely professor here is to be commended for her ingenuity!"

"How soon until we can do a long-range test?" Moscow asked in a whip-crack tone.

Vilhjalms bridled in response, but maintained a cool demeanor. The wise hunter tiptoed past the cave of a bear. "As soon as Gunnar returns, and I install the turbines and fuel cells," she replied honestly. "After that, the range becomes unlimited."

"Very well. In the meantime, can your laptop establish a link to an oceanographic satellite?" Belgurovski said, blowing a smoke ring at the ceiling. "You must have planned for some way of tracking the torpedoes all the way to England...." He paused, expectantly.

"Yes, we can track them across the world. Hrafen got the access codes to a NATO spy satellite before leaving the UN," she replied hesitantly, not sure where the question was leading.

"Excellent!" the colonel said, then smiled around the cigarette. "Then find me something local, say, within a hundred miles."

Without moving, Thorodensen spoke. "There should be nothing that close except for those atolls to the north, and some commercial shipping, oil tankers and such."

"An oil tanker would attract too much attention," Moscow said. "We don't want that this early."

"Then expand the range and choose another target," Belgurovksi ordered, levering himself off the desk and walking to the window. "A cruise liner will do nicely."

Attack civilians? Utterly horrified, Vilhjalms opened her mouth to object, until Thorodensen caught her eye and shook his head. With some effort, she managed to control her breathing.

"You mean a British cruise liner," she stated.

Exhaling smoke, the colonel smiled. "If you can find one."

Staying perfectly still, Thorodensen said nothing. After the previous night, he felt hollow, devoid of any emotions or feelings. The urge for revenge was gone, replaced by a numbing cold that seemed to emanate from his very soul.

Opening the laptop, Vilhjalms typed steadily for a few minutes, then turned it around. On the screen were a dozen blinking icons of various sizes and distances from Butterfly Island.

"We have a cargo freighter from Libya that is eleven hundred miles away," she read off a scroll at the bottom. "There's a fishing trawler from Brazil at nine hundred miles. A Japanese whaler at seven hundred miles and a yacht from America at four hundred."

"Do you know who owns the yacht?" Moscow asked breathlessly, clearly excited.

"There's no name, just a holding company in the Cayman Islands."

"Then that could be anybody," Thorodensen said dismissively.

"Anything else?" Belgurovski asked with a dark scowl.

"There is also a British submarine—no, that just went out of range—and an aircraft carrier from Argentina at three hundred miles," the professor continued. Why where there so many military ships along the equator? It was almost as if they were searching for the Icelanders. That was an unnerving thought.

"An aircraft carrier," the colonel said thoughtfully. "How thick is the hull?"

She typed for a few minutes. "According to the Jane's military website, it is thirty-four inches."

Almost a meter thick? He smiled. "It is fully armed, of course? Not some old wreck on the way to be sunk and turned into a reef for tourists to dive around and take pictures?"

"NATO has it listed as fully battle worthy, with sixty AMX jet fighters, four gunships, cannons, depth charges, deck guns and over a thousand sailors."

"A thousand. Yes, that will do nicely," Belgurovski said with a nod. "Time to target?"

"Thirty-two minutes."

"Take it out."

"As you wish," Vilhjalms said, typing briefly again, then tapping a button.

Outside the repair shop there was an enormous boom of compressed air, followed by an even louder eruption of seawater. The patter of falling drops lasted for several minutes.

"Hard-firing was successful," she reported. "Loki is live, and tracking."

A new icon appeared on the monitor, a tiny red triangle. Going faster than anything else on the screen, it moved away from the island, heading straight for the oblong circle that identified the Argentine warship.

"Speed is 400 mph and accelerating," Vilhjalms said. "Five hundred…five-fifty…full speed."

Nobody spoke as the minutes ticked away and two icons grew ever closer. Then they merged, and vanished in a brief flash.

"The carrier is destroyed," the professor announced, feeling sick to her stomach. She hated the British, but the Argentines had done nothing to her or her homeland. Those sailors were innocent of any crime, except for being in the wrong place at the wrong time.

"This was too easy," Moscow growled suspiciously, cracking her knuckles. "Could it have been a trick?"

"Bah, nobody is that good an actor," Belgurovski replied smugly. "Look at their faces!"

Moscow scowled, then broke into laughter. "Yes, I see what you mean!"

Catching her reflection in the plasma screen of the laptop, Vilhjalms turned away in shame. She was now a mass murderer, and didn't have to be. There was a button on the laptop that she had installed for just such a situation. All she had to do was press it twice and the Loki in the launcher would misfire.

The resulting back blast would take out the repair shop and detonate all the other torpedoes. That explosion would kill everybody on the island. No more civilian lives would be lost. Tap-tap, and the deaths stopped. But just considering taking her own life made her feel numb, and stopped her cold. Was it cowardice or self-preservation? She simply didn't know, and that was tearing her apart inside.

"Do...you want another test?" she asked, massaging her wrists. Both her hands were aching for some reason.

"Most certainly." The colonel leaned back in the chair. "But take out something big this time."

"Bigger than an aircraft carrier?"

"Maybe a bridge or a cruise ship—" He was interrupted by the strident roar of a Hercules passing low over the island, then another.

"Gunnar is back!" somebody yelled through the open door. "We're taking a truck to get the fuel cells!"

Vilhjalms closed the laptop. "I should assist," she said carefully, feeling as if she were walking across a minefield.

"Then do so," Belgurovski said, removing the cigarette

and blowing on the end to make it briefly flare. "I look forward to hearing good news within an hour."

"Absolutely."

"Perhaps I should accompany the professor," Moscow purred, brushing a muscular hand across her pale crew cut.

"No, I work better alone," Vilhjalms snapped, and turned on a heel to leave as fast as possible.

Crossing the repair shop, she felt dizzy, almost drunk from the rush of events. She had no idea how everything had gotten out of control so quickly, but now they were pawns for the Russians, and Hrafen was dead. Oh, he still moved and breathed, but the man she had fallen in love with was gone forever.

Leaving the boisterous Quonset hut, she strode along the sandy street with grim purpose, trying desperately not to look down at the tiny electronic object in her clenched fist.

Exhaust Tunnel 9, Butterfly Island

"I MUST ADMIT, you are a clever bastard," Fernando Mescal muttered, keeping the flashlight steady as he walked through the dark tunnel.

"Just keep moving," Bolan replied, following the beam of his own miniature flashlight, which was taped to the barrel of his XM-25 grenade launcher.

Before leaving the atoll, Bolan had removed all the spark plugs from the Albatross, then given one to every pirate. Since it would need at least a single working engine for the plane to fly, that meant nine of them had to join forces to escape. In a group of such individualists, Bolan considered that highly unlikely. In case several men were killed, he had a full set of spark plugs hidden inside a spare tire in the rear cargo compartment.

The midnight journey between the atolls, around the bubbling volcano and finally to Butterfly Island had been relatively easy to accomplish. One inflatable raft couldn't have held sixteen men, but Bolan had two of them, and the pirates had been hard at work assembling pieces of driftwood into a crude raft. Combined, the assorted crafts had proved sufficient for the task.

Approaching the main island, Bolan had studied the shore through the powerful monocular, regularly switching the settings between IR and Starlite. But there had been no patrols along the beach, only near a Quonset hut, and what the pirates had formerly used as an airfield.

As expected, the lone sewer pipe and all the old exhaust tunnel had been securely locked with steel grating, and armed with a Claymore mine. According to Mescal, that was new. Bolan found that interesting. This UN ambassador was proving to be highly resourceful.

However, as promised, there was a secondary entrance to one of the tunnels, a concrete plug that had to be removed by brute force. The opening was cramped, but once they were inside, the tunnel was roomy enough to walk upright, even if tiny roots from jungle plants hung from the curved ceiling and constantly tickled their faces, making everyone think they were covered with crawling insects.

Reaching a fork in the tunnel, Bolan saw muddy footprints going down one side. They didn't come back out.

"You had a spy among the prisoners," he stated.

"Just to keep a watch on things," Mescal said with a grin. "To prevent escapes, and such."

"And to find out when and where a rescue might come from," Bolan added, "so that you could also hijack that ship, and double your income."

"Sometimes triple!" Mescal laughed, then cut it short as they heard a muffled noise. "Quiet now! We're very close."

"About time," one of the pirates growled, squinting to try to see in the thick gloom.

"Damn roots!" another man muttered, swatting at his itchy face.

After only a few more yards there was a break in the tunnel wall, where ceramic bricks had been removed to make an irregular opening. That led to a tunnel with plank walls, which ended at a brick wall that had a small wooden door set near the floor. The passage was no more than two feet high, probably so that it could be hidden behind something—a pile of hay, or maybe a slop bucket. Nobody would want to inspect those too closely.

"There it is," Mescal said with a note of pride. "My cousin stayed with the prisoners, and we used this to sneak her food and blankets. We had to keep her healthy, just not too healthy, eh?"

"She was a good sport," Bolan said.

He shrugged. "She was a half-wit, and did whatever I told her. A good heart, mind you, just not too bright."

Since this was coming from a pirate, Bolan kept his opinion on the matter strictly private.

Going to the small door, Mescal scratched several times and waited. When nothing happened, he tried again, but there was still no reply. "If they harmed her, there will be blood to pay," he growled, taking a small crowbar off a hook on the wall and prying open the door.

The flickering light of multiple candles reached them, along with rhythmic sounds of snoring and mumbling.

Using the XM-25 to wave the pirates away from the opening, Bolan bent to look through. He saw sleeping prisoners in the other cells, and a rusty metal door, but nothing else. There were no guards or security cameras.

Turning, Bolan crawled backward through the opening so that he could keep watch on the pirates. Brandishing their knives and machetes, they stayed at the extreme edge of his flashlight beam, only partially illuminated. However, they closely watched his every move. So far, Mescal had proved to be a man of his word. But how much longer that would last was anybody's guess.

Standing up in the cell, Bolan wrinkled his nose at the reek of strong disinfectant, and saw that the floor had been freshly scrubbed. Somebody had recently died here.

As Mescal entered, his face took on a savage expression, and he hunched both shoulders, like a bull getting ready to charge.

"We don't know if it was her or a member of Penumbra who was killed," Bolan said quickly. "She might just be in another cell."

"If she is not, don't get in my way," Fernando growled, the tendons in his neck visibly tightening.

"Fair enough." Going to the cell door, Bolan sprayed the hinges with lubricant, then used a keywire gun to trick the lock, which opened without a sound.

"Just who are you, really?" Mescal asked, shifting uneasily. "CIA or the Mossad?"

"The Boy Scouts of America."

"What?"

"Just go back in the tunnel," Bolan said gruffly. "We can't let them see you."

Moving to the next cell, the soldier found an elderly woman asleep in her underwear on a canvas cot. The floor was clean, the blankets new, and there were remnants of a large meal on a table, including wine. Whatever other crimes he had committed, Thorodensen clearly didn't abuse prisoners. But that earned him no leniency with Bolan. If for nothing else, the ambassador had to die for slaughtering everybody on board the British convoy.

Unlocking the door, Bolan eased to her side and clamped

a hand over her mouth. She awoke with a start and started to kick and claw.

"U.S. Navy SEALs, ma'am," Bolan whispered. "Get dressed. We're here to take you home."

"Thank God." She exhaled as the hand was removed. Then surprised Bolan by kissing it in gratitude. "Let's get out of here!"

He stood. "First I have to free the others."

"Yes, of course, Lieutenant...?"

"Matt Cooper."

"God bless you, Lieutenant Cooper."

"Sure hope so," Bolan said, heading for the next cell.

In short order, he had all the prisoners free of their cells.

"Now what, Lieutenant?" an elderly man asked, rubbing the sleep from his eyes.

Going to the secret door, Bolan wasn't overly surprised to find it closed, and locked from the other side. Clearly, the treaty with the pirates was over. Mescal and his men were probably raiding a stash of weapons and preparing to attack the terrorists. All Bolan had to do now was wait for a few minutes.

"Anybody have weapons training?" he asked without much hope. These were dilettantes, millionaires and socialites. Probably everything they knew about firearms came from watching movies.

"Well, I shoot skeet every weekend in the summer," a woman said hesitantly, holding a candle.

"Twice a month I play laser tag," a young man offered.

"Of course! I'm the paintball champion of my sorority!" another woman stated, tightening the sash on a filthy robe.

"Just a little, sir. I served two years in the Canadian Coast Guard," a slim man replied. "Small arms only. I don't know shit about antitank launchers or such."

Without a word, Bolan reached behind his back to pull out his reserve piece, an S&W snub-nose .38 revolver.

"Five rounds?" the sailor asked, cracking the cylinder.

"Full load of six."

He closed it with a snap. "Trusting fellow, aren't you?"

Smiling, Bolan added both HE grenades attached to his harness. "Kill anybody who gets in your way."

"Not a problem," the sailor said, pocketing the military spheres. "Where should we go, sir?"

"Head for the shore, find a raft and head north. There's a plane on a small atoll, an Albatross. Remove the radio, inflate the spare raft and paddle out to sea. Once you're outside the radio jamming area, call for help."

"Can do," he said, hefting the revolver. "How long should we wait for you?"

Somewhere distant, an explosion sounded, and the roundhouse rocked slightly, the open doors rattling as a sprinkle of dust rained from the ceiling.

"Don't wait. I'll be busy elsewhere," Bolan replied, aiming the XM-25 at the wooden door inside the cell.

When he stroked the trigger, the grenade launcher boomed. The distance was short, but just far enough for the warhead to arm, and the 25 mm shell hit the half door like the fist of God. A staggering detonation filled the cell, chunks of burning wood and acrid smoke blowing everywhere. The candles died, but Bolan quickly lit them again.

"Now run for your lives, and don't stop until you reach the ocean!" he commanded, chambering another shell.

As the billowing smoke cleared, they saw a gaping hole in the wall, and the prisoners needed no further urging. They broke into a run and disappeared down the exhaust tunnel in record time, with the young Canadian sailor in the lead, the cocked revolver in his fist.

Turning, Bolan aimed at a metal door and fired again. The blast tore it off the hinges and sent it tumbling wildly along a long tunnel.

CHAPTER EIGHTEEN

Slowly, a siren started to howl from on top of the Quonset hut, and in the jungle the sputter of assault rifles sounded.

As everybody started to scramble, Vilhjalms maintained her pace and went directly to the little radar shack on the top of a knoll alongside the landing strip. A large crowd of Russians were waiting nearby, the few Icelanders among them clearly discernible by their lack of weapons.

Inside the radar shack, sitting at a table in front of a beeping screen, was an old friend of hers, Arjard. Vilhjalms was greatly relieved that he was alone, but she also saw that the gun rack on the wall was now empty. Even the signal flare gun had been removed.

"Do you have a computer?" Vilhjalms asked urgently. "A cell phone, video game console, anything with internet access?"

"No, the Russians took all of that," Arjard said, tugging on his beard. "Along with the radio jammer and all the guns."

"So, they control the airwaves?"

"Completely."

"Damn!" Going to the window, she looked down at the airfield. "How many of them do you think are here?"

"Unknown. A couple dozen showed up last night from out of nowhere," Arjard replied, minutely adjusting the dial on a portable radar scanner. "Then this morning, six of them took a Hercules back to Africa for additional supplies and more personnel."

"More?" she gasped. "How many of them are coming here?"

He shrugged. "I have no idea. But I am starting to think that the original plan of attacking England, then retiring to Belize, is dead and buried."

"Belize," she repeated, as if never hearing the name before. "Agreed. I also do not think that we will ever see it." Once more she looked at the thing in her hand, and this time sighed. "To be honest, old friend, I really don't think we will ever see any place other than this accursed island again…"

DESCENDING GRACEFULLY from the sky, the Hercules flew along the paved landing strip on the island and briefly touched down its wheels with a squeal. Almost instantly, the engines surged with renewed power, and it rebounded back into the blue sky.

"Dear God, I wish that I could warn them," Eldjarm growled, soaring over the tops of the waving palm trees.

"Warn them about what?" the copilot asked in confusion, his safety harness already released.

"Better buckle up again before you break your neck!" he commanded, reaching for the hand mike, but then stopping. Thorodensen had the radio jammer in operation 24/7 in case any of the prisoners escaped and tried to call for help. That tactic was now going to bite them in the rear, big time, Eldjarm thought.

"Goodbye, my friends," he whispered, watching the second Hercules gracefully land and brake to a gentle stop at the edge of the tarmac.

"What are you babbling about?" the copilot asked suspiciously, reattaching the harness.

"Tell me, how many people do we have remaining?" Gunnar asked, looking out the side window as the airplane sharply banked along the coastline.

"Very few." The man sighed, looking down at all the people busily moving along the sandy streets. "Especially after our recent losses in Brazil."

"How many! Give me a number!"

The copilot scowled. "Thirty-six! We should have only thirty-six people remaining from the original..." His voice trailed away as comprehension dawned. "Hey, there's easily that many just at the airfield, and even more scattered around the rest of the island!"

"The pirates must be back," Eldjarm growled, swinging toward the landing field once more. "And they brought along some friends."

"But then we need to land immediately!" the copilot sputtered. "Our APC might be the only intact one remaining, and it could make all the difference in a fight!"

"What fight?" Eldjarm muttered angrily, sailing again over the landing field. "Do you hear any gunfire or explosions?"

"No, I do not, only the fire alarm," the man muttered, studying the other plane. It had been down only a few minutes, and there was a trickle of smoke rising from the cockpit. However, nobody was running to or from the airplane, even though the cargo ramp was fully descended. Then he heard the soft chatter of an assault rifle, closely followed by the dull thud of a grenade.

"They're dead, aren't they?" he asked softly, clenching his fists.

"Most likely, yes," Eldjarm replied, swinging around the island once more. "And the Russians have the fuel cells."

"Then we have nothing to bargain with," the copilot said

tersely, "and we're dangerously low on fuel. What should we do?"

"Go to the APC and get it ready!" Eldjarm snarled, throttling back the engines again. "Once I land this bitch, we're going for a little drive..."

AT THE END of the brick tunnel, Bolan paused at the unexpected sight of hundreds of bright yellow plastic containers, each carrying a Flammable sticker. But those weren't really necessary, as the air was thick with the pungent reek of gasoline. A combination jail and fuel depot? Clever. That would certainly slow down any possible rescue attempts. One wrong move and there would be nothing to rescue but bones and ash.

Outside the roundhouse, the siren was still wailing, and the noise of combat was steadily increasing, the occasional pistol bang or shotgun boom replaced by hammering machine guns and chattering assault rifles.

Keeping out of the glow cast by electric lights strung along the sandy streets by staying in the entranceway, Bolan carefully scanned the running people. There was a lot more of them then he had estimated, and since the pirates couldn't have brought in any support this quickly, it meant these were newcomers.

Unexpectedly, a loudspeaker began issuing orders in a language Bolan recognized as Russian, and crowds of armed men dashed about in different directions. He took an educated guess as to where the newcomers came from: West Africa. Thorodensen had to have gone to that crazy Russian colonel in Senegal to obtain more supplies, and unknowingly brought back a small criminal army intent on taking control of the island base.

Then Bolan remembered that Pyotr was a former member of Spetsnaz, the elite special forces of the Soviet

Union. The soldier would have to do his best to keep any confrontation with the Russian at long range. They were some of the best knife fighters on the planet, every bit as good as Navy SEALs.

Adjusting his grip on the XM-25 grenade launcher, Bolan frowned. That meant there were at least four different groups interacting in the night, and he couldn't be sure who was a civilian technician forced to be here, and who deserved hard justice. That would slow down his reactions, which could easily get him killed. He'd have to do something about that, Bolan decided grimly.

From his vantage point, he looked over the base and quickly found his goal. Situated behind numerous machine gun nests was a large Quonset hut. That had to be the former command center for the pirates, and most likely the new headquarters for the Russians. Oddly, behind it was a row of upright steel cylinders attached to some kind of a compressor.

It took a moment, then Bolan recognized it as a steam-powered launcher to hard-fire the Squall torpedoes into the water at a hundred miles per hour. Immediately, he started to unlimber the XM-25, then noticed that the launch tubes were empty. Either they hadn't been loaded yet or the Squalls were already on their way toward the civilian oil rigs. That sent a chill down his spine. The numbers were falling. Time to move.

Just then, a VW truck braked to a squealing halt across the street, and a pile of men got out to start quickly erecting a sand bag nest for a Remington .50-caliber heavy machine gun. Feeling the pressure of a ticking clock, Bolan impatiently waited. As soon as the Russians were done, he cut them down with the Beretta, then charged across the street to take cover behind the sand bags.

Swinging the XM-25 grenade launcher, Bolan pumped

a shell into the roundhouse, then ducked. A split second later, the entire world seemed to explode as the thousands of gallons of gasoline simultaneously ignited.

At first he could only hear the destruction—shattering windows, splintering timbers, cracking cinder blocks and wild screams. Then the sand bag wall roughly slammed into him as the concussion arrived, closely followed by a searing heat wave that threatened to cook the very flesh off his bones.

CHAPTER NINETEEN

Outside the windows, Belgurovski heard assault rifles chattering nonstop, then came a polite knock on the office door.

"What is it?" he demanded, looking up from the collection of maps and charts. Every major offshore oil rig around the world was marked with a crosshair, including those off the coast of Mother Russia. When the newly elected democratic government had expelled him to Africa, it had signed its own death warrant.

As the door swung open, a young Icelandic technician grinned in victory. "Sir, the fuel cells have arrived!" he announced proudly. "We have already started installing them, and the first long-range Loki should be completed within a few minutes!"

"Good man, well done!" the colonel declared, placing a hand over the map on the desk. "We'll smash England yet!"

Just then he heard an explosion outside, and a volley of pistol shots and a scream of pain.

"Filthy pirates," the technician growled, then glanced at Belgurovski and Thorodensen.

"Don't worry, we'll stop them," Thorodensen said stiffly, rubbing a palm across his sore chest. "Back to work, old friend."

Sighing in relief, the technician hurried away, his clipboard tucked tightly under an arm.

"Who was that?" Moscow asked, tugging on the scarf around her scarred neck.

"Just some drone," Belgurovski answered curtly, uncovering the map. "Okay, as each Loki is finished, I want it immediately launched at these targets."

"Yes, sir. Who do we hit first?"

"England!" Thorodensen exclaimed, then slouched down in the chair, terrified that his outburst might invoke more retribution.

"England...why not?" The colonel chuckled. "Then we hit America on both coasts, followed by Mexico, Brazil, France, Egypt, India, Greece, China, Spain, Russia, Denmark, Australia, South Africa, then England and America again."

"Spread the destruction and keep them guessing," Moscow said, hitching up her gun belt. "Ha! This will be child's play! We can blow up an oil rig a million times faster than they can turn them off, much less clean a spill."

"Exactly!" His face became twisted, alive with emotion. "By God, this is going to work. The end of the world starts today!"

"Yes, your majesty!" Moscow chuckled, reaching for the laptop. Then she stopped and bitterly cursed. "What the... It's gone! That bitch took the wireless router! Without that we can't talk to the NATO satellite!"

"Find it!" Belgurovski snarled, looking around the room. "Find it! Then kill her, and bring it back here undamaged! At any cost!"

"She will not want to tell me."

"Make her! You know how."

Grinning widely, Moscow drew her 9 mm HK pistol and worked the slide as she strode from the office and into the mounting fray outside.

Sitting very still in his chair, Thorodensen said nothing,

but a muscle twitched in his cheek at the thought of them torturing his friend, and his features subtly changed into a feral expression of raw, unbridled hatred.

AT THE AIRSTRIP, a warm breeze blew across the field, carrying away the reek of exhaust, gunpowder and burned rubber. Then the last Hercules touched down on the smooth pavement, renewing the bitter stench.

Dropping the airfoils, Gunnar Eldjarm cut the forward speed, then applied the brakes and come to a full stop before killing the engines. Slapping the release on his safety harness, he charged down the stairs to the main deck. Outside, the propellers kept rotating for a few minutes on sheer inertia, then abruptly ceased.

With a hydraulic whine, the aft cargo ramp began to cycle down. But before it even reached the ground, an Uberpanzer charged out of the plane, roaring off the descending ramp to crash onto the pavement.

Just coming out of the jungle, the group of Russians were caught by surprise by this unexpected move, and barely had time to raise their weapons before the APC plowed through them in bloody ruination.

Then the last Uberpanzer charged off the pavement and straight down the middle of the sandy street, the 25 mm Bushmaster and both machine guns cutting loose in strident fury.

STAYING LOW, Bolan rode out the searing wash until the temperature eased and a cool ocean breeze blew over the base.

Carefully peering over the smoldering sand bags, he saw that the roundhouse was completely gone, removed at ground level. There was only a scattering of hot debris among the score of steaming corpses. Instantly, he ducked again, and a moment later there was a fusillade of gunshots as the ammunition on the dead men began cooking off from the residual heat.

Stray bullets went flying everywhere as several Jeeps arrived carrying more men, some of them equipped with fire extinguishers. As the ammunition continued to bang, Bolan took out a dozen enemy gunners with silenced rounds from the Beretta.

Only one Russian seemed to realize what was happening, and just as he swung up a shotgun, Bolan silenced him forever. As the man fell, the shotgun discharged into the ground, removing the boot and foot of another Russian.

Grabbing the ragged end of his leg, the man screamed in agony as a Hercules seaplane appeared out of the darkness to streak low over the base. Dozens of men opened fire with M-16 assault rifles as the aircraft began dropping North Korean mines from the aft end. They exploded thunderously on contact, generating huge fiery coronas of people and debris.

Then the streetlights winked out, and the only illumination came from a scattering of small fires caused by the destruction of the roundhouse.

As Bolan took off at a run, the gloom became alive with the flickering flowers of muzzle-flashes from the assault rifles.

Reaching an undamaged bungalow, he spotted a Jeep, the man in the back standing to aim a Stinger. Not wishing to get bombed by the Hercules, Bolan let the Russian launch the missile before taking him out with a 9 mm Parabellum round to the back of the head.

Half a heartbeat later, there was an earsplitting blast in the sky overhead, and the burning Hercules spiraled down into the jungle. A few seconds later there was a loud explosion, and a tremendous wave of plant life was thrown high into the starry sky.

Suddenly, an Uberpanzer braked to a halt across the street, and the rear doors opened to reveal a double row of men and women wearing Dragon Skin body armor, and loading AK-47 assault rifles. Quickly swinging up the XM-25, Bolan pumped a single shell into the APC. The results were spectacular and horrific at the same time.

Heading for the destroyed APC like everybody else, Bolan tried to get lost in the angry crowd, but then peeled off to sprint for a grassy knoll nearby. It would offer an excellent view of the entire island. However, he traveled only a few yards before a hail of bullets stitched across the street, kicking up little dust clouds and missing him by inches.

Spinning, Bolan took refuge behind a chunk of the fallen Hercules, and found the sniper on a nearby rooftop. He replied with a tight burst from the Beretta 93-R, but the 9 mm rounds fell short. Switching weapons, Bolan stroked the trigger of the Desert Eagle. With a strangled cry, the blond sniper tumbled off the roof and out of sight.

From out of nowhere, a grenade rolled across the street, past Bolan and into the jungle, where it detonated harmlessly.

Sounding a horn as if it were rush hour, another Uberpanzer appeared from the smoky jungle, the deadly Bushmaster cannon on top chugging out high-explosive death at the Russians. They scattered, and fought back with small-arms fire and grenades, both of which had zero effect on the experimental Swiss juggernaut. Then a LAW rocket streaked down from a rooftop to slam into the side of the Uberpanzer with just as much result.

Holstering the Desert Eagle, Bolan drew the Beretta and headed for the grassy knoll once more. When anybody carrying a weapon turned his way, he responded with hot lead.

At the halfway point, a LAW rocket zoomed out of the darkness to violently explode nearby. The Executioner's body armor took the brunt of the blast, but the concussion sent him tumbling down the hill, and the Beretta sailed away into the jungle.

CHAPTER TWENTY

Suddenly, the wooden door to the radio shack was kicked open, and in walked Ludmilla Moscow, her guns out and sweeping for targets.

"Hello, Professor," she whispered sweetly, the twin 9 mm pistols barking a dull staccato of death.

With a cry, Arjard tumbled from the chair, his life splattered across the riddled and sparking radar equipment.

Diving behind the desk, Professor Vilhjalms came up with her .22 Remington banging steadily. The first few rounds merely ricocheted harmlessly off Moscow's molded body armor, then she was hit in the arm, the tiny bullet going deep.

"Bitch!" Moscow shrieked, deliberately shooting the professor in the upper shoulder instead of the face.

The impact of the 9 mm round knocked away the Remington and spun the woman in a half circle. Gushing blood, she collapsed onto the wooden planks of the floor.

Taking her time, Moscow strolled around the desk to find the Icelander kneeling in blood, her white lab coat removed to press against the wound in an effort to staunch the flow.

"Oh, don't whine, it is only a flesh wound," Moscow told her.

"But it hurts!" Vilhjalms cried, trembling all over.

Breathing deeply, Moscow said nothing. She was captivated by the sight of the woman. Her long hair was thrown back, revealing her beautiful face, and several of the buttons of her shirt had to have come undone when she ripped off the jacket. Encased in a white lace bra, her generous breasts were now in sight, the supple flesh almost spilling out.

"Give me the router and you can walk out of here alive," Moscow said, holstering one of the guns to snap her fingers. "Now, bitch!"

Reaching into a pocket, Vilhjalms produced the wireless router and passed it over.

As their fingers touched, Moscow grabbed her by the wrist and twisted hard. The professor cried out, dropping the lab coat, the bullet wound in her shoulder starting to bleed freely once more.

"Pretty, but stupid," Moscow said with a laugh, grasping her hair and forcing back her head until she was looking upward.

"Please, I'll do what you want," Vilhjalms cried out, tears flowing down her cheeks. "I'll do…anything you want…."

Moscow smiled. "Show me."

Lifting both hands, Vilhjalms unclasped the front-closing bra and let go. Her breasts burst free from the tight confinement.

"Nice, very nice," her tormentor purred, leaning in close to cup a breast, then pinch the nipple, excited by the delicious contact.

Forcing a smile, Vilhjalms tried not to whimper as she raised her face to be kissed. Feeling almost drunk with lust, Moscow shoved the other gun into her belt to cup the beautiful face and tenderly kiss the inviting lips…then recoiled as a terrible pain erupted in her throat. As she straightened, a geyser of blood shot across the room to splash against the window.

Unable to speak, Moscow grabbed her aching neck and stared in horror at the woman on the floor.

"That is—or rather was—your carotid artery," Vilhjalms said, brandishing a sharp pencil smeared with red. "You'll be dead in ninety seconds…bitch!"

Furious over the unbelievable betrayal, Moscow kept one hand on the pumping wound, and clawed for a gun with the other—only to realize that the pistol was gone, and now in the bloody hands of the busty Icelander.

Frantically, the Russian went for the other gun, but Vilhjalms shot first. Two rounds drilled into Moscow's chest, slamming her back against the wall. She tried to recover, but tripped over the corpse of Arjard and went sprawling.

Lowering her aim, the professor fired directly into her opponent's knees. She shrieked in pain and collapsed, unconscious. Rising stiffly, Vilhjalms tied a proper field dressing on her wound before straightening her filthy clothing. Thorodensen had personally trained every member of Penumbra in the basics of combat, weapons handling, first aid, explosives and such. The professor only hoped that he was still alive, so she could thank him properly.

Retrieving the router, she started to smash it, then decided to err on the side of caution, and tucked it into a pocket. It was time to end the madness.

Opening the door, she heard a noise from behind and turned to see that Moscow was painfully dragging herself forward, leaving a wide trail of blood as she attempted to reach the .22 Remington pistol on the floor.

"Thank you, I forgot about that completely," Vilhjalms said, reclaiming the weapon and tucking it into a pocket. Then she took the second 9 mm pistol and fired it several times directly into the snarling face of the dying Russian, until there was no further doubt about her demise.

THROWING OPEN the office door, Belgurovski whistled loudly for attention. Everybody working in the repair shop stopped whatever they were doing and turned toward the man.

"Barricade the hut!" Petrov bellowed over the growing sounds of combat from outside. "Let nobody in! Not even one of us!"

"What about Ludmilla, sir?" a man asked, thumbing a 40 mm shell into the grenade launcher of an AK-105 assault rifle.

"Only her! Nobody else!"

"Yes, sir," he replied, then began shouting orders.

Almost at once, all the doors and windows were closed, and the wooden shutters locked tightly. Then heavy workbenches were dragged over to block the two doors. The former owners had prepared for the day when their island might be under siege from invaders, and had taken the logical precaution of installing the heavy shutters over both the doors and windows. There was even a storm cellar in the reinforced basement, fully stocked with enough supplies to outlast the worst possible tropical typhoon.

"Is the CIA here?" Thorodensen asked woodenly. "Remember that Major Salvatore told me—"

"Be quiet," the Russian growled, typing on the laptop. Without the router, he had no access to the NATO targeting satellite, so he could send off the torpedoes, but not aim them at anything. However, he might have a solution for that.

"They may be here soon," Thorodensen continued doggedly. "Salvatore said the Agency had their best man hunting for me—for us. A large man with black hair."

"I told you to shut up!" Hard-wiring the cell phone to the modem, Belgurovski was delighted when he got a flickering response, then full contact was made. "Yes, we're back online!"

"Then call for help. Or even better, surrender while you can," Thorodensen said, briefly roused from his stupor. "Because the CIA—"

"This is your last warning," the Russian growled menacingly.

The impulse of rebellion gone, Thorodensen meekly nodded, when something in his mind screamed to attack. Moscow wasn't here, the colonel was alone and the base was under attack. There would never be a better time!

For a moment, he wavered, unsure if there was any courage remaining inside him after the humiliating torture of the previous night. The shame of the surrender burned in his mind, sapping his will. Then from deep within Thorodensen there welled a surge of unbridled rage that exploded into a mindless fury unlike anything he had ever before known.

"No," he said slowly, the impossible word fueling his resolve. "No!" he yelled, almost berserk with anger. "This is your last fucking warning, you piece of dog shit!"

Startled beyond words, Belgurovski actually took a step back in surprise as Thorodensen gave an animal roar and rose to his full height, a dozen stitches ripping open, his clothing becoming blotchy with fresh blood.

As the Icelander lunged for the other man, Belgurovski drew the Pfeifer Zeliska revolver and clubbed him across the face. But the blow seemed to have no effect, as if the former ambassador was now immune to pain. Once more Thorodensen charged, and this time he caught his adversary by the throat. As their eyes locked, the Russian saw only madness in the Icelander, and his own approaching death. Raw panic hit, and Belgurovski desperately shoved the revolver into the stomach of the bigger man and yanked the trigger.

The discharged sounded louder than thunder, and the titanic .600 Nitro Express round lanced completely through Thorodensen, breaking his death grip and throwing him backward against the corrugated steel wall, hard enough to shatter bones. But instead of falling, Thorodensen rose once more, muttering obscenities in his native language.

As he advanced, a blood-splattered hole was visible in the curved wall where the .600 bullet had come out of him and continued to punch through the corrugated steel.

Now outright terrified, Belgurovski emptied the massive handgun, using the last four rounds to blow away portions of Thorodensen's head until the decapitated body finally dropped lifeless to the dirty floor.

Almost immediately, somebody rattled the doorknob, then hammered a fist on the locked door. "Sir, are you okay?" a man shouted, trying the knob again.

"Fine! I...I'm just fine!" the Russian replied, fumbling to reload the revolver. "Somebody tried to get in through the window!"

"Do you need any help?"

"Stand your post! This might have been a diversion!"

"Whatever you say," the man muttered, walking away.

Taking a minute to regain his composure, Belgurovski holstered the big revolver and went to a liquor cabinet to pour himself a stiff drink. The fiery spirits burned his throat, but sent waves of soothing warmth through his trembling body. He could still feel the strangely cold hands of the man around his throat.

Stumbling to the desk, the Russian set the bottle aside and reached for the laptop, dismayed to find the keyboard covered with blood and gore.

Using a handkerchief and some vodka, he wiped it clean, and the computer proved to be undamaged. Slowly, he began to type in commands, his movements becoming faster and smoother as he warmed to the task. As the master menu appeared, he fed in the coordinates and hit the launch button. The first torpedo went to England, but the next two he directed toward Iceland in revenge. After that, he returned to the original plan, and targeted the best-producing oil rigs to maximize the level of pollution.

Outside the Quonset hut, the steam-powered launcher on the shore began thumping loudly as it built pressure, then a Loki was hard-fired into the ocean with a tremendous splash. First one, then another and another, until the tubes were empty and the pump exhaled to a gradual stop.

THE SOUNDS OF BATTLE were reaching a fevered pitch as Bolan wrapped his hand in a clean bandage. Shrapnel from the LAW had almost taken him out, but not quite. He was battered and bruised, but still very much alive.

As the soldier tied off the field dressing, he saw rockets crisscrossing the darkness, mostly blowing up swatches of jungle or the beach. Grenades and shotguns occasionally boomed, but the chattering of assault rifles never ceased. It merely rose and fell in volume as magazines became exhausted and were replaced. By now, the white sand streets sparkled golden with all the spent brass.

Tracers filled the air, and assorted bodies lay everywhere, as did the charred wreckage of Jeeps, trucks and even a crumpled Hercules. A flock of seagulls was feasting on the dozens of tattered corpses.

Flexing his fingers, Bolan grunted. The original plan had been to stage a diversion to help the prisoners get away, but that was fast becoming moot. From what he could hear, the fight for Butterfly Island seemed to be taking an unexpected turn as Russians began attacking other Russians, age-old grudges boiling to the surface in the heated caldron of combat. Which was fine with him. Bolan had always been a strong proponent of fighting fire with fire.

Testing his right hand, he found the muscles were sore, but otherwise undamaged. That was good news. If that LAW had hit any closer, he would be fertilizer by now, a fresh repast for the all-conquering worms.

Unfortunately, his body armor was trashed, the ceramic plates cracked and splintered. Peeling off the Velcro straps, Bolan shrugged out of the rig and let it drop. Stretching until his joints popped, he then conducting a brief search for the Beretta, but it was nowhere to be found.

Checking over the XM-25 and the Desert Eagle, he was pleased to find them in perfect condition, aside from being speckled with blood, all of it his. But that was nothing new.

Starting up the knoll, Bolan saw that the radar shack was gone; even the transmission tower was missing. Amid all the other explosions, he hadn't noticed the blast that leveled the place. He tried his cell phone again to try to warn Brognola, but the transmission was still blocked.

Changing direction, Bolan used the monocular to look over what remained of the pirate base. The lights were still out, but several bungalows were on fire, the flames highlighting the savage carnage.

The airstrip was dark and strewed with the wreckage of numerous airplanes, a couple helicopters and even a Soviet Union–style hovercraft.

The only undamaged structures seemed to be a couple concrete machine-gun emplacements he hadn't noticed before, some bungalows, the rusted French gantries out on the point and the Quonset hut near the lagoon. Most of the base was totally destroyed, or in flames and well on the way to becoming a pile of smoldering rubble. Where was that jammer hidden?

Deciding on the Quonset hut, Bolan proceeded that way, curving through the jungle, the Desert Eagle ready to blow thunder at anything that got in his path.

Reaching the outskirts of the base, Bolan encountered numerous private fights, and ended many of them with a round or two from the Desert Eagle.

Inside the ruins of a bungalow, Fernando Mescal and a bald Russian were having a savage knife fight. After watching a moment, Bolan shot the Russian. Mescal nodded his thanks, then raced away into the night.

Trying to cross a street, Bolan saw a shotgun barrel in a window, and he fired from the hip. Inside the building, a man cried out and tumbled forward, to land sprawling on the littered sand.

Circling a bomb crater, Bolan discovered two Russians dragging away a woman. Recognizing her as one of the prisoners, he instantly aimed his gun. But before he could fire, the Canadian sailor charged out of the shadows swinging a fire axe. The first Russian died on the spot, the axe buried in his chest.

As the second Russian drew a .357 Magnum Smith & Wesson revolver, Bolan took him out with a single booming round from the Desert Eagle.

"Thank you again," the woman said, struggling to her feet.

"What are you all still doing here?" Bolan demanded.

"We wanted to help," the Canadian replied, snapping off a shot into the darkness. A strangled cry announced a kill.

"Well, get away from here right now!" Bolan commanded sternly. "You're in the way."

"I'll do my best," the man said, taking the Smith & Wesson revolver from the corpse. "But have you ever tried to herd cats?"

"Constantly," Bolan replied, and turned to fire the XM-25 at an approaching jeep. The vehicle exploded, the tattered bodies of a few Russians flying far and wide.

"You heard the lieutenant!" the sailor boomed, poking the civilians with his gun. "Move it or lose it, people!"

As the group moved off, Bolan covered their retreat until the jungle swallowed them. Then he swiftly proceeded.

Cutting across the intersection of a dirt road and the sandy street, he paused as an Uberpanzer charged around a corner, rolling over corpses and slamming aside crippled Jeeps. Bolan started to dive aside, then noticed the ammunition belts for both the Bushmaster and the machine gun were missing. This particular tiger was toothless.

"Time to die, Mr. Cooper!" Gunnar Eldjarm called from inside the APC, and the vehicle lurched forward.

The use of his cover name startled Bolan for a second until he remembered that Major Salvatore had been a spy for Penumbra. As the Detroit engines revved to full speed, Bolan dropped the Desert Eagle to swung up the XM-25 grenade launcher.

As the APC steadily accelerated, Bolan aimed at the tiny viewing slot assigned to the driver, and squeezed the trigger. Instantly, the built-in computer in his weapon lanced out a UV laser beam to learn the precise distance of the oncoming vehicle, then added a yard, armed the warhead and fired. The 25 mm shell shot through the viewing slot, completely missing Eldjarm and the copilot, but then violently exploded in the interior.

Filled with a roiling fireball, the Uberpanzer veered about wildly as Eldjarm and the copilot were both obliterated. Crashing through the blackened remains of a collapsed bungalow, the APC went airborne, then nosed down into a bomb crater and crashed. Flipping over, it rolled away, to come to a stop against a palm tree.

Bolan wasted a precious moment checking to make sure the people inside were dead, then continued on toward the Quonset hut.

About a block away, the soldier slowed his approach and slipped back into the jungle to do a fast recon. Through the monocular, he saw that the hut was a hardsite, surrounded by trip wires and machine-gun nests, the curved metal roof frothy with razor wire.

In addition, the doors and windows were sealed with rusty iron shutters. The XM-25 at his side could easily punch through the corrugated steel of the hut, but that fist-size hole wouldn't get him inside to find the controls for the torpedoes. His grenades were gone, and Bolan needed something a lot more powerful than a 25 mm shell to breach those thick walls.

Going directly to the steam-launcher, Bolan smashed open the control box and began to hot-wire the compressor, when there was a movement in the nearby shadows. He glanced up just in time to see a pipe wrench swing out of the darkness, aimed for his head. Pivoting out of the way, Bolan almost fired the Desert Eagle at the woman holding it, until when the wrench came down on a safety valve with a hard clang.

"Well, don't just stand there, help me smash this thing!" she commanded. "You're certainly not a Russian, a pirate or a member of Penumbra!"

"Matt Cooper, CIA," he replied, keeping a finger on the trigger.

"Excellent! It's about time you people showed up!" she snarled, continuing to pound the valve flat. "I'm Professor Vilhjalms! This is how they launch the torpedoes! If we can make it blow up, they're helpless!"

"Good plan," Bolan said in a measured tone. "But the torpedoes have already been launched."

"Damn! Then we must get inside quickly," the professor stated, casting away the wrench. "Unfortunately, the place is a fortress, full of armed men!" Staring at the Quonset hut, she began to tremble with impotent rage, and a wound in her shoulder started to bleed.

Making a battlefield decision, Bolan lowered the gun. Obviously, the woman had switched sides in the conflict, probably sickened by all the killing. That didn't clear her of blame, in his opinion, but it did make her an ally. Temporarily, at least.

"We'll get inside," he stated. "However, first I need to know if there are any civilians or hostages there."

She looked at him anew, obviously amazed that anybody on the island would care about such things. "There are no innocent people inside the hut," she stated honestly. "Only lunatics and murders…like myself."

"Good to know," Bolan said, swinging up the XM-25 grenade launcher.

"No, don't!" she cried, blocking the barrel with a hand. "If the Loki have launched, then we need the laptop in the office. I can stop the torpedoes, assign them new targets, but only if that computer is undamaged!"

"Any suggestions?" Bolan demanded, lowering the weapon.

"Yes," she replied, pulling a wireless router out of her pocket. "Kill me."

CHAPTER TWENTY-ONE

Walking to the front door of the Quonset hut, Bolan pounded on it with a fist. "Hey, I found it!" he shouted, shifting the body draped over his shoulder. "Let me in, comrades!"

A small peephole opened and a man looked out. "Found what, and who the fuck are you?" he demanded suspiciously.

"I used to be a pirate, but now I'm on your side," Bolan said with a wide grin, then slapped the backside of the woman he was carrying. "This is that professor bitch with the thing. You know, the wireless router. Ludmilla said to bring it here immediately and get a big reward!"

"Absolutely, my friend," the Russian said eagerly. "Now, pass it through!"

Bolan tried, but the router was much too big. "Aw, shit, you want me to leave it on the ground and back away or something?" he suggested, scratching his head with the device.

"Yes…no… Come on in!" the Russian growled, and the peephole slammed shut. Bolan heard the sound of something large and heavy being dragged aside, then the squeal of rusty bolts disengaging.

As the door cracked open, Bolan dropped the professor and charged. Ramming forward, he dived inside and came up in a roll, the Desert Eagle blowing hot death in every direction.

The closest Russians didn't even have a chance to cry out as the .50-caliber hollowpoint rounds took their lives. Then the rest scrambled for cover, and started wildly shooting back. But by then Bolan had already taken a position behind a stack of oil drums.

Swinging up the XM-25, he switched it on autotarget and fired the remaining shells. The 25 mm grenades shot across the repair shop to violently detonate in the open air, spraying out shrapnel. Supposedly safe behind the large pieces of machinery, the Russians briefly screamed, more in surprise than pain, then went silent forever.

Quickly reloading, Bolan took out a couple men hiding behind stacks of Squall torpedoes. The Russians shrieked as the barrage of shrapnel musically zinged off the armored casings and tore them apart.

Suddenly, the overhead lights went out.

In the blackness, Bolan heard the sound of a door opening, then running feet. But that abruptly stopped. Easing off his own boots and socks, Bolan proceeded barefoot through the darkness, switching the U.S. Army monocular to infrared.

Under the IR setting, everything radiating heat glowed faintly—the newly deceased bodies, cups of coffee, gun barrels, spent shells, cigarettes, the electric motor of a recently used lathe, the fuse box on the wall—and a human figure with a strangely lumpy head.

Jerking aside, Bolan felt the passage of a big bullet going by even before he heard the roar of a truly massive handgun.

"Nice try, CIA, but I also have IR goggles!" Belgurovski boasted, firing his massive hand cannon twice more. A drill press toppled over in a deafening crash, and the door was ripped off a refrigerator, some of the foods inside tumbling out.

Soft white light issued from inside the fridge, illuminating a wide portion of the shop. But there were only corpses sprawled on the floor, along with a scattering of spent shells.

"You're not a very good shot for a Spetsnaz," Bolan answered, sending a 25 mm shell that way. It exploded directly above a large winch, the shrapnel hissing as it passed through empty air, then clattered off the machinery and tools. But there was no cry of pain announcing a hit.

"Good enough!" Belgurovski retorted, his words followed by the unexpected chatter of an AK-105 assault rifle. The muzzle-flash strobed brightly in the gloom, the stream of 5.56 mm rounds spraying randomly among the machines, oil drums, stripped down Uberpanzers and dead Russians.

Just then, the open door slammed shut.

"So the lovely professor was not dead," Belgurovski said, slinging the spent assault rifle away. "She must have been very compliant if Ludmilla let her live!"

The weapon landed on a distant workbench, dislodging dozens of tools hanging from a Peg-Board. The resulting clamor seemed to last for an inordinate length of time. When it eventuality stopped, silence reigned.

"I wouldn't mind taking a ride on her myself!" Belgurovski finally said, trying to rattle the other man. When there was no response, he fired the huge revolver a fast three times. Twice, the huge caliber bullets slammed into machinery. The third bullet punched a hole in the corrugated wall, allowing in a tiny beam of moonlight.

"Time is on my side." The colonel laughed, as nervous sweat trickled down his back. "Why not join me? The Spetsnaz and the CIA working together at last. Think of what we could accomplish!"

A murky shape moved in the dark, and the Russian

instantly fired. Someone cried out in pain, and a body dropped into the glow of the refrigerator.

"Then again, why share the world?" Belgurovski chuckled, pulling out a large knife even as he shot the body twice more. The second time, the .600 round flipped over the battered corpse to reveal the face of a pale Icelander holding a clipboard.

"I'm not going to share it with you, anyway," Bolan whispered, firing the XM-25 downward from the top of a tall pile of oil drums.

The warhead of the 25 mm shell still didn't have enough distance to arm properly, but it punched through the Belgurovski's chest like a cannonball. As blood exploded from his mouth, the Pfeifer discharged harmlessly at the concrete floor, then the dying Russian staggered away, to topple sideways into an open grease pit.

Climbing down from the curved ceiling, Bolan hurried over and put a final round from the Desert Eagle into the Russian, ending the matter.

"Lily, he's dead!" Bolan called into the darkness.

Suddenly, the lights crashed on, to reveal the professor, standing in the open doorway of the office. "Stop shouting! It's done. They're stopped," Vilhjalms said, the laptop tucked under her good arm.

"You blew them up, aborted the mission?" Bolan asked, hurriedly walking closer.

"No, I was not allowed to install a self-destruct," she replied, shuffling over to a wooden chair and sitting down heavily. "So, I merely changed the coordinates to a safe location."

"Where, exactly?" the soldier asked.

"Right back here, to this repair shop. The blast will destroy all the data files and remove the rest of these accursed things, so that nobody else can get their hands on them."

She gestured at the rows of Squalls resting silent and potent in their dark wooden cradles, death incarnate waiting to be released upon the unsuspecting world.

"Good enough," Bolan grunted. "What's the time to target?"

"Twenty-two minutes and counting."

"Well, I better make sure those civilians are very far away from here by then."

"What about everybody else?"

"The pirates and the Russians? Let the universe choose which of them live and die."

"Okay. The rest of my friends are dead. What about me?" Vilhjalms asked in a small voice, her hands moving aimlessly.

As he considered the details of the matter, Bolan said nothing for a moment. The professor had been at the heart of this madness from the very beginning, but she had also paid for her crimes, and saved many more lives than she had ever personally taken. There was no way to know for certain, but Bolan felt sure she would never cross the line again. In his savage world, redemption was almost unheard of, but not impossible.

"Come with me," he said, holding out a hand. "I'll get you away from here safely, with the others. What happens afterward is up to you."

* * * * *

Don Pendleton's Mack Bolan

Shadow Strike

**Unholy allies plot to drown the globe
in a sea of oil**

Eco-Armageddon is the goal of a far-reaching
plan with the scope, vision and power to
strike oil rigs around the globe. With disaster
looming, Mack Bolan begins the hunt
to identify and stop the terror-dealers behind
the threat. It's a long and dangerous trail...
and the enemy is all but invincible.

*Available January
wherever books are sold.*

TAKE 'EM FREE
2 action-packed novels plus a mystery bonus

NO RISK
NO OBLIGATION TO BUY

GE11B

The Executioner®
Don Pendleton's
NUCLEAR STORM

Ecoterrorists plan a deadly strike.

An ecoterrorist group in Yellowstone National Park
has a plan to save the planet. The group has set in
motion a plot to kill millions in seconds and leave
the rest of the human race on the verge of extinction.
Nothing and no one will throw them off course—but
Mack Bolan isn't your average outdoorsman.

Available February wherever books are sold.

JAMES AXLER

DEATHLANDS

JAMES AXLER

DEATHLANDS

Hell Road
Warriors

Humanity's shattering battle
for survival continues

Hell Road Warriors

Humanity's shattering battle for survival continues.

Canada hides a trove of Cold War-era secret government installations known as Diefenbunkers, filled with caches of weapons, wags and food. Ryan Cawdor and his companions agree to head west to retrieve four portable nuclear reactors—enough power to light up a ville for years. But they have death on their tail....

Available March wherever books are sold.

Don Pendleton
ARMED RESISTANCE

Sudanese extremists tap a new arms source— the U.S. military

Sudan's political situation is a nightmare as guerrilla forces rule the violence-torn region. Able Team moves in stateside, while Phoenix Force goes deep into the bloodiest regions of Sudan and Uganda. Stony Man is hunting predators who kill for profit and pleasure—battling long odds to bring some justice to a ruthless land.

STONY MAN®

Available February
wherever books are sold.